Books by James Stewart Thayer

The Hess Cross
The Stettin Secret
The Earhart Betrayal
Pursuit

RINGER

JAMES STEWART THAYER

CROWN PUBLISHERS, INC.

NEW YORK

Copyright © 1988 by James Stewart Thayer

Published by Crown Publishers, Inc., 225 Park Avenue South, New York, New York 10003 and represented in Canada by the Canadian MANDA Group

CROWN is a trademark of Crown Publishers, Inc.

Manufactured in the United States of America

Library of Congress Cataloging-in-Publication Data
Thayer, James Stewart.
  Ringer.
  I. Title.
PS3570.H347R56   1988   813'.54   88-354
ISBN 0-517-56970-1

10 9 8 7 6 5 4 3 2 1

First Edition

Thanks to
José Aleaga, John Brenneis, Víctor Borrota,
Earl Doan, Lorenzo Pérez, John Reagh, Jay McM. Thayer,
John L. Thayer, M.D., Silvio Rogríguez Vila,
Amy Wallace, Richard Yeamans,
and to my wonderful wife,
Patricia Wallace Thayer.

Cuban history, curiously, has a dark strain of treachery. . . .

Castro biographer Herbert L. Matthews

PART ONE

Quien hace su cama con perros,
se levanta con pulgas.

(He who lies down with dogs gets up with fleas.)
CUBAN PROVERB

Chapter 1

Hector Perez and his family had been hiding in a guava thicket near the beach for two hours, waiting for the sun to settle into the sea. Only then would light angling off the waves hide them from shore patrols, and only then would the MIGs no longer be flying.

The fighters never flew at dusk. He had been assured of that by his friend Rafael Crespa, an oyster farmer who lived two kilometers north of the base.

Leaving at night would be too dangerous because a mile offshore were the reefs of the Archipiélago de los Colorados, where sharp coral could rip apart his raft. Perez needed enough light to see his way through the gap in the reef. The only break in the coral within two dozen kilometers of his home near La Panchita was near the air force base.

Perez scratched at a sand flea bite on his ankle and waited. Hidden under guava bushes was the raft Perez had built. It had taken him a year to find the eight oil drums and to save enough pesos to purchase the oars and his meager supplies. Perez was a *machetero*, a cane cutter, and had never been to sea. Using oars fastened to sawhorses hidden in Perez's back room, Rafael Crespa had taught him to row.

Perez and his family were about to cross the Puente de la Libertad, the Freedom Bridge, as many Cubans call the sea between Cuba and Florida. Perez caught the scent of eucalyptus and wondered whether such trees grew in Florida. He knew little about Florida. His cousin had fled Cuba from Mariel in 1980. Perez occasionally received letters from him, and each contained a photograph of his cousin embracing some new acquisition, a portable stereo, an automobile, a clothes washer. Perez was fleeing Cuba because he wanted the freedom of the United States, but he admitted to himself that his cousin's snapshots worked on him. All those unimaginable luxuries. How could his cousin, who had been a simple cane *guajiro*, obtain such things?

Perez's six-year-old son, Miguel, called out to him from near the raft. His wife, Sylvia, hushed him. Crespa had said that Cuban DAAFAR sentries patrolled the area. Perez had seen no soldiers as they had dragged the raft down the gully and across the *manigua*—the rough ground cover of prickly pears and salt grass—to their hiding spot near the beach. The sun was a large orange disk in the western sky, visibly dropping to the water. He could not look at the water without squinting. Only a few more minutes now.

Perez wore a white *guayabera*, Cuba's ubiquitous cotton jacket-shirt, and a pair of khaki pants stained brown from cane juice. He had a thin, pensive mouth. His eyes were prematurely surrounded by wrinkles, making him always look thoughtful. Sylvia often teased him that he had a professor's face and a peasant's hands. After years swinging a machete in the cane fields, where leaves and stalks lacerated skin, his hands were covered with purple scars. Perez knew he would never see a cane field again.

Miguel playfully banged on one of the raft's drums. His

4

mother snatched his hand away from it. The raft was a pathetic thing, eight empty fifty-five-gallon oil drums tied together with rope. Perez had stolen a wood door from Miguel's school building. The door was held between the rows of drums by a web of ropes running under it. Rafael Crespa had fashioned oarlocks out of rope. Strapped to the door were plastic bottles of water and tins of food. Sylvia had been able to find bananas, and about fifty of them were tied to the top of a drum. Two weeks' wages went for the small life jacket that Miguel was squirming in.

The Florida Keys lay two hundred kilometers to the northeast. Perez knew he could not row that distance and that he did not have enough food or water for such a trip. But the United States Coast Guard patrolled the area. The Americans would find them.

The glare off the water was now so brilliant that Perez could not look at it. It was time. He turned to his wife and nodded. Both rose to grab the oarlocks, and they dragged the raft from under the guava bushes. Their heels dug into the loose soil, and the raft left shallow grooves marking its passage. Miguel happily skipped behind them.

They left the *manigua* and gained the dune at the edge of the beach. Breathing heavily, Perez glanced east and west. No patrols. They would make it to the water.

Sylvia tripped on her cotton skirt and fell to her knees. She had refused to go to America in pants. She was a strong woman, and she immediately gained her feet and tugged at the raft. They had known each other since childhood, and she had lost none of her beauty in all the passing years. Glittering, even teeth, walnut-colored skin, and burnished black hair that fell to her shoulders. She grinned unexpectedly at her husband, hiding her fear.

With his thin nose and sharp cheekbones, Miguel had inherited his mother's looks, for which Hector often laughingly thanked the Virgin. The boy trailed after the raft, smiling as if they were on a picnic.

They reached the water's edge. The reef blocked rol-

5

lers from the Florida Strait, but the waves were still strong enough to knock Perez off balance as he shoved the raft into the sea.

"*¡Empuja!*" he ordered. Push.

When the drums floated free of the sand, he lifted Miguel to his position forward, then climbed over a barrel to his place at the oars. He slipped them through the oarlocks and began rowing against the waves.

Sylvia put her shoulder to the raft's stern, shoving it away from the shore. When the water was to her waist, Perez called, "*Sube.*" Climb in.

She gripped ropes at the stern to pull herself in, but a wave broke over the aft barrel and washed over her. She disappeared below the surface long enough for Miguel to scream.

Perez dropped the oars to reach for her, pulling her to the surface by her hair. She sputtered saltwater.

"*¿Qué paso? ¿Estás bien?*" he yelled over the roar of the waves. Are you all right?

Without waiting for an answer, he pulled her onto the raft. She coughed and wiped water from her eyes. Her wet dress was pasted to her, and her hair clung to her neck. This time her grin was feeble. She waved him back to the oars.

The raft began drifting back toward land, and water rushed over the bow, skidding Miguel along the door and against his father. The boy rolled onto his stomach and grasped the line between two barrels.

Perez pulled again and again on the oars, and the cumbersome vessel broke free of the waves and into deeper water. The ride leveled. The raft had never before been in water, and it had survived the breakers.

Between strokes on the oars, Perez looked at his homeland, the beach and the green hills rising behind it. His last look, he knew. He should be melancholy or exhilarated, but he had no time for such feelings, not with the reef ahead.

The coral was a low, menacing white apparition rising from the sea. Waves crashed into it, shooting spume into the air. He pulled toward it. After they were through the gap in the coral and after darkness covered the sea, Perez would allow himself a moment to rejoice, and perhaps a moment to weep.

Esteban Martinez had walked his route fifteen years, along the dirt road from the small dairy commune to the creamery. He led a donkey named Ponce, once his, now the commune's. The donkey pulled the commune's milk wagon, which carried fifty milk cans.

For five years the commune had been promised a tractor to pull this wagon and to harvest alfalfa. Finally the Russian Komintern tractor arrived. It lasted less than a week before its block cracked. Tractor parts were impossible to obtain. Ponce had been a few hours away from the slaughterhouse when he was given a reprieve and brought back to service on the milk route. Purple bougainvillea was now growing over the tractor. Martinez laughed and patted Ponce on the nose.

Martinez was only a little taller than the donkey, and the animal's long ears frequently flicked the rim of Martinez's straw hat. The Cuban sported an enormous, drooping black mustache that hid his mouth and much of his jaw. His skivvies and pants smelled of a barn.

The road was narrow, squeezed between the cliff overlooking the Florida Strait and the razor wire fence that surrounded the airfield near La Panchita. The airport was used by DAA-FAR, Defensa Anti-Aérea y Fuerza Aérea Revolucionaria (Revolutionary Air Force and Anti-Aircraft Defense), and each day MIG-25s and 21s took off on training runs. The runway had been built six years ago. The commune's cows had taken three months to become accustomed to the screaming MIGs before they could produce milk again.

Martinez led the donkey past the end of the runway, where the road turned inland to parallel the airstrip. The DAAFAR base was built on a promontory that jutted out to sea, and here the cliff also turned inland. Martinez always paused a moment to look out over the archipelago, beyond the reef to the setting sun. He had done it so many times that Ponce stopped without a pull on his bit.

This was the Cuban's moment of solitude each day, and he savored it. The brilliant colors of the failing sun playing off the waves. The fresh breeze from the sea.

After a moment Ponce led him away from the cliff, anxious for his day's work to be done. They followed the road south along the fence. Across the airfield were several hangars, one just recently built. Their doors were closed. Parked near the hangars was a line of fuel trucks and two fire trucks. Above the northerly-most hangar was the control tower, its glass windows throwing back the red and orange of the sun. Half a dozen antennas reached into the sky from atop the tower. On a rise behind the hangars was a barracks. Many of the MIGs were rolled into the hangars each night, but three of them were tied down on the edge of the runway near the tower. Their cockpit hatches were open. With their long landing gears and stubby wings, the fighters reminded Martinez of mosquitoes.

Across the runway were several DAAFAR military police- men, lounging near the door to the tower. Their rifles were slung over their shoulders. One threw back his head as if he were laughing. Martinez could hear only the soft sough of wind through the palm trees bordering the road.

A truck painted in khaki camouflage drove around the end of the north hangar and sped to the hangar's door. A soldier climbed down from the truck and pressed a button in a box on the side of the building. The hangar door began to slide open. Esteban Martinez slowed his donkey. He saw the truck inch ahead. He resisted the urge to run up to the fence and peer through it. The door opened farther. The interior of the hangar was flooded with light.

A plane was inside, much larger than a MIG. Martinez could see only a third of it, from the cockpit to the middle of the jet engines under the wing. The wing seemed to be dis- jointed and to have several parts. And unlike the MIGs, the fuselage was black, a polished sheen that made the craft look particularly sinister. He had never before seen such a plane.

8

He walked toward the milk wagon, giving Ponce's rump several nervous pats. Martinez's footfalls on the dirt sounded oddly loud to him. He rolled a milk can to one side and dug at the wagon's wood floor with his fingertips, prying loose a small piece of panel. He brought out a 35-mm Leica camera with a 200-mm telephoto lens.

Martinez stepped behind Ponce. Using the donkey as cover, he raised the camera and found the plane with the viewfinder. His practiced hands managed to take three quick shots before the hangar door rolled shut.

So intent was Martinez on the camera that he didn't hear the approaching DAAFAR vehicle until it was fifty meters from him, coming rapidly on the road and trailing a brown plume of dust. A soldier was behind the windshield and another manned a mounted DSh KM machine gun. The truck was a Soviet GAZ field car, an imitation of the American jeep. Martinez's throat tightened and his knees wobbled. He leaned into Ponce for support. Somehow they had seen him. Or maybe they had suspected him a long while and the glimpse into the hangar was a trap.

The field car roared down on him. Martinez simply held the camera, knowing there was no sense trying to hide it. He had no defense. They will send him to the infamous El Príncipe Prison where he will stand in front of the *paredon*, the firing squad. He crossed himself, his hands shaking with fear.

The jeep's siren sounded and the driver downshifted. A siren? Why would the DAAFAR be using a siren to arrest him? Martinez glanced at the jeep. The gunner was waving him off the road. Martinez surged with hope. Turning to hide his hands with his body, he tossed the camera between two milk cans, then grabbed Ponce's reins and led him into the *maruba* at the side of the road. Ponce snorted his displeasure at being taken into the thorny shrub.

The GAZ rolled by. Martinez stared after it through its trailing dust cloud. The gunner suddenly pointed out to sea and yelled something, and the truck stopped, only ten meters from Martinez. Knowing he would be safer continuing on his route, he nevertheless stepped farther into the brush for a better view of the sea. His gaze followed the gunner's gesture. He narrowed his eyes against the sun.

It took Martinez a moment to find the raft, but there it was, a black speck in the flash of the water. A slight pucker in the sea. Surely too small to be of significance to anyone. But Martinez knew better.

Carrying a bullhorn, the driver climbed out of the GAZ. He put the horn to his mouth.

"*¡Vuelvanse a la playa!*" The order to return to shore crackled out of the bullhorn. The driver barked it again.

The gunner watched the raft through binoculars. When the driver looked up at him, he shook his head.

"*¡Vuelvanse a la playa!*" Return to shore. The bullhorn's flat, steel tone crawled up Martinez's back. He was afraid, more fearful for the people on the raft than he had been for himself a few moments before.

Another moment passed before the gunner indicated the craft had not changed directions. Martinez could not tell how many people were on board. It must have been a cumbersome, jerry-built raft, as it was moving so slowly it left almost no wake. He could just make out the rapid dip and rise of its oars.

The gunner lowered the machine gun and pulled back its bolt. He gripped the dual handles tightly and leaned back. He looked at the driver.

Martinez closed his eyes.

"*Escoria,*" the driver said. Scum. It was a term originated by Fidel Castro for those who tried to flee the revolution. It was also a death sentence. The driver signaled with his hand.

The machine gun erupted with a long burst. Red fire shot from its snout, and spent casings arced into the air, sputtering into the ground near Martinez's feet. The startled donkey bucked in its tracings. Martinez's eyes opened involuntarily. The raft was still afloat.

But the machine gun kept on firing and firing.

* * *

10

Facing the rear of the raft, Hector Perez had seen the GAZ's dust trail on the hill. Over the waves brushing against the oil drums, he could not quite hear the bullhorn order, but he had no doubt what it was.

Sylvia was smiling at him, unaware of the DAAFAR patrol. She held Miguel on her lap. The boy was chewing a banana, pressing the mash into one cheek and making funny faces at his father. Perez pulled harder on the oars.

There was no going back, not to the camps and the separation from his family. One way or another, Cubans never returned from the Puente de la Libertad. Perez frantically worked the oars.

The first bullets tore into the water fifty meters behind them, looking like a school of herring churning to the surface to escape predators below. The boiling water quickly drew near as the gunner found his range. The first sounds from the machine gun reached them. Sylvia's eyes grew with sudden alarm. When she turned to look aft, her husband dropped the oars and went to his knees to embrace his family.

The water boiled toward them, then bullets slashed into the first oil drum. Steel and wood splinters erupted from the raft. Hector Perez's last thoughts were of his wife and child, and then the warm water was streaked with red.

Sick and weak, Esteban Martinez leaned against Ponce. The gunner licked his finger, then playfully touched the machine gun's barrel. He made a sizzling sound and laughed. The driver scowled at him and returned to his place behind the wheel. The GAZ backed away from the ledge, then turned toward Martinez. The gunner waved cheerfully at him as they drove past.

Martinez drew his hands across his eyes, then looked toward the reef again. The sun was almost below the horizon, and the water danced with the last of the colors. There was nothing left of the raft. Not a drum, not a piece of wood, not a body, nothing. Those people had just disappeared in a vapor.

11

A small sound escaped him, a moan of loss and despair. With great effort, he firmed his legs and walked to the donkey. Cubans gone forever, without leaving a trace. Their families would never know what happened to them. Cuba was a land of tragedy. This one would be lost in all the others.

Martinez had lived with his anger for many years. It flamed again. He jerked on Ponce's reins, leading him back to the dirt road. The donkey brayed at the unusual treatment.

That plane in the hangar. Surely it was a DAAFAR secret. His photos might make a difference. Esteban Martinez prayed they would.

Chapter II

The *Carolyn May* was called a three-island vessel because its superstructures—the fo'c'sle, bridge, and poop—looked like three islands when the hull was hidden below the horizon. The freighter was a six-thousand-tonner, and it worked its way through the Government Cut between Miami Beach and Fisher Island.

An air of weariness lay over the *Carolyn May*. It moved slowly, as if against a brisk current, and it rode low in the water, burdened with cargo. The ship's lines were blocky and rigid. Rather than with a modern ship's smooth sweep, the freighter's prow descended straight into the sea, and its gunwales precisely paralleled the water. The wheelhouse was made of teak, and the portholes were small and round in the old fashion. Like liver spots, exposed rivet heads speckled the ship bow to stern. Dried salt spray coated much of the hull. The single stack was blackened with diesel exhaust residue. Ketchup stains marred the hull midships where the cook threw scraps overboard each evening. All evidence of a long journey.

A glittering white cruise ship, its passengers lining the forward rails, was gaining steadily on the freighter. Spirited chatter could be heard over the dull rumble of *Carolyn May*'s old diesel engines.

The freighter was built in Liverpool in 1949 and spent twenty-nine years sailing the timber routes between Scandinavian and British ports. Timber ships usually have short, battered lives, but the *Carolyn May* had been purchased and converted by the Maurice Shipping Company in 1978. Two forward holds were now for bulk cargo, and two aft were for containers and pallets. The ship was a tramp, carrying cargo on irregular runs in the Caribbean.

The freighter came abreast of the MacArthur Causeway, a main link between Miami Beach and the mainland. Children in the backseats of automobiles leaned out windows to point at the enormous cruise ship, ignoring the *Carolyn May*. The sun was setting below the western horizon, made jagged by the buildings of Miami. There had been no wind that day, and haze made the distant city seem soft and forgiving. Shimmers of heat still rising from the baked land crossed the sun, rippling it like a flag in the wind. Reflections off the water dappled the cruise ship with orange and red.

Solid and stodgy, the *Carolyn May* seemed untouched by the beauty of Biscayne Bay at sunset. The hull was gunmetal gray with a bottle-green stripe running its entire length just above the waterline. Below the anchor was the Maurice Shipping Company's logo, a black *M* inside a black circle. Fore and aft of the bridge were the masts, each supporting three cargo booms, the largest a thirty-tonner. The masts and booms were secured by an intricate web of lines and pulleys that filled the sky above the ship. The *Carolyn May* had been built to work and had never known anything else.

The freighter veered to port, out of the main channel. The cruise ship glided by, slicing through the calm water, its wake rolling against the *Carolyn May*. A tug was waiting, and as the freighter slowed, the tug crossed its bow and turned its bumpers against the ship's hull. The tug was owned by the Lopez Tug and Launch Company, whose boats were identifiable by their electric-blue stacks and trim. When its bumpers gently pressed against the *Carolyn May*, the tug churned white water and nudged the freighter toward its mooring.

Ricardo Ferra stood on the ship's fo'c'sle, impatiently rocking on his heels as the ladder truck was driven along the dock to the freighter. This had been his first voyage, and now he was as anxious to disembark as he had been to board. He had so much to tell. The things he had seen and done. His mother and sister would not believe him.

Mr. Maurice had told him to try it out, see if the sea suited him. And now the boy knew he would spend his life at sea. This knowledge, its purpose and promise, exulted him. It was as if Mr. Maurice had grabbed him by the shoulders, shook some nonsense out of him, and set him on a straight course. Which is precisely what the old man had done. The boy would be forever grateful to him.

As the *Carolyn May* was secured to the bollards, and the accommodation ladder raised to the gunwales, the boy surveyed the pier. Three-story warehouses lined the dock, and the fading sun threw long shadows from one building to another. The pier was littered with stacks of pallets, rolls of hemp, barrels of molasses, crates of bananas, boxes of shoes, and idle forklifts. Uninterested in the *Carolyn May*, a security guard walked leisurely along the warehouses, his thumbs hooked in his Sam Browne. The boy almost waved, as he had seen tourists do from the decks of the cruise ships. But he was an old salt now, and it would be undignified to signal the landlubber.

Ricardo Ferra was fifteen. His mother claimed he was growing an inch a month, which was not far from the truth, as he was six feet and climbing fast. Ricardo was as thin as an egret, with bumpy knees, spindly arms, and a stretched neck. His dark hair was normally in a careful wave, the product of

15

fifteen minutes in front of the bathroom mirror, but was now wind-tossed over his brown eyes. He thought his best feature was the deep dimple in his chin, which he was still learning to shave without drawing blood. Ricardo was wearing jeans and a clean Hawaiian shirt, donned for the arrival. He had two Cuban cigars in his bag for Mr. Maurice.

He moved aft along the gunwale as a crewman in a watch cap secured the ladder. Emerging from hatches on the deck-house and wheelhouse, other hands began drifting toward the ladder, but the seaman in the watch hat gallantly swept his arm toward the ladder and bowed low, indicating Ricardo should be first off the ship.

The boy laughed at the honor but was only too happy to sling the bag over his shoulder, step over the rail, and begin the descent. He moved swiftly, letting the ladder's safety rail slide through his hand. Three rungs above the cement, Ricardo leaped and landed on the dock. He turned toward the dock's street gate.

Twilight had hidden the men, but now they stepped from doorways and alleys. Like apparitions, they emerged through the mist of falling darkness, appearing where there had been nothing before. A dozen of them, carrying badges and side-arms. They fanned out, stepping around pallets and crates, moving quickly toward the *Carolyn May's* bow and stern, some to the accommodation ladder. The men all wore blue wind jackets with patches on their chests, and blue pants. Some had on baseball caps with emblems on the front. They carried rifles across their chests, muzzles toward the sky. They closed in on the freighter.

As he walked away from the ship, Ricardo Ferra was gazing with pride at his new shoes, made of lizard, purchased in Kingston for a pittance. When he looked up and saw the Bureau of Alcohol, Tobacco and Firearms agents closing in on him, he panicked. His first thought was of the two contraband Cuban cigars stowed in his bag. An illegal act, the first in his life. Smuggled Cuban products, and the feds had come for him. For an instant, he saw himself behind bars, five years for each cigar.

Ricardo began to run. He held the duffel bag with its incriminating evidence tightly and churned his legs, jumping over a box of engine parts. He dodged right, away from an ATF agent who moved to intercept him.

"Hey you, stop," the agent called, unsnapping his holster. The boy reached the *Carolyn May*'s bow and feinted once, hoping to twist away from another agent who was reaching for him. In a grease slick, his right foot slipped out from under him, pitching him forward against a cleat.

With Ricardo's full weight behind it, his hand jammed against the iron cleat, snapping back two fingers. The breaking bones sounded clearly over the cry of a black-headed gull, circling over head, hoping to profit from the commotion. Ricardo rolled to his knees, tried to rise, then fell back to his seat, grasping the broken fingers with his good hand. The fingers jutted at an odd angle. His mouth pulled back with pain, but he would not cry out.

"You all right?" a man in a gray suit asked before he saw the fingers. When he did, he knelt near the boy and pulled Ricardo's hand away from him, clinically examining it. The man was tall, over six-two, and his suit was precisely tailored to his thin frame. His coffee-brown hair was in short curls and had only recently begun to recede. His features were sharp, with a long nose and chin, but his mouth was less severe, with a full lower lip. His cheeks were sunken, making him appear hungry. "We'll get you to a hospital. You'll be fine."

The man released Ricardo's hand. The boy grimaced again and tucked his hand into his belly, as if the warm Miami air were hurting it. Tears of pain rose in his eyes.

"Come on, let's get up." The man in the pinstripe suit hooked his hand under Ricardo's arm and gently helped him to his feet. The man's voice seemed disassociated from the scene at the dock, and his eyes swept the dock and the *Carolyn May*. None of it seemed to register on him.

17

One of the ATF agents hoisted Ricardo's duffel bag onto his shoulder and took the boy's elbow. Other agents began climbing the ladder. The man in pinstripes ran a hand across his forehead. He chewed on his lower lip, then asked Ricardo, "You're not a bad omen, are you? Not like the Flagler Street Bridge?"

Ricardo's cheeks were damp, and he was unaware of the low moans escaping him. But he had been raised in a polite family, and, still gripping his sprung and cracked fingers, he turned to the man. He stammered through his agony, "What? An omen?"

"You're not a sign that we should run away from this thing, are you? Learn our lesson, and not get involved with those bastards again?"

Ricardo shook his head, not understanding the man, not even hearing him clearly, because his hand hurt so much his ears were ringing.

The man in the pinstripe suit nodded at the ATF agent, who led Ricardo away. The man's gaze followed Ricardo, and under his breath he said, "Christ, I hope you're not a Flagler Street Bridge."

Chapter III

Brigade 2506 lived again, as it did every year on April 17. There were fewer of them now. Some had died, some had lost interest. But every year since the disastrous Bay of Pigs invasion, many of the survivors had met in this hall on Calle Ocho in Miami's Little Havana.

Merriment and melancholy filled the hall in equal portions. For those Cuban Americans who had grown wealthy and had moved on to Hialeah and Miami Beach, the annual visit to Little Havana was their pilgrimage, a return to their impoverished, noble past. For those who had stayed in the neighborhood, the reunion was a rededication to their Cuban heritage. And for all, it was a misty-eyed look back at those terrible days trapped on the beach and in the swamp at Bahía de Cochinos on the south coast of Cuba, and the capture and imprisonment that followed.

The hall had once been owned by the Odd Fellows, but

now, except when used by the local Boys Club for basketball tournaments and a few banquets, it was empty most of the year. On the night of the brigade dinner, it came alive with intense festivity.

Because of the dense cigar smoke, anything seen at a distance of over thirty feet was blurred. The ceiling was all but invisible. On one wall was a large blue-and-white banner that read in Spanish, "Next Year in Cuba." The banner had become a bit tattered over the years. Another one, new this year, proclaimed *"Cuba Libre."* Enormous bouquets lined the walls and stood in front of the podium; yellow and red roses, birds of paradise, and, in tribute to the homeland, white gardenias and showy jacaranda, all courtesy of a Brigade 2506 veteran who had prospered with a half dozen florist shops in Miami. The basketball nets were stuffed with balloons, and crepe paper streamers were everywhere. The gay decorations always seemed forced.

A band played to the left of the podium, and a small dance floor was roped off between the musicians and the dining tables. Along with brass horns and electric guitars, this group featured Cuban instruments: a gourd used for percussion called a *guiro*; another gourd with pebbles inside called a *maracas*; a small guitar called a *requinto*; and a *trest*, a nine-string Cuban guitar. They played rumbas and puntas, and once in a while a *zapateo*, where partners were separated as if doing a minuet. The dance floor filled when the band played *"Malaguena"* and *"Siempre en mi Corazón"* ("Always in My Heart"), songs by Ernesto Lecuona that had been popular for half a century.

The room smelled of prerevolution food, spicy ground hamburger, roast pork with black beans, and chicken with rice. Before Castro, Cubans ate little fish and green vegetables. There were none on the plates here. The fragrances of these dishes mixed with the jasmine and rum odor of the cigar smoke and the earthy fragrance of strong coffee, producing an intoxicating aroma. And if that were not enough to inebriate, most tables were covered with glasses of daiquiris and *mojitos*, juleps made of rum, lime juice, crushed ice, and a minty sprig called *yerbabuena*.

Shouts of recognition sounded above the music. Men unabashedly hugged each other and slapped each other on backs. At each table, veterans took turns offering toasts, raising their glasses to each other, to the south, or to the banners. Raucous laughter came from every corner of the hall, and, at this stage in the evening, a few slurred words could also be heard. Waiters rushed through swinging doors to and from the kitchen. Occasionally one of *los exilos* would look wistfully south, as if he could see the shores of his homeland through the walls.

One table near the podium was more sedate than the others. Many Cuban Americans would claim this was because the only Anglo in the room sat there. They were gloomy people. This one was William Maurice, and everyone would also admit, some grudgingly, that he deserved the honor of attending the annual brigade reunion. Maurice had stayed with them even during the time of Gorbachev—inspired euphoria when exile-Cuban anticommunism was in bad order. With the collapse of the expanded SALT talks earlier in the year, opinions had changed.

Maurice pushed his plate away. It had been heaped high with *cerdo asado con frijoles negros*, and there was not a bean or a shred of pork left on his plate. With a swizzle stick on which was a plastic replica of La Geraldilla, the maiden who is the symbol of Havana, Maurice stirred the dregs of a Scotch he had ordered before dinner.

He always anticipated this dinner with a mixture of hope and dread. He saw many friends from the old days only once a year now, at this reunion. There were quick updates, congratulations, and commiserations. A war had bonded Maurice and these men together. A dirty, quick, tragic war, but a war nevertheless. It had produced a deep, mutual attachment that had survived for decades. Maurice had been accepted by these brigade veterans, and that should have been his redemption. But

21

there was always the knowledge, endlessly gnawing at him over the years, that he, and only he, had ultimately sent these men to the beach head. Guilt would accompany Maurice to his grave. Until then, it flared with a vengeance at the brigade reunion.

Maurice sipped his watery drink. He was a tall man, but thick, with the look of an aging athlete. His belly sagged comfortably against his belt, a recent development his wife enjoyed teasing him about. He was wearing a blue blazer, and his heavily muscled thighs pushed against his slacks. His brown hair was peppered with gray and was closely cropped to hide its sparsity, showing his scalp's deep tan. His eyes were the color of a winter sea, a silver gray, and were harnessed by wrinkles. The rest of his square face was surprisingly unlined for a man in his early sixties, deceivingly cheerful, with a wide, turned-up mouth and a square jaw. He had a young man's smile, sudden and full, but quickly gone. Maurice rolled an ice cube around his mouth and glanced at his wristwatch.

"Impatient for Fidel?" Luis Cuervo asked over the noise. "Remember, he's as punctual as the summer solstice." Cuervo had been a radio operator at the Bay of Pigs. "My one regret in life is that I never fired a shot," he always said. Cuervo had a pencil mustache and meticulously combed hair. He favored silk suits, with a white handkerchief always in the jacket pocket. Cuervo was crisply handsome, and there was some truth to his claim that he was still breaking hearts all over the Caribbean. Maurice called him a dandy and a womanizer and a Beau Brummel, all to his face, accusations Cuervo proudly accepted as his due. Cuervo was an exporter of computers and software to Latin America. In the tense days before the invasion, late at night when there was nothing to do but worry, he taught Maurice how to play dominoes. In the years since, he had relieved Maurice of a minor fortune using the same set of tiles, so worn by now that the corners were rounded.

"When's he taking the podium?" Maurice asked, smiling at his own question. They were speaking Cuban Spanish, clipped, with some words bitten off. Mexicans can barely understand Cubans.

"Couple more minutes. He's probably putting on his watches now." Cuervo blew cigarette smoke—adding to what Maurice suspected was a toxic level in the hall—and said, *"El relajo"*—the fun and games—"begins in earnest when the Cancer takes the stage." The exile community had dozens of names for Fidel Castro, but "the Cancer" was preferred. Castro had as many names for Cuban Americans. *Gusanos*—worms—was among his favorites. At times the dictator and the expatriates seemed to be children angrily yelling across a fence. "Last time I almost choked on my fried bananas."

Luis Cuervo hailed a waiter for a brandy and pulled a cigar from his breast pocket. He asked, "I saw you favoring your leg tonight, Bill. How's the knee doing these days?"

Maurice pursed his lips, then gave the same answer he always did: "It creaks a little when it rains."

Compared with some of the others, his wounds had been insignificant. And they weren't even received on the beaches at Girón or Larga, making them less honorable. But Maurice had paid doubly, and this had made him a veteran in the eyes of brigade members. Following the Bay of Pigs, Castro had ordered a number of the Cuban invasion planners murdered on American soil. One of them was Jorge Gonzalez, who had supervised and funded a training camp for the brigade in the Florida Everglades, and who had escaped capture on Girón Beach. Three months after the Bay of Pigs, Gonzalez and his wife, Rosa, and Maurice and his wife, Anne, had just entered Gonzalez's car on their way to a restaurant when a bomb wired to the ignition detonated. With the random illogic of such a device, Gonzalez and Anne Maurice were killed instantly, Rosa Gonzalez suffered severe internal injuries, and Maurice's great toe on his left leg was severed, his patella smashed, and an eardrum ruptured. With the help of two stainless-steel pins and some wire his kneecap healed, but the resulting grainy joint surface and the loss of a weight-bearing toe had given him a small limp, exacerbated when he was tired or walking downhill. He tried to minimize his uneven gait when around his Cuban friends, but the day had been a long one, and Cuervo had picked up on it. Maurice always dismissed the loss of the high tones in one ear by saying he had never liked the piccolo anyway.

In 1961 Maurice had been one of the top people in Clandestine Services—now called the Directorate of Operations—for the Central Intelligence Agency, the youngest person ever to hold that position. President Kennedy was his mentor, taking him from his professorship at Princeton to the agency, then pushing him up the ladder in Clandestine Services. He had been one of Kennedy's golden boys, above criticism or direction from CIA lifers. Cocksure and puffed up, he had urged the invasion on Deputy Director Charles Cabell, on Director Dulles, and finally on the president.

Maurice had believed that an armed and trained Cuban underground existed. He convinced the president they were only waiting for a signal of support to rise and overthrow Fidel Castro. A grenade, just waiting for President Kennedy to pull the pin. Christ, the utter foolishness of the idea. He believed it because he trusted both the Cuban informants and the agency's own self-deceiving evaluations of what turned out to be dismally poor information. Kennedy had relied on Maurice to give the final "go" or "no go" signal. But he hadn't told Maurice that he would withhold air support at the critical moment.

After the Bay of Pigs, Kennedy told reporters, "Victory has one hundred fathers, and defeat is an orphan." An orphan with a lot of company, as Cabell, Dulles, and Maurice were forced out of the agency shortly after the disaster.

He had waited a year after the bomb blast to marry Rosa Gonzalez. Despite their grief, the truths of their situations had become quickly apparent, and they did not try to deceive each other about their motives. She needed a father for her two boys. He finally had a focus for the crushing guilt he suffered over his role in the Bay of Pigs.

24

Maurice had been fortunate, he knew. He would have married Rosa Gonzalez regardless of her personal qualities. He owed it to Gonzalez and to the brigade. He had met her only a few times before her husband's death. Maurice quickly learned she had an unwavering will, a vast intelligence, and a cutting wit. She could make Maurice laugh at will, a therapy he often needed. When he emerged from his crippling depression after the invasion and the car bomb, he found he was in love with Rosa. By then, he had been married to her more than a year.

A line of *comparsa* dancers formed in front of the band. The women were dressed in colorful peasant skirts and the men in white *guayaberas* and pressed slacks. Their movements were tightly syncopated with the band, bringing applause from the veterans.

Maurice lifted a *guanabana* from the dish of fruit. With his knife he halved it, avoiding the briers on its thick skin, then used his spoon to scoop out the white pulp, which had a taste and texture like vanilla ice cream. The *guanabana* and the other Cuban fruit on the tables—guavas, papayas (called *fruta bomba* because they resemble hand grenades, and never called "papaya," which in Cuban slang signifies female genitals), mangoes, and *zapotes*—were provided every year by Maurice, huge baskets of them, pungent reminders to the veterans of their homeland. The fruit had been illegally imported from Cuba on the *Carolyn May*. William Maurice had arranged it.

When the dancers finished and the musicians put down their instruments, Cuervo said, "They're opening the door." He laughed. "There's the wall. I love this."

A hush fell over the crowd. It was the same every year, the same door on the north side of the hall, the same Styrofoam bricks blocking the entrance, the same expectant grins spreading across the crowd. Fidel Castro had once attempted to prove his machismo by riding a bicycle at high speed into a brick wall. Friendly Castro biographers claimed the story was apocryphal, but brigade veterans believed it as an article of faith.

The drummer began a roll on his snare. Those at the rear

of the hall stood for a better view. Many put their cigars in their mouths to free their hands to clap. A few began anticipatory cheering. The drum abruptly ceased, and Fidel Castro burst through the brick wall on an old Zenith bicycle.

A wild roar of laughter and applause went up from the crowd. Castro wagged his head, shaking off the impact of his dash through the bricks. He rode the bicycle unsteadily to the podium. The Zenith had red plastic streamers hanging from the handlebars and bulbous balloon tires. Castro dismounted and lowered the kickstand with his foot. He clasped his hands above his head and swaggered to the podium.

This was not Fidel Castro, of course. It was a Cuban American named Eduardo Mederos, a brigade veteran who made an annual appearance as the dictator, always the highlight of the evening. Each year Mederos embellished his Castro lampoon with enough new mannerisms and jokes to keep the veterans talking about it until the next reunion.

Maurice glanced around at the crowd. Years before he had noticed a phenomenon that occurred a few seconds after the impersonator made his preposterous entrance. Once Castro was behind the speaker's stand, the crowd suddenly quieted, as if doused with cold water. For half a minute there was not a sound in the hall, not the clinking of utensils, not a cough.

Maurice knew why. Mederos's resemblance to the Cuban dictator was eerie. Despite the impostor's deliberately scraggly false beard (a play on Castro's thin beard, which was touched up in propaganda photographs and posters), Mederos could have been Castro in the flesh. He had the same expansive forehead and weak chin with a small double chin just below it. His hair receded, but not quite to the temples. His lips were malleable and wet, always on the verge of a long speech. The eyes were set deep, almost feminine, with long lashes, yet his gaze was unnerving. His frame was large, and he moved with the grace of a cat, just as Castro did. Those who were acquainted with Mederos—almost everyone in the room—knew the impostor's nose was too lean. Castro's had a high bump just under the brow and a downward turn at the nostrils. A broken Greek nose. Mederos used bits of putty to transform his nose into Castro's. Mederos's hair was too dark, and he used a wash-out gray dye.

In those first few seconds, before Mederos began making fun of himself as Castro, the brigade veterans saw the real Castro, the man who had driven them from Cuba, who had confiscated their property, who had imprisoned many of them, who had killed their loved ones. Even after decades in the United States, Castro was still the fulcrum of their existence, an inescapable tormentor. Mederos behind the podium brought back waves of pain.

Maurice saw faces flinch. Some looked away. Hands balled into fists. Some took a half step toward the podium, the first motion of a lynch mob.

Then the act began. Castro's face screwed up with worry, and with an exaggerated motion he brought his arm up to look at his wristwatch. The real Castro was known to frequently wear two watches, cheap East German models, the only brands available in Cuba, so he would not be late for appointments should one watch stop. Mederos-cum-Castro rolled up his sleeve to display a dozen watches, fitted on his arm up to his elbow.

The tried-and-true joke broke the tension, and the crowd again launched into laughter. Castro stepped to one side of the podium and pulled up one leg of the green army pants. Six more watches were strapped around an ankle above the combat boots. Every year there had been more wristwatches. The crowd clapped for more, and Castro pulled up the other leg. More watches. Loud laughter. Castro turned his back to the crowd and lifted his shirttail from his pants. Sewn to the shirttail was a row of wristwatches, a new twist this year. Deafening applause and laughter. Castro's struggle to tuck in his shirt popped a button on the uniform blouse, which hid a large pillow, put there to imitate Castro's recent weight gains. The crowd howled.

Luis Cuervo laughed as much as his reserved manner would ever let him. Maurice grinned, more in sympathy with the crowd than with humor.

The impersonation only emphasized how utterly powerless they were against Castro. They were reduced to mocking him at a safe distance. Laughter was the exiles' only revenge, gained once a year, and it had to carry them through the year. Luis Cuervo once told Maurice that laughter was not enough.

Castro pulled a foot-long cigar from inside his shirt. He took his time lighting it, bellowing his cheeks and blowing smoke from the side of his mouth. In an accurate impression of Castro's Galician accent and chronically hoarse voice, the impostor said, "You've read I quit smoking cigars." He paused for effect. "I didn't know Prensa Latino had an office in Miami."

The veterans laughed and nodded knowingly. Prensa Latino was Cuba's notoriously mendacious wire service and propaganda arm.

"On my way to this dinner tonight," the impostor said, "I crossed the Flagler Street Bridge. No guns on the boats today, so the revolution is safe another year."

Same lame joke every year. The veterans laughed, but there was a hard edge to it. In the days before the invasion, the CIA assembled a ragtag navy to transport the brigade and its equipment to the beaches. They did little to disguise the vessels. One gunboat with a .50-caliber machine gun on its stern was moored under the Flagler Street Bridge in full view of Miami rush-hour traffic. Miamians took to calling the CIA the Cuban Invasion Agency. Thus the Flagler Street Bridge became a metaphor at the agency for a bad omen. Mederos mentioned the bridge every year, and Maurice's ears always burned. He had purchased that boat and rented its mooring.

Castro puffed on the cigar and continued, "As you know, I am a man of few words, as you will find out in the next two hours. There will undoubtedly be a lot of this speech left over at the end of my ideas. Fortunately, I can talk fifty percent faster than anybody can listen."

28

Maurice chuckled along with his friends. He had met Eduardo Mederos a number of times. Mederos had been among the first to land on Playa Larga, which before the invasion Maurice had labeled Red Beach. Girón was Blue Beach. There was to have been a Green Beach, but the operation collapsed before that landing was established. At the time, Maurice thought the colors lent the invasion a proper military air. His use of colors was only embarrassing now. Twenty months after the invasion, Castro exchanged the imprisoned brigade members for $53 million in food and medical supplies. Mederos returned to Florida to open a small auto parts store. He now owned sixteen of them throughout Dade and Broward counties.

Maurice settled back in his chair. The act would continue for another ten minutes. Mederos would hilariously ridicule Castro's peculiarities, real and imagined. His talkativeness, his wide gestures, his enormous appetite, his indifference to religion, his ignorance of virtually everything outside Cuba, his failure to remarry, and on and on.

Every year the biggest laugh came when the impersonator introduced Castro's brother Raul, for whom the veterans reserved a special hatred. He was viewed as a talentless sycophant and leech. Raul was Castro's second-in-command and head of Cuban military services. The Raul impostor—a friend of Mederos—always took the stage dressed as Harpo Marx, with frizzy blond hair beneath a DAAFAR *comandante*'s cap, a long coat, and a squeeze horn tied to a belt. In the course of sixty seconds, Mederos would yell out a dozen comical non sequiturs and ask after each one, "Isn't that right, Raul?" The impostor would grin idiotically and honk the horn. Even Maurice would laugh.

Just as Castro was to introduce his brother, the doorman hurriedly wound his way between tables toward Maurice. The man's features were creased with anxiety, and he did not take his eyes off Maurice as he dodged between the veterans rocking back in their chairs with laughter. Maurice did not see him approach.

29

The doorman was short and did not have to bend far to speak into Maurice's ear. At his first words, Maurice jerked upright in his chair. Maurice asked tensely, "Who impounded it?"

"Alcohol, Tobacco and Firearms, Captain Pearson thinks. But he isn't sure. They've got armed people all around the *Carolyn May*, and they've boarded the ship. Pearson is walking them around the ship, cooperating, like you've told him to if this happens."

Maurice sat back in his chair, ran a hand through his thinning hair, and said under his breath, "Damn it to hell." He shook his head wearily. "Well, there's nothing I can do about it now. I'll call. . . ."

"There's more bad news, Mr. Maurice. Ricardo Ferra has been hurt."

Maurice stood so quickly his chair tipped back against the next table. He towered over the doorman. "How badly?"

"Don't know. It happened as he was getting off the ship. They've taken him to Jackson Memorial."

Maurice brushed by him and squeezed between tables toward the door. The veterans craned their heads around Maurice as he passed, watching the door where Raul Castro was due to make his appearance. No one noticed Maurice's troubled expression, except Luis Cuervo, who tossed his napkin on the table and followed him. Thick smoke swirled behind Maurice as he dodged around a waiter and ducked blue crepe paper over the door. With Cuervo close behind, he stepped onto the street.

Calle Ocho was a river of people, lively and loud, and Maurice and Cuervo were swept along with them. Cuervo pointed down the street where his car was parked. Maurice pushed through the strollers, Cuervo in his wake. The street smelled of coffee and cologne, and the lilting sounds of salsa could be heard from the doorways of shops open late. Young couples walked arm in arm, while older people stopped to stare into store windows, some featuring ornately mounted photos of John F. Kennedy and Cuban patriot José Martí, draped in American and Cuban flags. Children held their mothers' hands and tried not to spill their sugar cane juice. Garish neon streaked the pedestrians with light. Staccato Spanish and bright laughter made Calle Ocho sound like an aviary.

Maurice heard none of it. Worry pressed his mouth into a grim line. When he reached Cuervo's Jaguar, he impatiently rattled the door handle until Cuervo unlocked it. Maurice sank onto the sedan's seat, and they pulled out into the traffic.

Cuervo asked, "Who's hurt?"

"Ricardo Ferra." Maurice rubbed his chin with a knuckle. "The kid I put on the *Carolyn May* this trip."

"He's one of your extended family?"

Maurice nodded. Cuban Americans often said the Bay of Pigs produced only two things, propaganda for Castro and widows for Miami. Attempting to manage his guilt and grief over the lost lives, Maurice tried to console a number of the widows in the weeks after the invasion. There was nothing he could say to them, but soon he was helping the widows with the Immigration Services' unfathomable bureaucracy, with getting their children into school, with the language, and with a loan now and then. Some of the women eventually remarried and had more children. Maurice still helped when he could. Many of the kids were grown now, and he got them jobs or advanced them funds for college. Maurice's accountant recently told him his extended family was costing him seventy thousand nondeductible dollars a year. Maurice had replied, "Coffins don't have pockets."

Ricardo Ferra was having trouble in high school. Too much a dreamer, his mother said. Maurice had thought exposure to a maritime sailor's life might convince Ricardo to continue his schooling. He had assured Mercedes Ferra that her son would be worked hard but would be completely safe at sea. Now this. Maurice bunched a hand.

"Easy," Luis Cuervo said. "The dashboard is real wood. Your fist print wouldn't look good in it."

They crossed the Miami River on Northwest Eighth Avenue and moments later pulled into Jackson Memorial's emergency entrance. The last time Maurice had been on this driveway, he had arrived in an ambulance. In his dazed condition, he had not realized that his wife was on the stretcher next to him. A sheet covered her face.

Maurice got out of the car before it was fully stopped. He rushed by several uniformed drivers leaning against their ambulances and into the admitting area. Expecting to be told to go to the intensive care unit, he asked for Ricardo Ferra. Without looking up from her computer monitor, the nurse pointed to an examining room.

Maurice was instantly relieved. An examining room was not an operating room. The kid wasn't critical. He walked around the admitting desk. He could see into the room, where a white-coated physician stepped to a supply drawer, revealing Ricardo Ferra, who was sitting on the examining table. When the boy saw Maurice, he grinned sheepishly. Splints held two fingers.

As he stepped into the room and nodded at the doctor, Maurice could not keep the delight out of his voice. "I let you out of my sight a couple weeks, and look what happens."

"It's just two fingers. The doc here says I'll be like new in a month. If I wasn't so fast with my reflexes, it would've been my handsome face getting the cast." Percodan was doing Ricardo's talking.

"What happened?"

Ricardo Ferra began an answer: "These guys with guns . . . "

A man in a pinstripe suit appeared at the examining room doorway. "William Maurice?"

Maurice turned.

"That's him." The boy pointed with his good hand. "His men have taken over the *Carolyn May*."

"Mr. Maurice, I'm sorry this happened." There was a clerical air about the man, with his modulated tones and assured expression. "I'm also sorry to report that we've impounded your freighter and its cargo."

Maurice squared himself to the man. "Who are you?"

"I'm Jack Cantrell, deputy director for operations for the Central Intelligence Agency. Your old job, if you'll remember."

"I remember," Maurice said. "What do you want?"

"Your help."

Maurice laughed abruptly. "Little chance of that, don't you think?"

"We knew you'd be difficult, Mr. Maurice, so let me be blunt. You are a smuggler. The *Carolyn May* is filled to the gunwales with illegal Cuban goods. We are going to direct the Justice Department to indict you and to auction off your ship." Cantrell smiled irritatingly. "That is, unless we have your help, and we think we'll have it."

Chapter IV

J ack Cantrell turned his Buick into one of the warehouse's truck loading slips. The headlight beams swept only a portion of it, as the building was a block long. Its cement walls were painted white, and the doors were bottle green. There were no windows.

"I thought the agency's office was in the federal building downtown," Maurice said, levering himself slowly out of the car. His mended kneecap grated. Years ago, the first time Rosa heard that sound, she began searching for her sewing basket, thinking her new husband's pants had split.

Cantrell answered over the car's roof as he locked the door. "Still is downtown, but the DGI often puts a watch on the building, and makes notes on who comes and goes. We can't take that chance, not this time." The DGI, for Dirección General de Inteligencia, was Cuba's CIA.

Maurice followed Cantrell away from the car. The air was

humid and hot. Maurice was a Maine native and had never adjusted to what he called the "six-step sweat," the suffocating walk between an air-conditioned automobile and an air-conditioned building. Rosa laughingly called him a wimp, and he would counter that he didn't have the heat dissipation system evolved by her swarthier race.

The warehouse was on the Port of Miami's mile-long island, a thousand yards off the mainland, accessible by a causeway. The night sky high above the warehouse was filled with lights festooned along the decks of four cruise ships moored bow to stern on the island's north shore. Maurice knew his ship, the *Carolyn May,* was berthed farther along the line with a few other freighters, out of view behind the building. He hoped it would still be his ship at the end of the evening.

Cantrell stepped across the pavement to the warehouse. A small slot was in the door at chest level, and Cantrell slipped his fingers into the narrow aperture.

"Back when I joined the agency," Maurice offered, "one of our first lessons was to open the door and get the mail from the other side. You'll discover it's considerably easier."

Cantrell smiled, softening his austere features. A bolt sounded loudly. The DDO said, "There's a laser in the slot, much like the one at the supermarket. It reads my fingerprints, and feeds them to a computer upstairs to compare them with those on file. Takes one second. Then the computer throws the bolt."

From the sawdust on the cement near the door, Maurice guessed the mechanism had been installed that day.

Cantrell pushed open the door. "We'll redundate tomorrow by installing a camera to view the door."

Redundate. Lasers or no, some things never changed at the agency. Maurice had a sense of coming home. He didn't like it at all.

Maurice followed Cantrell through the door, expecting the warehouse's crates and barrels and sacks to be pushed back for a desk with a single phone. Maybe a file cabinet. In his time,

Maurice had set up more than a few of these impromptu branches. He had called them "tomcat offices." Gone before the neighbors knew anything.

This was on a different scale. Seven workmen were erecting shelving and installing overhead lighting, working at a fast pace, even at ten o'clock at night, and filling the building with the sounds of hammers and a table saw. One worker was laying telephone and power cables. An electrician was installing a circuit-breaker panel near the back wall. Six desks were already in place, each with a computer terminal and a phone. Agency people were manning them, some removing documents from portable files. Unused desks lined the back wall, along with a small mountain of cardboard boxes. At the base of the pile was a large wood crate, its top pried off and lying across it at an angle. Maurice saw the wire stock of a semiautomatic weapon protruding from the packing. One of the agents had a ghetto blaster on the floor near his desk, and from it came classical music. Maybe Wagner, Maurice couldn't tell. The only time he listened to classical was at his dentist's, and Maurice had finally told him he preferred the drill's whine.

The warehouse was divided by a wall into two areas, this office, and the remainder of the long storehouse that paralleled the ships. East of this building, nearest the city side of the island, was the port's cruise ship building, resembling a modern airport terminal.

Sitting behind a steel desk was a stout, bespectacled man of about thirty. Cantrell introduced him as Gerard Jones and cautioned that he never went by "Gerry." "But some people around here call him 'Toothbrush.' "

Maurice shook his hand and came away with a smudge of chocolate. Next to a computer monitor on Jones's desk was a slide rule encased in a lump of clear plastic on which was etched "RIP." An empty McDonald's bag and a Coke cup with a straw protruding from it were pushed to one side. Jones must have had ketchup with his fries, as he was wearing some of it on his navy-blue tie. A ketchup smear suited him. His eyes were set close and were bright blue, enlivening his pallid skin and dusty brown hair. Jones may have had a chin once, but extra pounds had padded most of it away. With his full cheeks, canted eyebrows, and blunt nose, Jones had a face that would always be cheerful, irrespective of his mood. And he looked like he had a basketball beneath his shirtfront. Maybe the agency didn't have fitness standards anymore. Probably thank Jimmy Carter for that. He'd tossed out all other standards, so Maurice had heard.

Jones said in a slight voice, "The DCI called ten minutes ago. You're to contact him right away."

"Entertain Mr. Maurice for a moment with your Castro bit, will you, Gerard?" Cantrell walked to the next desk to lift the handset of a telephone, which with its extra buttons and read-out panel looked more purposeful than a conventional phone. Cantrell inserted a plastic key into the phone and turned his back to them.

"All right," Jones said, spreading his hands as if showing there was nothing up his sleeves. "Give me a date since 1959, and a time of day."

Maurice looked balefully at the young man. Maurice's stomach was sour, and he could feel his heart in his chest. He had no idea what his old employer wanted. But no good could come of it, no mistake about that.

"Go ahead," Jones urged. "A date and a time."

Maurice exhaled, billowing his cheeks. "June 4, 1975, two o'clock in the afternoon." What in hell?

Jones thought a moment, his stare in the distance. Then he beamed. "Fidel Castro had just left his room at the old Havana Hilton, one of the many places he keeps in the city, and had joined Ernesto Delgado for a snorkeling outing west of Havana. They arrived at the dock at Salado forty minutes later. They spent two hours snorkeling." Jones grinned widely, as if expecting congratulations.

Maurice wouldn't give him anything. "January 15, 1968, noon."

Another short pause. "Castro was meeting with his brother Raul and DAAFAR *Comandante* Emelio Vasquez at the presidential palace to discuss the acquisition of Soviet antiaircraft guns. The meeting broke up at one o'clock when Castro suffered a flare-up of the influenza that had been bothering him for three days. He spent the next twenty minutes in one of the palace's second-floor bathrooms."

Maurice challenged, "You're making this up."

Gerard Jones's grin did not falter. The monitor was on a universal joint, and he spun it to Maurice. He pressed several keys to call up the program, then typed in Maurice's last date. The green phosphor screen filled instantly.

Maurice bent toward it. After a moment he muttered, "I'll be damned." I'm dealing with an idiot savant, Maurice thought. "You're a case for a clinic somewhere."

Jones laughed. "Believe me, I've been studied. Too bad the computers make my small talent even smaller."

"Some computer."

"It's an Apollo workstation, flown down here just this morning from Washington."

Maurice liked this bizarre fellow. Jones had a passion, and nothing endeared someone more quickly to Maurice than a passion, even an eccentric one, like knowing of Fidel Castro's every bowel movement.

Cantrell returned from his desk, his face a shade lighter and his mouth pressed into a straight line. The DDO slipped into a rolling secretary's chair next to Jones. "Bring up Mr. Maurice's business file. Let's start with Dallas Lyle, shall we?"

At that name, Maurice knew they had him.

The Apollo must have had a tape tie-in, because when Gerard Jones stroked the keys several times, a video of Dallas Lyle appeared on the screen. Lyle was shuffling along a dilapidated neighborhood Maurice knew was in Port-au-Prince. His long white hair was tousled, and his pink face was pinched and creased, a miser's face. Lyle stepped around a mound of garbage and a naked toddler playing with a length of twine, and continued on his way.

38

"Dallas Lyle is only forty-four years old"—Cantrell paused with a comic's timing—"if you don't count the twenty-four years he has spent in prison. He's a counterfeiter of modest talents, having never quite mastered the artistic intricacies of the twenty-dollar bill. But Lyle has been singularly successful in his latest parole. In fact, he has had no contact with American authorities for almost ten years."

Cantrell nodded at Jones, and another image appeared on the monitor. "This is the inside of Lyle's shop on Merita Street in Port-au-Prince. You can see his IBM copier and a cylinder press. He's got a desk full of styluses, inkwells, writing brushes, penpoints, nibs, even some old quills. And, more interestingly, that open cabinet you see to the right of his desk contains blank U.S. Customs and FDA forms, and assorted other blanks from Haiti, Jamaica, the Dominican Republic, and Cuba."

Another nod. "Here you see one of Dallas Lyle's better works. It's a fraudulent Food and Drug Administration May Proceed Notice, green form number 702, indicating that no sample will be taken by the FDA of a shipload of Haitian cigars, and that there'll be no detention of the goods. With this, the cigars can breeze right into this country without the inspection that might show the tobacco was grown and the cigars rolled somewhere other than Haiti, say, in Cuba. Lyle also counterfeits invoices, bills of lading, ship manifests, waybills, and anything else that might be needed. Most of these documents have Maurice Shipping Company and *Carolyn May* on them, by the way."

That it was perhaps the dumbest thing he could ask didn't stop Maurice. "So what are you saying?"

Cantrell waited for a nearby table saw to wind down before he answered, "You've given a comfortable retirement to an old con. Not necessarily out of compassion, though. Lyle is one of your assistants running a double transport system out of Cuba, Mr. Maurice. Cuban products—cigars, cloth and finished apparel, fruit, chemicals, and sugar—depart Baracoa or Santiago de Cuba in Cuba and arrive in Port-au-Prince or Kingston, sometimes Santo Domingo. On this leg of the journey, the goods are transported in coasters owned by Jamaicans and Haitians licensed by their governments to import from Cuba. All legal so far, at least at the first glance. You're still with me?"

Maurice scratched his chin, as neutral an answer as he could come up with.

"Some of the goods departing Cuba are approved for export by the government there. Others, deeper in the holds, are purchased on Cuba's black market at much lower prices. Everybody makes out; the Cuban farmers, the warehousemen, the boat owners, all making more than if they had sent the goods through the Cuban system. And then the dance really begins when the products are offloaded in Haiti or Jamaica."

"Have you got a couple of Tums?" Maurice asked.

Gerard Jones typed something onto the keyboard, then said, "Coming right up."

"You've got an antacid program in there?" Maurice asked. Jones had probably been caught in one of the agency's regular sweeps of Cal Tech.

Jones replied with delight, "I've got an in-house procurement menu, and—"

"Please, Toothbrush," Cantrell cut in. "In Port-au-Prince, say, the goods end up in dockside warehouses, and your document sleight of hand begins. New invoices, showing Haitian rather than Cuban origin. New manifests, new warehouse tickets. The FDA forms, a Customs Consumption Entry Document 7501, and anything else you might need are forged by Dallas Lyle."

A young man in a white shirt rolled to the elbows appeared and dropped a roll of Tums into Maurice's hand.

Cantrell went on, "Payments are made to certain Haitian customs officials and warehouse owners. Not much per load, but it's proved to be a steady, long-term income for them. Then the goods are loaded onto the *Carolyn May* headed for Miami. The result is that you can beat the prices of legal imports into this country."

"You have proof of all this?" Maurice asked, chewing two tablets.

"Your file takes up fully a quarter of the space on a twenty-megabyte hard disk," Jones answered sternly. "We've got proof."

"Show him something, Gerard."

Jones grinned again, a crease above his chins. His hands flashed over the keyboard. "What you now see on the monitor is a photograph of several crates of bananas on a dock at Santiago de Cuba, in southeast Cuba. The picture was taken twenty days ago by one of the air force's high-resolution film recon satellites ninety miles above Cuba."

Jones flicked another key. "Here is the same crate eleven days ago being offloaded from the *Carolyn May* in Miami, two hundred yards from where we're sitting right now. I suppose we could have stationed someone on the warehouse roof to take the second photo, but the satellite was in position, and it's easier for the program to have input from the same camera."

"It's pretty tough to tell one crate of bananas from another," Maurice said hopefully.

"Not at all. I'm putting on the screen a computer-generated line drawing representing all observable angles of the crate slats and the bananas as they sat at the Cuban dock. The computer reduces the photo to stick representations, exaggerated to the frame edge for clarity. No two crates of bananas have the same angles, like fingerprints."

Angles of bananas? Maurice began to wonder if this whole event wasn't one of his wife's pranks. She'd been known to yank his leg in the past, sometimes conspiring with Luis Cuervo and others to put one over on him.

"Now I'll decrease the first image's size and move it over, and next to it show the angle map for the crate in Miami, also run through the geometric reduction program. Looks like pick-up sticks, doesn't it? Now I'll lay one image over the other."

On the monitor, two sets of lines melded perfectly into one.

"See?" Jones asked in triumph. "Same crate of bananas."

"What happens if the Russians ever find out we've got a

banana-crate comparison computer program?" Maurice asked. Maybe levity would save his ship.

Cantrell looked at Maurice. "Gerard has a software program showing that normally there's a sixty percent chance I'd laugh at that. Not tonight, though. I'm too tired." Cantrell smiled weakly.

He's human, Maurice decided with relief.

Cantrell quickly reverted to form. "Your ship will be sold at public auction, and you'll probably go to prison."

"The hammer and the slammer," Gerard Jones summarized cheerfully.

Maurice ate another Tums.

Jones added, "In the old days, you called it having someone by the nads, if you'll remember. Short for gonads."

Maurice rubbed his upper lip with a finger. "I remember."

"We still call it that," Jones said despite Cantrell's hard stare. "That term is your great legacy at the agency."

"What's the trade-off, then?" Maurice asked. "What do I have to do?"

"Try as we might, we can't quite develop a computer that completely replaces Jones here," Cantrell said, not unkindly. "Try the Castro game again. Give Jones a date from the 1980s."

Jones immediately looked uncomfortable. He stared at Maurice, his brows raised and his mouth parted, as if silently pleading with him not to pick a date.

"Independence Day, 1986."

The agent's gaze turned to the ceiling, then back to Maurice. He shook his head and slumped back in his chair.

Cantrell said tonelessly, "As you know so well, the agency was obsessed with Castro for decades. From 1959 until 1979, we knew his precise whereabouts and activities, every minute of every day, except for a total of ninety-two days."

"Ninety-two days, four hours, and twenty minutes," Jones corrected softly, as if in the presence of the dead.

The young agent mourned those missing days, Maurice supposed.

"Our current information on Castro, and on anything in Cuba, is patchy at best," the DDO said. "A number of things contribute to this. Less effort on our behalf over the years. Fewer Cuban walk-ins. And the most important reason has been Cuban G2's success in eliminating our humint resources."

G2 referred to the Departamento de Seguridad del Estado, a combination Gestapo and Doberman pinscher. Maurice guessed "humint resources" meant spies. Soon he'd ask Jones's in-house procurement program for a dictionary.

"Not knowing Castro's whereabouts is only one symptom of our problem, which is getting worse all the time. Did you ever work with Armin Chacon in the early sixties?"

Maurice shook his head.

"Chacon was a reporter back then, but he rose steadily to become the newspaper *La Tarde*'s city editor, which Cubans call a town editor. He has worked for us since before the Bay of Pigs, and was our cell director in Havana. Two months ago G2 arrested him. Undoubtedly under dire stress, Chacon talked. Since then, it's been like falling dominoes. In the next week, twenty-eight other *agentes informativos* vanished. And to date there've been almost three hundred other arrests, most of people we aren't connected with. It's one of those berserk G2 sweeps, just like the one during and after the Bay of Pigs. Because of the vast number of people they round up, they're bound to net our people. And they have. We didn't have much of an organization in Havana. Now we've got nothing. A complete disaster for us. And the arrests are continuing."

The sudden realization what the agency wanted shoved Maurice against his chair. His people. Cuban cigars and fruit didn't just find their way down to the dock in Santiago de Cuba and into the boats. Maurice's people got them there. Maurice's contacts had resulted from twenty years of taking risks, of culling and grooming, and of patience. Now these bank clerks wanted him to hand them over.

"You think I've got some sort of network in Cuba," Maurice said. He gripped the chair arms. "A few middlemen, sure.

43

But they're warehousemen and truck drivers, not much good to you." Some truth to that.

When Cantrell impatiently waved at the Apollo monitor, Gerard Jones's hands passed over the keys, and a photograph of a seaside building appeared on the screen.

Jones leaned forward to share the view of the monitor. He said, "This is the Workers' Dock Number Four in Santiago Bay. Those mountains you see rimming the city behind the warehouse are the Sierra Maestras, and that's the Santa Iglesia Cathedral rising behind the warehouse." He pressed a key. "This is the same scene, magnified several times. Standing on the wharf between the warehouse and that coaster is a man we think is Lieutenant Gustavo Tamayo of the Santiago police."

Maurice tightened his hold on the armrests. "The distance and heat shimmers have made that picture fuzzy. That could be anybody."

Jones replied without malice, "Not really. It's clear the person has no mustache. Now take a look at this." He entered a command. "Now this photo was taken by a McDonnell Douglas RF-4 Phantom, with a lateral oblique camera, a Zeiss KA-116A, in a multisensor pod hung externally under the plane's wing. The photo shows the roof of the workers' warehouse and the safety railings, deck, and a portion of a hatch of the coaster docked at the wharf. In between you can see a person wearing a uniform cap. On his shoulder straps, you can see the single star and bar of a Cuban police lieutenant."

"That still doesn't—"

Cantrell cut in, "The Phantom photo and the sea-level shot were taken within four minutes of each other. It's the same man in both. Although the pictures are not as clear as we'd like, we know it's Gustavo Tamayo. There are four lieutenants on the Santiago de Cuba force, and only one doesn't wear a mustache. Tamayo."

"So what have you figured is his connection to me?" Maurice asked.

"Nothing concrete," Cantrell admitted. "But every time

that coaster is about ready to depart Santiago, Tamayo appears and stands beside it on the dock. We've got photos of him on three occasions. And that ship is the same one that delivered the crate of bananas to Port-au-Prince."

Cantrell leaned back and crossed his legs. "We've got some other items on your network in Cuba. Nothing too impressive. But the telling fact remains that you couldn't do business with Cuba's black market unless you had greased a lot of wheels. We want those contacts."

"They won't work for you. Most of them learned the hard way not to trust the CIA."

"But they'll work for you," Cantrell said. "We want you to run them. That's part of the deal."

Maurice glanced between Cantrell and Jones. They had him by the nads, no question about that. As if looking for help, he glanced around the warehouse. Work continued at a fast pace, even this late at night. Carpenters were walling off a corner of the building, perhaps a conference room. They must have been adjusting the air conditioning, as the temperature seemed to be dropping quickly.

Maurice said, "You've spent a lot of money trying to persuade me. Sending out the recon planes, positioning the satellites, who knows what else. The agency must be on to something very big."

"The Cuban photo, Gerard." Cantrell's voice imbued his words with reverence, making him sound like a priest.

On the monitor appeared a portion of a large airplane inside a hangar. Near the building's door were a military jeep and several soldiers. "This photo was taken four days ago by one of our few remaining operatives in Cuba. Jones, extrapolate it out."

The visible portion of the plane remained on the screen, but the hangar and soldiers disappeared, replaced by a royal-blue field. At another keyboard command, a line sketch was added to the plane, completing a hybrid photo-drawing of an entire plane. Yet another keyboard entry instantly colored the plane in black and gray, filling in textures and shadows on the windows, wheels, and engine intakes.

"That's what our Office of Weapons Intelligence believes the rest of it looks like," Cantrell said. "Rotate it."

The plane came alive on the screen as it turned slowly toward Maurice. Now Maurice could see the second square engine intake.

"I've programmed in some fantastic sound effects, if you'd like," Jones said. "I borrowed them from the Nintendo Company, same people who make Donkey Kong."

Cantrell grimaced, the pained expression of one enduring tight shoes, but otherwise ignored him. "We don't know what the Soviets have named their new bomber. NATO calls it the Blackjack. One or more of them is in Cuba."

Maurice stared at the plane. He had never seen a meaner piece of equipment. It reminded him of a dagger. "So what do you want of me?"

"The president has decided they cannot stay in Cuba. You are going to help us get them out."

Chapter V

William Maurice's home in Coral Gables was a fortress. Tons of cement, iron doors, and barred windows were ingeniously disguised by its Mediterranean design, and the palm trees and ferns in the driveway island softened the house, but it was a fortress nevertheless. The agency had concluded that Jorge Gonzalez was the bomb's intended victim, not Maurice. But Maurice had never been sure. No sense making it easy for them to try again, he had figured.

Time had lessened his fear of another attack. Now the bulletproof windows were often left open. The property was surrounded by a six-foot-high cement wall, but the driveway gate was usually rolled back these days. Easier for the kids to come and go. He had junked the annoying television security system. When his German shepherd died of old age, Maurice hadn't bothered replacing him. Wasn't much of a guard dog anyway. Twelve hundred dollars to train an animal whose only stunt turned out to be the balls-up back roll.

Maurice drove his Ford along Granada Boulevard to his driveway near the intersection of Osorio. It was ten-thirty in the evening, and light from stagecoach lamps on the gate columns cast a pearl glow on the manila palms lining the street. He turned into the blue cobblestone drive and drove through the reinforced picket gate, painted white and ornamented with wrought-iron scrolls.

Maurice maneuvered around Aurelio Moreno's ancient and unsteady Fairlane station wagon, parked where it usually was, blocking access to the garage. He stopped the car near several bicycles leaning against an enormous pottery planter in which grew a rubber tree, its leaves shining like oilskin in the moonlight. As he emerged from the car, he heard the distant laughter of several teenage girls, sounding like wind chimes. Maurice smiled at the sound.

Much of the driveway was under the flat canopy of a royal poinciana, a tree of the tropics covered with a sweep of blood-red flowers. Out of habit, Maurice paused under the poinciana to survey the house. In years past, he did so to detect movement or sounds. Now he just enjoyed the moment each evening.

He and Rosa had built the house. She liked to call its style Provençal-Moorish-Mediterranean. He called it Spanish-but-with-running-water. The exterior walls were white stucco, and the roofs were unglazed terra-cotta tile. The house was L-shaped, with the driveway fronting the crook of the L. Hip roofs were on three elevations, recessed and rising behind the main entrance, lending the house a stateliness. Lady palms and orchid trees graced every corner.

The home's casement windows and doors had semicircular stilted arches. Tiled brows shaded ground-floor windows, which were covered with *raja,* elaborate Spanish ironwork. Facing the driveway and garden, the second floor opened to a loggia, an arched-roof gallery along the side of the building.

Once a year Maurice had to cut back the ivy that ranged along the side of the house and over the front door up to the arcade. Another loggia rimmed the back of the house, overlooking Coral Gables Canal, a narrow waterway running south and east to Biscayne Bay. Across the canal was the Riviera Country Club golf course. Maurice was not a member.

He walked around the bikes and under the overhanging archway to put his key in the lock. He pushed the door with his shoulder. It was carved oak bolted onto metal, and it weighed three hundred pounds. Rosa had to use her tush and back, leaning mightily against it. Years ago Maurice had also wanted to install a gun port, but she had adamantly refused. Vigilance could only bend a life so far. Someday they would replace the door with one more manageable.

"Rosa, I'm home," he called loudly as he entered, thinking she was in the den.

Her closeness startled him. His wife was standing in the entrance hallway just behind the door. She was wearing a simple white cotton skirt and a flower-print blouse, a work outfit. She was also wearing an expression Maurice had not seen in almost three decades. Utter fear.

He gripped her shoulders. "Honey, what's wrong?"

Her eyes were brown and luminescent, with lashes that did not blink but rose and fell languorously like the fronds of a fan palm in a soft breeze. Rosa's skin was chamois, and her lips were ruddy and full. Her hair was the color of coffee with a few new hints of gray, and even its businesswoman's style, tucked in at the shoulders, could not subdue its luster.

He was so attuned to her emotions, so open to the slightest shifts in her feelings, that he rose or sank according to her mood, like water seeking its own level. Maurice had been fearful since he was pulled away from the reunion dinner earlier in the evening. Now it was fanned anew.

"What's wrong?" he repeated urgently.

Rosa was the city editor at the *Miami Herald*. After nine hours of wrestling with reporters and breaking stories, she arrived home feeling as if she had gone ten rounds in a ring. Same with Maurice, with his endless work to get the *Carolyn May* and its goods through. At the end of such a day, their eyes always caught and held each other for a long moment, each drawing strength from the other, recommitting themselves. Tonight Rosa's eyes were veiled and remote. Her arms, usually open and welcoming, were locked in front of her. Somehow she already knew about the agency.

She said, "Wilfredo called a couple minutes ago. Some men came by his house to talk to him. Some government men."

Rosa's voice was faintly exotic, faintly guttural. Now it was strained, and she was speaking Spanish, always reserved for romance or anger. With her mouth pulled back and her dark eyes boring into him, Maurice was sure her Spanish wasn't an invitation to go upstairs.

Wilfredo was her brother, a grade school principal in Hialeah. "What else did he say?"

"They asked a lot of questions about him and me, and about our parents. They are your old people, aren't they? What does the agency want, William?" He was always William in Spanish and Bill in English.

She became more vulnerable with her question, and with her half step toward him. Her eyes glistened with her anger and sadness. She turned her head away, revealing the wisps of silver hair on the back of her neck that looked like clinging smoke. He felt a peccant longing, an echo of the night before. She was asking questions that went to the very heart of their relationship, to promises they had made long ago, yet he was suddenly thinking of the flowing curve of her shoulder and throat, and of her full blouse and narrow waist. Even at the end of this long, troubled day, he found Rosa's voluptuousness diverting and undiminished by her fear as she stood in the dim light of their entrance hallway.

"William . . ."

Her voice brought him back. "It's the agency," he said. "I had a long talk with them tonight."

"What about? And why would they question Wilfredo, and why . . ." She brought her hands up to her temples, a gesture of despair that cut her off. After a moment she said, "Damn it, William. You said those people were all in your past, that they were through with you and you with them."

Maurice gently squeezed her arms. "They're talking to your brother to check you out, because I told them I wouldn't even consider their offer if I had to hide anything from you."

She drew herself up stiffly. "What offer did the CIA make to you?"

"Have you rousted the kids?" he asked, looking into the living room.

She shook her head coldly.

"Let me do that before we talk."

Maurice left her in the hallway, walking past the hall stand to the basement door. As he descended he let his shoes smack loudly against the stairs. He didn't want to startle anyone.

He found Calvo Cubela and Celia Pazos in the rec room with the lights turned low. The smell of popcorn filled the long room. Maurice knocked against the wall and said, "Once again it looks like I'll have to pry Calvo's arms from around you, Celia."

Calvo was a high school junior, with a distressingly thin mustache and a batch of black hair that swept low over his forehead. His shirt was opened to the middle button. Celia was a year younger and prone to wearing lipstick an ounce at a time.

Calvo stood and took Celia's hand. "We might see you tomorrow, if my mom kicks us out."

"Your mother is a smart woman, so she'll probably give you the boot, and I'll see you tomorrow."

Celia pecked Maurice's cheek as she passed. Two dozen or so young people called the Maurice house their second home. They came and went any time the light in the master bedroom was on. After that, the house was off limits. And Maurice had made sure they knew the signal. Every night Maurice flushed them out like quail from a bush and sent them home. He called it his taps tour.

They were the children of the Bay of Pigs widows, some from their marriages to deceased brigade members, some from later marriages. Maurice and his wife had not planned to make their home a Boys or Girls Club back in the early sixties, when some of the brigade widows would arrive at their doorstep with a problem and he would do his best to help them. Soon the widows learned to make their own way, but the kids kept coming by. Some of them were now bringing by their own children.

Maurice liked to put on a gruff act, complaining to Rosa that they never had the house to themselves. But eight years ago, after the *Carolyn May* first started sailing in the black, he and Rosa moved to Palm Island, the posh, secluded residential neighborhood in Biscayne Bay midway between Miami and the South Beach. Too far for the kids to come on their bicycles, they had quickly learned. After a month Maurice and Rosa moved back to Coral Gables. Buying their old house four weeks after they sold it cost them a markup of fifty thousand "unbelievably nondeductible and stupid dollars," according to Maurice's accountant.

Maurice checked the locks on the rec room's windows, then moved into the billiard room, little more than a storage bay with a pool table surrounded by shelves sagging under the weight of dusty boxes, some containing college textbooks he had been unable to throw out. A clothes washer and dryer and a sink were in a corner.

Aurelio Moreno was bent over the table, his cue sliding repeatedly through his fingers. He said without looking up, "Quarter on three banks?"

Maurice rounded the table, peering under the stained-glass lamp hung low over the slate. He fished out a coin and snapped it onto a rail.

Moreno cocked and fired. Three bumpers later the ball dropped into a pocket under his chin. He grinned, flipped Maurice's quarter into his palm.

"Too much time down at Dinty's, Aurelio."

"I'm paying my way now, Mr. Maurice."

That he was. Four years ago, when Aurelio was thirteen, he'd wandered into Maurice's pool room and had scarcely bothered to leave since. He had worn a moat in the linoleum around the table. He was perhaps the best pool shooter in Florida. Last summer he beat Marvin "Two Balls" Strudy at three-cushion to prove it. Maurice had fronted the thousand-dollar wager, and Aurelio had taken Strudy's money. If Rosa ever found out, she'd use the pool table for a fire grate. Aurelio's mother stopped speaking with Maurice years ago, but Maurice believed a person's destiny couldn't be denied. The pool players had tried to stick Aurelio with a nickname—"Eight Ball," after his dark complexion, an honorable handle—but Aurelio preferred his given name, as it had all the vowels, something none of his friends' names had.

"Time to pack it in for the night, Aurelio."

The young man immediately put down the cue. "Thanks again, Mr. Maurice." He crossed the room to the sink. He dared not go home with blue chalk on his hands. He asked as he lathered, "You doing all right?"

"Sure. Why?"

"No offense, but you look a little drained."

"I'll let my doctor know your diagnosis next time I see him. Maybe he'll have a pill or something."

Aurelio laughed as he scrubbed. Maurice walked through the rec room to the basement's side door, then up a few steps to the outdoor swimming pool. The pool edged the south side of the lot. From the garden chairs near the pool's shallow end was a view of the canal and its homes, docks, and pleasure boats.

Maurice had built the pool for laps. It was fifty feet long but only four feet wide, except on the canal side, where it flared out for a wading area. They'd installed it a few years ago, at the height of the exercise craze, and in all the years since Maurice had swum a grand total of eighteen torturous laps. Trouble was, he was a sinker, not a swimmer. For every four crawl strokes, one was for forward motion and three were to save him from drowning.

The pool area was brightly lit at night. At the shallow end three young ladies sat dangling their feet in the water, giggling and leaning together conspiratorially. All three wore string bikinis Maurice doubted their parents knew anything about.

"You girls are here late tonight," Maurice called as he walked toward them on the pebbled surface.

They straightened and smiled as one. "Lots to talk about, Mr. Maurice," Julie Porlocarrero answered for the three of them, as she always did. At fourteen, she was the oldest.

"I can well imagine. It's too late to bike home. Aurelio will drive you if you ask him. Bikes and all."

Often they tried to cajole him into swimming a few laps with them. A futile endeavor, they knew. Tonight they must have sensed anxiety in his voice, as they quickly gathered their radio and towels and empty Coke cans and hurried into the changing hut between the house and pool.

He entered the kitchen, his favorite room in the house. Maurice specialized in Cuban dishes, which require little more than pans and a spoon. His *picadillo*, a fiendishly seasoned minced beef served with *moros y cristianos* (rice and beans, called Moors and Christians), was legendary among the Cuban kids for its authentic taste and for authentically causing an outbreak of sweat about ten minutes after the last bite.

He found Rosa sipping coffee, sitting in the breakfast nook overlooking the waterway. Steam from the cup rose across her face like a lace veil. He stopped at the liquor cabinet, poured himself a shot of B&B into a snifter, and slipped into the nook next to her. When she lowered the cup from her lips, he poured half the B&B into it. She studied her husband as if he were a stranger.

He bravely played their game. "As Dickens said, 'To make your child sufficient of billiards is the beginning of honesty.' "

She wouldn't bite. He took a long breath and reached for her hand. It lay limp in his.

She said dully, "Carol Pearson called earlier. Her husband phoned her from the bridge. I know about the *Carolyn May* being impounded. Was that the agency?"

Maurice nodded. "They put ATF up to it."

She sighed heavily. "They must want a lot."

Maurice told her of Ricardo Ferra's injury and of meeting Jack Cantrell at the hospital. Then he said, "They took me to a temporary office at the port."

She whispered, "The problem is in Cuba?"

He nodded. "They've discovered a Soviet plane there. A bomber called the Blackjack."

"The Russians have long had bombers in Cuba."

"Prop engine Bears, some thirty years old. Nothing like the Blackjack." He sipped the liqueur. "Before discovering the Blackjack in Cuba, the only hard evidence the bomber even existed was a fuzzy satellite photo of a test prototype taken over the Ramenskoye flight center in 1985. Because the photo showed it parked between two Tu-144s, the supersonic airliner NATO calls the Charger, the agency thinks it has a good idea of the bomber's dimensions, even its capabilities. And suddenly it pops up ninety miles from here."

"Is there only one?" she asked. She wrapped both of her hands around the cup, as if she were cold.

"They've only seen one. But Cantrell says the mode of attack with such a bomber would require at least six, maybe more. The Soviets are building them at a new complex at the Kazan airframe plant. The agency has a computer that generates a picture of the Blackjack. They can spin it around, or explode it to see the cockpit, or turn it over to look at the engines or bomb bay."

"What does it look like?" Rosa asked.

Maurice thought her question was to delay the inevitable crisis to come. He dreaded it. His favorite praise from her was that they made a good team, and when they argued, rarely but with fire, he felt miserably alone.

"Very slender, with variable geometry, meaning that its wings mechanically sweep back for high speeds. It's got a massive dorsal fin, and its horizontal tail is mounted high on the dorsal, and is very sharply swept. It looks like a fighter, but bigger, much bigger."

"And I suppose it's fast." No mistake this time. Her voice was purposely low and silky. She was saving it for the quarrel to come.

"They've got good guesses about its capabilities. Fifteen hundred miles an hour, with a combat radius of forty-five hundred miles. It's a whole new plane, not just a scale-up of the Backfire, the Soviets' last bomber. It's about twenty-five percent longer than the Backfire, longer even than the air force's new B-1B."

"I thought bombs were old-fashioned."

"The Blackjack carries air-launched AS-X-15 nuclear warhead cruise missiles with ranges of eighteen hundred miles. It has a similar design to the U.S. Tomahawk missile."

"How can the agency know what kind of weapon the plane carries, if it only has dim photographs of it?"

"From engine configurations. The agency thinks the plane is powered by four Koliesov single-shaft turbojets. They are affixed in pairs, with the inside two separated by wing ducts. The gap between the ducts indicates the kind of weapon the plane carries."

Maurice put his cup down. "Cantrell was almost whispering when he told me the plane could be over Miami in five minutes and Washington in less than three-quarters of an hour. A single Blackjack's cruise missiles could be splayed out along the East Coast, targeting all the major cities."

"But I don't get it," she said, renewed irritation in her voice. "Why the fuss over this new plane, when the Soviets have had hundreds and hundreds of missiles pointed at us for decades?"

"The Defense Department claims the Blackjacks are more dangerous to the United States than the nuclear missiles placed in Cuba in 1962."

"They'd say that as a reflex. That's how the Defense Department works."

"Rosa, they're dead serious up there. Frightened, I think, and with good reason. The Blackjacks give the Soviets the third prong of the nuclear triad, one that due to their lack of bomber bases near the U.S. has been denied them. The Blackjacks can be launched, then recalled, which increases the Soviet's ability to bully. Unlike a missile, the Blackjack can change targets in midflight, giving greater flexibility to an attack."

She looked skeptical, and he rushed on defensively, "The Blackjacks are equipped with computer and laser guidance systems, and can fly thirty feet above the waves, far below American radar. The agency thinks the plane has a lot of stealth technology in it. Special composite, low deflection skin, and a very low radar profile. And most U.S. radar points north, the old DEW line. Southern radar defenses are woefully inadequate."

"They've convinced you, haven't they?" she said. "William, you're glowing."

He tried to hear some humor in her words. There was none. He rushed on, "American satellites, like the Code 647, can instantly detect missiles launched from Cuba, but to a satellite, the Blackjack's takeoff is indistinguishable from a MIG's launch, a daily occurrence."

Maurice spread his hands on the table, a broad gesture he unconsciously used when he was about to conclude. "What all this means is that for the first time in history, the Soviets have a weapon that we can't see coming. It's too fast and too quiet, and most importantly, it's too close."

She smiled grimly. "I'm sure they primed you with some melodramatic statistic, some all-the-dollars-laid-end-to-end-would-reach-the-moon type of thing."

Embarrassed, he looked out the window, across the canal to the fairway. Two kids with flashlights were walking along the bank looking for golf balls.

"Well?" Rosa challenged. "Didn't they?"

"One Blackjack carries fully four times the total explosive power spent by all combatants in all of World War Two."

She laughed mirthlessly. "You always were a sucker for

comic book science." She exhaled slowly. "What does the agency want?"

"My people in Cuba, and me."

"Why? Why can't they just tell the Soviets to remove the bombers? It worked with the missiles."

Maurice said, "This time the Russians will fully realize what they have to lose. The Cuban missile crisis—the way in which Kennedy made the Soviets back down and remove the missiles in front of the world—was the gravest humiliation to the USSR this century. Soon afterward the Politburo dumped Khrushchev. The Russians won't let it happen again."

He searched his wife's eyes, measuring her resistance. It was still there, a shine of willfulness and fear. "The White House has concluded that bluff won't work this time. And nobody up in Washington wants to risk a war by confronting the Soviets. So the agency has been told to get rid of the missiles, one way or another."

"You sound impressed."

"The agency certainly is. They've moved a slew of people down here, including no less than the operations deputy director." Maurice grinned narrowly. "I remember when I used to mount this kind of thing. . . ."

"You've spent almost thirty years trying to forget exactly that." She leaned forward, gripping both his hands. "We now have each other, but that shouldn't lessen the memory of our losses. Jorge and Anne, gone in an instant. It still tears at me, and I know it does you, too. Grief and fear."

"I've been involved with Cubans all along," he argued uselessly.

"With market people, growers and shippers, some policemen, a few officers in their army. William, you've been successful because you've found a nice little niche. With drugs pouring into the U.S. and with Castro always afraid of counterrevolutionaries, neither country makes much of an effort to chase a black market banana importer. And now you are considering throwing it all away."

"The agency made it clear we'll lose everything. I'm going to help them."

His words seemed to make her physically smaller. Her voice was dark with resentment. "It's not the house or the ship, William. Admit it to yourself. You've suddenly been offered a chance to pay the Castro government back, and you're going to grab it like a life ring."

"What do you mean?" he asked softly.

"Your embarrassment and anger over the Bay of Pigs and your abrupt dismissal from the agency have never been resolved. And then there was Anne's murder. You were left with nothing back in 1962. You were almost destroyed. And you blame Fidel Castro personally. All those emotions have been festering ever since."

His heavy shoulders were hunched forward protectively, and his fists were so tight his knuckles gleamed. "I screwed up last time. The lives lost. The careers thrown away. My fault. Now I'm getting another chance."

She sat back in her chair, her gaze out the window into the broken darkness. Overhead was a high, white, indifferent moon.

He said, "Not many people recognize their last chance until it's too late. This is mine. I don't want it to slip away. Please, Rosa."

"Then it isn't simply revenge. It's redemption." It was a revered word from her Catholic childhood, and it softened her.

They had learned to gauge each other's resolution, knowing when the time had come to see the other side. And both of them had an infallible sense when an argument had gone long enough, when there was nothing left to say that wouldn't cripple. It was a mark of their love that they never felt bloodied after an argument. Spent, but never wounded.

Her wondrous brown eyes took him in. For the first time that evening, she spoke in English. "All right, Bill. Let's talk about your redemption."

Chapter VI

I n thirty years, the revolution has brought San Roque very little, so the villagers are grateful for the three blocks of paved road, for it is three more than the town ever had before. At the ribbon cutting for the new pavement, the town's main street was renamed Juan Almeida Avenue, after a hero of the revolution who crossed the sea to Batista's Cuba with Castro on the leaking yacht *Granma,* but the townfolks still call the street the Prado.

San Roque is twenty-five miles west of Santiago de Cuba on the narrow road to Cape Cruz. The road clings perilously to the Sierra Maestra mountains, wedged there by the sea. The wilderness pauses only briefly at the town. San Roque is in the Oriente, Cuba's wildest province, which proud locals call "the only province." In San Roque there are few roads, and Cubans there are fond of saying that Oriente would extend to Venezuela, if only the rugged mountains could be pulled flat. Even the local plants have rugged names: *rasca-barriga* (scratch belly), *volador* (thief), *revienta-caballo* (burst horse), and *cagadilla de gallina* (chicken dung). In 1956, Castro landed in the Oriente to begin his revolution. He stayed only as long as he had to and seldom 'returned.

Despite the new asphalt, San Roque is so dusty that it looks like a cracked and fading sepia photograph of itself. A veneer of brown powder lies over the town, muting colors and subduing angles. When a truck passes, eyes must be closed against the cloud. Each day women use wet mops to wash down their wood living room and porch floors. Dragging carts carrying fifty-gallon drums of water, donkeys make use of the dust, lowering their nostrils to the road and snorting loudly, raising puffs to cover their muzzles against the flies. Vendors kindly pass rags over bananas and grapefruit before placing them on the scales, lightening the purchases by a layer of dirt. Children play in a nimbus of dust.

The buildings along Prado Street are all one or two stories, and none has had a new coat of paint since the revolution, so they have faded to dun. A grocery store, filling station, lawyer's office, pharmacy, and two bars are interspersed with wooden houses. The homes have porches right up to the sidewalk, and passersby can peer into living rooms, through the kitchens, and into tiny backyards. The homes are sparsely furnished, but all have sturdy rocking chairs, ubiquitous in rural Cuba. Deep ditches line the sidewalks, and to get into the street requires a considerable jump.

San Roque is a fishing village, and the small dock jutting into the water is covered with *jaulas,* small wire cages made of netting, which are driven into the seaweed-covered seabed at low tide to catch lobsters. Also on the dock are *nasas,* funnel-shaped fish traps made of loosely woven reeds. Before the revolution, San Roque red snappers were ordered by name in Havana. Now, because of engine parts shortages, the fishing boats seldom even feed the town.

The people of San Roque stubbornly hold on to their heritage despite the nonsense Fidel sometimes sends their way. A paved road they'll accept, but not the edict to abandon using *"adios"* because of its reference to God, as it literally means "go with God." The stern, peeling portrait of Che on the side of the Ministry of Construction (MiCons) building is tolerable, as is the poster pasted on the grocery store wall showing a CIA agent dressed as a priest trying to sneak into Cuba, but the folks strolling on the Prado still call each other *"señor"* and *"señora,"* not "comrade," as is required in Havana. And to save cloth and leather, Fidel decreed that the wearing of shorts and sandals was fashionable, but to do so in San Roque is still to be taken for a homosexual. A few of the revolution's ideas are more practical. The government pays for burials. The people of San Roque like to say that the communists starve you to death, then give you a free funeral. The revolution was like a stone thrown into a pond. The farther from Havana, the weaker its waves.

There is no movie theater in San Roque, and the mountains blur the television signal from Santiago de Cuba. The townfolks are their own amusement. Standing on corners watching passersby is a Cuban tradition. On this April evening, clusters of farmers and fishermen and tradesmen lingered on the Prado's corners. Hard work makes people look alike. Burned faces, gnarled, knuckle-heavy hands, eyes squinting against the sun even after it has gone down.

Citizens of Havana call villages like San Roque a *pueblo sín sopa,* a town without soap, but the *campesinos* gathered on the corners wore *guayaberas* and white crash trousers, and all were spotless, as it is an undying Cuban tradition to put on clean clothes for dinner and the evening. A few wore *enquatadas,* heavy T-shirts. Few Cubans wear hats in Havana, but in the villages straw hats with upturned brims are still essential. Most men wore heavy boots called rock crushers, Russian army surplus. Cuban women do not have a distinctive, traditional dress, and most along the Prado this particular evening wore sleeveless blouses and simple print skirts.

The men smoked mild cigarettes called *suaves* or Cuban cigars called *puros habanos*. Some folks crowded around the two outdoor bars, drinking Hatuay beer or coffee. Others gathered near the town's chess table in front of the grocery store. Batista had played canasta, and Fidel dominoes. But chess is the game of Cuba. To *norteamericanos*, it is a game of intellect. To Cubans, muscle and macho make a good chess player.

The villagers of San Roque savored the evening. The ocean breeze blew away the day's blanket of heat and the mosquitoes, making tolerable a stroll along the Prado. The three blocks might take an hour, as there were friends to greet and gossip to be exchanged. Young men crowded the corners, baldly watching girls walk by. With knowing smiles, the town's elders said these men were *muy enamorado*, too apt to fall in love. The Prado had a festive air after the long week, with gay laughter and teasing, the squeals of children and rattle of glasses. The street was filled with the Oriente accent, more lilting and higher in pitch than elsewhere in Cuba. The scent of cooked onions and peppers drifted along the street. Three men sat in the doorway of the closed grocery store sharing a flask of rum. One of them laughed mightily, tossing his head back and exposing black teeth. Cubans used laughter as medicine, and on the Prado the treatment was intense.

At ten that evening, a silence spread down the street, a palpable force that hushed children and broke off sentences. The people of San Roque turned to stare east along the Prado, then stepped out of the street to the boardwalk. One of the rum drinkers whispered, "*¡Vamanos el carajo de aquí!*" Let's get the hell out of here. He stood to walk quickly away from the grocery, but not too rapidly, not fast enough to be noticed. Other people slipped into doorways. Some turned their heads away, the smiles gone, eyes furtively looking anywhere but the street, stepping around corners and into alleys.

Escorting the silence down the Prado was a Russian Zil automobile, an ungainly sedan weighed down to its axles by the four men inside. The license plate—reading *Estatal*, the state—

gave them away, but, also, no one in San Roque would mistake the grimness and singularity of their faces for anything other than those belonging to G2 agents. They always traveled in fours. Two to hold the arrested man's arms behind him, one to do the beating, and another to hold a pistol on the whole process, lest the victim escape the other three. At least this was consensus of the people of San Roque.

The villagers melted away in front of the car, reappearing on the street after it had passed, like sea grass blown down by the wind, only to spring back at the first calm. Black cars had always been sent to San Roque, by Castro, by Batista, by Machado. Now and then a villager would disappear into the trunk of one of the cars. G2 visits were as much a part of Cuban heritage as *carnaval* or the *zafra*, the sugar cane harvest. They came with being Cuban, and it would always be so.

The townfolks looked with relief at each other and shook their heads in sympathy with whomever G2 was visiting that evening. But it was none of their concern, as the Zil rolled off the paved road and onto dirt, plowing up a skirt of dust, apparently intent on one of the villages west of San Roque. The villagers' collective sigh of relief was premature.

The baseball diamond marked the west end of town. It was the only flat acre in San Roque. Several dozen *bohíos*—peasant huts—crowded the road on the hill above the playing field. The folks of San Roque knew *"el proceso de la revolución"*—the process of the revolution, a term uttered frequently by the faithful —may never reach this road, not if the twentieth century had not, and it surely had not. The huts had a dispiriting similarity and were direct descendants from those of the Taino and Ciboney Indians. A popular Cuban folk song was entitled *"Amor de mí bohío"* ("My Bohio Love"), but in truth they offered little to love. The huts had a skeleton of poles, with walls of palm bark. The roofs were made of a palm thatch called guano and were steep to allow quick runoff of tropical deluges. These huts had been here a century, and the dirt road between them was only as wide as a carriage.

The *bohío* at the west end of the road abutted a steep embankment and was tucked under a hawthorn tree covered with trumpet-shaped white flowers. Spotted with boulders and patches of grass, the embankment rose above the tree, toward the Sierra Maestra foothills. A boy perhaps twelve years old sat in front of the door, in which was a *postigo*, a small barred window fitted with wooden shutters on the inside.

The boy whittled on a piece of soft pine, not carving anything, just reducing the stick to nothing, letting the chips fall at his bare feet. He wore a cotton pullover shirt and *pitusas*—jeans—made in Yugoslavia, a Levi's knock-off that had black buttons where the famous rivets should have been. He was a handsome youth, with carefully parted hair, brown eyes set wide, and teeth as even and white as the picket fence in front of the church. His cheekbones were pronounced, and his face was without the roundness so common in the Oriente hills. He never looked at the stick or at the view over the baseball field to the ripple of moonlight on the black water, just down the road. He was a lookout.

He heard a woman cry out above the cicadas' whine. The pitiful sound came from the hut, but the boy was accustomed to such noises. The woman in pain was in good hands, as the boy's mother was also inside. His mother would see her through. She always did. The blade bit again into the pine, and another wood sliver was added to the pile.

With boarded windows and no electric lights, the interior of the hut was dark. Other than the wood floor, the *bohío* looked as it had since it was first inhabited. Furniture was limited to several stools, a table, and two cots. A wood door led to the back room, a kitchen containing a kerosene stove, a washstand, and another cot.

A woman lay on the cot, with her knees raised and spread. She had been in labor for almost twenty-four hours, and her cervix was dilated to almost six centimeters. She was naked and was covered with sweat. Her eyes were wide and rolled up as

65

she stared blankly at the wall above her head. She groaned, then shrieked, but kept her legs in position.

The midwife knelt at her feet. She said in a low voice, "Fina, I'm going to check again. Just hold on."

The midwife reached between the pregnant woman's legs into her vagina to slide her fingertips over the cervix. She had no sterile gloves, but she had washed her hands as carefully as she could. "I feel the baby, Fina. Things are fine. Just a few moments now."

The woman on the cot wailed, "It is too much. Too much. I can't do it."

"Yes, you can. You aren't the first woman to have a child, Fina. You'll be just fine. A few minutes now. Push a little if you can."

The woman was exhausted and could do little to help the baby. She gripped the cot's rails and moaned again. She twisted her head wildly, her eyes screwed up against the pain.

The woman was in fact a girl, just seventeen. Her newborn would be what Cubans call a Fidelista baby, illegitimate because condoms were impossible to obtain. The midwife had not asked the girl the name of the father. It was none of her concern. She had helped perhaps five hundred children into the world.

With her finger, the midwife again checked the baby's progress. "Not long now," she said. "Did you say you were hoping for a girl, Fina? We'll soon see. I know I wouldn't trade my Segundo for any girl I've ever met, and that includes you and me." She grinned widely and nodded, inviting Fina to smile with her. It seldom worked. The midwife kept up the patter, knowing it was something other than pain for the women to focus on. Her voice was full and reassuring, and later many mothers said it had helped them through.

The midwife's name was Carmen Santana. Her face was Castilian, with a retroussé nose, hazel eyes, full and curled lips, and dark hair that under sunlight shone with mingled wisps of gold and auburn. For the birth, she wore her hair in a net. When she smiled, a series of deep dimples formed at the sides of her mouth. She wore no makeup, but her burgundy lips and black eyelashes and sculpted brows made her look like a Havana woman ready for a rare night out. For a Cuban woman she was tall and had to bend low over the cot. Her high neck, thin arms, and narrow waist added to an elegant appearance unusual in a *batay*, a rural town. Her fingers were long and not marred by scars from cane cutting or stains from tobacco rolling, like most country women.

There was more to her face than Cuban loveliness. Lines at the corners of her eyes and a pensive turn to her mouth gave evidence of a hard life. Some of her movements—jerky glances as if she were startled, and frequent pulls at her arms with her opposite hands, as if she were trying to draw herself away— spoke of enduring tension. All her adult life, Carmen Santana had been a prisoner or a fugitive.

It should not have been that way. Her father had been the owner of the *Havana Record,* a newspaper that in prerevolutionary days had been scrupulously nationalistic but supported neither Batista nor any of the dissenters. That delicate balance had prevented Batista from closing the publication. But Castro hadn't seen it that way. A month after his triumphant entry into Havana, Pedro Santana disappeared. Three weeks later, Carmen was told to report to Morro Castle, the massive stone structure in Havana harbor started in 1587 in response to the unwelcome appearance of Sir Francis Drake a few years before, which had been used as a prison by every regime since. She found her father in a row of bodies, bloated and flyblown, with deep slashes across his arms and chest. His face was locked in a horrifying mask of a cruel death. She rented a mule and cart to take the body to the family burial plot in the cemetery several blocks from their home. Gravediggers put Pedro Santana's body into a crypt beside her mother, who had died years before of a severe flu called One Hundred Eleven, so called because it began with one, stayed with one, and finished one, a pun that works better in Spanish.

Carmen lived in the big house for several more weeks,

alone except for the cook and gardener, who had refused to leave even though Castro had announced there was no longer a servant class in Cuba. Then she learned that two friends at the University of Havana, the son and daughter of a sugar refinery owner, had vanished, apparently following their father into Morro Castle. Castro's deadly purge had spread to the families of counterrevolutionaries. Carmen purchased passage on a ship to Miami, leaving everything except what she could carry in her valise. Not long after, she learned that the Santana home in the Vedado district had become a regional office of the CTC, the Confederation of Cuban Workers.

Carmen had been a semester away from her medical degree at the university, one of only six female students in the department. She was not in Miami long, as she volunteered to be a medic for Brigade 2506. Again and again she was turned down. Finally, brigade leaders realized they were desperately short of medical personnel and relented. When the brigade assaulted Playa Larga at the Bay of Pigs, she was one of only four women in uniform. As it turned out, she fought harder to join the brigade than she did for the brigade. A minute after she landed, a mortar shell blew her off her feet. Dazed and useless to anyone, she was left on the sand.

Her next clear memory was of the *granja*—concentration camp—at La Ruda, where she would spend six years. A fence separated her from the women *comunes*—the common prisoners—and she wore a yellow uniform, and they wore blue. She lived in a barracks crowded with other prisoners, none of whom were from the invasion force. She was denied food and medical assistance, and the barracks crawled with rats, lice, and bedbugs. There was no ventilation from the heat or insulation from the cold. She never knew who might have tried to visit her, because visiting rights were never granted. In those six years she did not receive one letter.

She heard that brigade veterans were returned to Miami twenty months after the disaster at the Bay of Pigs. When she asked the camp's *jefe supremo* why she was not allowed to also return, he confined her in a *tapiadas,* a dark, totally walled-in cell, where she slept naked on the floor and defecated at the rear of the cell, which was never cleaned. For one reason or another—insubordination, insolence, lack of cooperation—she was sent to the *tapiadas* many times, for weeks, and once for two months.

Carmen never learned why she was not sent back to Miami. The puzzle dominated her life, an inescapable, heartbreaking mystery she knew would never be answered. Perhaps she was simply forgotten. Or someone in the revolutionary government was carrying out a vendetta against her, but she didn't know who or why. Or her card got into the wrong file. Most probably that, she guessed.

After six years, she was allowed to join a UMAP, a forced labor gang called a Unit to Aid Production, where she tended the injuries of cane cutters for two weeks before she simply walked away from the cane field. But all Cubans need papers from the Census Bureau, from their place of work, and from the military, and without these they cannot find work or a place to live. She wandered in the country for three weeks before G2 caught her.

There is a saying in Cuba, *"Quién no cruza tras los moros de la cárcel muere un niño."* Whoever does not pass through the walls of a prison dies a child. The people's court made sure Carmen Santana would not die a child. Although she never learned the length of her initial prison sentence, the judge added another five years to it. She was labeled a hardened counterrevolutionary and sent to Havana's most famous prison, El Príncipe, on a hill not far from the university.

El Príncipe was housed within an ancient Spanish fortress, and the dungeons were used as cells. For the first month, Carmen was fed nothing but *gofio,* a drink made of flour and water. The guard's favorite game was to enter a prisoner's cell and announce he was free to leave. They would follow him into the main yard, their rifles across their chests. Sometimes the prisoner was indeed free, and he would walk through the gates

69

into the Havana streets. At other times, the guards were carrying out a sentence and with their rifle butts would push the prisoner into a run, then shoot him. Often the first bullet was not fatal, and the condemned man would rise and run again, only to be shot again. The game continued until he could no longer get to his feet. The firing squad joked and laughed all the while. If the prisoner was not quite dead, they put another bullet into him as he lay on the cobblestones, usually into his rectum. The guards then paid their bets, wagered on who got the best shot, and dropped the body into a mud pit. Prisoners dreaded the day of release, for they did not know if they were being released from prison or from life.

Carmen was interned at El Príncipe for another three years and again was sent to a UMAP, this time in the Oriente province. Either the prison officials did not learn their lesson, or Carmen did not, because a week after she arrived, she again walked away. This time G2's bloodhounds never found her.

She had been a fugitive for almost fourteen years. Because she had no papers, her life was on the run. Never did she stay more than three months in a town. Never did she live anywhere but in the poorest of housing in the poorest of neighborhoods. She confined herself to remote areas, where police were fewer and cooperation with the government was more hesitant. For much of that time she lived in the Oriente, where all of Cuba's revolutions began and where there were fewer friends of Castro. Several times someone suspected her and informed G2, and she narrowly escaped. She did not know if they were still looking for her. She seemed to herself such a small prize, how could they be looking after all the years? Twice she was detained by local police, and both times she bought her way out of custody with the only thing she had, herself. She had no choice. She would not survive another prison sentence. If she were arrested again, she knew it would be the end of her. El Príncipe and the UMAPs and life as a fugitive wrenched her dreams from her and killed her hope. She lived, but she was without a future, and that was a living death.

Her son, Segundo, was the result of a few days with a carpenter in Bayamo. The carpenter was later drafted and killed in Angola, and Carmen had given him little thought since. But Segundo had been the burning flame in her life, her only link to her humanity. She would not have bothered getting up in the morning were it not for the boy. She thought El Príncipe had dried her tears forever, and she never cried for herself. But there were times when her son's plight left her weeping. Other than what she could teach him, he had had no education. He did not make friends, because he knew his mother would take him elsewhere in a short time. She tried her best not to instill in him her fear and watchfulness and suspicion, but he picked it up like other children learned baseball or swimming. How could he not, when he had known nothing else?

Fina tried to twist away from her, moaning, then yelping like a kicked dog. Carmen again checked the baby's progress with her fingers. "A few more minutes. Don't worry, Fina."

Carmen snapped upright at the sound of an automobile grinding to a halt on the dirt road outside the *bohío*. The few cars in San Roque were treated like members of the family, never driven hard. Yet this car's brakes squealed as it stopped. Only the police drove like that. She heard car doors opening.

She stood quickly, glancing at the door between the rooms, then out the back door. She desperately wanted to bolt, to leave the woman and her coming child. Fina wailed again, and her body trembled. Loud voices came from the street, and Carmen heard Segundo responding, but she couldn't make out his words.

"Oh, God. Help me. . . ." Fina's words trailed off into a wail.

Fear held Carmen. She was an animal caught in the blinding light of an automobile, wildly wanting to run yet frozen to the spot. Car doors slammed. She heard a gruff laugh and a slap. She had a chance, if she could just make it through the door.

"Never again—oh, God." Another moan.

Carmen closed her eyes and swayed as if being pushed. Pushed through El Príncipe's gates again. This time she would be thrown into the mud pit.

With a wrenching effort—the greatest of her life—she opened her eyes and lowered herself again between Fina's legs. She could not leave her.

"Push now, gently," Carmen breathed, forcing her raging thoughts back to the *bohío*. "Help the baby, Fina."

When the mother pushed, the baby's head appeared at the opening, and when she relaxed, it disappeared again.

"Push again, Fina. You can do it. Help your baby."

After a few more contractions, the baby remained visible. A red prune of an infant's head.

"He's got a lot of hair already, Fina. I can see him, so your work is done. Don't push any more." Memorized words. Carmen's thoughts were now out in the street with Segundo. She prayed that they would not take him away.

"Now push again. We'll get the shoulders out." Carmen pressed downward gently on the infant's head to help him slip through. She wanted to scream at them, Go away, leave us alone, but she talked quietly and reassuringly to the woman, waiting for the baby to slide into her arms.

Segundo had seen the car when it was two blocks away, as it rounded the curve and started toward him on the road above the baseball field. There was no thought of running. His mother was inside. They had never been apart, and he wouldn't start now. He whittled as the car stopped, and he whittled as the men climbed out and walked toward him.

No, he hadn't learned to play baseball, and he knew no mathematics. His lessons were of a different nature. His utter calm was surely learned from her. And thinking lucidly under dire stress. And his capacity to boldly lie.

They were secret policemen, Segundo knew. Their car, their swagger. The man who had been in the front passenger seat approached him and wordlessly held his hand out for the knife. Segundo stood and instead gave him his pine stick.

The policeman, wearing the cloying odor of Russian after-shave, a perquisite of the G2, rocked Segundo with *un pinazo*, a strike with the fist to the chest, literally a pineapple blow. The boy staggered back against the *postigo* but would not fall. He held out the knife.

The other G2 agents leaned against the car. One repeatedly cracked his knuckles, sounding like gunshots. The leader opened and closed the pocket knife and said, "We were told there is a new person in town, someone who tried to buy some chickens at the *tienda del pueblo*, but didn't have a ration card. We also heard she was somewhere on this road. Do you know anything of her?" The policeman glanced over the boy's head at the door.

"All I know is whittling, and as you can see, I know very little of that. Perhaps if you told me more about this person." Segundo had heard enough births to know the pace of his mother's encouraging talk. He had to stall these men a few more minutes. His mother would never leave the pregnant woman. Carmen may not have known that about herself, but Segundo knew it. The baby must be born, then Segundo would take care of himself. Whenever he and his mother entered a town, they always identified a place to meet should they become separated. A few more minutes of talk with the G2.

The policeman's stomach hung over his belt. Sweat stains had spread from his arms almost to his buttons. "We are looking for a traitor to the revolution, a woman who returned to Cuba from the United States a month ago, and whom the CIA has trained. But why should I tell this to you, I ask myself."

They weren't looking for his mother, but Segundo was not relieved. If they found her, they would question her and discover she was a fugitive. Segundo and his mother had no way of knowing that G2 stopped searching for her a decade ago.

"Well, I can tell you, comrades, that there is no one in this *bohío,* or anywhere else on the road. They are all down on the Prado, parading for each other."

"And why aren't you there? You're old enough for *la enfermedad.*" The policeman used the vernacular for the sickness

73

that attacks young men, making them want to wear tight pants and gold chains and stroll the streets looking for girls.

Segundo shrugged. "I'd rather work on a piece of pine, and . . ."

He was cut off by a cry from the house, the gurgling chirrup of a newborn. The policeman's face knotted, and he struck Segundo again. This time the boy kept his feet under him. The policeman drew his pistol and kicked the door, which flew open and bounced against its hinges. Another policeman followed him into the *bohío,* while a third ran to the rear of the hut, also drawing his weapon.

The G2 agents pushed into the back room and found a mother lying on a cot cradling her newborn. The floor in front of her was slick with afterbirth, and the room smelled of old heat and blood. The mother cooed at her baby, wrapped in a blanket and held to her bosom, and did not even look up at the intruders. The back door was swinging as if by a gust of wind.

The policeman waved his pistol at the door, signaling the other to give chase. He scowled at the mother, then turned to leave the hut. He was going to settle the score with the lying boy.

But when he rushed through the door to the street, the boy and the other policeman were gone. He squinted into the night and could just make out the flapping shirttail of one of his men giving chase. The shirt was quickly lost in the darkness. The boy must have sprinted away. He had looked fast and would never be caught. And now they had come to San Roque for nothing.

Chapter VII

Maurice drove deep into the swamp, not liking one minute of it. He had come west from Miami on Highway 84, called Alligator Alley, and turned south on a dirt road into the muck. In a restaurant, Maurice was comfortably on top of the great food chain. Here in the swamp, he was somewhere in the middle. He preferred a restaurant.

He was behind the wheel of his Ford, a map of south Florida on the seat beside him, next to foil wrap that had been around a BLT. At least Rosa called it a BLT, although there was no bacon in it. She had warned him to eat it before the sun turned the mayonnaise bad. He had complied by downing most of it by the time he had cleared their driveway in Coral Gables. Lately for breakfast she was serving him health cereal, granite-like nodules that a goat could not chew. She was afraid for his heart. So Maurice had begun to eat his lunch earlier and earlier, complemented by a second lunch later in the day.

He was on land bordering Everglades National Park, and he passed a sign warning that trespassers would be prosecuted. The road was rough, with rain washouts sunk deeply into the dirt. The Ford acted like it was at sea, climbing and descending huge rollers and leaving a spray of dust behind it. The area was limestone pineland, and he drove through a grove of slash pines. The pines' bark was blackened by the latest fire, and their lower limbs had been burned away. The ground between the trees was studded with saw palmettos, their green leaves looking like explosive bursts. The road had once been a rail bed, built for logging. Maurice drove by a rusted steam-engine boiler and a washtub sitting on its side with its bottom rotted away.

The land softened, and the road turned onto a dike built over ooze and water. The pines gave way to pond cypresses that were covered with air plants called wild pines, looking like pineapple plants and clinging to their host trees forming an impenetrable wall of sharp foliage. The cypresses grew in black muck, which resulted from millions of years of vegetation rotting in nearly stagnant warm water. Here were the alligators and other animals that made Maurice feel like bait.

He visited the swamp frequently, forced to by the kids who hung around his house. Maurice had a theory that a primordial connection existed between alligators and children. Something deeply imbedded in their genetic code made kids demand to see one of the serpents the instant they learned such monsters existed. Gators called kids into the swamp. Time and again Maurice trekked into the Everglades in search of alligators, five or eight kids in tow, and he always found several. Once, after a heart-rending appeal by little Celia Recabbaren, he had taken a carload of kids to an excruciating ordeal called the Gator Jumparoo, a tourist trap where alligators leaped into the air to snap at dead chickens hanging from an overhead wire. The slithering and hissing and growling and snapping had actually nauseated Maurice, and he adamantly refused Celia's pleas for a second visit. Maurice figured it was mankind's hard luck that the comet that got the dinosaurs didn't raise enough dust to also get their cousins.

The car rolled deeper into the swamp. The Ford's interior stank of Cutter, as Maurice had virtually showered in it before he left the house, but it was either that or be phlebotomized by the mosquitoes. He consulted his map. Not much farther. The Ford dipped down onto a flat. The wheels threatened to bog, and Maurice withdrew pressure from the accelerator so the wheels could gain purchase. He passed a wild bouquet of butterfly orchids, their delicate yellow petals hanging from a cypress tree, seemingly in flight. Several cardinals, vivid red against the sky, stared down at him from a perch in a cypress viand. At the staccato racket of an automatic weapon, the birds scattered.

Maurice turned the car to follow the narrowing road as it wound under a canopy of trees. When he emerged into the sun, he was in a clearing surrounded by cabbage palms and yuccas, spiky trees that formed a fence around the area. Beyond the trees, the water and cypresses began again. It was a training camp.

There was little to it. One dilapidated, weather-grayed slat building, perhaps once a railroad toolshed. Four automobiles and a pickup with a camper. A picnic table covered with green backpacks and a Styrofoam cooler. Smoke rose from a barbecue.

Six men formed a firing line, aiming an assortment of small weapons at paper bull's-eyes that were tacked to posts sunk into the soft ground. A drill instructor, also dressed in green-and-black camouflage, walked behind them, occasionally saying something or repositioning a weapon. Maurice recognized an Uzi submachine gun and a Heckler and Koch assault rifle. Firing was infrequent. Maurice supposed they were saving ammunition. One of the men turned to see who had driven up, but the instructor yelled at him, and he quickly twisted back to the target.

They were a ragtag lot. Two wore olive campaign pants,

the others wore jeans. All had on T-shirts or sport shirts. Tennis shoes or work boots. Headgear were either berets or campaign caps or nothing. Maurice supposed the extent of their uniform was the blue bands on their left arms. He couldn't make out the insignia on the bands. It looked as if they'd been prancing around in the swamp, practicing assaults, as the legs of their pants were wet.

As Maurice climbed out of the Ford, the shack door opened, and Eduardo Mederos stepped into the light. He was wearing an olive kepi and a matching blouse with epaulets and black buttons. His boots had laces wrapped around behind. The boots and his pants were wet up to his knees. When Mederos walked toward Maurice, a fountain of grasshoppers leaped out of his way. Maurice wrinkled his nose against the sickly odor of orchids and decay. He looked around for alligators.

Without his Fidel makeup, Mederos looked the executive he was. His seal-brown hair was closely cropped, and his face was well shaved. Mederos's small chin was dented with a deep cleft. Maurice couldn't remember from early photos whether Fidel's chin was similarly notched. Mederos's large and expressive eyes and broad nose were still Fidel's. Maurice thought the resemblance startling, even without the beard, so much so that when Mederos opened his mouth, Maurice expected a boisterous speech.

Mederos said only, "How'd you find this place, Bill?"

"The FBI told me. I wouldn't be surprised if half those fellows playing with guns over there aren't feds."

Mederos flinched, then glanced at the men on the firing line. Maurice and Mederos were acquaintances, not friends. Maurice bought his auto parts from Mederos, back when Mederos only had one store and could usually be found behind the counter, bent over a parts catalog.

"What brings you out here?" Mederos asked. His tone was of a boy caught in a petty crime, chagrin mixed with a touch of defiance.

Maurice waited for an Uzi's clatter to subside. "You must be real tired of selling fan belts and water pumps to be out here with these kooks, Eduardo."

Mederos ran one of his bony hands across his jaw. "I might be, all right." They were speaking Spanish.

"My friends at the FBI say these guys aren't Omega 7 or Alpha 66, so your group must be new. I thought this kind of paramilitary, anti-Castro crap went out in the seventies, along with avocado-green refrigerators."

"There are things you don't know about, Bill. Not even you, with all your connections."

Maurice ran his gaze along the firing line. "Your soldiers look like they couldn't fight their way out of a church bingo game. Tell me, what Cuban beach have you selected for them to land on? I can already see the headlines. 'Six Guerrillas Led by Wealthy Auto Parts Executive Storm Castro's Island Fortress.' "

Mederos said equably, "I won't consult with you on picking a beach, I know that much."

"Good reason for that, I suppose." Maurice paused while the drill instructor emptied a .45-caliber government-issue pistol at a target. He held the weapon in both hands, and his shoulders bounced with each recoil. Veterans of only their imaginations, his students nodded knowingly. "It's sad, you out here in the bugs and mire, shooting away. Some sort of middle-age crisis, maybe?"

"This is a gun club, Bill. Leave it at that, will you?"

"Well, I wish I hadn't found you out here with these juveniles. It complicates matters."

"You are being unusually vague today."

"Now I'm going to have to see if you're really the person for the job. Do some more checking."

Mederos laughed harshly, a sound that mingled unpleasantly with the bray of an Uzi. "A job with you? No thanks. I worked once for you at the Bay of Pigs, and ended up in a Castro prison camp for over a year." Mederos sobered quickly,

79

and his eyes shone with emotion. "I lost more than those months of my life, believe me. Much more than those months." He added kindly, "I know you did, too, Bill."

Maurice nodded, and they were silent a moment. Usually the swamp was filled with the trills of cardinals and warblers and the honks of herons and egrets, but the target practice had chased them away. Mederos leaned against a strangler fig, also called the vegetable octopus, which over the course of decades wrapped itself around and around its host tree, this one a cabbage palm, and prevented it from expanding, eventually enclosing and killing it. The strangler fig was knotty, grasping, and suffocating, to Maurice a metaphor for the entire swamp.

He flicked his hand at a mosquito undaunted by the Cutter, then asked, "You were with Erneido Oliva?"

Mederos nodded. "I was on the troopship *Houston,* and I transferred to Oliva's landing craft. The landing craft pilot fell into the water, a bad start. And then the frogmen reported coral reefs we weren't expecting. We landed at Red Beach at Playa Larga, at the top of the Bay of Pigs, right at the impenetrable Zapata swamp. Nothing went right, as you know."

"You get any military training before the invasion?"

"More than some. Two weeks. I had been at the University of Havana. There were about two hundred and fifty of us students. We hardly knew which end of the rifle was which. But we knew which end of our rifles made the best paddle, because before we got to shore our landing craft's engine failed. Then our craft bounced off a reef and started taking on water. The CIA had told us that based on their aerial photos, that reef was seaweed. So we rowed with our rifles and bailed with our helmets."

"How long were you on the beach?" Maurice asked.

"The beach . . ." Mederos's eyes fogged. He said nothing for a moment, and Maurice felt as if he were forgotten. "I don't remember much of the beach. We were being shelled."

Another long pause. Mederos might have been talking to himself. "I ran across the woody area next to the beach, hard soil under my boots, I remember. I was a mortarman. I ran as best I could, an old sixty-millimeter M2 mortar, forty-three pounds' worth, weighing me down, right into the swamp. I never did find the road. Zapata swamp, a place like you've never seen."

Mederos looked around. "Not like this friendly place here. We crossed the swamp, at times up to our waists in mud and water. We had been told that our target, a little town for some reason called Australia, was defended only by a militia of charcoal burners."

Mederos squinted into the sun a moment. "Well, I never thought charcoal burners could fight like they did. And soon the Stalin tanks and T.33s arrived. And, of course, the U.S. Navy planes never did come. I later heard President Kennedy was at a dance that night, and couldn't be bothered authorizing attacks from the *Essex*, which was lying off the Cuban coast. I don't believe that about Kennedy. Plenty still do, though. Might've been Dulles's decision."

Maurice didn't want Mederos to spend too much time talking about the operation's chain of command. He asked, "How were you captured?"

"After three nights in the swamp, there were only six of us left from our platoon. Two had drowned, including my shell carrier, and the others had wandered off, sick of stupid orders. Finally we were captured by a couple dozen charcoal burners. We lost another two fellows in my platoon, crushed to death in the cramped troop truck taking us prisoners to Havana."

"Ever had a desire to return to Cuba, Eduardo?"

"Go back? Sure, all Cubans in America do. Once Fidel is gone, maybe we will." Cubans called him "Fidel," almost never "Castro."

Maurice waited as another Uzi clip was fired, then said, "Fidel is in Cuba to stay, which is something some of our friends on Calle Ocho have yet to figure out. But I'm not talking about idle daydreams about returning. I mean really go back. *A oler tierra mojada.*" To smell the wet soil, a common

81

phrase among Cuban expatriates for returning. "Ever thought about it?"

Mederos dipped his chin. "Sure. But when exile Cubans talk about returning to the homeland, solemn plans and frivolous dreams often get confused." His voice gained a bitter edge. "I saw you in the audience at the brigade reunion again this year. You know that's what they all talk about. Next year in Cuba. It never changes. It's almost laughable."

"Not so laughable now," Maurice said. "At least for you."

"I'm not following you."

"I've been approached by the CIA. They want to send some people in."

"Why?"

"There's a big problem down there, and Washington is more worried than they were during the missile crisis. They've told the CIA to fix it, and do it quickly."

"And the agency came to you?" Mederos asked, astonished.

"I'm heading the operation."

"Mother of Mary, that's all I need to hear to turn you down." He stepped away from Maurice, waving his hand in front of his face as if Maurice's suggestion were a bad smell. "The last time you led me anywhere, it was into one of Fidel's *granjas*." The Cuban continued to wave his hand.

"When your theatrics are completed, you might want to listen to the rest of what I have to say."

Mederos laughed. "You keep away from me." He backed farther, almost tripping on the sun-bleached skeleton of a small raccoon. "You and the CIA. Christ, that's like dropping a match into a can of gasoline. A truly frightening combination."

"You owe Castro a debt, don't you? You've forgotten what he did to you, Eduardo. Your parents were owners of a *latisfundios*. At least, the revolutionary tribunal claimed their five hundred acres of sugar cane was a large estate. And for that terrible offense, your father was sent to the Manacas camp at

Las Villas, and your mother to Taco-Taco. Then they just vanished."

"I know all of this, Bill."

"And then G2 came looking for you at the University of Havana. The only thing you did was to contribute several poems to a pro-Batista magazine. Bad poems, if I recall. You and six others were about a dozen oar strokes ahead of the secret police. How many days did you spend at sea?"

"Eighteen," Mederos replied. His face knotted with the memory.

"I've just reread your medical file from the Coast Guard. Severe dehydration and malnutrition. Exhaustion. Second-degree sunburn. You were a wreck. One of your compatriots suffered a burst appendix while you were adrift, and he died horribly, and you had to push his body overboard. And you don't claim you'd like to get even?"

Mederos shifted on his feet, and the raccoon bones cracked under him.

Maurice went on, "Isn't that why you're out here in the swamp playing soldier with these idiots? Shooting up the bush, fantasizing about getting even with Fidel? Well, I'm offering you a real chance."

The Cuban bent to scratch a leg. "I thought the CIA was out of the business of assassination?"

Maurice held up his hand like a traffic cop. "Nobody said anything about assassination. Washington has given us two rules, and they've said under no circumstances can we consider breaking them. First, we can't harm Castro. And second, we can't work to overthrow him. They've made it very clear that they'll have my ass if I even think of doing anything along those lines."

Mederos pulled a pant leg from his boots and rolled it up to his knee. A black leech, about three inches long, was stuck to his calf. The Cuban gently lifted its shiny, squirming body away from his leg, but the head stuck. He pulled, and the leech stretched but would not let go with its sucker. Mederos pulled a little harder, until it seemed it would snap in two, and only then did it pop off. The leech injected an anticoagulant, and the leg bled profusely. Mederos tossed the leech away, then spit into his hand and rubbed the saliva into the wound. "When I climbed out of the Zapata swamp I had so many leeches on my back it looked like I was wearing a shirt made of them."

Christ almighty, Maurice loathed the swamp.

Mederos rolled down his pant leg while he was still bleeding and asked, "If you can't do those two things, kill him or topple him, what's left?"

Maurice wet his lips before continuing, "I've got an idea, and you're a large part of it."

"I don't want anything to do with you," Mederos replied.

Maurice smiled. "I can be pretty persuasive."

"Frankly, Bill, you couldn't persuade me to rise to the surface of a lake if I were drowning."

One of the trainees laughed, a hysterical sound that startled Maurice. He turned to see an alligator—five feet long and fiercely lashing out with its tail—being dragged to the firing line by one of the marksmen. The man—actually a boy, no older than seventeen—had found the animal in the bog's edge behind the targets as he was checking scores, and he held it by its snout as he pulled it over the ground. When the alligator's feet found purchase on the soil, the boy rolled it onto its back and slid it along.

With his hands locked around its mouth, the boy lifted the gator into the air like a trophy. He grinned fiendishly as he held the reptile to the target post as another marksman tied it with a length of rope. The second marksman kept well away from the alligator, walking in wide circles as he wound the rope around the gator and the post, then cinched it tight. Anticipating high sport, the other trainees pushed clips into their weapons and pulled back bolts. The drill instructor stood by, his hands on his hips.

Maurice began walking toward them, giving the leech a wide berth. The trainees lifted their weapons, and Maurice sprinted the last forty yards to them. "Hey, hold up there."

84

As if the instructor had given them a marching order, they turned as one toward Maurice, who was holding up a hand as he approached. "No sense shooting up the wildlife, is there?"

The drill instructor laughed mirthlessly, and the trainees recognized their cue and joined in. One of them—a fellow in his mid-twenties who had removed his shirt and wore a scar from his left nipple to his belt line—said in a voice Maurice guessed was an octave below his normal, "Doesn't look like you've got a whole lot of say out here, does it?"

A trainee wearing a bandolier over his shoulder added, "We ought to just tie you up next to the gator."

The DI laughed again, and the trainees followed his lead.

Mederos walked up behind Maurice but said nothing. Maurice glanced at him. There might have been a smile on Mederos's face.

Maurice said tonelessly, "It doesn't take any *cojónes* to fire at a gator."

He walked across their firing line toward the alligator. Despite the heat, his backbone felt as if it were a rod of ice. His hands were trembling as he reached for the knots tied across the gator's back. The animal snapped its jaws but was tied too tightly to turn to Maurice. Maurice didn't know what was worse, standing in front of a firing squad or touching the alligator's skin as he worked the knot.

The drill instructor had a jug jaw and a nose bent out of line. He called, "Mister, I'm going to have my boys carry you away from there, and they do whatever I tell them with enthusiasm."

Maurice undid the first knot. The gator whipped the end of its tail and hissed, a sound that seared Maurice. He pressed his fingers against the gator's scales to stop his hands from trembling.

"Go get him, men."

They started toward Maurice and the alligator, but Eduardo Mederos brought them up when he said, "That's William Maurice."

They looked at Mederos, then back at Maurice. The scarred trainee asked, "Maurice? From Coral Gables?"

Mederos nodded. "The same."

One of the trainees lowered his Uzi and said, "My kid brother learned to swim in his pool."

The drill instructor cleared his throat with embarrassment. "I should have recognized you, Mr. Maurice. I used to go to your house when I was a kid."

Maurice was working on the last knot. He had no idea what he would do when the alligator was free. The animal was staring at him, its yellow eyes rolled back in its sockets. Maurice grabbed the end of the line and walked around the post. The gator began to squirm as the rope slackened. Then it slid down the post, backed away, bared its teeth at Maurice, then ran on the soft ground toward the cypress trees on the swamp's edge. Damn, they're fast, Maurice thought. And they don't drag their stomachs when they run, he noticed. Just footprints, no belly prints. Precious little thanks I get from you, I suppose.

The trainees muttered apologies and turned away. Their mortification added to the day's heat. They fairly ran to their vehicles.

Maurice brushed his hands together. "So, you'll think about it, Eduardo?"

"Not at all."

"Sure you will. Have one of your boys here drive your car back into town. You come with me. We'll talk along the way."

"No way will I do that."

Maurice put his hand on his elbow. "Your lips tell me one thing, but your eyes say another."

"Charm and wit don't work on me, Bill."

Maurice led him to the Ford. "I want to show you some photos taken at an airfield in Cuba."

"Goddamn it, Bill, will you listen to me a moment?"

By the time he had the words out, Maurice had pushed Mederos into the car. He walked around the vehicle and climbed in behind the wheel. "As Dr. Johnson said, 'He who does not yearn for a return to his homeland can yearn for nothing.'"

"Emeliano Johnson, the Cuban American psychiatrist on Calle Ocho?"

"No, but close." Maurice waved away a second guess. Mederos could not have known the rules of Maurice and Rosa's little game. "Anyway, Eduardo, you'll be amazed at what's going on in Cuba these days. Flat amazed."

Chapter VIII

Jack Cantrell squinted at the monitor. He placed his hands on the keyboard and scrolled down through the memorandum. Not reading, as he had it virtually memorized, but catching key phrases as the words rolled by. Nothing changed. The amber screen stared dumbly back at him.

Gerard Jones leaned over from his terminal, which carried the same memo. "You were hoping, maybe, that in loading Maurice's proposal the words might have been scrambled, and that they now made more sense? No chance. I checked it against the hard copy."

Maurice's hard copy was a thirty-two-page proposal submitted to Cantrell that morning. When the DDO read it the first time, he had begun to tremble, something he could not recall doing before, cold showers excepted.

"Well," Jones asked happily, as he always was behind his machine, "are you going to send it?" Five strokes on the Apollo keyboard would instantly display the memo on the CIA director's desk at Langley.

When Cantrell lifted his fingers to the keyboard and hesitated, Jones added, "You've been doing that for two hours. You remind me of a kid the first time on the swimming pool's high board. Back and forth, back and forth. Hugging his chest. Can't quite jump, but doesn't dare climb back down the ladder in disgrace."

"We should have done tests on Maurice before we gave him this job. The last one anybody has on him dates back to the early sixties. He may have gone way downhill since then." Cantrell spread his hands in front of the monitor like a faith healer, then removed his glasses and peered myopically at the screen. "This proposal may be symptomatic of something."

Jones laughed. "Still reads the same, glasses or no?"

The operations director balled his fist. "Goddamn it. I just can't send this."

Jones smiled again, unaffected by his boss's quandary. "If you'll excuse the impertinence, this is a side of you I've never seen. Indecision, confusion, hesitation. A bit of humanness. Actually, you don't wear it well. It's like seeing you in an ill-fitting suit, something no one at operations would ever dream possible."

"Toothbrush, that you are irreplaceable does not mean I wouldn't try my hardest, given sufficient provocation."

Mindless banter to hide his tension. Cantrell did not remove his eyes from the screen. He put his glasses back on, and the display was reflected in both lenses. It made him more a part of the office, which five days after the beginning of construction was a fully equipped command unit and was decorated primarily with computer monitors. Sixteen analysts and controllers manned the desks, but the hectic activity during the setup had calmed. The carpenters and electricians were gone, although the sound of construction could be heard from beyond the east wall. Two agents were playing gin, and another was diving deeper into a labyrinthine adventure game on her computer. Another was reading the *Herald*'s sports pages. They were waiting for Cantrell.

He said, "You haven't told me what you think of this."

"I ran it through the Berlin 8.5 gameware," Jones said, bringing the results up on his monitor. He had designed the model. On his free time at home, he swore. He had once determined that fully 15 percent of the world's humint operations took place in Berlin, three times that of the next busiest city (New York). So Jones named the game Berlin. He added 8.5 to the name because much of what the agency did reminded him of a Fellini film.

The game was a cloak-and-dagger variation of a war-room simulation, where an entire battle could be fought without a shell being fired or a soldier leaving his barracks. Jones had access to almost all of the agency's files and had culled from them over the course of two years certain patterns in intelligence operations. He had quantified these and reduced them to programmable variables. It had taken him another eighteen months to design the software. He claimed that given sufficient information, Berlin 8.5 could predict the percentage chance of success of a given operation, plus or minus five points, a boast the director of the agency's Office of Research and Development scoffed at. However, due to the mass of data Jones had reviewed and entered into the hard drives, and to the novel and complex nature of the game, neither could Jones's boast be disproved. When Jones had the temerity to offer the program to the agency for $250,000, agency lawyers pointed to four laws Jones was violating by even suggesting such a sale. In truth, all the agency could do was buy it and insert a letter of reprimand into Jones's personnel file, which Jones deleted the next time he tapped into it, which he did with some frequency.

Cantrell realized there were drawbacks working with a person who had the fifth-highest intelligence quotient ever recorded (218 points), but he saw no alternative in light of Jones's talents. Particularly galling was that even though Jones was two grades below Cantrell, Jones made fully three times the salary.

90

Every time Jones received an offer of employment from IBM or Microsoft for wages that made Cantrell burn, Jones marched into the director's office for a salary adjustment. The director threw him out the door the time Jones asked for more than the director made. But, as always when dealing with Jones, the agency eventually granted his request.

Jones looked at his screen. "Of the game's five hundred and fifty-eight variables, I could fill in only three hundred forty, but of these, one eighty-five were with greater than ninety percent probability, due to our familiarity with Castro. Normally with the Berlin system, the object of manipulation is the great imponderable. But knowing Fidel like we do, we can eliminate much of the guesswork, at least with the one eighty-five." A few keystrokes. "Berlin normally would have given us a probability percentage, based on the 558-340-185 input."

"Gerard, I'm sinking into a stupor of boredom here."

Jones was undeterred. "But Berlin wouldn't venture a percentage chance of success because its endgame—the hoped-for result—was not one it recognized. It kept asking me to redefine what we want. I'm afraid I couldn't do it adequately, not in terms the program would understand."

"You designed the program," Cantrell charged. "I thought you could make it comprehend any endgame."

"Not this." Jones grinned. "Not Maurice's proposal."

Cantrell pulled open his desk drawer for a pack of cigarettes that wasn't there, forgetting he had quit two years ago. At times like this his need for a smoke reached truly primitive levels, approaching the need to breathe. The doctor at the agency's stop-smoking clinic had promised the nicotine grip would lessen over time. A cruel lie. Not for one waking minute in those years had Cantrell not needed a cigarette. He angrily closed the drawer.

Jones went on, "I did, though, run through Berlin the three plans you came up with. None of them scored higher than the plus-or-minus factor."

"What's that mean?"

"None scored more than a five percent chance of success."

"Your game is just that, Toothbrush. A game. Not once since you extorted all that money from the agency has a decision been made based on Berlin's conclusions."

Jones renewed his smile. "But no one these days undertakes a humint operation without running it through my little game. So there seems to be an anomaly here, *nicht wahr?*"

Cantrell swore to himself. Jones frequently injected simple foreign terms into his conversations, hoping Cantrell would again be tempted to wager on Jones's ability to learn a language. Jones had once bragged that within one week he could learn any language for which the agency had tapes. Cantrell bet $500 and picked Farsi. Seven days later, Reza Mossadegh of the Iranian desk, after a fifteen-minute conversation with Jones, swore Jones was fluent, but "with a slight Azerbaijan accent we from Tehran find irritating," and Cantrell was $500 poorer.

Knowing Jones was not without its small pleasures, though. He was an amateur card counter and visited Atlantic City every few months to sit at the blackjack tables. In a fit of puerile spite, just before Jones's last visit to New Jersey, his co-workers in operations persuaded an operator in SIGINT Tasking to fax a photo to the Atlantic City Harrah's, with a false Reno Harrah's origination, alerting Harrah's that a counter might be headed their way. Such information flashes through a gaming city, and Jones, who never bet more than twenty dollars even when the remaining deck was full of face cards, was turned away from every table in Atlantic City before he could get comfortable on the stools. Jones returned to Langley that Monday, his usual smile gone. Cantrell felt a touch sorry for his subordinate, but not enough to tell him of the plot.

"So what's your own conclusion?" Cantrell asked.

"I think it'll work, Jack. And so do you. Maurice has you convinced. Admit it."

Cantrell turned to his assistant. "Maurice's effort back in 1961 was a half-baked plan." He stabbed a finger at the monitor. "And this is less. Maurice lost his job because of it."

"Our jobs aren't the most important consideration here."

"Easy for you to say, when you've got Big Blue waiting to escort you to Armonk if the agency tosses you out." More of the same banter. "You really think it'll work, Gerard?"

"Yes, even though Maurice is quirky."

Cantrell raised an eyebrow. "That from you?"

"Jump, boss."

One final long grimace, then Cantrell pressed the five keys. Secrecy and confirmation codes appeared at the bottom of the screen. He said, "There. It's on the director's desk."

"I'd love to be there when he reads it, just to see his face."

Cantrell exhaled loudly, blowing smoke he wished was there."Then you're very brave, despite all appearances."

It had always seemed to Domaso Redono such a small thing to lose his career over. Even now, with the perspective of sixteen years, it grew smaller, not larger, unlike other regrets, which were amplified by memory out of proportion.

No, this truly was small, and so remained distressing. In a speech from the Plaza of the Revolution, Fidel had said that unlike in the United States, Cuba did not need an election every four years, because the Cuban people voted every day. Redono had been a writer for *Granma*, the official newspaper of the Cuban Communist party. In a story on the speech, otherwise lauding Fidel, Redono had questioned how Cubans voted every day. Perhaps the line that lost his job was, "The mechanism by which we vote is not visible to most Cubans." Redono and the editor who let it slip into print were on the street the next day.

Redono searched for work a year, finally finding a job as a bus driver in Havana. The buses are called *guauas*, pronounced "wah-wahs," and are always crowded, so much so that Redono developed a chronic ache in his neck where passengers' rear ends and shopping baskets pushed against him. It was a menial job, one beneath his education and dignity, in the true spirit of the revolution.

He never quite gave up his profession. In 1979, during one of the infrequent thaws in U.S.–Cuban relations, dozens of American journalists arrived in Havana. At great risk, Redono approached a *Miami Herald* reporter at the Conejito Restaurant—serves rabbit one hundred ways—and offered to send the *Herald* periodic articles on Havana and Cuba, if the reporter would determine how to get the stories out of the country once relations soured again, as they surely would. It was easier than Redono expected. The next day the reporter told him to leave the articles in a mailbox at a home in the Miramar district, a block from the Mexican embassy.

Redono was amused that the reporter probably notified the Americans of a new intelligence agent, a walk-in. Redono had in mind only soft news stories, features on Havana and its people. He may have had a quarrel with the revolution, but he certainly was no traitor. At first he wrote articles about the improvements to the historic district in Old Havana, and of Cuban teenagers' penchant for Levi's, even though the city was flooded with East German knock-offs. His crisp, often humorous articles appeared in the Spanish-language edition of the *Miami Herald,* using a pseudonymous byline and the thrilling subheading "Our Man in Havana." He wrote an article a month and often found a little money in the box, and once there was a sparkling new Honda moped leaning against the box with his name taped to the saddle.

Over the years, his articles had become more adventurous as his sources improved and his dissatisfaction with the government increased. Redono, a practicing Catholic, wrote a bitter article about children in Cardena, seventy miles east of Havana, who were being dissuaded from their religion by their teachers, who asked them to lean over their desks and pray to Jesus for a pet duck. Nothing happened. But when, moments later, they prayed to Fidel, the teacher gave them a duck.

His best piece was about the crash of an aging Bristol Britannia, with fifteen passengers and two crewmen on board, in the Sierra de los Organos southwest of Havana. In Cuba, relatives of those who die in plane wrecks are never notified, as the crash is a state secret. Loved ones are left waiting at the airport with no explanation. After the story appeared in Miami, a note

94

was left in the box saying G2 was now looking in earnest for our man in Havana. They never found him.

Knowledge of a new Soviet bomber in Cuba came to Redono by accident. One of his contacts from the crash investigation, a runway maintenance worker at the La Panchita airport, journeyed to Havana to report his suspicion that someone in the state-owned construction company was making illegal profits by digging only a meter-deep foundation for a new hangar at the airport, instead of the two meters called for in the specifications. The cement truck delivered every other load to one of four sites off the base, which the worker suspected were the foundations for luxurious private homes. The worker had complained to his supervisor, who threatened to fire him if he mentioned it again. The worker was outraged. A meter of concrete would not withstand *una tromba terrestre*—a strong whirlwind—much less anything like Hurricane Flora, which devastated Cuba in 1963. And who was making money stealing the cement?

With nowhere else to turn, he visited Domaso Redono. He knew Redono investigated the Bristol Britannia crash, and that the worker had later heard the story on Radio Marti, from a copyrighted *Herald* article. Maybe Redono would be interested in a construction theft.

Indeed he was, particularly when the worker indicated the larger hangar was needed for a new airplane. You mean the Blinders or Backfires that occasionally visit Cuba? The worker paused with his coffee to vigorously shake his head. No, this plane is new. An old Bear? Another shake.

"I'm telling you, Domaso, this is a new plane. I've seen it, but only once at night, when I had to work late. I don't think they bring it out during daylight. A big plane, sleek and beautiful."

Redono wrote the story, one about corruption in the state-run construction industry. There were only three sentences about the new plane, which included the worker's description of it.

Redono dropped the article in the box, wondering what

responsable—official in charge—would lose his job when the news filtered back into Cuba. He was unaware of the stir his story would cause in the *Herald*'s newsroom.

His house on Indian Creek in Miami Beach was an embarrassment to him now. Eduardo Mederos had purchased it in a spate of denial of his heritage and his past and his obsession. He had hoped to cut himself off from it all. One deft stroke at all the memories. It hadn't worked, of course. Nothing would, it seemed. He was left with a six-bedroom Georgian home, so jarringly English that it pained him to look at it. He had never overcome the urge to apologize to the Cuban American gardeners and pool repairmen and window washers every time they drove up. He felt like apologizing again, this time to Maurice as he dropped Mederos off.

Maurice waved cheerily as he pulled back onto Pine Tree Drive. Mederos was relieved to be rid of him. The ex-CIA operative was at it again, apparently having learned nothing from the 1961 debacle. Maurice back with the CIA? I can die content now, Mederos thought, because I've seen it all. Mederos had laughed aloud several times during Maurice's presentation, which didn't even slow Maurice. But by the end of their drive in from the swamp, Maurice had made his plan appear to have some crude sense.

Mederos stamped mud off his boots, entered the house, and closed the heavy oak door behind him. The sound echoed. He had tried everything: moving furniture, adding thick drapes, carpeting all horizontal surfaces. Nothing eliminated the echoes. The home's emptiness taunted him. He had been coming home to echoes for many years.

His housekeeper had left a telegram on the parson's table, carefully set apart from the other mail. Mederos closed his eyes a moment. He had been expecting news one way or the other, and the telegram this early meant his latest attempt had failed. He pulled his reading glasses from a pocket and put them on. He slowly ran his thumb under the seal. How many of these had he received? The telegram had been sent from Madrid, forwarded from Santiago de Cuba. The telegram shook in his hand. It read in Spanish, "Trail ended. No further trace. Apologies. Pelayo."

He crumpled it slowly, as if it took all his strength, and dropped it onto the table.

"What am I doing?" he asked aloud. His gaze found his boots. "Tracking mud into the hall, and not much else." He took a long breath. "Not much else at all."

Mederos walked down the hallway into the den. He pulled off his boots, then stripped off his wet socks. His brows furled as the news in the telegram settled on him. Pelayo was a code name for a Yugoslavian import-export official stationed by the Belgrade government in Havana. Mederos had hired him to do the searching this time, one of a long line of tenuous contacts that had come to nothing. Mederos never knew whether he was being taken or whether they were doing the investigating for which he was paying them. And what could a Yugoslavian civil servant do? Or the rum distillery manager before him? Mederos should have had better luck with the Havana police captain who claimed to have spent his entire two-week holiday searching and to have traveled to Matanzas, but that too came to nothing. Mederos had no better contacts, no one with any authority to do the investigation.

He unbuttoned the camouflage blouse. The den was overdone with leather furniture, books he had never read, and Oriental carpets he always hesitated to walk on. The interior designer had also insisted on filling the room with expensive pseudoart, as if quantity could hide mass production. Mederos's least favorite was a two-foot-high rose-colored marble obelisk—presumably patterned after the Egyptian tower at the Place de la Concorde—that sat on the end table. Mederos tossed his hat onto it. He opened the small refrigerator built into the cabinet along the north wall and twisted off the cap of a bottle of mineral water. He finished half the bottle before lowering it.

Maurice's question came back to him. What in hell was he doing out in the swamp? He muttered an oath under his breath. Fooling around with a bunch of thick-skulled adolescents with severe cases of arrested developments, with a so-called drill instructor who once proudly told Mederos that he had paid a *muchacha perdida* to rub his thing with an Uzi's barrel. Even had the searches been successful, nothing could come of such slop. He had known it then, and he knew it now. What had he been thinking? Desperation makes sense of nonsense.

And he was desperate, even after all the years. Mederos opened the cabinet drawer where he kept the only photo of her he had. It was framed in silver, and he lifted it out. Keeping it in the drawer was a childish compromise, but a necessary one. Not so apparent in the room as to bloody him every time he entered, but there in the drawer, not too far away, should he need it.

He raised it to his eyes. The black-and-white photo was taken in 1960 and showed a young woman sitting on the Escalinata steps at the University of Havana. Wind played with the hem of her skirt, and the photo caught her tucking it under her legs and laughing into the lens. A wisp of hair crossed an eye, and her other hand was trying to tame it. A textbook lay on the steps next to her. An unposed moment caught by Mederos with a Brownie.

The photograph was of Carmen Santana, taken during her days as a medical student. Mederos lowered himself slowly into a wingback chair, his eye never leaving the photo.

In every person's life there is a crucial moment that if bungled reverberates down through the years, unrelenting and mocking, never allowing one to forget. It can be pushed around by memory, but not much, and it remains a hard little burr of unappeased truth. The killing truth for Eduardo Mederos was that he had left Carmen Santana on the beach at the Bay of Pigs.

They had volunteered for the brigade together and had trained together. She was a medic and he a mortarman, and the brigade leadership was so in need of soldiers they could not refuse Mederos's demand that they sail in the same invasion ship, the *Houston*.

They were only a dozen yards up the beach, sprinting in infantrymen's crouches for the safety of the brush, when a mortar round exploded, instantly killing the man running next to Carmen and knocking her to the sand. Mederos had been five feet in front of her, manfully leading the way, when he heard the sound, first like canvas ripping as the shell arced in on them, then a surprisingly muffled explosion. He turned to see Carmen sitting next to the body. She was seemingly uninjured. His mortar bouncing against his back, he rushed to her, asked if she was all right over the sound of more incoming, and tried to lift her to her feet. All around him soldiers were scrambling up the beach. She did not respond, just sat there staring. When he lifted her by her arms, she slumped back to the sand. He could tell she was breathing, and he saw no wounds. She just would not move.

Mederos's corporal was running along the beach, urging frightened soldiers into the cover of the brush. He came to Mederos and roughly pushed him away from Carmen.

"Get moving. Up to cover." Corporal Delgado gave Carmen a cursory glance. "I'll call the medic for her."

"She is the medic," Mederos replied dully.

The corporal yelled, "Get going," and he ran on.

That was the moment crystallized in Mederos's memory. He had replayed it incessantly, and, inescapably, he made the wrong choice. He obeyed the corporal and left her on the beach. Someone would take care of her, he remembered reasoning, not yet suspecting that the brigade's assault was already falling apart and not knowing that the first soldiers to give Carmen attention would be DAAFAR troops who would take her to a prison hospital.

Mederos was frantic when, after twenty months in a prison camp, he and the other brigade soldiers were ransomed, and she was not among those returning to Florida. He made inquiries at the CIA, the Departments of Defense and State, and anywhere else he could think of. He also tried many times contacting the Cuban government but was rebuffed again and again.

He received one letter from her, in 1969, sent via the State Department. She wrote that she did not know if he had survived, and if so, why she had not heard anything. She had not received any of his hundred letters, which he attempted to send to her through DAAFAR, the Federation of Cuban Women, the Ministry of the Interior, wild stabs at finding her. He had no idea where she was or why she had not returned with him and the other prisoners. Not knowing tumbled him into bouts of depression, anger, and bewilderment, symptoms that should have lessened their grip on him over the years but had not.

He saw her once. In 1967, a *disgustado*—one of the unhappy, the cure for which, the revolution believes, is a prison sentence—was released from a camp at La Ruda and had stolen a fishing boat at Cardenas. He was found by American fishermen several miles from Key West. Trying to find her, Mederos was interviewing all former Cuban prisoners as soon as they were released by U.S. Immigration. This one said Carmen Santana had treated him for a cane cut at La Ruda just two months before, and he believed she was still interned there.

Mederos went back to Cuba, smuggled in on a boat from Caracas. He carried passably forged documents. Traveling to La Ruda was fairly easy, as internal passports are not required in Cuba and there are few travel restrictions on Cubans within their country. Journeying by bus, Mederos arrived at the camp four days after he entered the country.

He had no plan. No plans were possible, not with the prison camp within the La Ruda FAR base. He spent three days in the oak and cedar glade on a hill overlooking the camp before he saw her through his binoculars. Mederos was shocked. Her six years in the camp had crushed her, he could tell from a hundred yards. Her youth had vanished. She looked more like her mother than the young student he had known at

100

the university. Not that she still wasn't beautiful. She was, heartbreakingly so, but he had irrationally expected their time apart to be time halted. She shouldn't have changed. The ghastly unfairness of it. Both of them were being robbed of their youth spent together.

Then she was gone, disappeared back into a barracks. He waited two more days until his water ran out but never saw her again. As arranged, Mederos was picked up several days later at Santa Clara Bay by a Keys fisherman who had charged him roughly the cost of a new boat. Mederos had heard a number of rumors since then, that she had escaped and was in hiding, that she had died in the camp, and others. He thought he had come close to finding her a few times but in fact did not even know if she was still alive.

Mederos had carried the memory of that thirty-second view of Carmen like another might carry a photo in a wallet. He pulled it out and examined it frequently, minutely. Over the years the risks of his return to Cuba were largely forgotten, but her face, with its new lines, fretful eyes, and turned-down mouth, was indelibly impressed on his mind.

Mederos sipped his water, his eyes unfocused. He had long ago recognized that his feeling for this woman had mutated beyond love. Love implies an innocence and freshness and, in its maturity, respect and renewal. And love nurtures love. The give and take of it all. The kindnesses and the laughter and the touching. He had had none of it, not for three decades. None of what sustains love.

So his love had not grown. It had hardened. Mederos was well aware that his emotion was no longer normal. It was a storm-driven tide, receding, then reappearing in force. It had allowed him to build his business and home. But it always roared back, washing over him. A psychiatrist once diagnosed these struggles as depression, a clinical imbalance of something in his body that could be controlled by injecting something else into his body. That Mederos had never been able to move on to other relationships was part of the illness, the psychiatrist

101

claimed. Mederos did not believe a word. Love should not be worn down to nothing with the passing of the years, like a stone in a river, made smaller and smaller as water sluiced over it. But, the psychiatrist countered, your love was fixed by guilt, just as your photo of her was fixed by a solution. Passing years change us all. You are no longer the same people you were thirty years ago. She is irretrievably gone, and you should let go. Release yourself, Eduardo. And let her go.

He let the psychiatrist go. All those years of education, and the shrink couldn't understand Mederos's simple need to see again the only woman he would ever love. A driven, implacable, blinding need, but a simple one nonetheless.

Mederos glanced at his watch, at the day and month display. When he was seized by the melancholy, he told time not by minutes, but by days. And the morose spells were increasing as time passed, prompting him to do irrational things, like playing soldier in a swamp.

He carefully placed the photograph on the table and lifted the phone. He needed a way out. For Mederos, it was a matter of life or death.

He withdrew a slip of paper from his shirt pocket and dialed the number on it. "May I speak with a Mr. Cantrell? William Maurice asked me to call."

Chapter IX

Rosa Maurice was startled by the scratching at the front door, which sounded like their German shepherd, long dead. She dropped her magazine and walked quickly to peer through the peephole. She was startled again by the tiny, distorted image of a man's face swathed in bandages. The head rocked to and fro, as if only loosely attached to its body. She was frantically securing the safety chain when her husband called out, "It's me, Rosa. Open up."

She swung the door open. Eduardo Mederos's arm was draped over her husband's shoulder, and Maurice was bent with the effort of keeping the Cuban upright. Mederos's nose was crossed with a white bandage, and his ears had gauze pads on them, held by a wrap around his chin and head. Two points on his right cheek and another on his left were covered with smaller bandages. His lower lip was also covered with a bandage. He smiled weakly, revealing metal braces.

"Two ears, a nose, three moles, a lip, and some teeth," Maurice summarized, walking Mederos down the hallway to a back bedroom. Rosa hurried ahead of them to turn down the bedspread and sheet.

Maurice lowered Mederos onto the bed and lifted his feet while Rosa closed the curtains. Mederos immediately began a deep, stertorous breathing.

She asked as they left the room, "If the resemblance is so close, why all the plastic surgery?"

Maurice opened the *Herald* and spread it over the coffee table in the study. "The cutters—one from McGill, two from Massachusetts General, two from Stanford—studied photos of the two men for several days. Also a couple of tooth benders from the dental school at Columbia. Hours and hours of meetings. Slides and models, computer-generated alterations, like Detroit designs cars these days. They saw dissimilarities a group of half-bombed veterans at a banquet can't. It pained me just to watch what the surgeons and orthodontists were doing to Eduardo."

"Probably not as much as it pained Eduardo."

Maurice looked contemplatively a moment, then said, "No, probably not as much." He read a headline, then said, "I was on my way with him from the clinic to the agency's warehouse when he started sliding back into the anesthesia, so I came here. Figured I'd give him a couple more hours."

"For heaven's sake, Bill, why did you drag him out of the clinic so fast? He looks terrible, and can't even walk."

Maurice pointed to an article on the front page of the newspaper. "Because of this. Somehow the *Herald* got wind of the Blackjacks in Cuba. They don't name the plane, and they don't have any details, other than that it's big, black, and new, and unlike any other Soviet planes previously in Cuba. Then the writer does some guesswork about what armament such a plane would have." Maurice lifted the paper. "The writer ends the piece by speculating what such a plane could do to the 'fragile balance of power' in the Caribbean."

"It's accurate, isn't it?"

"Very. So Cantrell called while I was in the clinic's waiting room, reminding me that a newspaper leak is precisely how the missile crisis began, and that if the public and especially the politicians in this election year decide to grab on to this news, things might accelerate. He pointed out that press and popular opinion rapidly closed off many of Kennedy's options, and that mounting pressure seriously damaged the president's negotiations. Cantrell has people down at the *Herald* right now trying to find out where this came from. The director is pressing Cantrell. They talk every three hours or so. Cantrell complains that he is spending too much of his time managing his boss and, by turns, the White House."

"Are you going to like working with him?" Rosa asked.

"It's been two days since Mederos said he'd go along with my idea. Since then, Cantrell has largely been a buyer for me. I'm impressed with what he can get and how quickly he can get it. It reinforces what he told me at the outset, that the weight of the agency is behind this operation. And Cantrell is as dry as dust, but I like working with him."

Rosa glanced out the window, perhaps carefully forming her words. "You were left adrift the last time you worked with the agency. They abandoned you. You don't think it'll happen this time?"

Maurice waited while Julie Porlocarrero leaned around the den's door frame to ask if she could make some popcorn for the crowd in the rec room. Rosa said, "Of course. Don't put too much salt on it. It's bad for you." The girl disappeared.

Maurice said, "All they can do is seize the ship again."

Her smile was false. "The *Carolyn May* no longer matters, does it, Bill? Ever since the agency got the ATF to release it back to you, and you turned it over to Captain Pearson, you haven't given it another thought."

"Some thought, sure." Maurice knew what was coming.

"I've never seen you like this before. These past five days you've been like a kid on Epiphany. So many presents to open,

105

so much color and light, so much going on. You've been positively beaming. Four hours of sleep a night. Sudden meetings, late-night phone calls, all these plans whirling around. Not even when you first began your importing business, those first risky months, were you like this." She sighed heavily. "I don't know whether to be happy for you or frightened for you."

"Be happy. As Dorothy Parker once said, 'Happiness is the absence of things that will eventually kill you.' "

She looked hard at him, trying to read him. Sometimes his mouth would twist with a nascent grin, but this time he wore a poker face. She said finally, "Dorothy Parker never said that."

Maurice frowned and reached into his pocket for his wallet. He withdrew a five-dollar bill, walked across the study to an empty Spanish vase inlaid with crushed lapis, and dropped the money into it. "No," he admitted, "I suppose not."

He had begun the game during their honeymoon, when, after ecstatic lovemaking at night on a pink Bermuda beach, he'd breathlessly whispered, "As John Dos Passos said, 'The pulse of the waves and you are one.' " Well, she'd thought then, a lovely thing to say, but Dos Passos must not have been as good a writer as I remember from my college course. Then the next night, at dinner at the Pink Beach Club, Maurice raised his glass of wine, looked into her eyes, and said grandly, "As General Eisenhower said at Normandy, 'With enough wine and women in, this war would not have been.' "

She remembered her mouth falling open. She said, "Dwight Eisenhower never said any such thing, on Normandy or anywhere else."

Maurice pursed his lips. "Maybe not." Then, without other explanation, he gave her five dollars.

The exchange of money was not a one-way proposition. Once in a while he would quote some notable figure, she would challenge it, and he would walk to his *Great Quotations* or the Bible or his annotated Shakespeare or one of the other thousand volumes in his den and gleefully show her the quote. Then he would demand five dollars. Only if she couldn't be sure did she remain silent. Regardless of who paid, they put

106

the money in a vase and every few weeks treated themselves to an elegant dinner somewhere.

They heard footfalls in the hall and turned to see Eduardo Mederos leaning against the door frame. "I'm rallying."

"You don't look any better," Maurice said.

"How can you tell, when most of me is hidden under bandages?"

"What hurts most?"

"My teeth. Or maybe my ears. Hard to localize it." Because of the braces, Mederos's words were puffed and rounded. He straightened himself and patted out the wrinkles in his shirt. "I'm ready to go."

"You're still wobbly, Eduardo," Rosa said, rising from her chair to take his elbow.

With a finger, he gently explored the bandage across his nose. "I've got a touch of nausea, but I'm tougher than I look."

Maurice found his rain jacket in the hall closet. "I just got my car cleaned last week. If you have to vomit in the car, lean your head out the window."

Mederos tried a smile.

Rosa exclaimed, "Honestly, Bill." She opened the door for them.

Maurice asked her, "You're coming, aren't you?"

"To the agency's warehouse?" She looked surprised. "Of course not. That's your business."

He vigorously shook his head. "Remember, I told them you were to be in on everything. I meant it, and they had no choice." He turned fully to her and lowered his voice. "There might be losses for us if things go wrong. At least this way, you'll know what happened."

She got her coat.

Maurice said as they walked to the car, "Eduardo, let's go see how we're going to turn you into Fidel Castro."

The hall was somber, with carpeting that sank like sand underfoot and a row of paintings, probably of presidents. Neither man had ever looked at the gloomy, crusted artwork, as they had never before dallied here. But dallying they were, because behind the door, in the Oval Office, the president was meeting with Senator Richard White, and the president had sworn he would talk some sense into White, which they all knew might take a while.

The secretary of defense stood with his arms behind his back, as if hiding the thin folder in his hand. He wore a black suit, and his initials were monogrammed in small gray letters on his shirt pocket. He had an undertaker's face, carefully composed and dignified, with a square chin and charcoal eyes. His gray hair was precisely combed. He said in a muted voice, as if out of respect for the august personages of the portraits, "You've been hurt in Havana, I hear."

Standing opposite the secretary, and in full contrast, was the director of the Central Intelligence Agency. The DCI's rumpled herringbone sport coat looked as if it doubled as his pajamas. He cut his faded brown hair short to avoid having to comb it. His face resembled a bloodhound's, with sizable dewlaps, a broad, wet nose, and malleable lips. His expression was one of eternal preoccupation.

He said, "It's worse than after the Bay of Pigs, when G2 rounded up twenty-five hundred of our people. We were expecting it then, and we had inactivated a lot of them. We didn't have the warning this time. Now we're not getting anything out of Havana. And we couldn't mount a simple mail drop there now if we had to."

"I've always wondered," the secretary said, flicking his eyes at the door, "how many times the agency went after Castro."

"We don't do that anymore, not on a country's leader, no matter how deserving."

"But how many times?"

"Five that I'm aware of. Castro thinks there have been over twenty attempts on his life. And we've dinked around with him, too."

The secretary wondered if "dinked" had ever been used in the White House before. "How so?"

The director sucked on a tooth, lost in recall. In the secretary's view, the CIA director was a compendium of irritating habits, from his screwed-up face, kept that way to wrinkle his nose so his glasses would not slip down his face, to his constantly collecting spit in his mouth, as if swallowing were difficult, which made his words sound moist. The secretary overlooked them all, as they had been improbable friends since the president's first senatorial campaign eighteen years before. The secretary often thought the director's quirky mannerisms were an act to disguise his pitiless competence.

"Well"—the DCI rubbed his skull as if to warm a memory —"once the agency's Technical Services Division studied how to impregnate one of Castro's cigars with botulism toxin. And there was a plan to dust his shoes with thallium, so that when he inhaled its dust, it would cause his beard to fall out. We also studied a plan to put a hallucinogen in one of his cigars just before a televised speech."

"Christ almighty. . . ."

"All those people were gone, though, long before I came to the agency."

The secretary asked, "Are you bringing one of them back?"

"William Maurice? At this point, he has more contacts in Cuba than we do. And there's some things you don't know about him. Maurice is a hard case, not the type to mess with trying to get Fidel's hair to fall off. Maybe his head, but not his hair."

"What about this, then?" The secretary held up the file. "Is this plan any better than thallium dust?"

"Remember the limits we're working under. No dispensing with Fidel, either with his life or with his rule of Cuba. Those are good rules, too. You don't want an open season."

The secretary of defense rose on his toes and settled back, then glanced again at the door. "You agree with me, then, that the Soviets won't take the Blackjacks out of Cuba if we demand it."

109

"My people are certain, as am I." The DCI gurgled, then swallowed visibly.

The secretary said, "The Soviets must have known they couldn't keep the Blackjacks secret for long."

"The Soviets are squatters. They think that if they do something long enough, it becomes legal and acceptable, like adverse possession of land. Remember back in 1980 when Frank Church caused a storm by revealing that the Soviets had a combat battalion in Cuba? The administration quickly insisted to the Soviets and Cubans that the troops be removed. Turns out they had been in Cuba over ten years. When the Soviets refused on this ground, the administration let the matter fade away. Maybe they're trying the same thing. Get them in there long enough, and nobody can protest with any success." The DCI removed his glasses and rubbed the lenses on his tie. "When is the president confronting the Soviet ambassador with what we know?"

"He's calling him in tomorrow morning. The message will be blunt. Take the Blackjacks out of Cuba within thirty days or the United States will view their presence as an act of aggression."

The ponderous door opened, and Senator White stepped into the hall, escorted by the national security adviser, who whispered one last plea or promise into Senator White's ear before saying louder that he would hear from the president shortly. The senator, wearing a cream-colored suit, a handkerchief in his pocket, and an enigmatic smile, nodded a greeting at the others as he passed them.

The adviser, a clerical man in his late forties, turned to the secretary and the DCI and said, "The president and I have had a good laugh with your plan."

"It'll work, John," said the CIA director. "We both think so."

"I'll watch as you convince the president of that. After Senator White's visit, I could use some comic relief."

Traffic was light, and the Ford arrived at the Port of Miami ten minutes later. The port's guard, who manned the gate booth just beyond the passenger terminal, was gone, replaced

110

by an agent whose shoulders were so broad they almost touched glass on both sides of him. There had not yet been time to tailor the port uniform, and his shirt buttons were strained almost to breaking. He leaned out of the booth to look into the Ford.

"Afternoon, Mr. Maurice, Mr. Mederos." He winced at Mederos's dressing. "May I ask who the lady is?"

"My wife."

"I'm afraid this is a restricted area, and—"

"Call Cantrell."

"I've been given my orders, Mr. Maurice."

"Call Cantrell. He'll change them."

The agent lifted the phone. A moment later he said, "Sorry, Mrs. Maurice. Please go on through."

They found Cantrell on the telephone, pacing behind Gerard Jones, who was absorbed with his terminal. Cantrell was flushed, and despite the chill of the air conditioning, the back of his white shirt was damp. He dipped his chin repeatedly, silently agreeing with whoever was on the phone.

Jones looked up. "What you are seeing is Jack jumping."

Cantrell lowered the phone. "That was the director. Senator White's office is calling the agency and the National Reconnaissance Office and the Defense Department, demanding to know more about the plane reported in the *Herald* this morning." Cantrell bared his teeth. "As you know, the senator's opponent in the primary election is a popular Cuban American. I'm sure White wants to beat him on this issue, to be the most strident in his denouncing the Soviets for sneaking a new weapon into Cuba, further enslaving Cubans, and on and on, so he won't lose all of his traditional support in Florida's Cuban community."

"When you pause to catch your breath, let me introduce my wife, Rosa. And in case you don't recognize him, the mummy here is Eduardo."

Cantrell shook hands with Rosa, his eyes still on the telephone. "Eduardo, you're going to be seeing a lot of this building. You'd better have Bill show you around."

111

A new door had been cut through the east wall. While Cantrell's office remained the same—a dozen or more agents, the computers, the communications equipment, and the file cabinets—through the door was Maurice's complicated factory. He escorted Rosa and Mederos into it.

The warehouse beyond Cantrell's office resembled a trade show. A number of booths and curtained rooms were arrayed around a central aisle, each manned with several people busily solving whatever was at hand. The room was spotted with bright lights from numerous large monitors. Recorded, amplified voices mixed with each other. Out of sight behind a portable wall covered with photographs of Havana street scenes came the sound of hammering. There had not been time to install fixed wiring, so much of the floor was covered with winding electrical cords, and an electrician was bunching the cords together with duct tape and trying to tuck them out of the way along the aisle. Fluorescent lights hung in a patchwork design, obscuring the warehouse's ceiling. The scent of solder was sharp. Filling in the gaps of noise was the hum of an air-conditioning unit. Every twenty feet along all walls were round clocks, the kind familiar to schoolchildren. Everyone in this portion of the warehouse seemed in a hurry, from the young woman taking sandwich orders to a man, apparently a mime, who appeared to be walking rapidly forward against a breeze, but who in fact was moving smoothly backward, to the delight of a fellow wearing a badge on his belt, who was applauding with gusto.

Maurice led them to the mime and introduced him as Jacque DeLong. "You may remember him in every film of San Francisco in the 1970s. Face painted white, making a fool of himself and embarrassing tourists at Union Square."

DeLong laughed and extended his hand to Rosa and Mederos. He was pole thin and moved gently, as if he were fragile.

Maurice went on, "And this is Lieutenant Dale Thompson of the Los Angeles Police Department. He has successfully convicted ten or eleven felons, based on a lineup identification not

112

of faces, but of walks. The victims identified the accused by watching them walk."

The lieutenant wore a pencil mustache, at odds with his shiny suit and scuffed shoes. He said, "A person's walk is as distinctive as his face."

Maurice said, "These fellows have been reviewing the agency's film file of Fidel. Studying his walk."

"Over eight hours of Fidel walking," DeLong said. "Gerard Jones also used a program that reduced Castro's walk to an animated stick figure on a computer screen, much like the ones Olympic javelin and discus throwers study. They might help."

"Walking in crowds, walking on a hunt, walking to a podium," Maurice explained. "Jacque and Dale are going to teach you to move like him. Like most of us, Castro's gait often depends on the situation. We've got them cataloged and are ready to begin."

"Castro's walk is more distinct than most," Thompson said.

Maurice went on, "After Castro's failed attack on the Moncado barracks in Santiago de Cuba in 1953, several of his planners, Melba Hernández and Haydée Santamaría, were already imprisoned on the third floor of the Santiago jail when the soldiers brought Fidel to the jail. From behind the bars, Hernández and Santamaría's view down to the entrance was partly blocked, and they were only able to see part of Fidel's body as he was escorted into the jail, yet they knew immediately it was him from his stride. They spread word in the jail that Fidel had survived the attack, giving the imprisoned revolutionaries new hope."

The portion of Mederos's face showing under his bandages registered puzzlement. "I thought I already walked like him."

"A little, maybe," the lieutenant said. "Yours is a bulky, somewhat ponderous walk, but we'll refine it."

Maurice added, "They've also been studying Castro's gestures. He uses his hands and arms and body in certain ways in certain situations. An example is that in informal, one-on-one conversations, Castro always draws closer to the person as he talks. If he's on a couch, he slowly inches along until he's close enough to hug you. His boot will tap your foot, then withdraw. His knee will wedge against yours, as his voice gets more insistent. If he's standing, he gets near enough to walk on your shoes, so close that the listener sees Fidel's gestures only by peripheral vision. Castro reaches for the listener, tapping him, patting him on his shoulders. It's a physical invasion."

"Another example," the mime said, "one we've noticed repeatedly, is that Castro typically plays with his cigar midsentence. Taps ash, inserts or removes it from his mouth, stares at the burning end. It's a display of power, as no one dares interrupt him during such a pause, like anyone else would be interrupted."

Rosa said, "I read that Castro quit smoking."

Mederos added, "And I don't smoke."

"He's been smoking cigars since he was fifteen, and he still does," Maurice replied, "and you'll learn. I've got a crate of Cahiba, Castro's brand, which happened to be on the *Carolyn May* last trip, and you'll seldom be without one from now on."

Maurice led them down the aisle, past a corkboard partition. Here an elderly man appeared to be nodding off over his desk, his hands casually on a cassette recorder. He wore earphones, and his eyes were closed. After several seconds, his finger hit the rewind button. He listened intently, unaware of Maurice and the others. Again he pressed the rewind.

Maurice said loudly, "Excuse me, Mr. Alvarez."

The old man looked up, then smiled and removed the headset. He had white hair, yellow at the roots, and horse's teeth, also yellow. He stood and bowed slightly to Rosa. A cane with a carved ivory head leaned against the table.

Maurice asked, "Eduardo, do you remember an act called 'The Professor Knows' on the *Juan Cruz Radio Show*, broadcast live Saturday evenings from Havana in the 1950s?"

"Sure, I think."

Rosa said enthusiastically, "Of course you do. I loved that

game. Listened to it every week, right before the Coca-Cola commercial. Evelio Alvarez. You remember that the professor was—"

Alvarez cut in, "The professor is a stage name. I don't have an academic credential to my name." Age had pulled his voice tight.

"But a perfect ear," Maurice said. "As part of the Cruz show, between big-band numbers, the professor would invite a couple up to the stage from the audience, and would talk with them for, what, no longer than sixty seconds."

"That's all the time Juan Cruz could go without the spotlight on him," Alvarez said with a touch of bitterness that thirty years had not erased.

"Then, based only on that short conversation, the professor would tell the couple where they came from, invariably getting it correct within twenty miles."

"Usually fifteen."

"Their accent and colloquialisms gave them away. The Juan Cruz show was enormously popular all over Latin America, and a ticket for an out-of-towner visiting Havana was a must. Whether they were from Bayamo or Carnaguey or Cienfuegos, the professor would get it right. Not just Cuba, either. They could be from any part of Mexico or Venezuela or Puerto Rico, any town or province, and he'd nail their address within fifteen miles."

"I'd also catch contestants faking. A phony accent is as obvious as a belch." He paused, then said, "The contest would be harder these days, with the kids from all over the Caribbean trying to talk like Julio Iglesias sings."

"The professor is going to teach you Fidel's every inflection, probably the most important thing you'll learn here," Maurice said. "Castro is enchanted with his own voice. Once his son Fidelito was injured when the jeep he was riding in overturned in Havana. He was taken to a hospital with serious internal injuries that required an immediate operation. The surgeons would not operate until the boy's father gave permission. Well, Fidel was in the middle of one of his long stemwinders, and even though he was notified of his son's critical condition and of the surgeons awaiting his approval, Fidel was so involved in his speech, he kept on talking for another hour. Finally, after many begging calls from the hospital, Raul convinced him to end the speech and go to the hospital. His wife, Mirta, was furious with him, as you might imagine."

Alvarez added, "Castro tailors his accent a bit, depending on where he is speaking. In Havana, he talks more quickly, shortening his vowels. In, say, the Oriente, he is more languorous, and even adopts a higher tone by half a note."

"I hate to repeat a theme," Mederos said, "but I already can sound like Castro."

"You do." Maurice moved him along the aisle. "But there's always room for improvement. And if things go like we plan, the whole country is going to hear you."

They came next to an open area that was littered with shining pieces of chrome and heavy disks of what looked like pig iron. Three attendants were bent over the shapes, wrenches in hand.

Maurice said, "Weight equipment. They're putting together five Nautilus machines and a Universal gym."

"I've got a sinking feeling," Mederos said sourly, "that this equipment isn't for the agents here, for a noon workout program."

"An important part of Castro has always been his strength. He's a big man, six feet three, with large arms and powerful legs. When he was in college he ran track, eight hundred and fifteen hundred meters, high jump, and hop, skip, and jump. He even tried out twice for the Washington Senators, back when their scout Joe Cambria lived in Havana. He was a good, but not a great pitcher, and wasn't given a contract. Anyway, he's always been boisterous with his strength."

"A show-off, if you can believe the films of him released by La Prensa," Rosa said, lifting a ten-pound disk and turning it over in her hand. "Olympic" was stamped onto the metal.

Maurice said, "Castro's strength is legendary throughout

Cuba. It's part of his charisma, and he keeps weight-lifting equipment at all his places. But more than that, agency psychologists believe that being stronger and bigger than those around him shaped his personality, and continues to affect many of his daily decisions. They've convinced me."

The weight-lifting area was lit like a surgery. White mats lay on the floor, and a water cooler was against the wall. On a counter near the lat machine was a Braun juicer and a pea-green milkshake mixer. A rugged-looking man in an olive tank top, with the hair on the side of his head cut almost to the skin, walked across the mat toward them. He had a military bearing, with a ramrod-straight back and squared shoulders. He carried a large stainless-steel mixing glass filled with a cream and handed it to Mederos.

Maurice said, "This is Lieutenant Commander Ralph Smith. He's sheep-dipping from the navy, and he's your trainer."

Smith's face looked carved in wood by an axe, nothing but chips and angles. He said, "I've been told to put fifteen pounds on you in fifteen days."

"What's in here?" Mederos asked, peering at the drink as if it were a petri dish.

"Two thousand calories of cream, bananas, coconut, bran, yeast, and, against all regulations except in the Royal Navy, a modest dash of rum to make it tolerable."

"I'll be your taster." Rosa took the glass from Mederos and sipped it. She had to swallow several times to get it down. "A little thick, but not bad."

"You'll get sick of these drinks, and of me, Mr. Mederos," Smith said. He smiled. "I've been consulting with the warehouse's new resident physician about a touch of anabolic steroids. It'll slap the muscle on you. Any problem with that?"

Maurice's eyes opened. "Hell, yes, there's a problem. That stuff crystallizes your liver, gives you breasts, and lowers your brows, makes your face look like a gorilla. None of those chemicals, and that's an order."

The lieutenant commander had been told of the chain of

command. "Yes, sir. We'll do it all with weights and my pushiness, then."

As they moved on, Maurice said quietly, "Smith is a navy SEAL. Gung ho. I heard that when he was in Vietnam he had Donald Duck tattooed on his peter, in such a way that when he gets hard, Donald smiles."

"Honest to God, Bill," his wife said in a well-used tone, "why must you always inflict these little facts on me?"

"You wanted in on this operation. You've got to take the bad with the good. And wait until I fill you in on Eduardo. Makes Donald Duck look like kindergarten stuff."

Mederos grinned, then winced as it pulled against the sutures. They came to an area separated by curtains, and they entered to find two men and a woman sitting around a card table on which was a brass lamp.

Maurice introduced them as Susan MacLeish, a professor of organization behavior, and Segundo Blet, a political science instructor, both from the University of Miami, and Emeliano Porro, a professor of psychology at Yale.

"You'll spend a lot of time here, Eduardo. These folks are going to teach you how to dictate."

Mederos shook his head. "Surely not how to run the Cuban government."

Porro said, "Not at all. We've been asked to help you learn to fit the role, to order and know it will be done." Porro wore a business suit with a silk tie. His gray hair was in tight waves.

Mederos lightly scratched at the gauze covering an ear. "I didn't build an auto parts company with sixteen retail outlets by not knowing how to give orders."

"There's more to it than that," Susan MacLeish said. She was dressed in a carefully tailored linen suit with a red scarf. "We've been told you won't be in Cuba long enough to do much ruling. What we'll prepare you to do is meet the expectations of those Cubans you come in contact with. Ruling a country, with absolute power, answerable to no one, brings about predictable changes in the ruler."

"In Castro's case, a few unpredictable ones as well," Segundo Blet said. He looked as if he had been dragged in from vacation, with a week's growth of stubble and a T-shirt that read "Club Med—Cancun."

MacLeish went on, "Very few people are ever in a position of unquestioned authority. Yes, Mr. Mederos, you run a large company. But even though you own it, your day-to-day relations are with employees who are certain of their rights and have a strong bargaining position with you."

"You must be talking about Local 503 of the Retail Clerks," Mederos said without a smile.

Susan MacLeish was not receptive to small talk. "Those who future depends on your utter whim act in ways which we'll teach you to manage."

"The sycophants and grovelers," Porro said. "Your method will be: Never apologize, never explain."

"Eduardo will be back," Maurice said as he led Rosa and Mederos farther into the warehouse. "Since his mother died in 1963, nothing has been mentioned in the Cuban press about Castro's private life, with the exception of a few photos of him fishing or hunting or skin diving. Castro has imitated Soviet leaders in going to great lengths to assure his privacy. Most Cubans, for instance, don't know he has grandchildren now. But we are gathering people who over the years were close enough to Fidel to know his personal habits, and who later came to the United States."

"Like who?" Mederos asked.

"We've found a maid and two housecleaners, one of his physicians, a military chauffeur. Also, like most others, Fidel's revolution has eaten many of its children. A number of his old friends who began the revolution with him, called the 'Generation of Fifty-three,' have been tossed out of government, some into jail. Plotting, counterrevolutionary activity, sedition, spying. We've got one of Castro's old fishing pals, and an ex-minister of agriculture, a fellow Castro grew up with in Biran on the north coast of Oriente Province, and a number of people he went to college and law school with. I have a battery of people right now asking them questions about Castro. Personal things, the smallest of things. We'll know if he brushes his upper or lower teeth first. We'll know when he takes his boots off at night, how long it takes him to read the newspapers. Thousands of things. We'll reduce it to manageable lessons, and you'll start to memorize and practice, Eduardo."

"It seems to me," Rosa said, "that you're letting a lot of people in on this big secret. Aren't you afraid of word getting back to Cuba?"

"The agency is trying to winnow out anybody whose allegiance is suspect. Nevertheless, it is also sending many people we talk to on vacations to Tahiti, Australia, India, anywhere that's remote, so they won't have many people to chat with. They take very stern warnings with them. And some folks we must talk with about Castro, yet whom we might suspect, are watched closely after the interviews."

Rosa said, "You are using 'the agency' and 'we' interchangeably. It didn't take them long to get you, Bill."

He stepped ahead of them, so as not to answer, and led them through a partition into a small area with a low ceiling and cordoned off with wallboard, a room within the warehouse. The area was dark. Two agents sat on metal folding chairs at a Tektronix computer station. Maurice walked too far into the room, blocking the agents' view of a man wearing a mustache, generated on the system's three-dimensional shaded surface modeling screen. He stepped out of their way.

He explained, "Castro sees roughly thirty-five of the same people every day. These include his brother, who is chief of Cuba's military services, and the heads of the ministries, a number of advisers, several friends, and those in his personal staff, his driver, bodyguards, and the like. Another forty-five or so he sees irregularly, but almost certainly two or three times a week. In this room you'll learn to identify these people, and learn more than you'll possibly want to know about each of them."

120

Maurice told him the names of the agents at the computer, who nodded in a no-nonsense way. Maurice said, "For example, up on the monitor right now is someone you'll deal with every day, precisely at nine in the morning. This is the chief of G2, Carlos Galvez."

Rosa and Mederos inhaled as one.

"Galvez," Mederos whispered, as if the G2 chief might hear him. "I've never seen his face before."

"He likes to think there aren't any photographs of him, but we've got a basketful. For many Cubans, it's the last face they ever see on this earth."

The photo of Galvez was taken as he was leaving a stately government building—a ribbed stone column was visible behind him—and was enlarged so the lines of his face were indistinct and his eyes were murky. Galvez had a narrow nose above a broad band of a mustache that covered his lips, except at the corners where they curved down in a snarl that he looked comfortable with.

"I heard Galvez was bald," Rosa said, leaning toward the screen for a better view, but carefully, as one might lean over a safety rail above a canyon.

"That hair is real, we think." Galvez wore it brushed back and weighted with oil.

"And I thought he carried a lot of weight," Mederos said with a new hoarseness in his voice. "His face looks thin, with cheekbones sticking out. You sure that's him?"

"That's Galvez all right." Maurice looked at the agents at the workstation. "Let's see a few more of him."

The screen blinked and Carlos Galvez appeared again, this time a profile showing a strong nose with a bump on it. The visible ear was attached to his head at a slight cant, as if designed to reduce drag. He was caught by the camera just as he stepped from the backseat of a car.

"Now roll some of the video."

One of the agents tapped a command into the Tektronix. The screen darkened for an instant, then four men appeared, all in black suits, but only the man in the center, Galvez, wore a thin tie. The camera had apparently been stationed in a third-floor window across the street from Galvez and his bodyguards. The video began as they emerged from a sandstone building on a busy street and followed them for forty yards as Galvez walked toward a waiting Zil. Midway through the moving image, the cameraman had zoomed up close to Galvez. Every fourth step, the G2 chief looked quickly over his shoulder. The magnification increased again, and the screen was filled with his face. Nothing moved on it. He didn't even appear to blink. It could have been a still photo. Then he disappeared under the Zil's roof.

Mederos said heavily, "If you knew the grief that man has caused Cuba . . ."

"We know," Maurice said. "He's very, very good at his job. If you fool him, you'll fool all the others."

Another photograph of Galvez lit up the monitor, and Maurice said, "Run some of our recordings, please."

From the speaker came the words in Spanish, "I don't care if he isn't scheduled to arrive until three. I want everything in position at least two hours before then. Understood? Now, what else have you got?"

Maurice waved briefly, and the voice quieted. "That rough-sounding fellow is Galvez. The NSA routinely picks up his telephone calls and two-way radio communications, using equipment I don't begin to understand."

"It sounded like he was right in the room with us," Rosa said. She had taken a step away from the screen.

"Conversations lifted off a wire always sound tinny, as the wire usually only sends between three hundred and twenty-six hundred hertz, missing the low ranges. The agency has a Comrex machine that adds the bass tones, from one hundred to three hundred hertz. Because of the digital reader on it, it doesn't need a box at both ends, unlike most such machines."

Maurice turned to Mederos. "Eduardo, in this room you'll be listening to Galvez as if it were over the phone, and as if he were in person. Also, the whiz kids up in Langley have assembled and constructed thousands of phrases, all using Galvez's voice. You'll be able to carry on a conversation with that speaker, and it'll seem as if Galvez is making the proper responses to your questions and comments, all in his actual voice. It's called a voice interaction and simulation, VIS. They've got the same thing for dozens of other people you'll come across in Havana."

Maurice thanked the agents and ushered his wife and Mederos into the next room, another tack-up job that looked as sturdy as a house of cards. It too was a studio, and there again was a Tektronix station. On the wall opposite the door was a floor-to-ceiling map of central Havana, from Miramar east to Habana del Estes and from the harbor south to Vibora. On the map a long row of tiny lights was glowing red, from the Palace of the Revolution to the Habana Libre Hotel. When Maurice escorted them closer to the map, they saw that many of Havana's streets had the pinhead-sized lights marking them.

Gerard Jones was manning the workstation. He said, "Took me a couple hours to get over motion sickness the first time I played with it. Where do you want to begin, Bill?"

"Let's try Malecon."

Jones entered it, and the light path on the map flicked off, and another path glowed. Jones said, "Looks just like something you'd see at a world's fair, doesn't it? Showing you the miracle of our city's proposed monorail transit system, to be installed sometime in the twenty-first century, God and the taxman willing."

"Start the show, Gerard," Maurice ordered. "Somewhere on Malecon."

On the monitor appeared a video of Malecon, taken through the windshield of an automobile. Old stucco buildings, some painted yellow and blue and trimmed in white, all fading, passed on the left, while on the right was a rock seawall. Malecon had been a central avenue in Havana for three hundred years. The six-lane road had almost no cars on it, but many

123

Russian trucks, one in front of the camera's car. On the water side of the road, a Ford Comet was perched on oil drums, and the mechanic's legs stuck out from under it. Pedestrians crowded the walkway, some pausing to peer over the wall to the harbor. Beyond the truck, Havana's skyline was visible, appearing as it did in 1959. Almost no buildings have been built in the city since the revolution.

"Jesus, how many times have I walked along that wall," Mederos said softly.

Rosa wiped away a tear and looked around for her husband, but he was standing next to Jones, unaware of the effect the video was having.

Maurice said, "The CIA hasn't had many successes in Cuba. But Castro knows we overthrew Arbenz in Guatemala in 1954, and Allende in Chile. So he is eternally afraid of it."

"One wonders why, with some of the people we used to hire to go in there," Jones said dryly.

Maurice ignored him. "So he never travels to a destination on the same route twice in a row. He and his entourage use side streets and make sudden turns. However, the agency long ago determined Fidel's twelve most traveled roads in Havana."

Jones piped in, "They did so for reasons we can only guess at, and probably guess quite accurately."

"We have each of these routes on video, going both directions for each route. Eduardo, we want you to spend your spare time in here reacquainting yourself with the Havana you'll see when you get there. This'll refresh your memory, which may have faded."

Mederos glanced at Maurice as one might a traitor. "It hasn't faded."

"Well," Maurice said after a moment, finally realizing the melancholy in the room, "a few things have changed on Havana's streets, and these will fill you in. You won't have much spare time anyway."

"I don't remember all the orange," Rosa said, perhaps trying to divert Mederos and herself from the memories.

Many buildings were a garish orange, as were numerous automobiles, lampposts, and fire hydrants.

Jones said, "Several years ago, the Soviets sent Cuba three or four shiploads of paint, every drop of it orange. Fidel was furious, but rather than throw it out, Cubans painted everything that couldn't run away and hide. Orange has become the country's unofficial national color."

Maurice led them through another door into a bedroom, so out of place in the cavernous warehouse that Rosa started to tiptoe and asked in a whisper, "Castro's bedroom?"

"One of them. This is a precise replica of his room in the Palace of the Revolution, at least as it was twenty months ago, the last time anyone we've talked to went in there."

The room was Spartan, containing a twin-size bed with a pine headboard, a blue cotton bedspread without a design, an oak table with four captain's chairs around it, and several dressers. There were no rugs and only one chest of drawers on which were five telephones, four black and one red, all older, dial models. The walls were bare.

Rosa said, "That's a picture of Castro's father on the chest of drawers, isn't it? I thought he disliked his father."

"Not enough to put the photo away, apparently."

Mederos opened a drawer, then another. "Nothing's in these, not even a bathrobe."

"Nobody wears bathrobes in Cuba since the revolution, because Batista loved them, and was often photographed in them. We don't know what's in the chests, nor what's in that closet"—Maurice pointed—"nor where that door goes. We've got copies of the architect's drawings for the building, but they don't show that door. You can put some of your clothes in that closet, Eduardo. You'll be sleeping here."

"What about my home in Miami Beach?"

"Your sister is caretaking for you."

"I don't have a sister."

"Yes, you do. I'll introduce you to her sometime. Even after all these years, Castro only rarely sleeps in the same bed-

125

room two nights in a row. Next door is a mock-up of room 2406 of the old Havana Hilton, now called the Habana Libre, which Castro appropriated his first triumphant night in Havana, and has never given up. He stays there frequently. You'll learn to be comfortable in those rooms before you go."

As they left the bedroom, Maurice said, "We've got other people here we don't have time to introduce you to right now. A memory expert is going to help you retain what we'll teach you, and a marine sharpshooter is here, because Fidel is a crack shot, and a makeup artist to help you with that kind of thing, and some others."

"Aren't I going to resemble him closely enough after this surgery?"

"We think so, but you've got to learn to put on a fake beard and make it look real, since you won't have time to grow one. And Castro has a wide scar from an appendix operation that got infected. I don't know why you'd show your belly to anybody in Havana, but we want you to be prepared if you have to, with makeup."

They approached a roped-off area where four dollhouses rested on the floor. Maurice introduced Rosa and Mederos to Mike Phillips, a slender man in overalls who had smears of paint and dabs of dried glue on his fingers and a streak of white on his mustache where he had absently brushed it with his hand. Maurice said Phillips was the leading Atlanta architectural model artist. Phillips had a crew of three, each man bent over a replica building.

Maurice said, "We're constructing miniatures of Castro's residences and offices, as well as we know them. Eduardo, you'll sit on a chair staring down at these small rooms, at their furnishings and floor plans, learning your future surroundings. Mike has promised they'll be done within twenty-four hours. We don't think you'll visit these other places, but you need to be prepared."

Cantrell was hanging up the secured telephone when they entered the office. He said jubilantly, "I just received word that the president has approved our plan."

"What?" Mederos exclaimed. "You mean all this didn't have approval?" The local anesthesia was wearing off. He said his words like a ventriloquist, almost without moving his lips.

"On his own authority, the director gave a preliminary okay, enough for Bill and me to set up shop. Now it's a full go."

The skin visible through Mederos's bandages purpled. "You had my face operated on without knowing whether your plan was approved?" He turned to Maurice, and his voice climbed the scale. "Goddamn you. I ought to walk away from here while I still can."

"We had to let the surgeons work on you right away. It'll be a while before you lose your black eyes from the operation and for your face to heal enough to be presentable." Nothing in Maurice's words sounded like an apology.

"I ought to walk away from here."

Rosa tried to come to Mederos's aid. "Bill, don't you think you should be a little more forthright and—"

"We don't have time for that."

Mederos was so angry he was breathing heavily.

Maurice glanced at his wristwatch. "You're due in the weight room in five minutes. We've installed a shower and change room at the back of the warehouse. You'll find trunks and workout shoes there. With that senator snooping around, it looks like we're going to need a new Fidel faster than we thought."

P A R T T W O

Más vale maña que fuerza.

(Stealth is better than force.)
CUBAN PROVERB

Chapter X

Rosa could have walked back to work, as the Miami Herald Building was just across the inlet and past Bicentennial Park, but she had been on her lunch break for over two hours. Maurice was happy to drive her. When they were in a car together, the radio and tape deck were never on. They enjoyed each other's conversation too much.

But now she was silent as they drove by the guard booth and the cruise ship passenger terminal and onto the short causeway to the mainland. On their right was a seaplane anchorage, and to the left was a small marina of charter and sightseeing boats. Behind the marina was Miami's new skyline, with its glass boxes filled with lawyers' offices.

Maurice flipped on his blinker for the turn onto Biscayne Boulevard. He said, "I don't ever remember either of us being quiet long enough for me to notice the hiss of the air conditioning like I am now."

She didn't say anything. Her fingers were laced tightly together on her lap.

"Come on, Rosa, what's going on?"

She looked at him. "I'm frightened, Bill."

"I know, and I think—"

"Not like that. Before I was talking about losing your business and all we've built. Now I'm talking about just being fearful. Afraid for our lives."

He absently slowed the car, keying on his wife's words. "The risks aren't like that this time."

"Do you still dream about the bomb blast?"

The Ford was traveling so slowly that a car honked behind them. Maurice pulled over to the curb. "Not much anymore."

"I didn't either, until this week, when you got involved again with the agency. Now the terrifying dreams are back, almost every night. There, sitting next to me again, was Jorge, behind the wheel of our car. You know, I don't really remember the explosion. It was like somebody bumped me, and I went to sleep. No more than that. But my dreams have filled in the gaps. Fire and glass and metal, and Jorge's head . . . his head disappearing in a splash of blood."

Maurice put his hand on her shoulder.

She went on, "Last night I woke up shaking and bathed in sweat. And I lay in bed awake for another hour, terrified. Not for you or the *Carolyn May* or for our home, but for me. A very selfish emotion, but I was truly afraid, Bill."

"You should have woken me. "

"What could you have said to comfort me? That I was just dreaming? Well, you know better than that. We lived through that nightmare once. You can't tell me there's no reason to be afraid. All you can say is that as long as you deal with the agency and Cuba, I'll have to get used to it. I'll have to fit those nightmares back into my life." She wet her lips. "It's like turning my life back to all those years of fear and pain. I just don't know if I can."

"The agency is taking some precautions, you know."

She waved his words away. "They couldn't do anything last time."

"This is different," he insisted. "Let me show you something." He looked over his shoulder, then pulled away from the curb. He turned west toward the freeway entrance.

"Where are we going? I've got to get back to work."

"Not as much as you need to see this."

After they entered the stream of traffic heading north on I-95, he asked, "Have you noticed anything unusual in our neighborhood?"

She must have been lost in her thoughts, as a few seconds passed before she replied, "No, nothing."

"How about the white van over on Osorio across from our house?"

She shook her head.

"That van or a light blue one has been there continuously night and day since I agreed to help the agency. Inside it, two fellows watch our home."

Rosa shrugged, unimpressed.

"Out back, over on the golf course across the canal, two gardeners watch the house. Only they aren't gardeners. They are armed, and Cantrell tells me they are very good at what they do. And the *Herald* has just hired a new copy editor, right?"

She thought a moment, trying to follow him. "Just last Monday, a fellow named Rolando Cubalo."

"He's from the agency, and he spends most of his time watching you, not his screen. Same with the new busboy at that cafeteria on Biscayne where you usually eat lunch. You and Maria Aricos play golf after work every Wednesday. Next time you'll get a caddy who has never caddied before, also from the agency."

They exited the freeway to the 36th Street Expressway. The neighborhoods began to deteriorate.

"Your car, the Honda. It's going to be very sluggish when you drive it home after work this afternoon. Well, it'll look like your car, same silver color, same plates, same Sony tape deck, same hairline crack in the rear window. But it's going to be a proxy car, one the agency has altered by adding almost a thousand pounds of steel on the fire wall, along the door frames, under the floor, even under and behind the front seat. The switch has already been made."

Rosa looked around at the interior of the Ford. "What about this car?"

Maurice smiled. "You know those little punctures in the upholstery near your knee, where Javier Rego's damned dog sank his teeth into the cloth when it realized Javier and I were taking him to the vet?"

She moved her leg to look at the seat. She declared, "They're gone!"

"This isn't my car. It only looks like the Ford. There's more metal in this rig than on Eduardo's teeth. The agency made the switch last night."

She leaned back in the seat. "Well, I should be mollified, but I don't think I am."

They were driving along Northwest 27th Street, in the heart of Liberty City, an area of town where there weren't enough pedestrians to prey on, so muggers often ran up to a car, smashed the side window out with the pistol butt, stuck the other end of the gun in the driver's face, and demanded money. Miami is the most violent city in America, and Liberty City is the heart of it.

"What are we doing here, Bill?" Rosa asked as he slowed the car.

"Going for a stroll." He looked intently at the storefronts, which had iron grates across their windows and doors, making the street look like the view from a prison guards' catwalk. He found a parking spot and backed into it.

"Here? Good God, I'm not leaving the car." She glanced over her shoulder, as if someone might be sneaking up on them.

They had stopped in front of a small appliance store.

Taped above the doorknob was a sign that read "Ring for service." Through the bars, the proprietor peered warily at them. It was common for such a store to be robbed every two weeks. Spray-painted in red on the tile below the window was "Dagger Runners." Sitting on the sidewalk with his back against the tile was a man wearing a week's stubble and a stained shirt, with his hand tightly around a bottle in a paper bag. On the corner near a fire hydrant were three teenagers laughing at something. All were wearing new black Reeboks, but their jeans were grimy. All shirttails were out. Two elderly men loitered in a nearby doorway. With their aimless gazes and rooted stances, they had the look of those who have surrendered to poverty. Near them was a scratching mud-brown mutt who was bleeding from a scab-matted hot spot on its back.

Before his wife could protest further, Maurice emerged from the car, to the accompaniment of his abrading knee. He hurried around to open her door and said, "Let's walk a while."

Nervously she glanced up and down the street. "Bill, what are we doing here? You're always telling the kids to stay away from this place."

He put his hand on her elbow and escorted her around the teenagers. Shoelaces dragging, a panhandler approached, but Maurice's glare dissuaded him before he could ask for change. They walked by a check-cashing joint that had a gun portal in its iron door, then by an off-price clothing store with a rolling grate that was down even during business hours. On the corner was a bar with a wrestling poster pasted on its door. The street smelled of Mogen David and damp cloth and old urine. They passed a fellow in a filthy Pilson coat who leered at Rosa. She leaned into her husband as if she were about to fall.

They walked for two blocks, and Maurice kept pulling Rosa back when she wanted to break into a sprint. "Bill, will you please tell me what we are doing in Liberty City?"

"I'm proving a point," he said.

They came to an alley, where the curbs were buried under piles of rubble. Rosa resisted when he turned into the alley, but he gently pulled her along, between dilapidated walls of a liquor store and an abandoned building, which blocked the light of day. They moved into a gloomy dusk where shapes were softer and odors close and strong. They walked over a flattened cardboard box, avoiding a wet mound of nameless material piled against the brick wall. Three ripe garbage cans lined the opposite wall below a swarm of droning flies.

Rosa gasped at a sound behind them, a step on the cardboard. She spun to see two men approaching, spreading out to cut them off from the street. One was the man in the Pilson coat. He wore a black cap and was hunched at the shoulders like a fullback. The other had a wide mustache that blended into stubbly whiskers. His hair was stringy and down to the collar of the shirt. He closed in, holding a knife near his belly with the point up. He knew what he was doing.

He said with a mean smile, "Your wallets. Quick like. Hand them over."

Maurice said with utter calm, "You fellows are making a mistake."

The knifeman stepped closer, and his partner circled to Rosa's left, his eyes on her shoulder bag. He moved with a rat's scurry.

"Your wallet, asshole," the knifeman demanded. "Don't make me cut you."

"My God, Bill, give it to him, anything. . . . "

Maurice waited until the Pilson coat reached for his wife's bag. He said in a low voice, as if to himself, "That's enough. Do it now."

From above them came an abrupt hiss, like the sudden escape of steam from a pipe. It filled the alley with a sharp sibilance that died as suddenly.

The man in the Pilson coat staggered back, then collapsed as if his legs had been broken from under him. He landed loudly on his back. His chest quivered and his legs jerked. Protruding from his coat was a rod that looked like a crossbow bolt, except that it had a tip forked into two points, both buried

136

in the coat. Attached to the bolt was a thin wire that trailed skyward.

His eyes wide, the knifeman glanced at his partner, then backstepped away from Maurice, shifting the blade left and right to cover his retreat. Five steps back, he turned to run.

He made four more strides. A huge man dressed in a blue nylon windbreaker and jeans had followed the muggers into the alley. Against the wall, behind the garbage cans, he was unseen until he shot across toward the fleeing knifeman. His fingers closed around the mugger's collarbone and tripped him over his hip. The mugger's legs flew into the air in a large circle before he bounced off the pavement. The knife skittered along the alley. The man in the windbreaker then sprayed the mugger's face with a finger-size aerosol can. The mugger lay still.

Maurice glanced to the roof. Two heads, their features lost in the sun's backlighting, hovered over them. Without a signal or a word, the man in the windbreaker disappeared toward the street.

Maurice again took his wife's elbow and guided her from the alley. She stared at the man in the Pilson coat, at the weapon protruding from his chest, and said breathlessly, "I don't know what just happened."

Maurice led her around the prone knifeman. "That was a Faser rifle, much like some police departments are using, but modified to be shot out of a gun that looks like an over-under shotgun. Air-propelled. It puts a lot of volts into the target. That's what the wire was."

"But . . . but how did they know we would be robbed?" At the street they turned toward their car. Her hands were still shaking, and she gripped them together.

"And that other guy, the guy with the judo, he's one of them, too."

"But who? Who are they?"

Maurice said, "The agency. Castro has a history of striking at people in this country, and I told them I wouldn't get involved if there was any danger to you. You haven't noticed, but agents have been on you like green on a pea for five days."

The panhandler again considered approaching Maurice and again declined. Maurice opened the Ford's door for her. When he got behind the wheel, she said, "There's something wrong here."

The car was like a sauna. Maurice started the engine. Rosa pressed, "Why did we come out to Liberty City? And walking down that alley, you were asking to be mugged. Something smells, and it's more than that alley."

The Ford pulled into traffic. "Well, I told Cantrell that I wanted a test of his guards. He said he'd arrange it. Those muggers were with the agency."

She was aghast. "You knew we'd be mugged?"

He put a palm in the air, suggesting it was nothing. "I didn't know where or when, but I figured if I gave them a dark alley like that, they'd try. I also knew our guards would intercept them."

"That mugger works for the agency, the one they shot?"

"He'll be all right. Couple of puncture wounds in his skin. The gun only stuns. Same with the other guy. He'll come around with not even a headache."

She inhaled through her teeth, a bad sign. "Goddamn it, William, you promised never to hide anything."

"All I did was show you there's no need to be fearful. As John Keats said, 'Fear will clip an angel's wings.'"

"I'm too mad to play your stupid game," she said.

"You're not mad. You're relieved. You feel a lot better about this whole operation, knowing those people are all over. You just don't realize it yet." He made a U-turn to head downtown. "And you just missed a chance to make five dollars."

In the hearing chamber, eleven United States senators had gathered for a session of the Select Committee on Intelligence that had been called only moments before by their most junior member. The senators, weary from a long day on the floor,

138

leaned back in their chairs or slumped forward over the long, curved desk, thankful that the chairman had barred reporters and spectators from the meeting. Ties were loose and tempers short.

The chairman, a statesman from the Southwest who brooked no nonsense and knew that their junior member was a font of it, rapped his gavel and called them to order. "Let's begin, shall we?" He gave the members another few seconds to settle in, then said, "Our colleague from Florida has called this session. Without objection, I'll give the floor to the junior senator from Florida."

Richard White cleared his throat and rattled his papers in front of him. He leaned forward to the microphone, even though the chambers beyond the green felt–covered witness table was empty. White had a media face, a montage of perfectly proportioned features that didn't add up to much. He looked like a pitchman in an investment house television commercial, with his gray-white hair, concerned eyes, and finely set mouth. It was widely understood in the Senate that White's sole talent was campaigning.

He tapped the microphone, and the sound echoed in the vast room, making the chairman scowl. "Thank you, Mr. Chairman. I have asked for an extraordinary meeting of the committee this evening, feeling obliged by the confidence the Senate leadership has placed in me by appointing me to the committee, to come before my fellow senators before I went to my constituents with this information. As you all know, I have always believed that the voters should make the choices, but in such a sensitive area as Cuba, I felt this forum should be informed first."

Glancing at his wristwatch, the chairman said, "It's on the late side, Senator. Can we make this brief?"

"Of course, Mr. Chairman. I have reason to believe that the communist government in Cuba has allowed the Soviet Union to install offensive weapons of enormous destructive power in Cuba."

"You're talking about the unconfirmed report of a new bomber in today's *Miami Herald*?"

"Yes. This matter is of vital interest to my constituents, as it should be to all Americans. The Soviet Union agreed in 1961 that they would not put offensive weapons in Cuba. It appears that they may have violated that agreement. If there are such bombers in Cuba, they must be removed."

"This is only a newspaper reporter's speculation, Senator."

"But it caused an immediate stir among my constituents. I ask this committee to subpoena the director of the Central Intelligence Agency and the director of the National Security Agency to testify before this committee on what they know about the new bombers."

"That's a bit premature, don't you think, Senator?" the chairman asked over the rumble of his stomach. He had not eaten since breakfast.

"It's got to be before the primary," the senator from Oregon said with bite, secure in the knowledge he was not up for reelection for four years.

White countered, "If the report is true, and we wait, the bombers will become a fact. Now is the time to discover the truth. We owe it to the country—"

"And our Cuban voters," interrupted the senator from Oregon.

"—to insure our country is not threatened by a new weapons system this great deliberative body knows nothing about."

The chairman said, "Why don't I give the DCI a call on the quiet, see what he says. I'll let you know. It might save a lot of wasted time and effort."

White scanned the table, gauging his support. He saw none but plunged anyway. "I'm afraid, Mr. Chairman, that I must exercise my right to insist on calling the DCI and the DIRNSA before this committee. This matter is of too much importance to my constituents to rely on informal communications."

The chairman rubbed his temple and sighed loudly. "All right. I'll check with their schedules. . . . "

"Their schedules should be at this committee's leisure, Mr. Chairman," White said.

The chairman glared at the senator from Florida. "As I said, Senator, I'll check with their offices, and see when they can appear before us. That will have to do."

White had an infallible instinct on how far he could push someone. He had reached the limit with the chairman. He said, "Thank you, Mr. Chairman."

As the others rose from their chairs, White added petulantly, "This situation must be resolved, and the sooner the better."

At the same moment the Senate hearing was adjourning, a small boat rolled in gentle swells fifteen miles north of Havana. Its diesel engine was stilled, as fuel was too precious to waste, even if it meant not being able to maintain the boat's bow into the swells to reduce rolling.

The boat was a *práctico,* a thirty-foot wood pilot boat that guided ships into the Port of Havana. Its mast had a white light over a red light, but this night both were dark, as were the running lights. William Maurice had said they would find him without his lights.

Mario Plata owned the *práctico* and was at its helm. At least, he still considered it his boat. In a tersely worded letter ten years ago, the Cuban government had appropriated the boat, but that was the last he had heard from them about it. Funny thing was, now he didn't have to pay license fees, but he still had his boat.

Plata had worked for Maurice for thirty years, ever since Plata had been a disillusioned private in the young revolutionary army and had provided the Americans with estimates of the number of troops guarding the airport. Amazingly, after the aborted invasion at Bahía de Cochinos, when G2 arrested thousands of suspected American agents, they had missed Plata. A year later Maurice contacted him, asking him to arrange the onloading of cases of Havana Club rum onto a short-hauler. They had been making money together since.

141

Maurice deposited Plata's income at the First Security Bank in Miami. Four times a year, Maurice sent him the bank's deposit statement. American dollars, a staggering amount now.

But this, meeting him at sea, was a first. He did not even know what Maurice looked like or how he would come to the *práctico*. After all these years, how could he refuse such a request from Maurice? Plata's cover was foolproof, should he be stopped by the MGR, the Marina de Guerra Revolucionaria, the revolutionary navy, always patrolling against an American invasion, they claimed, but actually searching for Cubans in homemade boats. He was meeting a Polish freighter to guide it into Havana harbor. Plata was just early and farther to sea than he should be.

Plata was disagreeably thin, so skinny that those near him often felt guilty because of their weight. His head appeared haphazardly balanced on his stick neck, almost ready to topple. His mouth was little more than a slash across his face, and his cheeks were drawn inward, as if he were sucking at a straw. Plata believed he was as fragile as he looked, and he always moved carefully to avoid cracking something.

Plata cocked his ear at a low rumble coming from the north. He squinted into the darkness, but a high cloud had drifted across the moon, and he could see nothing. Was it a ship? He glanced at his radio, hoping they wouldn't contact him over the air. MGR monitored the frequencies.

The engine sound grew louder, now mixed with a windy flutter. And it was coming fast. On the sea or in the air? Plata couldn't tell. He was afraid.

The cloud passed, and suddenly the helicopter was visible in the gray moonlight half a mile north, its twin rotors angled forward and its aft end raised as it sped across the top of the waves. Plata was unaware this was a U.S. Navy Sea Knight, made by Boeing Vertol. The helicopter was traveling at 165 miles an hour ten feet above the water, its twin General Electric turboshaft engines whining and its blades pounding against the air. The Sea Knight was capable of lifting five tons of cargo. As it drew near, Plata could see the number "18" on its nose and a stylized rabbit's head painted on the cowling below the front rotor. He had no idea what that meant. The water under the rotors was a froth.

The helicopter closed quickly on the *práctico*. It was surely going to ram him. Coming too fast. Plata dropped to the deck, but the copter abruptly angled back, soared over the boat's gunwales, seeming to miss the pilot house by inches, and rose twenty feet into the air, where it hovered. Plata's cap blew off and slid along the deck, finally flipping into the sea. He rose slowly, whipped air weighing him down. He grabbed the gunwale and looked skyward.

A derrick had been rigged from the helicopter's hatch, from which a crate on a line was descending rapidly. He jumped out of its way. It was the size of two large crab pots, and it landed gently on the aft deck, a feat of piloting given the rolling boat. A crewman signaled from the hatch. Plata immediately understood. He unhooked the line. The hook sped back to the helicopter.

Next came a man, hanging from the hook on a bosun's chair. He was dressed in black and landed just as easily next to the crate.

Plata walked gingerly across the deck and heartily hugged him. "After all these years, so good to meet you, Bill," Plata yelled over the engine noise.

The man struggled out of the embrace, then jumped off the seat. It was raised to the Sea Knight.

"Sorry," the man said in Spanish. "My name is Roberto Ramos. I'm a technician."

Ramos stared fully at the boatman, smiling. Plata felt uneasy, as if the man wanted something from him but wasn't going to tell him what it was.

Another man lowered from the helicopter. Ramos steadied the chair until the second man's feet found the deck.

This time Plata waited until the man was off the bosun's

rig. He stepped up and vigorously hugged the second man. "Bill, so good to finally meet you."

The man shook his head. "Name's Ernesto Pazos. Maurice sends his regards." Pazos wore a purple scar at the end of an eyebrow.

Plata unwound his arms. "He's not coming?"

Pazos was already checking the crate, so Ramos answered, "Not this trip."

"Maybe I shouldn't have expected him, after thirty years." He looked hurt. Finally, he shrugged and said, "I've got no complaints." He pointed and asked, "What's in the crate?"

"Technical things," Ramos said with an apologetic smile.

"I see." He looked sternly at Ramos. "You're with the Central Intelligence Agency, aren't you? Somehow you've got Bill Maurice working for you again."

Ramos answered, "Sorry."

Plata crossed himself. "Poor Bill. Poor me."

The second technician checked the condition of the crate.

"I've heard rumors of a lot of arrests in Havana," Plata said loudly, unsure the technician could hear him over the helicopter engine. "Morro Castle and El Príncipe Prison are filling again. Passersby are hearing screams at night for the first time in years. G2 dealing with CIA suspects, I guessed."

"You guessed right," Ramos said. "That's why we need you and your boat." He waved at the Sea Knight's co-pilot, whose head was protruding from the window. The helicopter instantly tilted away from the boat and sped to the north, keeping low and stirring the water under its blades.

"You know, the freighter I'm meeting to guide into the harbor probably saw your helicopter on its radar. The ship is only ten, twelve miles off."

Ramos grinned. "We've got a navy Grumman EA-6 Prowler in the neighborhood just for that reason. That freighter's captain is seeing nothing on his radar screen but laundry. He thinks his radar is broken."

Plata did not know what a Prowler was, but Ramos spoke with confidence. Plata asked, "Now what do I do?"

Ramos said, "Meet the freighter and lead it into port, like you always do. We'll take care of the rest. We don't need anything more from you."

Plata started for the pilot house. He said, more to himself, "That's not how I remember the CIA works. There's always something more."

William Maurice opened his dinner, a sandwich Rosa had packed when she learned he would be late again. He said, "A sprout sandwich and a little plastic bag of celery. Cows eat better than this."

Gerard Jones dug into his meal. He had ordered out, a Dagwood sandwich six inches high that to Maurice smelled of a dozen wonderful things. He also had a strawberry milkshake, four small bags of potato chips, and a pickle the size of a flashlight. Jack Cantrell had settled for a taco and a glass of iced tea. It was almost ten o'clock, and the rest of the office was empty except for two code and communications specialists and the plainclothes guards near the door. Behind the wall, the factory was still working on Eduardo Mederos.

Jones tossed a package of chips to Maurice, who grabbed it as he might a life ring. "I know what it's like being a hostage to your belly."

Maurice tore open the package. "So how many places does he sleep?"

Cantrell said through his taco, "As you know, he still rotates where he sleeps. Toothbrush, bring up the Havana Hilton."

An exterior shot of the hotel appeared on Jones's monitor. It was the international style so common to hotels built in the 1950s. Jones switched to photos of the interior of Castro's suite. Dumbbells were stocked at the foot of the bed.

"When Castro stays at the hotel, the entire twenty-second floor is emptied. Also, the rooms above and below are vacated. We've studied it, and we don't think it's vulnerable."

"Where else?" Maurice asked.

The screen went blank, then showed a well-maintained

duplex. Cantrell said, "This is where Celia Sánchez lived in the Vedado area. Castro often stayed here during the twenty years of their relationship. After Celia died in 1980, he has still slept here, but less frequently."

"Is the place defended?"

"Castro had some communications equipment installed, but did nothing to the structure. But when he stays here, the entire block closes down. There are usually fifty guards spread through the area, including armed scout cars in back and front. We've run a number of penetration studies on the building over the years, and it doesn't appear we can get through."

"Where else?" Maurice asked, brushing the sprouts into a wastebasket until only the mayonnaise remained. He slapped the bread slices together again and took a large bite.

"You already know about the presidential palace where he stays frequently," Cantrell said, putting shredded cheese from the container back onto the taco.

"Thirty-eight percent of the time," Jones added helpfully.

"It, too, is solid."

Another photograph appeared on the monitor. Cantrell explained, "This is the mansion in the Cojimar suburb that an admirer gave Castro. He spends a night a week or so here. Whenever he has one of his marathon domino sessions with his friends from the exile days, he does it here. And we've got the same problem here. G2 floods the area with guards when Castro is in residence. Show the next one, Gerard."

A rambling one-story home in a brush wilderness appeared on the screen. "This is Castro's hunting villa on the Isle of Pines."

"It's now called the Isle of Youth," Jones corrected. The island was off Cuba's south shore. "Named after all the students who do so-called volunteer work on the farms there."

Cantrell said, "Here, out in the woods, Castro only has three or four guards around him. Trouble is, though, Castro doesn't go there with any frequency. We can't count on him visiting at any given time. Same with his small fishing retreat on a key just south of the Bay of Pigs."

146

"And he never announces his travels in advance," Jones said. "Secrecy was crucial to his success when he was in the mountains hiding from Batista's troops. To this day he never tells anyone all his plans."

Maurice leaned back in his chair. "Has he developed any weaknesses? Women, maybe?"

Cantrell said, "The longest love of his life, Celia Sánchez, died of lung cancer in 1980. Castro has been mostly celibate since then, as far as we can tell."

Jones did not have a napkin, so he resorted to the bachelor trick of wiping his hands on his socks. He pressed the keyboards several times. "He's no monk, though. He was poking around even when he was married to Mirta. I've got a list of his girlfriends here, and long bios on each of them. Naty Revuelta, Isabella Custadio, Maria Lorenze, Lidia Vexel-Robertson, Gloria Gaitan. Fidel has been a sex symbol in Cuba since the revolution. Not the ideal sex symbol, though. After the first photo of him skin diving was printed in a Havana newspaper in 1963, there was a lot of tittering among Cuban women about Castro's skinny legs. He wasn't perfect after all."

"What about a honey pot operation?" Maurice asked.

Jones laughed. "What? A honey pot? Isn't that one of those portable toilets at a construction site?"

Cantrell said, "You're showing your generation, Bill. No, Castro can't be reached that way. He has a deep puritanical streak, and a come-on from a woman offering herself for a one-night stand wouldn't tempt him."

Eduardo Mederos walked from the factory into the office. His hair was spiked from sweat, and he gingerly dabbed a towel at his forehead. His bandages were stained gray from perspiration. He was carrying another of Lieutenant Commander Smith's protein drinks. As if on sprung legs, he shuffled to the Apollo and stared longingly at an empty chair near Jack Cantrell.

Cantrell gestured toward the chair, but Mederos said wearily, "Smith said take five. I've learned he means exactly that, to the second. If I sit, I'll never get up again."

147

Cantrell asked, "He's got you lifting weights at ten at night?"

"Twice a day. I missed my four o'clock session because I was learning to paste on hair. The fellow who was showing me had to get back to Los Angeles tonight."

Maurice said, "Eduardo won't have time to grow a beard, so we had makeup artist Ray Martin come to Miami. Plus, Eduardo needed to learn how to put on a realistic appendix scar in case one of Castro's housekeepers sees him with his stomach out. We wanted the plastic surgeons to give him a real scar, but Eduardo refused."

Jones asked in a laughably stern voice, "Don't you know the meaning of sacrifice, Eduardo?"

"Is it too much to ask that just one part of my body be left intact?" Mederos sipped the drink. Chocolate milkshake dribbled down his chin onto his shirt. He was unaware of it until Maurice passed him a paper napkin and pointed.

Mederos wiped his shirt and face and said, "I can't feel a damn thing in my lip or chin yet."

"You won't for another day or so," Maurice said. He turned to Cantrell and Jones. "Eduardo's lower lip wasn't quite as prominent as Castro's, so some silicone was injected into it, just enough to give it that pendulous look. We had it done by Anthony Salisci, the same plastic surgeon who gives many New York ballerinas that pouty look they need to dance better."

"Let's go, Eduardo," Ralph Smith called from the doorway. "Couple more sets."

Mederos groaned, lowered his drink, and straggled back to the factory.

Maurice picked up the calorie shake and tasted it. He kept it in his hand. "What about Castro's weaknesses? Alcohol? As I recall, he doesn't drink much."

"Still doesn't," Cantrell said. "A touch of Armenian brandy now and then."

"Health troubles?"

"Not much. He occasionally has rounds with pleurisy, and

148

the dry coughs and painful breathing that go with it. He gets an intestinal infection once in a while. We know he has hypertension. Old wounds include a hairline skull fracture he received from a policeman's club at a demonstration during his student days. And the appendix."

"Doesn't give us much to work with," Maurice said, drinking Mederos's milkshake. "Any psychological weaknesses we can use?"

Cantrell said, "Castro suffers depression once in a while. He did when his mother passed away in 1963, and after the missile crisis, and he had a severe bout after Celia Sánchez died, and a number of other times."

"What else? Anything we can play on?"

Cantrell wadded up his paper bag and dropped it into the wastebasket. "Anger, certainly. We could count on that, if we gave him proper prodding. Castro gets as mad as any world leader we deal with, and he holds a grudge like the McCoys and Hatfields."

"Fidel does not like to be humiliated," Jones said. "The Russians have yanked his cord that way."

"He almost broke with the Soviets after they left him in the lurch during the missile crisis," Cantrell said. "The Russians backed down without even consulting Castro. He said on the record to a reporter that Khrushchev had no balls. He was red-faced with rage for weeks and weeks. Same thing when the Soviets went into Afghanistan. Castro thought it made him look like a fool, after supporting the Soviets so slavishly for so long, while trying to lead the nonaligned movement."

Maurice thoughtfully rubbed his chin. "That sounds like something we could bank on, given the right circumstances. What else?"

"Ruthlessness," Cantrell said grimly. "I don't have to tell you about that."

"We've got to find him alone." Maurice returned to the problem.

"More than that," Cantrell said. "We need to get to him when his black box is not within reach."

"An alarm?"

"Show him, Toothbrush."

On the screen appeared a photograph of Castro shaking hands at Martí Airport. Over Castro's shoulder was a sign reading "Free Cuba Welcomes You."

Cantrell said, "This shows him pressing the flesh last time he returned to Havana, a flight from Berlin where he attended an economic summit. The men on each side of him are G2 bodyguards. The guard at his back holds a briefcase, something like the president's football. But this is only an alarm. It calls in reinforcements."

"That briefcase is with him all the time?"

Cantrell nodded. "Show him, Gerard."

A series of photographs appeared on the Apollo's monitor. Castro walking into the Palace of the Revolution. Castro cutting cane. Castro shaking Daniel Ortega's hand. Castro on a podium with his fist raised. Talking to tobacco farmers. On the porch of his hunting lodge. Inspecting a new Soviet-made fishing boat. In each picture, the guard and the black briefcase were evident, always only a few steps from Castro.

"Well, hell. . . ." Maurice thought for a moment. "He just has to be alone, and without that damned briefcase from time to time. Gerard, use your overdeveloped brain and figure out when."

"Castro spends twenty-point-three-five percent of his time in closed-door meetings, nineteen-point-one percent at meals . . ."

"Put it on the screen, Toothbrush," Cantrell requested.

The photo of Castro and the boat vanished, and seconds later a list appeared. "This is a percentage breakdown of how Castro has spent his waking hours over the last ten years." Two keystrokes. "And here is the same record for the last year. I'll scroll it down."

The list rolled, revealing smaller and smaller percentages.

"There's fishing on your list. Does he go alone?"

Jones gave the computer a command, and Castro's fishing

expeditions were broken out on the screen. Location, date and time, people accompanying. "He always has one or more of his longtime friends with him. Same with hunting."

"I see snorkeling," Maurice said. "Castro spends one and a half percent of his waking time in mask and fins?"

"He skin-dives at least once a week, and has for thirty years. Sometimes twice a week. Two hours or so at a time. It's his favorite sport."

"What else do you know about that?"

"Every time he snorkels, he does so inside various coral reefs. Outside the reefs, usually half a mile away from Castro, a gunboat—a refurbished American PT boat—is always patrolling. Protection from sea or sky attack."

"Is the black briefcase around? And his guards?"

Jones tapped on his computer. A satellite photo appeared on the monitor. It showed a boat and what might have been a body in the water off its bow. Jones pressed another key, and the same photo was magnified. Clearly visible were two men at the boat's stern and another on the bow. Two of the men carried rifles. What might have been an oxygen bottle was also aft, as were several chairs. The boat was perhaps forty feet long, a cruiser with a flying bridge.

"Zero in on the swimmer, Gerard," Cantrell said.

The screen rotated the boat out of the picture and further enlarged the man in the water.

"Castro?" Maurice asked.

"Yep," Jones answered. "You can even see his fins."

"What's that in his hand?"

"A speargun. He's got a game net tied to his waist. The shot was taken by an NRO White Goose satellite, put up there last April by a Titan 3B."

"Where's the black briefcase?" There was an edge of excitement to Maurice's voice.

"Probably on the boat," Cantrell replied.

"When's the last time he went snorkeling?"

Jones answered without referring to the computer. "Four

151

days ago, two-thirty in the afternoon, near Baha Honda. Speared a thirty-pound grouper."

"What've we got on his skin-diving habits?"

"Quite a bit," Jones said, typing in a command. A menu appeared on the screen. "Dates, durations, locations, friends along, information on his catches, that type of thing."

Maurice stood. Elated, he said, "We've found him alone."

"That's not quite alone," Cantrell said skeptically. "Not with armed guards on the boat, and a PT boat within a few minutes' sail."

Maurice said, "It's alone enough."

Chapter XI

Tracking Fidel Castro was a case of American intelligence overkill. The U.S. Armed Forces, the National Security Agency, and the National Reconnaissance Office replied enthusiastically to Maurice's requests. Anything he wanted. Terse calls had been made from the White House.

Castro's personal helicopter was a Soviet-made Hormone A, a model used primarily for antisubmarine warfare. Before turning it over to the Cubans, the Soviet navy stripped it of its sonobuoys, dipping and optical sensors, and the chin-mounted radome, thinking, quite accurately, that anything they sent to Cuba and did not encircle with Russian guards would eventually be examined by the CIA. Even without the radome, which looks like a tumor on the helicopter's prow, the Hormone is an ungainly-looking machine. Rather than an aft stabilizing rotor, the helicopter has two counterrotating main rotors, one right under the other, and a fixed triple tail.

Unlike all other copters in Cuba, Castro's Hormone had no markings and so was not difficult to spot. Castro was an ardent fan of Franklin Delano Roosevelt and had sent him a congratulatory letter after his election to a fourth term. Roosevelt had traveled in an unmarked Pullman car named the *Ferdinand Magellan.* All other Pullman's in the United States had their names—the *Conneaut,* the *Hillcrest Club,* and so forth —emblazoned on their sides. Castro believed it was Roosevelt's bravura that led him to ride in so obvious a car, and what Roosevelt could do, Castro could do. The unmarked helicopter was never far from Castro.

On this Saturday, April 23, an air force McDonnell Douglas RF-4 Phantom found the Hormone. It did so as the Phantom flew 850 miles an hour just south of the Isle of Youth, the island forty miles south of Cuba's south coast. In a pod beneath its wing, the Phantom carried an ESSWACS (electronic solid-state wide-angle camera system). A small portion of the island was photographed through the ESSWAC's five independent lens assemblies, which focused the light onto five charge-coupled devices. The five electric currents were fed through a video processor, then through a multiplex system to break them down into a single burst of jam-proof digital pulses. The burst was sent through a stabilized transmitter that was under a helmet-sized blister on the aircraft, to an LOS (line of sight) ship lying another thirty miles south of the island.

The ship was a Spruance-class destroyer, the USS *Kinkaid,* which relayed the signal to a FleetSatCom 5 satellite in geosynchronous orbit, which instantly retransmitted it to a dish at Langley, Virginia. There the signal was rebuilt into pictures, much like a television screen, each line consisting of 8,640 pixels. Before the Phantom had sped through another mile, the agents in PHOTINT Tasking could agree that Castro's Hormone was indeed at the landing platform near his hunting lodge on the island. The pictures were relayed to the Apollo monitor in Miami.

"Funny-looking helicopter," Maurice said, chewing some of the fries Gerard Jones had sent out for.

At three minutes after ten that morning, a Castro aide at the lodge used a scrambled telephone to notify the Cuban Air Force that Castro would be returning to Havana in thirty minutes and to clear the standard three-mile safety zone around Martí Airport. Castro had been on the island more than a week, and the aide also suggested that a small welcoming crowd greet Castro at the airport. This conversation was broadcast across Batabanó Gulf to DAAFAR headquarters in Havana.

The National Security Agency's Vint Hill Farm near Washington, D.C., picked it out of the air. The farm was covered with log periodics, broadbands, and monopole antennas, but it was a rhombic array that lifted the transmission. Each antenna of the array was a wire three feet off the ground connected to four posts positioned as if at the corners of a diamond. The posts were ten feet apart. An underground coaxial cable connected the antenna with the farm's operations building. The array consisted of forty rhombic antennas spaced over several hundred acres. The intercepted signal was forwarded to NSA headquarters at Fort George G. Meade, halfway between Washington and Baltimore.

Unscrambling at Fort Meade was done within a split second of the words being spoken on the Isle of Youth. The NSA had eleven acres of computers in an underground bunker at Fort Meade. The agency had a policy of having computers at least five years ahead of anything available commercially, which meant it was a dozen years ahead of the Cuban scrambler. Had the Cray X-MP/48, the world's most advanced computer, been programmed to yawn, it certainly would have as it made short work of the scrambled message. The Cray next ran the message through its translation program, and within five seconds of the Castro aide's final word into his telephone, the NSA's Central Security Service provided a full English transcript of the conversation to Gerard Jones's terminal.

The Hormone's flight from the Isle of Youth north to Havana was monitored by a Boeing E-3 Sentry flying at twenty-nine thousand feet over the Florida Keys. The plane was an AWACS platform, a Boeing 707 with a rotodome secured on eleven-feet-high stanchions above the fuselage. It had an APY-2 radar with a beyond-the-horizon mode and a pulse-doppler elevation scan mode, capable of detecting minute changes in the helicopter's altitude and direction. This information was transmitted to Randolph Air Force Base in San Antonio, then instantly on to Fort Meade, then to the warehouse in Miami. William Maurice knew as much about the Hormone's location as did its pilot.

"Does Castro ever make last-minute changes in his flight plan?" Maurice asked. He and Jones were sitting next to each other in secretary's chairs, facing the Apollo monitor. Jack Cantrell was standing at his desk, speaking into the secured telephone. Pained expressions crossed his face repeatedly. He was talking to the director again.

"Not often, once the call has been made to Havana," Jones replied. "It'll be a while before he reaches the heliport at José Martí, where he lands when he wants a crowd to greet him." He leaned back and reached for a bag of pretzels he had kept in reserve.

Jones's telephone rang. He lifted it and listened for a moment. He looked quizzically at Maurice before handing him the receiver. "It's for you. A kid."

"Only my wife knows how to get me here," Maurice said by way of apology. He pressed it against his ear and said hello. After a moment he asked, "Did Mrs. Maurice give you this number, Eloy?"

It was Eloy Labrada, a fifth-grader whom Maurice had spent hours playing catch with and had taken to half a dozen big league spring training games, trying to wean him away from soccer, which Maurice thought was a pernicious influence.

"No, there's no problem calling here," Maurice answered. "How come you're so upset, Eloy? Nothing's as bad as that."

Maurice listened to a bubbling tale. He finally interrupted, "The English project is due in two days? Well, why did you wait until the last minute? . . . I know the book is thick, with long sentences, but that shouldn't have kept you from finishing it

156

and starting this project for school. . . . A Robinson Crusoe island? Sounds like a lot of work . . . I think—"

Maurice was interrupted in turn. He cupped his hand over
the phone and said to Jones, "Be right with you." He listened a
moment longer before saying with resignation, "What kind of
thing does your teacher want for this Robinson Crusoe island?"
Maurice blew a long sigh. "Now, Eloy, calm down. Listen, I'll
see what I can do. . . . Yeah, I'll come up with something. This
is the last time I bail you out, though. . . . Yes, I promise. . . .
Yes, I'm crossing my heart and hoping to die. I'll call you tonight. So long, Eloy."

Maurice hung up and said to Gerard Jones, "Big secret this
place is, when a fifth-grader can call right in."

The helicopter landed in Havana at eleven thirty-two that
morning. Whatever doubt there was in Miami that Fidel Castro
was aboard the Hormone was dispelled when an air force broad
coverage photo recon satellite on a north-south orbit passed
ninety-five miles above Martí Airport. This Big Bird satellite
was outfitted with radio transmission detectors, recoverable-
photo cameras, and infrared readers. Its capabilities were, as
the KGB station chief in Havana told Castro, "far beyond what
we can tell you." Castro knew the Big Bird, flying above a
Cuban parade ground, could distinguish between the two gold
chevrons of a *primer teniente* (first lieutenant) and the single gold
chevron of a *teniente* (lieutenant). He had ordered his troops to
replace the shiny insignia with those made with black anodized
metal, harder to detect.

But Castro did not know that his own polished boots, shining in the sunlight as he emerged from the helicopter in Havana, reflected an infrared signature as distinctive as a
fingerprint. NSA knew he had four pairs of boots, and the Big
Bird could read every one of them. Three seconds after Castro
stepped out from under the Hormone's blades toward his limousine, Gerard Jones in Miami pointed to his Apollo screen
and told William Maurice, "He's wearing his newest pair
today."

Castro did not wait until he had returned to his offices to

157

begin hearing reports and issuing instructions. His ministers often met him at the airport. On this day Raul Castro, Carlos Galvez, and Aristides Diaz Rabassa, chief of DGI, flanked Castro as he stepped away from the helicopter. They leaned toward him, briefing him in earnest, knowing Castro did not like wasting time. Wary of lip-readers, Galvez hid his mouth behind his hand as he talked.

They walked down a tunnel of soldiers of the Ejército Revolucionario, the Revolutionary Army. The soldiers were dressed in battle fatigues, but, like many other socialist leaders, Castro had created a vast array of medals and orders, and many of the soldiers wore colorfully decorated uniform blouses.

Pressing the flesh was never a waste of time to Castro, and he had spent his career acting as if he were up for reelection. On seeing the crowd behind a sawhorse barricade, Castro veered toward them, his ministers in tow. Many in the crowd were Young Pioneers, eleven- and twelve-year-olds, in their olive shirts and blood-red bandannas. Some carried small Cuban flags, and others held silver, red, and blue balloons on short sticks. A man in a straw hat was still passing out flags as fast as he could, but the balloon vendor had sold only a few—at two pesos each, a little dear—and was holding six balloons above his head. Also in the crowd were a hundred airport workers and several hundred others rounded up by members of the CDR (Comités de Defensa de la Revolución, Cuba's official block snoopers) from nearby workers' apartment buildings.

A shrill schoolyard cheer went up when the Young Pioneers realized Castro was heading their way. Raul Castro and the other ministers dropped back, and G2 bodyguards who had followed Castro off the helicopter fell in on both sides of him as he shook hands down the barricade. Castro moved quickly along the line, shaking the eager hands. Young girls shrieked when they made contact. The performance was perfunctory. When he reached the end of the barricade, he turned toward the waiting car, and the ministers regained their positions.

Aristides Diaz Rabassa leaned farther toward Castro and

said, "Your meeting with Yuri Sokolov is set for two o'clock. The bastard doesn't share our concerns. . . ."

No heed was paid to the balloon vendor, Roberto Ramos. One of his silver balloons was a parabolic listening dish. Another balloon was a high-powered amplifier, the underside of the balloon being the dish. The feeder was a small point on the top of the balloon. The power booster, called an exciter, was in Ramos's pocket, as were the battery and the electronics, each the size of a cigarette package. The voices were plucked out of the air and instantly transmitted to a FleetSatCom satellite.

Four seconds after the words had been spoken, William Maurice read on the screen, "Your meeting with Yuri Sokolov is set for two o'clock. The bastard doesn't share our concerns, I'm afraid. He's going to insist on keeping them at La Panchita. . . ."

"Who's that talking?" Maurice quietly asked Gerard Jones, as if afraid to rudely interrupt the conversation in Havana. Their heads were four inches apart as they studied the screen.

"I can run a voiceprint check on it," Jones said. He tapped his computer. "We've got a library at Langley on their prints." A few seconds passed. "It's Aristides Diaz Rabassa, head of DGI."

The screen scrolled. "Sokolov received a long message from Moscow this morning. We've got it, but we aren't having any luck with it."

It pushed those words higher, and then appeared, "That's because you got your decoding equipment from the Russians. They're not going to send you something that can be worked against them."

Jones pressed several keys. "That's Carlos Galvez."

The screen: "Keep working on it. I'd like to throw that pompous Soviet ass in the Circular."

"And that's Castro," Jones said. "God only knows what the Circular is."

Maurice said, "It's the colloquial name for the prison on the Isle of Pines, near Castro's lodge."

The screen: "[Fadeout: 6.7 seconds] advise against prodding Sokolov too much. Last time we irritated him, the Soviets canceled a shipment of scout cars they had committed to the FAR. Turned the freighter right around, sent it back to Leningrad. I think it was on Sokolov's recommendation. [Sound est: car door closing.] [Transmission end.]"

"That was Rabassa again." Jones smiled and reached for a Dr. Pepper. "Not bad, on such short notice. I didn't think we'd get Ramos into José Martí. Those crowds are invitation only."

"I know some people at the airport, " Maurice said vaguely. He leaned back in his chair. "We'll see where we pick up the *jefe supremo* next."

Jones swallowed loudly and reached for a box of Good & Plenties. Moments passed as he chewed the candy.

"So tell me how you ended up with the nickname 'Toothbrush'?" Maurice asked. "It has a nice ring to it. Toothbrush Jones."

"Damn, I hate that." Jones grimaced, then scowled over his shoulder at Cantrell, who had a finger in his ear as he continued to listen to the director. Jones turned back to Maurice and said, "I invented a sure-fire way to tell if someone is left- or right-handed. Find a photo of that person smiling, and measure his teeth."

"His teeth?"

"A person who is right-handed almost invariably brushes the teeth on his left side harder than on the right. Over the years, it causes the gums on that side to recede farther, making his teeth on that side appear to be longer."

"What's the point?"

"The point is that I discovered it, and no one else did."

Maurice laughed and shook his head. "Toothbrush Jones. I like it."

Jones glowered at Maurice a moment, then punched a series of commands into the Apollo. The screen blackened, then filled again. He read a moment and asked with acid sweetness,

"So you tell me, Bill, how'd you end up with the nickname 'Spade'?"

"You can do better than that, Toothbrush."

"Miami police took to calling you 'Spade' back in 1962, when for most of the year following your termination at the agency you prowled around Miami looking for the fellow who planted the bomb behind your fire wall. Says here you dug as thoroughly as any detective. Miami police gave you high marks, but you came up empty-handed."

"What're you reading?" Maurice chafed.

"What were you going to do to him, once you found him?"

"I had plans."

"I can well imagine."

Maurice rose stiffly from his chair, giving his knee time to lock. "I've got better things to do than listen to your nonsense, Toothbrush. Eduardo probably needs some encouragement. Call me when you get something more from Havana."

The Apollo beeped, and Jones said, "Sit down. It's coming in now."

Fidel Castro emerged from the limousine in front of the Palace of the Revolution. Soldiers guarding the door snapped to attention as Castro passed them into the building.

Three blocks north, a taxi was parked in front of another government building, a ten-story sandstone structure without a name in front of it. Most government buildings in Havana have Che Guevara's stern countenance pasted somewhere on them. Because this building had no blank walls, windows punctured Guevara's eyebrows, nostrils, beard, and lips. Just what the Bolivian soldiers did to him when they caught him. Here also, on another side of the building, was a poster showing Uncle Sam—who in Cuba is always drawn with President Kennedy's face—fishing in the Caribbean. Haiti and Grenada were in the catch basket next to him. Taxis in Cuba do not have meters, as they have established routes from which they cannot vary. But this one—a 1958 Chevrolet with every metal surface painted yellow, even the wheel rims, door handles, and grill, as

161

are most old cars in Havana—had what looked to be a fare meter mounted next to the steering wheel. The driver, Ernesto Pazos, could only hope no passersby would notice. There were few taxis in the city, and Cubans called them *los incapturables.*

The meter was a laser with its beam aimed at Castro's tenth-floor office window. A thousand times a second it measured the precise distance between the laser and the window. The office window acted as a tympanic membrane, vibrated by the voices inside. The measurements were digitalized, then transmitted over the taxi's antenna, which looked like a straightened coat hanger, common in Havana. The signal was snared by a shunt aerial flush with the fin on an air force Phantom flying four miles above the Gulf of Mexico.

The screen in the Miami warehouse read in English: "How long have they been waiting?"

"We've got him in one of his offices, the Guevara Building, near the plaza." Gerard Jones enthused. "He's got three offices in Havana. That's Castro."

The screen: "Twenty-five minutes."

"That's Chico Legro. How'd you get the taxi, Bill?"

"An old friend of mine who sometimes delivers money for me. Been a Havana hack for twenty years."

The screen: "Show them in."

"That's longer than he usually makes people cool their heels," Jones commented. "I figure him with a fifteen-minute average. Castro is upset."

The screen: "Thank you for seeing us, Comrade Castro."

Jones said, "That's translated from Russian. Must be Sokolov. I'll check prints." A few seconds elapsed. "The ambassador all right. Sokolov can't quite jump from Havana to the Politburo. Rumor has it six years ago he exited a helicopter door before Dobrynin, a bad breach of decorum in the land of equals. Dobrynin has kept him in Havana since."

The screen read again: "Thank you for seeing us, Comrade Castro."

Jones said, "Those words were originally said in Spanish,

162

so that'll be Victor Fedorin. Let's check." A brief pause. "Yep. Fedorin."

"Who is he?" Maurice asked.

"Fourth man at the Russian embassy in Havana. Sokolov is the ambassador, at least nominally on top. But, as you know, the organizational charts don't tell the real story. The second in command is chief of Line PR for the KGB section there, while the third man actually runs the embassy. Fedorin is fourth, officially a liaison officer between the Soviet embassy and Castro's people. He's a translator and provisioner and a general factotum. I'll have the monitor identify the speaker automatically, and I'll have the computer omit the translations." He entered several commands.

The screen: "Sokolov: 'We are concerned that the DAA-FAR has surrounded the hangar at La Panchita with military police. You know us to be capable of guarding our own equipment, Comrade Castro.' "

"Castro: 'Of course, but I was unsure [unintelligible—2.39 seconds] security.' "

"Sokolov: 'With due regard to your exceptionally well-trained troops, we must insist on complete responsibility for guarding the planes. If I may be blunt, comrade, the [unintelligible—3.75 seconds] DAAFAR is refusing to let us get our service trucks to the planes until after eight each night. This new development is viewed with concern by my government.' "

"Castro: 'Your air force troops were opening the hangar doors at dusk to get those trucks in there. That's too early. Too much daylight left. Despite warnings from our minister of the Revolutionary Armed Forces, this went on for three days. [Unintelligible—2.33 seconds] risk of detection.' "

Jones said, "Castro always refers to his brother Raul by his rank. Never says 'my brother.' It's as if he hopes the world will forget the nepotism."

"Sokolov: [Unintelligible—11.5 seconds.] 'I'll see what I can do, of course.' "

"Castro: 'Good day, then, comrades.' "

Maurice said, "Short meeting. Any way that computer of yours can let us know the tone of those voices?"

Gerard grinned. "We're working on it. But it's easy to tell that Castro doesn't have much tolerance for the Soviets, even though they give him ten million dollars a day in aid."

Jones rolled the words off the screen. "That's it for now, looks like. Castro has probably gone into an interior room. We'll pick him up in a minute. He does most of his work near the window."

Maurice said, "Gerard, call in Mike Phillips, will you?"

The model maker was quick to answer the summons. He was rubbing his hands in a towel as he approached the workstation. Maurice rolled Cantrell's chair over to the workstation for him.

"Mike, something's come up. Needs to be done right away. I need a model of an island, something like Robinson Crusoe would have lived on."

"That'd be no problem," Phillips answered, perhaps wondering why Gerard Jones laughed suddenly. "Can you give me a three-D of it on your shader here, or even an elevation map?"

Maurice shook his head. "This is quicker than that. All I need is a flat board painted blue like water, and a plaster of Paris mound on it, painted green and brown to look like an island. Some trees on it like Lionel sells. Then maybe a little cave poked into it where Crusoe hid out, and a fort on it, made of toothpicks stuck in a circle, where he lived with the loot he took off the ship."

Phillips looked at Jones. "Is he joking?"

"Maybe you could even paint a tiny footprint or two in the sand," Maurice advised. "You know, Friday's footprints. And Mike, I need it to look like a fifth-grader did it. A talented fifth-grader who spent a lot of time on it, but still a fifth-grader."

Phillips asked Jones accusingly, "Does Bill have a ten-year-old?"

"Nope," Jones answered, sincerity all over his face.

"Can I ask what you need a model of Robinson Crusoe's island for?"

"You're new to the agency, Mike," Maurice answered. "We operate on the need-to-know principle around here."

"Well," Phillips said, pulling at his mustache, "I suppose I could make that fairly easily."

"Before we close shop tonight?"

"Might not be dry, but it'll be able to travel."

Maurice thanked the model maker, who returned to his studio through the doors. Maurice turned to Jones. "I owe you one for keeping your trap shut, Toothbrush."

Jones said, "We'll call it even if you forget my nickname."

"Done." Maurice rose again.

Jones's face registered alarm, and he bent toward the computer, his hands poised over the keyboard for an emergency.

Maurice said, "That's not your machine on the fritz. It's my knee."

Jones glanced at Maurice's leg. "You ought to get that fixed. Sounds like a broken starter on a truck."

"I'll worry about my knee, Gerard. You just tell me when Fidel decides he needs a little R and R."

Had Victor Fedorin heard Jones describe him as a factotum, he would have bitterly agreed. His fall from grace in the KGB had been sudden, irreversible, and beyond his control. There was only some solace in that it hadn't been terminal.

Fedorin walked along a cracked and dusty sidewalk in the Vedado district not far from the University of Havana. His hands were deep in the pockets of his blue serge pants, standard plainclothes wear for KGB agents the world over. He had left his jacket and tie at the embassy, where he had dropped Sokolov off after their interview with Castro. Fedorin had told the ambassador he was off to procure oranges and beans for the embassy's larder. Sokolov had only nodded, unaware of or, more likely, not concerned with the irony that a KGB major would spend most of his foreign tour filling grocery orders from embassy cooks.

Fedorin stepped into an apartment doorway and waited for several minutes, watching for a tail. The embassy was filled with *stukachi,* the KGB term for informers. He brought a hand up to his nose, a shield against the smell. The government claimed Havana's pervasive brown odor was diesel exhaust and seaweed. They could not admit the new sewage system was already crumbling.

Fedorin's face had not been colored by the Havana sun and was as chalky as when he'd arrived. His face was dominated by eyebrows that grew together over his nose. His eyebrows were a straight, broad, black line that made his small nose and mouth seem incidental. His dark hair always looked as if it needed washing. The Havana heat made him sweat like a wrung sponge, and the handkerchief in his back pocket was already soaked through from wiping his forehead.

When he was certain he was not being followed, Fedorin walked around the corner to the Club Sharad. The door was black with a date tree and a veiled woman painted on it. He pushed through, into a hallway with a coat checkroom on one side. He moved through to the bar. The room's windows were covered with moth-ravaged cloth heavy enough to still block out most of the sun. The room was lit by an intricately shaped brass chandelier with eight sockets. Only three had bulbs, and only one worked.

Fedorin sat on a stool, and when the bartender approached he ordered a rum highball, called a *matarates,* or rat killer. The back bar had only eight bottles, all of them rum. A mirror hung above the bottles, but the room was so dim little could be seen in its reflection. From a portable hi-fi on the serving bar came the scratchy voice of Idalberto Delgado, modern Cuba's Bing Crosby. The grooves on the record had almost been worn smooth. Fedorin put two pesos on the bar, sipped the biting drink—Cuban bartenders are almost always generous with rum—and turned to survey the bar.

The dance floor was empty, and the band platform had no music stands and only one upended folding chair. Naugahyde divans lined the wall, most with strips of black electrician's tape holding them together. Low cloth partitions separated the

166

couches. A couple groped together on the far divan, his hands pressing her to his waist.

The prostitutes of Virtue Street were gone. They had been driven indoors to shadowy establishments like the Club Sharad. Fedorin knew one would approach if he waited long enough at the bar. The first time he went to the club he waited thirty minutes, during which he gulped down four drinks and looked lonely while the bartender watched him closely. Finally he sent over a woman. She sat next to Fedorin and ordered a drink. He paid for the liquor, but she wouldn't go to the couch right away. She talked, keeping her face partly hidden, trying to sense if he might be an *agente de policía*. After a while he led her to a divan. No money had been given the woman at first, but the divan cost thirty pesos, paid to the bartender. She spent an hour with him and refused to take all her clothes off. They kissed, unheard of with hookers in other countries. After she sat on his lap, she asked for another twenty pesos. Later trips to the Club Sharad had been quicker, but despite a compelling argument from below his belt, he didn't have time today.

He twisted on the stool to the barman. "Get Justo for me." Fedorin's Spanish was almost without an accent.

The bartender disappeared behind a curtain. There were some advantages to being a factotum, Fedorin thought, swallowing the last of his drink. Profit, for one. He traded on the left, and he made three times what the ambassador did. He had recently purchased a Fiat for his wife, Alexandra, in Moscow, had paid enough to skip the official waiting list. And she had just moved into a flat on Prospekt that had two bedrooms and a private bath. Still, it rankled Fedorin when he thought of the miserable turn his life had taken, abruptly away from the prestige and power for which he had worked all his life. He could thank his cousin for that, the bastard. The traitor.

At age ten, Fedorin had been selected for an experimental secondary school, where many of the classes were taught in foreign languages. Then came six years at the Moscow University's Institute of Western Languages, where he did postgraduate work in English and Spanish. He worked with the Soviet Peace Committee and the Latin-Soviet Solidarity Committee, where he proved to be a persuasive propagandist. He wrote articles for Radio Moscow's English and Spanish broadcasts and commentary for *Novoye Vremya* (*New Times*) magazine.

Fedorin was recruited by the KGB's First Chief Directorate, where he studied to be an illegals support officer, known as a Line N agent. There he learned to recruit and train Soviet citizens to be illegals, agents in foreign countries. He was then rotated to the Second Chief Directorate, the huge Soviet organization of internal repression that administers from its office in the Hotel Berlin near the Lubyanka.

Still rising quickly, Fedorin was admitted to the Foreign Intelligence School, near the village of Yurlovo, just off the Volokolamskoye Highway, one of only one hundred fifty students. Behind the yellow cement walls topped with razor wire, Fedorin became accomplished in ciphers, surveillance, drops, communications, and weapons. On graduation, he was commissioned a senior lieutenant in the KGB and was paid three hundred rubles a month. He was assigned to the Caribbean desk at the Center, as the KGB terms its Moscow headquarters. After exemplary work in Moscow, he did successful tours in Grenada and Nicaragua, was promoted to major, and then assigned to Havana.

Had he put in four good years in Cuba, he would have qualified for permanent assignment in Moscow, undoubtedly by then a lieutenant colonel. This sparkling path was so clear and so attainable. Then two years ago his cousin—of all the goddamn things, a high-wire walker with the Moscow Circus—defected in Ottawa. The bastard.

Bad enough the traitor had turned on the Motherland. He had also swept Victor Fedorin's career into the coal bin. Fedorin was guilty by blood relation. Had the defector been his brother rather than a cousin, Fedorin would have been sent to one of those villages in the Soviet east where hospitals are known only as frostbite centers. As it was, there would be no more advancement for Fedorin. He was stuck in Havana.

Fedorin glanced impatiently at the curtain. Instead of Justo, one of the girls pushed it aside and grinned at him. He remembered her name as Carla. She sauntered over, provocatively swaying her thin skirt. She wore her bronze hair to her shoulders. Her lips were painted vermilion, and she slowly wet them as she approached. She had two pockmarks on a cheek, which she had filled in with powder. She seductively ran her hand along the mahogany bar as she neared.

Customers who didn't know Carla by name asked for her by cupping their hands in front of them. Now her breasts almost spilled out of her scant oyster-gray blouse as she slipped onto the bar stool next to the Russian. She brought her elbows together, a seemingly casual gesture that pushed them up at him. There must have been an acre of flesh there. She had apparently not forgotten his tastes, or the inexpensive digital watch he had given her as a bonus last time, cheap anywhere but Havana.

"Are you here to visit me or Justo?" She glanced at her chest, hoping to lead Fedorin's eyes to her deep cleavage.

With an enormous effort, he wrested his gaze away from her to the curtain. "Justo, I'm afraid."

She slid out her lower lip. "You love business more than your Carla?" She reached for his hand. "Are you sure about that, Mika?"

It was the first name that had come to Fedorin when he had first visited the club.

She slowly trailed his fingers along her thigh. Her smile was inviting but faintly professional. She lowered her lashes demurely. "Why don't you talk to the barman about a couch for us?"

"You're tempting, Carla, but I'm here to talk with Justo."

"Always the businessman, Mika." She glanced quickly around the room. The barman had not reappeared, and the couple on the far divan were bouncing against each other, oblivious to all but their passion. Carla deftly opened two buttons of her blouse. She wore nothing underneath, and her breasts flowed out, filling the space between them as she leaned toward him. She playfully opened Fedorin's fingers. Looking at him with burning frankness, she pressed his hand against her breast.

Fedorin felt the warm skin flow between his fingers, spilling around his hand. Her nipple hardened under his palm. The scent of lemon blossoms drifted from the darkness between her breasts.

"I can hurry, Mika." She looked around again. "The barman will leave us alone. And he's still out back, anyway."

"I really can't today, Carla." He made no effort to retract his hand. He was breathing as if he had climbed four flights of stairs.

"Instead of a divan, why don't you rent a stool today?" she whispered. "Come on, we'll hurry."

When he took another breast in his other hand, she pulled up her skirt to her waist. Here, too, she was wearing nothing underneath. The inside of her thighs had fine, golden hair. She sidled against his front and pulled at the belt and buttons of his pants, a grin in place. She released him, exposing him to the room. The couple on the divan had collapsed into a rumpled pile and could not have been less interested.

"Business . . . really," Fedorin panted.

Gripping his member tightly in one hand and his neck with the other, she lifted herself. She slipped, laughed huskily, and hitched herself higher, climbing with her thighs. Fedorin would have helped, but he was still fixed on her breasts, which now had trapped his hands against his chest. They had a life of their own, squirming under his palms and heating him to his shoulders. She climbed onto him.

Just as she was about to lower herself onto him, she breathed, "The money, Mika. Even these stools cost pesos."

It took a moment for her words to register, and another before he could pull a hand away. Carrying her weight, he shifted forward on the stool to reach for his wallet. His first frantic stab at his pocket missed, and just as he pulled the wallet out, the police entered the Club Sharad.

At least, in the dim light, Fedorin guessed they were police, as they and the militia wore similar green uniforms. He panicked. Cubans view their forced relationship with the Soviets as anathema, and the police were no exception. They would delight in arresting him for soliciting, pretending they didn't understand his diplomatic status. They would drag him to the People's Court Building and only then call the ambassador to confirm Fedorin's position. Sokolov would have to come to the jail to obtain his release. It had happened before, to Gennadi Kisayev, the agent Fedorin had replaced in Havana. At the embassy, hilarious stories were still told of Kisayev's humiliation.

With Carla straddling him, Fedorin jumped off the stool. "Bastards. I've got to get out of here." He lurched for the back door.

She instinctively clutched him tighter and shrieked with alarm. The police came in once a week, ostensibly for an inspection, but in fact for *chivo,* literally a goat, but slang for graft. They wanted rum. She knew them well. She screeched because Fedorin began galloping toward the back door, making only three steps before she lost her hold on his neck and flopped backward, landing on her back on a stool.

He dragged her off the stool, and he yelled in pain as she fiercely clinched his organ to prevent falling to the floor as he tried to get to the curtain. Her leg lock around his waist was firm, and he could not shake her. She hung upside down, and her skirt slid higher, blocking her view. Her free arm flailed for an anchor. She found a stool leg, and she towed the stool across the floor behind her as Fedorin tried to escape. Then her hand caught the wood bar rail, and he was forced to a staggering stop. His eyes locked on the police, who were walking along the bar toward them.

She released him and fell to the floor. As Fedorin flew through the curtain, she rolled to a sitting position and probed her buttocks for bruises. The two policemen helped her to her feet. One asked, "Do you want us to go after that guy, Carla?"

171

"No, no, no." She patted her skirt into place and buttoned the blouse. "But you could have waited until he had paid me. Aren't you fellows early today?"

Victor Fedorin plunged through the stockroom, buttoning his pants and fighting his belt. He looked over his shoulder but saw no one in pursuit. Maybe dropping Carla in front of them had helped.

He trotted through the back door and almost toppled Justo Cantillo, who was rushing into his bar to investigate the commotion. The barman was behind him and continued inside.

Fedorin blurted, "The police."

Cantillo brushed away the Russian's alarm with his hand. "They come every week. Give them a little of the local product, and they're back out the door. Nothing like the Revolutionary Offensive." Cantillo referred to Castro's 1968 sudden fit of prudishness when he closed all of Havana's bars and night-clubs. Cantillo was a man in his fifties, with silver hair the same color as the square metal frames of his spectacles. He had a veined, bulbous nose and strong, irregular teeth. His skin was the color of an old banana. "Straighten out your pants, and I'll show you what I've got."

Wood crates leaned against the back of the building. Cantillo pried a plank off one and pulled out a bottle of Aquardiente Carta de Cano rum. "I've got twenty-four hundred bottles."

Fedorin glanced nervously at the back door. "Put fifty on the embassy's account, and I'll pay pesos for the rest, right now."

Cantillo whistled. "All of them? Big profits in our rum these days?"

Since Gorbachev had restricted production of vodka in the Soviet Union in an attempt to get workers to their jobs on Mondays, demand for Fedorin's Cuban rum had soared. "All of them."

"I don't know." Cantillo shook his head. "I've got an American I sell this stuff to, also. A good customer. I'll have to keep fifty cases for him."

172

Fedorin said, "I'll increase my price six pesos a bottle."

"Sold, every last one of them." Cantillo rubbed his hands together with undisguised greed. "The American can wait."

"Goddamn *norteamericanos*," Fedorin said, echoing his Center training with sincerity.

"No, you'd like this one, Victor. You really would."

Chapter XII

Maurice and Rear Admiral Bud Goldman stood on a short dock not far from a runway at the Key West Naval Station. To their left was moored a Chanticleer-class support ship, the *Sunbird*. It was difficult to talk over the takeoff roars of the F-14 Tomcats behind them, so Maurice remained silent. He had a manila envelope in his hand.

Goldman was commander of the Key West base. He had a pinched face and a small head, and Maurice guessed his hat size to be five and a half. Goldman's eyebrows were sharply arched like an inverted checkmark, and his eyes were set deep over dark pouches. He was wearing summer whites.

A hundred yards from the dock the sea stirred, then fell away from a rising tower. It was a red post under a dome light, followed by a windshield bubble atop the conning tower. Then the aileron wing and the rest of the tower emerged. Water bubbled around it.

The research submarine NR-3 drew near. Two crewmen emerged from a hatch to handle mooring lines. Several sailors from the base walked onto the dock and coiled lines, readying to throw them to the sub. The submarine moved silently and left almost no wake.

"About a hundred and twenty feet," the admiral offered. "Has a crew of ten."

"Doesn't sound too cramped," Maurice said. The sound of the fighters had faded.

"Over half that length is taken up by its nuclear generator. It's so crowded that the crew has to share hot bunks. Only half of them can sleep any one time."

"How long can it stay submerged?"

"We'll admit to forty days. If we could get the crew to eat nothing but high-energy pills, it'd be longer. The main restriction is the limited space to store food. The sub has only been out three hours today, training crew members and breaking in a new marine biologist."

The conning tower, aileron, and aft fin were the color of a fire engine. The hull was black, and water from the cooling system spilled down its side. A radio antenna rose high above the tower. A number of small gadgets—wires and bulges—were attached to the hull and the tower, and Maurice could only guess at their purpose.

An officer climbed from the tower's cockpit, landed on the hull, and jumped across to the dock. He smartly saluted the admiral and said, "We weren't expecting you, Admiral Goldman."

The admiral introduced the officer as Commander Edward Waite. Maurice knew Waite was a graduate of the Naval Academy and, like all NR-3's crew, was a veteran of the ballistic missile and attack nuclear submarine services before being assigned to the research sub. Waite was a thick man, with arms and thighs that pushed against his khaki uniform and a short, muscled neck. He had caps on two upper teeth that didn't quite match the white of his other teeth. Lost them playing football at the academy, Maurice had read. Waite was wearing a cap with scrambled eggs on its brim. He had a round face and a nose that flared at its base. His grin was quick as Maurice shook his hand.

When the admiral said Maurice was from the Central Intelligence Agency, the commander's smile grew even broader. Waite said, "Please tell me you're taking me away from researching sea slugs and anemones."

"Maybe, for a while," Maurice said. "I want to talk to you about what your sub can do." Maurice already knew about the sub. He wanted to take the pulse of its crew.

"Why don't I take you out for a few minutes. Nothing'll impress you more with NR-3 than a spin. If it's all right with you, admiral."

Goldman said, "I've been told by the secretary of defense, who had never deigned to speak with me personally before today, that Mr. Maurice's suggestions are my orders. Anything he wants."

"Let's go, then."

Maurice said, "The admiral said you've got a biologist on board. I want to talk to him, too."

They left the admiral on the dock. The hatch was made for a more slender man than Maurice, and he had to turn sideways to descend into the control station. He carried the envelope in his teeth. He landed on a circular worn spot on the station deck. Because it was one of the few spots on board with any headroom, the crew used the area to jog in place.

When Waite reached the deck, he quickly acquainted Maurice with his crew, who were surprised they were going out again. When the commander told them Maurice's affiliation, their interest was immediate and intense. They, too, were tired of photographing never-before-seen organisms in never-before-reached canyons of the ocean. All except Dr. Milt Wilson, of the Woods Hole Oceanographic Institution, who wondered in a crabbed voice what the CIA wanted with "his" boat.

Excited and speculating loudly, the crew returned to their stations. Muttering over his shoulder, the biologist climbed into

176

a narrow chamber beneath the control station's deck to a viewing station, where he would lie flat and peer out a circular port. The submarine sailed slowly away from land, and when Lieutenant Commander Charles Brickell descended the ladder, he screwed the hatch into place. He took his place at the pilot's console, which was lit by sonar screens, video monitors, and LCD readouts. The control station filled with the sound of water and air rushing through pipes as the ballast filled. The nose of the craft dipped gently, and Maurice could feel his ears as the boat pressurized. The sub seemed to press in on him. There was something morbidly final about the clang of a hatch closing and the hiss of water filling the cavities around him.

Maurice followed the commander three steps to the mess, nothing more than a two-person bench and a table as wide as a forearm is long. He slid in after Waite. In front of them, attached to the bulkhead, were a television set and a microwave, a coffee maker, and a crib of cups. A tape deck and VCR were near the television. In another rack were spices and A.1. Steak Sauce and envelopes of Kool-Aid, and in another stereo tapes and movies. Quite a collection, Maurice saw. Everything from *Empire of the Sun* to *Nurse Nelly's Naughties.*

Behind them was the wardroom, a small closet with four bunks, one on top of the other, giving each sleeper the height of his chest plus four inches. Little tombs within the tomb.

"Can NR-3 sit on the ocean floor?" Maurice asked, accepting coffee from Waite. It was strong but did not wash away the smell of the air, which had a tin-can scent to it.

"We've got small wheels on the underside. We can slide along the bottom, or we can rest there."

"What's its speed?"

"No more than four knots submerged, and not much faster on the surface. The ship you saw above, the *Sunbird,* tows us to our duty station. NR-3 is built for depth and duration, not speed. I don't know what the agency has in mind, but this is the most versatile sub in the navy. We've got bow and stern thrusters, and can do a three-sixty almost without any forward

177

motion. And for exterior work, we've got a forward manipulator arm that can pluck anything off the bottom. We've got camera and recording gear. We've got a gertrude, and can talk with surface ships. And we can go as deep as you'd ever want to go, and stay there for as long as you'd ever want to stay."

"What about an underwater hatch?"

"There's only one such hatch for the three subs in this class. It's used by the SEALs on occasion. It's up at the Undersea Warfare Engineering Station in Washington State."

"Are you trained to use it?"

"You bet. It takes about a week to ship it down here from Washington."

"I'll have it in Key West tomorrow, " Maurice said.

"Look, Bill, I'm tempted to lick my chops here. Can you tell me what's going on? Something other than squiring scientists around?"

Maurice nodded. "You'll be starting the training today, but before you get rid of the scientists, I've got to speak to one of them. I'm told Dr. Wilson below knows all there is about coral reefs."

"He'd use coral as a pillow if his wife would let him." Waite lifted the intercom and asked for the biologist. He appeared a moment later, a thirty-five-millimeter camera around his neck with a rubber ring around the lens to prevent it from scraping against the glass of the viewing port. When Maurice pulled several photographs from the envelope, Wilson sank onto his haunches to look at them.

Maurice said, "This is a satellite recon photo of a reef in the Caribbean. Would you mind telling me something about it, Dr. Wilson?"

Wilson wore a brown beard and hair to his shoulders, in stark contrast with the clean-shaven sailors. He had wire-rim glasses and ears that stuck out at an acute angle from the wild hair. The tails of his plaid Pendleton shirt hung free. His jeans had the deliberate prewashed look, and he wore black-and-red Air Jordans. "Well, there're three kinds of reefs in the Carib-

178

bean: barrier, atoll, and this type, a fringing reef. It's the kind that you find surrounding the islands here."

Maurice spread the photos out on the table and pointed at one. "What are these shadings?"

"A reef has zonations. I'd guess this particular reef is on the north side of the island."

"That's right," Maurice said. "How'd you know?"

"There are two kinds of zonations in the Caribbean. High-energy reefs are on atolls and on the windward portions of islands. And there are low-energy reefs, like this one. These tend to be more poorly developed, and are on the leeward side."

Wilson warmed to the work and spoke with enthusiasm. Maurice guessed the scientist felt like a sixth finger on the sub, not appreciated by the sailors.

Wilson lectured, "This is apparently a blowup of the first photo, and here you can see the sections of the reef. The outermost portion, here, is the reef front, usually completely submerged, sometimes as deep as seventy meters. Then behind it is the outer reef flat, which is often the shallowest part of a reef complex, in the Caribbean sometimes only a meter deep. Here you get the soft corals and the encrusting red algae. There's a lot of bare rock and gravel here, also."

Maurice withdrew a diagram from the envelope and handed it to the biologist.

"This is a bathymetric profile of the same reef, looks like."

"That's right," Maurice said.

"The structure of the reef is easier to see on the profile. Behind the outer flat is the inner flat, this wide area here. It's covered with white sand and rubble, and is a little deeper. Next is the lagoon, where you can see on this photo a few types of massive stony coral. From the profile we can see the lagoon is about ten meters deep. And then comes the leeward reef, that part of the reef closest to land."

"Lots of fish near a reef?"

Wilson looked at Maurice as he might the school dummy.

"Maybe I'd better switch to one-syllable words." He smiled to take the edge off it.

Undeterred, Maurice asked again, "Lots of fish?"

"Of course. A reef is an enormously productive ecosystem, except in the lagoon, where in the Caribbean the sluggish circulation of the lagoon water and the high rate of evaporation results in supersaline water. Lagoon water has a residency of one to two months. Too salty for many of the fish."

"Millions of fish near the reef?" the commander teased Wilson. "Or billions of fish? You should know these things, Milt."

Maurice pulled another photograph from the envelope. This shot, much less magnified, showed the same reef, the tidal water behind it, and a land mass south of the reef. On the photograph near an end of the reef were a dozen red ink dots.

"Let me ask you a hypothetical, doctor," Maurice said, pushing the photograph to Wilson. "These red dots represent locations where a person has gone skin diving over the past three months. You can see there's a lot of reef, about two miles of it here, but the dots appear only in one area. Why does this person repeatedly return to this spot?"

Wilson asked, "Where is this reef?"

"Sorry. What can you tell me based only on these photos?"

"Well, there's an easy enough explanation. You can see a break in the reef here. That's caused by the fresh water that pours into the sea from the river you can see here on your photo."

"Coral can't grow in diluted seawater?" Maurice asked.

"That's right. So, based on the scale graph on this photo, you've got a three-quarter-mile gap in the reef at this location. Due to the river."

"Then why does a skin diver like this location so much?"

"Simply because the gap in the reef is where the ocean fish can meet and eat the reef fish. It's a place for feeding. There'd be an incredible hodgepodge of predator fish and small reef fish here. An ideal place for skin or scuba diving." The biologist pointed at the dots. "At this point, just off the land side of the reef, a diver is protected from ocean rollers, but he would still have the fish mix."

Wilson paused, understanding suddenly narrowing his face. He asked indignantly, "Are you going after someone? Using this research sub for some sort of undercover high jinks?"

Maurice turned to Waite. "I've seen enough. Let's return to shore."

Chapter XIII

Grabbing the rim for balance, Maurice knelt next to Mederos on the catwalk that ringed the tank. He asked, "How's the mask feel?"

The diving mask covered Mederos's eyes and nose, and his voice sounded adenoidal. "I'm still tender."

The bandages were gone. He was sitting on the lip of the ten-thousand-gallon tank that had been reconstructed in the warehouse that day. The tank was made of formed steel sections and had a viewing window in one side, where Jack Cantrell was waiting for Maurice. Cantrell's face was tight with worry. The sound of a water heater could be heard over the soft lapping of waves.

Also waiting for Mederos, two navy SEALs were already in the water, staying afloat by slowly working their fins. One wore scuba gear including a wetsuit, the other only a mask, fins, and trunks.

Anthony Salisci, the plastic surgeon, was on the Cuban's other side. Water had sprinkled his wingtips and suit pants. He pushed his glasses up his nose, leaned closer to Mederos, and said, "Don't scrape the mask along your skin. Carefully lift it away from your face, then pull it up and off."

Mederos did as told. His eyes were blackened and puffy from the rhinoplasty. The surgeon tilted Mederos's head, examining the stitches behind his ears. Then he palpated Mederos's cheek, examining the tiny sutures. "Your stitches can take it. But be gentle with the mask." He looked doubtfully at the divers. "Nothing about those two fellows looks gentle, so go easy on yourself, Eduardo."

The doctor's casual assessment of the SEALs was accurate. The sailor with the air tank and regulator was Mouse Bretcher, so named because once during a session on plastic explosives a mouse had darted into the classroom toward Bretcher's chair. Bretcher had flattened it with his hand, lifted it by the tail, and dropped it into his mouth. He calmly chewed and swallowed it, without missing a stroke with his pencil in his spiral binder and not giving his awestruck classmates a glance. The instructor, a navy commodore who well knew his student body, asked indifferently, "How was it?" Bretcher replied without looking up, "Could have used a little marinara sauce." Even in a group known for bizarre acts of showboat courage, this was a bravura performance, and the nickname was a medal bestowed by his mates. Bretcher's body resembled a square knot, muscles twisted on muscles and tautly wrapped around a narrow frame. Under the mask, his hazel eyes flashed with amusement at Mederos's caution with the mask.

The other diver was a Mexican American named Miguel Sosa, who was the Pacific Fleet welterweight champion, who had also studied Japanese shito-ryu karate for ten years, and whose constant refrain was, "I'm quitting this chicken outfit and going pro." Sosa had twenty-nine wins and only one loss, a forfeit that occurred when, after an illegal head butt by his opponent, Sosa had twisted sideways on the ball of his foot and performed a *yoko geri*, a side kick with the flat of his foot to the opponent's knee, shattering the bone and sending the opponent writhing to the mat. Sosa laughed then, and he laughed now as the doctor probed Mederos's face.

Through Cantrell, Maurice had asked the secretary of the navy for the navy's two hardest men, which produced Bretcher and Sosa, members of the SEAL's Team Six. They kicked toward Mederos when he slipped into the water. The Cuban flinched as the pressure of the water pressed the mask against his sutures. When he waved he was all right, Maurice left him in the hands of the SEALs and climbed down from the tank rim.

He and Cantrell walked into the warehouse's office. "I just got off the phone again from Washington. This morning Senator White called a press conference. He announced that a new bomber has been sighted in Cuba. We don't know how he found out, but he called it the Blackjack, and he was accurate as to its flight and weapons capabilities. He has called on the president to demand the bomber's removal and, if that doesn't work, to establish an air and sea embargo around Cuba."

"I thought the Senate intelligence chair was going to keep White under control," Maurice said as they passed a booth where they heard Castro's amplified voice.

Cantrell said, "The *New York Times* and *Washington Post* are going to banner the story on their next editions' front pages, as are many other papers across the country. The president is considering addressing the nation tomorrow, to defuse what he fears will be a huge outcry."

Maurice rubbed his temple. "Our time is getting shorter."

"Shorter than you know. I was just given more instructions from the DCI. He wants you to limit Mederos's impersonation to two days."

"In and out within forty-eight hours?"

Cantrell nodded.

"That's cutting it close."

They arrived at the Apollo workstation. Jones was digging

184

into a box of Milk Duds. Maurice said, "This is the kind of second-guessing you said we would be spared."

"You should have known better. But the DCI is right. He thinks risks of discovery are so great that the best way to avoid them is to severely restrict the time of exposure. Can you get everything done in two days?"

"Maybe," Maurice said. He asked Jones, "During the missile crisis, did Castro completely alter his schedule?"

Jones did not need his computer. "Not as much as you'd think. He saw fewer people, but otherwise it was important to him to maintain the appearance of normality. Castro would view it as cowardly to alter his schedule." Jones smiled. "You're asking me if he went skin diving during those three weeks."

Maurice dipped his chin.

"Five times. And he went bird hunting twice. He apparently uses the outdoors to relieve stress."

Cantrell was called away to the STU-3 telephone. Maurice sat next to Jones and accepted a handful of Milk Duds. He asked, "When's the last time anything new came in on Eduardo?"

Jones's round face registered surprise. He chewed the gummy candy before answering, "Now is not the time to wonder about the main component of your scheme."

Maurice hadn't told Cantrell or Jones about finding Mederos in the swamp. The background check on the Cuban was still running, as they had recruited him before he could be fully certified. Time was of the essence, the agency had assured Maurice.

Jones brought up Mederos's file. "The FBI report came in forty minutes ago." Jones chewed on a lip as he read the screen. "Listen to this. Eduardo recently began an association with a Cuban exile paramilitary organization. One of their members is an FBI agent, and he reports that he was at their firing range east in the swamp country. Says here you showed up and took him away."

When Cantrell returned to the computer, Jones swiveled

185

the monitor to him. He read down the screen, then said, "Damn it, Bill, you should've mentioned something about that, instead of waiting for us to get the bureau report. We don't need anybody from a kook patrol around here."

Maurice asked, "Did the FBI give any reason Eduardo might, after all these years away from Cuba, have any dealings with these people?"

"Nothing on that," Jones replied. "You asked him about it?"

"I didn't get much of an answer. I'm tempted to ascribe it to middle-age crisis or homesickness. But have your people keep looking, will you, Jack? Gerard, show me a list of Soviets at their embassy in Havana."

The list appeared after a moment. Ambassador Yuri Kirillovich Sokolov was at the top, followed, as Jones scrolled the screen, by thirty-five other names in the order of the agency's estimate of their positions at the embassy.

"Can you ask your machine to list only those Russians with guaranteed access to Castro?"

"Nobody has that privilege, not even Raul, much less any of the Russians," Cantrell said.

Maurice suggested, "Try bringing up a list of those Russians who have had an audience with Fidel this past year, in order of the number of times they have seen him."

"I can do it off the top of my head, if you want." Jones's syllables were softened by a Milk Dud.

"The reason we trained you in computers, Toothbrush, is so we wouldn't have to listen to you list things all the time," Cantrell said. "Put it on the screen."

The list came up. Only eight Soviets remained, beginning with Ambassador Sokolov, then Liaison Officer Major Viktor Fedorin, Navy Captain First Rank Ivan Rogov and Colonel Fedor Gorshkov, both military advisers, Security Adviser Colonel Vadim Nilov, Economics Professor Rudolf Babkenovich, and two others.

Jones said, "All except the ambassador are presumed to also hold KGB ranks, and maybe even him."

"Print the list out, will you, Gerard?" Maurice asked.

As he lifted the pages from the laser printer's tray, an agent signaled Cantrell to the telephone. Cantrell listened for a moment and put the phone down. "Guillermo Callejas found the driver. You want him to do the interview?"

Castro's military driver in the late 1970s had been court-martialed and imprisoned for a crime spree that over the course of thirty-six drunken hours included battery on a superior officer, auto theft, AWOL, burglary, two further counts of battery, and resisting arrest. After serving a year in prison, he was put on a boat at Mariel.

Maurice looked at his watch. "I'm hungry, and am tired of takeout. Let's do it ourselves."

Thirty minutes later, Maurice and Cantrell walked into the Punta Gorda restaurant on Calle Ocho. Callejas had given the chauffeur fifty dollars to wait in the restaurant. The driver had used some of it to buy a drink, and the change remained on the table next to his glass, as if he were going to drink his way through the money.

Stationed next to an old brass cash register, a receipt spike, and open boxes of cigars, the Punta Gorda's owner grinned broadly at Maurice and Cantrell as they entered. The restaurant had a narrow aisle between the serving counter and a row of booths. Much of the day's cooking was in dishes under heat lamps on the counter. The glass dessert case contained porcelain cups of rum flan and *natilla,* vanilla custard. Behind the counter, the cook was partly hidden by a cloud of steam. Another *gastronamico* was bent over the sink. The restaurant smelled of spicy pork. From a jukebox came "Juana Mil Ciento" by the Cuban rumba-rock group Irakere. A yellow Shell fly strip hung in the doorway to the restrooms.

Callejas had posted himself next to the door. He nodded at Cantrell and left the restaurant. The DDO and Maurice slid into the booth opposite Faustino Queseda. They ignored Queseda while they both ordered steak with onions and *ajiaco.* Cantrell also asked for a red-beet salad. Maurice ordered his dessert early: *cucurucho*, a sticky mass of shredded coconut and pineapple wrapped in banana leaves.

Queseda nervously twirled the ice in his glass. For fifty dollars he had not bargained on two questioners. And one of them, the thick-necked, short-haired, gruff fellow, looked like he could tear the table in two.

"How long were you an army driver in Cuba?" Maurice asked in English without introducing himself. Queseda had bathed sometime the previous month, Maurice guessed. His thin hair was stuck to his scalp with oil, and he gave off an odor that made Maurice wonder if he'd be able to eat in the same room with him. Queseda looked hungry, with skin collapsed under his cheekbones and brown veins showing along his jaw. Skin was sucked up under his chin. His eyes were so sunken Maurice felt he had to grope for them. Queseda wore a length of cowhide around his neck, a chipped turquoise ring, and a filthy plaid shirt.

"You the police?"

Maurice withdrew his wallet from his pants pocket and threw two more fifties at the Cuban. "We're some people who want some answers."

Queseda's hand stabbed at the bills. "I've got all the answers you need."

"How long?"

"I wasn't just any army driver," Queseda puffed. "I drove Fidel. His personal chauffeur. He treated me like his son."

"He let you be drummed out of the army and right into prison," Cantrell said.

Queseda took a long breath, staring at his drink. "Rum put me into prison, not Fidel."

"How long'd you drive Castro?"

"Two years, 1978 and 1979."

"What kind of car?"

"Mostly a Mercedes-Benz. Sometimes an American jeep or a rebuilt East German scout car if he was going into the country."

"How many guards along usually?" Maurice asked. The

188

food arrived, and he lifted a dispenser to sprinkle ground peppers on the meat. Next came salt and pepper, then, on reflection, more salt.

"You guys are from the Central Intelligence Agency," Queseda said. "Those bastards are the only kinds who'd ask questions like that."

This time Cantrell reached into his wallet. Five one-hundred-dollar bills were pushed across the table to the Cuban. "This money buys your information. I should also tell you that there will be grave downside risks if you tell anybody about our conversation."

Queseda picked up the money, but slowly. "What are 'downside risks'?"

Maurice pointed his fork at Cantrell, switched to Spanish, and said with a smile, as if teasing Cantrell, "My friend here is a *botellero*." A government payroller. Maurice leaned across the table confidentially. "And they use fancy words like that. Downside risks means getting your throat cut."

Queseda jumped back against the booth. He dropped the money as if it were a hot plate. Maurice gathered it up and pressed it into his hand and rolled his fingers around it. "Silence keeps you healthy." He cut into his steak with a knife. In English, "So how many guards?"

The Cuban studied the money. He said finally, "Always one in the car with him, plus the driver."

"What weapons?"

"Driver and bodyguard have pistols, and there's a submachine gun on the floor near their feet, an AK-47."

"Bodyguards in following cars?" Cantrell asked. He had foolishly imitated Maurice with the pepper and was exhaling quickly, blowing off nearly toxic vapors in his mouth.

"Always at least one car in front and one following, unless he is away from the city. There is also always a sweeper car a quarter mile in front of him, just checking for trouble. When he hunts or fishes, the sweeper car is not there. Fidel feels safer in the country, he told me that himself."

"Does Fidel ever drive himself?"

189

"He hates to drive. Never does."

They questioned Faustino Queseda for an hour. Twice Cantrell had to drop a few more bills on the table. The struggle between Cuban patriotism and greed was evident in Queseda's twisted expression each time Maurice or Cantrell pressed him further. And he soothed his anger at being cashiered from the army with shots of rum, which Cantrell freely supplied.

Maurice ordered another dessert, *plantanos*, and slowly ate the baked banana slices while he asked Queseda about the security arrangements at Castro's usual destinations. His hunting and fishing lodges, Celia Sánchez's duplex, and the others. Finally Maurice got around to Las Paz, to the boathouse at the Bay of Mulata. "So where is the limousine parked when Fidel is out in the boat?"

Queseda mentioned that usually Fidel flew in his helicopter to Las Paz, and only three or four times did he use an automobile. Yes, he always dried off and donned his uniform on the boat on the way to shore. He always handled his catch until he got to the car, when he would hand the net to a bodyguard. Queseda didn't think Fidel cared what happened to the fish once he got them to land. He never gave orders to have them cooked for his dinner. Queseda didn't even think Fidel liked eating the fish, just hunting them. He also always carried the speargun until he arrived back at the limousine. No, Fidel didn't have a spare uniform with him. He didn't carry a personal weapon in a holster anymore. Fidel had taken to leaving his pistol behind, Queseda said, a sure sign the revolution was maturing. Hundreds of other questions. Cantrell had to excuse himself to the men's room once to change the tape in his pocket recorder.

By the time Cantrell paid for the meal, Queseda was too inebriated to leave the booth. Cantrell again invoked the term "downside risk," and the Cuban sluggishly nodded and made a gesture of sealing his mouth, missing his lips and poking himself in the nose. On their way out of the Punta Gorda, Maurice paid for a cup of coffee for Queseda, whom they left behind.

* * *

190

Nico Galvez had boosted the bathroom scales from the J. C. Penney store in Dadeland. He was fat enough so that no one noticed him stroll out of the store with both of them hidden under his shirt. He needed two scales. Because he had broken a number of them, he gingerly put a foot on the first machine and lifted his second foot to the other. He carried a pad and pencil in his hand.

Bathroom scales were not made for people who truly needed them. Every day Galvez performed contortions—bending forward while trying not to topple from the scales—to see around his stomach. Today each scale read 176. Before stepping down, he added up the figures. Three fifty-two. Not bad for someone seven-foot-four. Trouble was, Nico Galvez was a foot shorter than that.

His head looked like a rough plug, with his hair cut short and the roll of fat at the back of his neck. He had tiny ears, resembling coat buttons. His nose had a lump in it, the result of a rifle butt, and its base was almost as wide as his mouth. His sloping shoulders began at his ears. His arms were as large as anyone else's thighs, and not much of that bulk was fat. He wore a T-shirt, and much of his belly hung below it.

Galvez frequently tried losing weight, but in twenty-five years the longest he had stuck to a diet was an hour and a half. He had no testicles, so no women. And every man needed something. Food was his solace. Most of his waking hours, he ate. He had heard that men with no *cojónes* usually gained weight. Something about missing hormones. So his rotund shape wasn't entirely his fault.

The floor creaking under him, Galvez walked to the refrigerator and pulled out a dozen chicken drumsticks he had purchased already breaded and cooked down at Adolfo's Market. The refrigerator had broken years ago, and Galvez found no need to fix it. No food or drink lasted long enough in his home to need preserving. Galvez shopped at the grocery store daily, bringing back as much food as he could carry. The load was gone by morning.

Galvez lived in a clapboard house two blocks south of Calle

Ocho. A hurricane fence surrounded the lot. To the distress of the fastidious gardeners in the neighborhood, the lot had gone to weed. The azalea bushes on the side of the house were never trimmed and were ensnared in the black iron bars that covered the windows. The green composite roof had gaps exposing the lath planking. Blisters the size of pancakes dappled the house's white paint. And, scandalously, he had allowed a small brick shrine in his front yard to be overrun. Weeds grew around the Virgin and completely obscured the Child. Galvez had moved into the house ten years before and had done precisely no maintenance. Too busy eating.

Galvez tore into the sixth drumstick before reaching for a quart of milk. He drained the container in five seconds. Still thirsty, he opened a can of warm beer and emptied that without lowering it. Bananas were the staple of Cuban infants, and Galvez had never outgrown his taste for them. He tossed four down his gullet. Then back to the drumsticks.

He dropped the bones, beer can, and carton into a pyramid of garbage that completely hid his trash container. He lived in squalor. Using a wheelbarrow, he took his kitchen garbage out once a week, which by then was in a pile halfway up the refrigerator. At night his kitchen was a living thing, as everything he lifted—a cup, a spoon, a doughnut, a hunk of cheese—produced a stream of roaches darting for cover.

When he moved into the house, he had rented three rooms of furniture for twenty dollars a month. He defaulted on the payment after the second month, and when a truck driver arrived on his doorstep to reclaim the furniture, Galvez shoved a fistful of Fig Newtons into the man's mouth and told him next time it would be a brick. That was the last Galvez had heard from the furniture company. He had long ago shattered the dinette chairs simply by sitting on them, so for a chair he used a wood cable spool he had found next to the highway. The living room sofa was bowed to the floor, and its upholstery was in tatters.

Galvez used the sofa to play with his dog, Ass End, who

192

was sitting on its haunches in front of the couch, waiting for Galvez to toss him a couple of chicken bones. The dog was a 110-pound American pit bullterrier, a breed not recognized by the American Kennel Club because they were bred to a gameness standard rather than an appearance standard. Ass End was so named because when it was a puppy Nico Galvez thought its face resembled its behind.

The dog had a red coat with a white, wide, sprung chest. One of the dog's ears was cropped, and the other had been torn off almost at scalp level and looked as if it had been done with pinking shears. Its eyes were slits low on its skull. Its short muzzle was almost perfectly square, and its nose was a burnt red. Ass End had killed four dogs in the pit and a giant schnauzer on the street. All told, the dog had received 340 stitches in its career, done by Galvez with alcohol, a sewing needle, and thread. Ass End was spoken highly of by pit men in Florida.

Part of a fighting dog's training is tug-of-war. Galvez used whatever was handy—the sofa, throw rugs, a bedspread, the curtains, anything. There wasn't a piece of cloth anywhere in Galvez's home larger than a square yard. An automobile tire hung from a rope in the hall. Attached below the tire was a pad of leather.

Other than the couch, the spool, and a television set propped on a stool, the only items in the room were dog training equipment. A treadmill was against one wall, where Galvez could watch television and run Ass End at the same time. From a hat rack hung near a side window were half a dozen collars, including a choke chain and several leather collars with brass or stainless-steel studs. Most any dog man will say that a pit bull looks better wearing a studded collar. The collars originated in central Europe, where they were used to prevent wolves from mauling sheepdogs. Studded collars were used by American pit men only for their appearance, as they were not allowed in the pit. Nico Galvez had a variety on his hat rack, from a red cowhide collar with Levi's brass brads to an alligator-leather collar with half-inch, needle-sharp, steel barbs that were almost two inches long. Ass End's neck was as large as a man's thigh.

"You need a little training today, Ass End," Galvez said in Spanish. His voice was girlish. "Can't let you get soft."

Galvez pointed to the tire, letting the dog get set, its energy and enthusiasm building visibly. The Cuban ordered loudly, "Ass End, go."

Chicken bones forgotten, the dog rocketed off the floor, chomped down on the leather, and hung, its rear feet completely off the floor. Galvez pushed its compact, columnar body against the bathroom door, then banged it against the hall wall, but the dog remained hanging, its jaws savagely clamped on the leather.

Leaving Ass End suspended, Galvez returned to his chicken. He didn't like the dog. He'd bought the pit bull because it had *cojónes* enough for two. The dog had never understood whose house this was and was just as quick to piss on the living room's TV stand as on a tree outside. At those times, Ass End would stare villainously at Galvez, daring him to do anything. The house stank.

And once the son of a bitch had bitten him clean through his hand so that the dog's mouth was closed again. Snapped three bones and put the hand in a cast for two months. The only thing keeping Ass End from a bullet was that a New Jersey pit man had offered Galvez a thousand dollars for the dog, thinking no one in New Jersey knew the dog's reputation, and he'd be able to beat the odds up north. The New Jersey fellow was due in Miami at the end of the month. Then, so long, Ass End.

Galvez dropped the last bone on the pile and opened the cellophane around a half pound of cheese. He began rhythmically at one end of the bar. He gave Ass End another push, swinging him into the wall. The dog's evil yellow eyes rolled to the cheese.

The Cuban dropped onto the sofa, which groaned. When he ate, he often thought back over the cruel fate that had sent

194

him here, to this dump and this dog and this girth, which meant he dwelt on it interminably. The great love of Nico Galvez's life had been Fidel Castro. Galvez had been on the *Granma*, one of the original eighty-two who set sail from Tuxpan, Mexico, on the night of July 24–25, 1956. The spark of the revolution. Seven days later the ship landed in the southwest corner of Oriente Province, and Galvez should have entered Cuban legend, like Raul and Juan Almeida and José Smith and Che Guevara and Galvez's brother, Carlos, with whom Nico had shared one of the *Granma*'s bunks on the fearful crossing.

Instead, four months after the landing, Nico Galvez was captured near Pico Turquino, the Blue Mountain, by the Guardia Rural, troops of Batista's army intelligence chief, the barbarous killer Colonel Lorenzo Piloto. The Batistianos beat him senseless with their rifle stocks, then waited until he had regained consciousness before pinning him to the ground and pulling off his pants. Of all that would follow, Galvez's harshest memory was not of the Batistianos yanking his *cojónes* away from him as far as the sack would stretch, then slicing them off with a bayonet, but how ludicrous he looked, lying on the ground with his pants bundled around his shoes. No man should be seen without his pants.

Galvez had blacked out again, this time suffocating because his testicles had been stuffed into his throat, when Lorenzo Piloto happened on the scene. He ordered his men to fish them out, then throw water into Galvez's face. The colonel laughed at the sight, Galvez on his knees retching onto his *cojónes*, which lay in the mud under him. Although Piloto appreciated his soldiers' sense of humor, he told them to spare what was left of Galvez. A Fidelista might be useful.

They kept him in a *bartolina*, a cell so small he could neither stand nor lie. A week later Piloto dragged Galvez from his cell to stand in front of Galvez's mother, whom the Batistianos had found in Bayamo. Galvez had not seen his mother in three years. She was a withered peasant wearing a black shawl, so

195

terrified she had to be held up by two soldiers. They let him gaze upon her for only a moment before taking her away. The colonel told him he was to return to the rebel army, which was hiding in the Sierra Maestra range. The enormous scab on his crotch would be proof to Fidel that Galvez had not betrayed them. And Galvez would report weekly to Piloto on one of the rebel army's radios. Location and troop strength. The colonel gave him a frequency, a time, and an alternate time. If he did not receive a transmission, Piloto would murder Galvez's mother.

Galvez's mother was two steps from the grave anyway, so when he found the army, he told Fidel everything. Galvez was grateful when Fidel did not make him drop his trousers in front of Raul and Ramiro Valdes and Ciro Redondo and his own brother, Carlos. Fidel led him into the tent for a private confirmation of the truth. They knew anyway, as Galvez's voice already had lost its deep resonance.

The *guerrilleros* should have embraced Nico Galvez. He had paid dreadful dues. Yet Fidel, who survived by suspicion, could never trust anyone who had been in the Batista camp, not even when he heard that Mother Galvez had been executed by Colonel Piloto. "You'll be our soldier in the United States, Nico," he told him, and in late 1958 Galvez was sent to Miami.

Robbed of the rebel army's glorious entry into Havana. Posted beyond the rewards that had befallen other *Granma* veterans. No seat of honor on the podium behind Fidel during sessions of the National Assembly of People's Power. No home in the Vedado district. His brother, Carlos, had risen with Fidel and was powerful and feared. Yet Nico had remained in exile all these years, doing whatever jobs Carlos ordered. Paid a small amount every month. Never allowed to return home.

Carlos was an ingrate. Nico had always been stronger and harder. Back in the early days, it was Nico who had proposed they join Fidel. He had kept Carlos in training in Mexico, not letting him return to Cuba like some of the other cowards. He had fairly dragged his brother aboard the *Granma*. Carlos never

196

took the initiative, always wanted to take the easy way, never believed in the inevitability of Fidel's revolution. Carlos had always tagged along. Nico should have been chief of Cuban G2.

Instead, he lived in a hovel with a cur that would trade him in for a pound of hamburger. Galvez returned to the kitchen counter. He scooped a pint of sour cream into a mixing bowl and emptied a large bag of Fritos into the bowl. He stirred them with a serving spoon.

"Let's see how long you last hanging there, Ass End." He pushed the dog again, and it bounced against the bathroom door and the wall. It would not release the leather.

Galvez sank again onto the couch, steadily eating his way through the bowl of chips with the spoon. Nothing he did was enough to get him back to his homeland. Hadn't he done everything G2 asked? *A seco.* Just like that. No questions. Many of the enemies of the revolution had heard from Nico Galvez. On his brother's orders, he had destroyed them. It was his singular skill. Destroying.

Nico Galvez had placed the bomb in Jorge Gonzalez's automobile in 1962. One more traitor to the revolution put into the ground. Too bad about the others in the car. The dead woman was one Anne Maurice, the newspapers said. Two others were injured. Couldn't be helped. Galvez chuckled around the mash of Fritos and sour cream in his mouth. As good as Nico was, he couldn't shape a bomb blast.

There had been other bombs. Several pistol shots. One fellow falling from a fourth-story window. A hit-and-run on Calle Ocho. Always performed faithfully on Carlos's orders. And he did odd jobs, too. Depositing money. Making envelope drops. Doing some convincing with his fists. Faithfully and with skill. But it was never enough. I live in a twilight world, he thought sorely, holding the bowl just below his lip and shoveling the mix into his mouth. Not allowed to return to Cuba. Yet I can't refuse my brother's orders.

He was afraid of Carlos, truth be told. His people were everywhere. And they'd be only too happy to dispose of Nico.

197

In his messages, Carlos never made clear what Nico must do to earn his way back to the homeland. And it had been almost thirty years. All those years without balls, and he still was not home.

A knocking on the front door interrupted Nico's angry, self-pitying thoughts. He growled and continued gulping the Fritos. It came again, and with a curse he rolled himself off the sofa and trundled to the door. He opened it slowly, peering malevolently through the crack. It was usually enough to scare a salesman away.

"Hello, Nico. I got your address down at Adolfo's. Hope you don't mind."

Galvez tried to place the scrawny fellow at his door. His puzzlement must have showed in his face, because the man said quickly, "I'm Faustino Queseda. Remember me? We used to tip back the rum at Sixto's Bar and Grill." Queseda's voice fluttered. He planted his right foot squarely, ready to bolt.

Galvez rubbed his head, prodding a memory. Finally he said, "What do you want?"

"I've got some information that might make us both a little money."

Galvez pondered half a minute, then swung his door open. "Want a beer, Faustino?" He crossed to the kitchen counter and passed Queseda a Budweiser without waiting for an answer. He took one for himself.

Queseda squinted into the hall, which was darker than the living room. "You a boxer? That a punching bag?"

"Sometimes." Galvez chopped his fist into Ass End's rib cage. The dog swung silently, its narrow eyes on the visitor.

Galvez lowered himself onto the couch but left Queseda standing in the middle of the room. There were no other chairs. Galvez drank most of his beer in three swallows, then sat silently until Queseda spoke.

"You once told me you had some contact with Fidel's government," Queseda said nervously.

198

Galvez lowered the can. "I probably never said anything like that." Galvez's voice was always sweet. Nothing he could do about that. But there was no mistaking his expression.

Queseda glanced at the door. "Well, you and me'd had quite a bit of liquor. I probably said a lot of things, too. Who knows." He cleared his throat. "But I've got some information Fidel and Carlos Galvez would pay for. Got no way to get it to them, though."

Nico was known as Nico Brava. He'd never told anyone in Miami he was the G2 chief's brother. Never been that drunk. "Why don't you tell me about it, and I'll see what I can do."

Queseda shook his head, a slight movement so as not to offend. "I'm sorry, Nico. But I'm just like a Calle Ocho merchant. I'll need the money in advance. It's worth a thousand dollars, I figure. All I can tell you is that the CIA is up to something."

"That's a lot of money." Galvez belched. "You sure you don't want to trust me?"

"I know I should," Queseda answered unsteadily. "But I've got to protect myself."

Galvez nodded sagely. "I understand completely, *amigo*. I would do the same, were I you."

The vast, distended, pouchy man taking up most of the couch could move with a football lineman's speed. Unbeatable in a three-yard dash, he liked to think. He shot out of the sofa, a colossus in blurred motion. Before Faustino Queseda could make one step to the door, his neck was between Galvez's hands.

Queseda tried to scream, but Galvez increased the pressure. "Shush, now," he said in a warm voice.

He carried Queseda by his neck into the kitchen. Galvez swept aside the dirty pans, then pressed Queseda's right ear to a stove element. He said, "Let me know when you want to talk, Faustino."

Galvez reached across the stove and turned the electric burner on. Queseda screamed with fright as Galvez held his head to the unit. Galvez looked longingly at a box of doughnuts on top of the refrigerator. Ass End swayed gently.

Just when Galvez caught the scent of singeing flesh, Queseda cried, "I'll tell you, Nico. Please, please, I'll tell you everything."

Galvez held him there another five seconds for good measure, then lifted him away from the stove. He said, "You might want to hold one of those beers to your ear. They're still cold."

Queseda slumped to the kitchen floor, panting, his face congealed with pain and fear, and tears coursing down his indented face. A wisp of smoke came from his ear. He probed it gently.

Galvez stopped in the hallway. "Okay, Ass End. You can drop." He gestured to the floor, and the dog released the leather. It fell two feet to the linoleum like a dropped sack of cement. The pit bull followed Galvez to the sofa, but with a snarl the Cuban made it clear he was going to eat all the doughnuts himself.

After two of the powdered sugar ones, Galvez said, "You'd better come in here and tell me all about the CIA, Faustino. You don't want me to come back to the kitchen, believe me."

Carlos Galvez's temporary office was in Morro Castle, at the entrance to Havana harbor. G2 headquarters, called the Green House, on Avenida Quinta near the sea was too small to hold the prisoners of his victorious counterrevolutionary sweep. Galvez had broken the Central Intelligence Agency in Havana. He was sure of it. Three hundred twelve arrests. Find your weak points, Fidel always said, and you will find the CIA. Galvez had found them and was convinced the Americans were now paralyzed in Cuba.

Galvez was bent over an oak table, an ornately carved piece dating from the mid-1700s he had had delivered from his office. A cup of *manzanillo*—herbal tea—was at one corner on a silver coaster. A hundred-page transcript of an interrogation was in front of him. The room had once been a cell, and the

200

stone walls and ceiling pressed in on him. One small, barless window looked out over the sea.

At the foot of the castle, below Galvez's window, was the Battery of the Twelve Apostles, each ancient cannon bearing the name of an apostle. The castle appeared to be pushed up from the jagged rocks on the point. An irregular polygon light-house tower was added in 1844. The forbidding castle had no ornaments and no landscaping. It was barren and windswept and sobering.

In recent times Morro Castle had been used as a store-house, but Galvez found its tiny rooms and two-foot-thick walls ideal for a jail, and in the periodic mass arrests the prisoners were interned here. Galvez scanned the transcript, flipping over page after page. He was wearing an olive uniform and the four gold stars over crossed branches of a general. He looked up and asked, "Do you think that's all he knows?"

One of the interrogators nodded. "He's done."

In a corner of the office was Cuba's infamous garrote, an instrument of execution for a hundred years, ending when Fidel came to power and preferred the bullet. The garrote was a post, four feet high, with two steel bars forming a neckrest at the post's top. Below this iron collar were two parallel steel rails emerging from the post, with a connecting bar swinging from one of them, which fastened to the opposite rail, enclosing the victim's neck. A foot-long screw passed through the post, with a cross bar handle at the rear, the executioner's position. When he turned the handle, the screw tightened the bar around the condemned's neck. The iron neckrest projected slightly from the post, and as the bar tightened it struck against the upper-most vertebra, thrusting the head forward, snapping the spinal cord, killing the victim instantly.

The entire mechanism, including the condemned's seat, could be folded into a wood box, which resembled a bass guitar case. At the turn of the century, the *verdugo*—official execu-tioner—traveled in a circuit, doing his ghoulish business in all Cuba's towns. By this very machine, Cuban patriots Narciso

Lopez in 1851, Gaspar and Diego Aguero y Betancourt during the Ten Years' War, and the desperate murderer Gamoneda in 1897 were put to death.

If the handle was turned slowly, the victim would only black out. Then the bar would be loosened, and he would come to. Then the garrote's handle would be turned again. This torture might last for hours, which had been precisely the fate of the man now on the seat.

"He hasn't given us much." The G2 chief's voice was that of a bank clerk. Dry, bored, his mind elsewhere.

The second questioner was at the garrote's handle. He said, "He's to the point where he'd implicate his parents. He's through."

The victim was a nineteen-year-old newspaper delivery boy for the *Havana Post*. Galvez had suspected him of slipping messages into newspapers. The boy had confessed to that, and to anything else asked of him. Galvez again glanced at the papers. He was interrupted by a brisk knock at the cell door. It opened with a low creak. A messenger entered and handed Galvez a yellow slip of paper.

It was a message from his brother, Nico. Sent via his radio, which he was to use only in the most urgent circumstances. Galvez read it carefully, his mouth turning down, exaggerated by the heavy mustache.

"Comrade, are we finished with him?" asked the G2 agent at the garrote's handle.

Distracted, Galvez looked up. "What? Yes. We're done."

As Galvez went back to the message, the torturer spun the handle so the bar fell away from the boy's neck. The bar was unhooked, and they unstrapped his feet from the chair legs. The victim slumped forward and was caught by the other interrogator. They dragged him to the window, lifted him to its stone sill, and pushed him through. The sill was two feet deep, and they had to push the boy's legs as though they were tamping the apostle's cannons before the victim fell through.

The rocks forty feet below the window were called the

sharks' nest, and centuries of broken and bleeding Cubans have been further shattered when they hit the boulders. At high tide the ocean's predators work on the bodies. Not even the bones would remain in a day or two.

Galvez did not look up from the message. He chewed on his mustache as he read about Faustino Queseda, once Fidel's chauffeur, now apparently dabbling with the CIA. His brother, Nico, was a woman and a blustering fool. But he had the Galvez cunning. Something was happening in Miami. Knocked out of Havana, the CIA was stirring trouble in Miami, working again with expatriate traitors.

Most Cubans knew the CIA only by the cartoons plastered on buildings throughout Cuba. A CIA agent tempting a Cuban child with an inflatable raft. A CIA agent with enormous rat ears listening to a street conversation. A CIA agent mourning over Batista's grave. Feeble caricatures befuddled by Cubans' eternal vigilance. Galvez knew better.

He hurried from the room, almost knocking over the next victim being escorted into the cell for his turn at the garrote. Yes, Galvez knew better. He feared them.

Chapter XIV

William Maurice sat on the davenport with his ration of popcorn in a bowl on his lap. No salt or butter, dry and tasteless. Much like kitty litter, Maurice imagined. Rosa was next to him, proud he was sticking to his low-cholesterol diet. She didn't know about the two packages of peanut M&M's Gerard Jones had given him for the road home.

It was almost ten o'clock, and the president was about to address the nation. With ominous voices, network commentators were saying it was the latest in the evening a president had ever gone on national television to explain his policies.

Rosa massaged his neck. He usually did the rubbing, as he firmly believed her job at the newspaper was more tense than running his importing business. But he had left the house at five-thirty that morning and had just returned. His shirt collar was open and his tie was loose. His feet were resting on a pile of newspapers on the glass-topped coffee table. The television and a VCR were across the den in an open armoire. The remote control was on the table.

Sitting on a tan-and-black Chinese carpet near the windows, Julie Porlocarrero and her two friends, Maggie Suarez and Tessa Casuso, were huddling over a Yahtzee game. They hid their mouths with their hands as they whispered and giggled and frequently glanced at the Maurices. Only occasionally did they roll the dice. Maggie and Tessa pointed fingers at Julie, urging her on, daring her.

"What are they up to?" Maurice asked Rosa.

With a smile, she shook her head. "The minds of fourteen-year-old girls are unfathomable, even to someone who was there once."

"I'm so worried my bowels are loose," Maurice said abruptly.

She bumped him with her shoulder. "What a pleasant thing to say."

"You've read the newspaper today?" he asked.

"I put the newspaper together today, dear, just like every day."

Maurice lifted his feet from the table to reach for several newspapers he had brought from the warehouse. "Look at this from the *Herald*. 'President Declares Offensive Weapons in Cuba Unacceptable.' "

He pulled the *New York Times* to the top. " 'Forty Senators Send Cuban Bomber Letter to President.' The subhead reads 'Declares Cruise Bombers a Violation.' And this across the top of the *Washington Post* front page: 'Cuban Airport Hangar Construction Reported.' And finally, look at this in the *New York Post*: 'Missile Crisis Rerun.' Damn it to hell."

He tossed the newspapers onto the table. "Senator James Rogers, chairman of the Senate Intelligence Committee, called the director this morning. He apologized for the leak from his committee. The director asked him if the bigmouth was Flori-

205

da's own Senator White. He couldn't answer, but said he was looking into it."

"It isn't all a mistake, is it? I mean, those bombers are really in Cuba, aren't they?"

"The photos of it are irrefutable. Plus one of my friends in Cuba, a stevedore, has reported that coffinlike boxes were off-loaded in Cuba two days ago. There's an entire section at the CIA that just analyzes photographs of boxes. They've concluded from my friend's description that the coffins contain cruise missiles. And there's the construction at La Panchita we've detected by satellite and that was discussed by the *Herald's* Man in Havana. We're certain."

"Didn't you factor leaks into your plans?" she asked over another burst of tittering from the girls. On the television, network analysts were already second-guessing the president, telling the nation what the president meant in advance.

Maurice was silent for a moment. "Maybe I should have. Washington is more porous than when I lived there, as incredible as that seems." He clenched a fist. "We've lost the initiative. The leaks, and the press and public's reaction to them, are driving us now. They're going to force the issue."

"Just like in 1961?" she asked.

"The shrill outcry closed off President Kennedy's options. He was trapped, unable to negotiate, making brinkmanship virtually inevitable."

"You're blaming the press and public? That's inadequate and untrue."

"Says you, someone from the press."

Julie Porlocarrero dropped the dice and rose to her feet. Maggie and Tessa pushed her at the Maurices. She crossed the room, her face crimson. Julie was a blossoming coquette, but she didn't know it yet and so was still charming. With her full lips and auburn hair, she was going to be a heartbreaker, Maurice knew.

"Mr. Maurice, would you do us a favor?" She gestured toward her friends, lest there be any doubt this wasn't entirely her idea. "We need a fourth for Yahtzee. Would you go down to the billiards room and ask Aurelio if he'd join us? Just to play Yahtzee."

Maurice's face remained composed as he said, "Well, no need to ask Aurelio. I myself will be glad to play."

Julie's face dropped, and she inhaled with quick confusion. "No." It was almost a yell. "I mean, you and Mrs. Maurice are watching television and all, and we wouldn't want to interrupt."

"No problem, Julie." He gathered his feet under him to rise. "I haven't played the game since I was a kid, but I remember being pretty good at it."

Rosa jabbed him with her elbow. "Stop torturing her, Bill. Go get Aurelio."

Maurice looked crestfallen, but to Julie's delight he pushed himself out of the couch and wound his way to the basement. He heard the satisfying thud-plunk, thud-plunk of repeated bank shots before he got to the storage room. He pushed open the door. Aurelio Moreno was leaning over the green felt, methodically banking and dropping one ball after another.

"That's beautiful to watch, Aurelio."

"Thanks, Mr. Maurice." He grinned but did not look up.

"This will be difficult for you, Aurelio," Maurice said in somber tones. "How about coming upstairs and playing Yahtzee."

Aurelio sniffed. "You play Yahtzee, Mr. Maurice? That's kind of surprising."

Maurice rubbed a finger along his nose. "Not with me. Julie Porlocarrero and her little friends need someone for a foursome."

Knowledge washed over Aurelio's face. "Aw, goddamn it, Mr. Maurice . . ."

"It wouldn't be for long, and you'd make their day."

"I'd rather visit a bad dentist than play Yahtzee with a bunch of kids."

"You'd also make my day."

That was enough for Aurelio. He laid the stick on the

table. He struggled to remove the grimace from his face. He followed Maurice away from the pool table. "I'm not sure I remember how."

"You'll have very willing teachers, Aurelio. And believe me, three or four years from now, you won't turn down an invitation to play Yahtzee or anything else with Julie."

Maurice led him up the stairs and into the den. Wearing a sheepish grin that might have been a scowl, Aurelio sank onto the rug next to the girls. They were so excited they could hardly look at him.

"You're my partner, Aurelio," Julie said after a moment, branding him before Maggie or Tessa could recover.

Maurice returned to the couch. The television screen showed the presidential seal, which faded to the president, sitting at his desk in the Oval Office.

"My fellow Americans," he began. The familiar face, with the sorrowful, knowing eyes and the narrow mouth, was at once comforting and alarming. He was a popular president, rare in the second half of the century. But Maurice had never seen him appear tired before. Tonight the pouches under his eyes resembled dark oysters, and his cheeks were drawn. "I want to talk to you about recent developments in the Caribbean, and I want to tell you directly what we know, and what this government intends to do in response to the changing situation there. Earlier this evening I spoke again with the director of the Central Intelligence Agency, and he informed me . . ."

The president's speech lasted less than ten minutes. He said there were unverified reports that the Soviet Union had introduced a new bomber in Cuba, one with an unknown weapons configuration, but which might carry cruise missiles. He acknowledged that such bombers—he called them Blackjacks —and their cruise missiles were offensive in nature, and that their presence in the Caribbean might constitute a breach of the 1961 agreement between the United States and the Soviet Union that ended the missile crisis and by which the Soviets pledged not to introduce offensive weapons into Cuba. He said the bombers' presence had not been confirmed, nor the presence of the cruise missiles. Ever cautious, the president said that if confirmation was received, his administration would formulate an appropriate response. He blessed his countrymen and said good night.

When the network switched back to the analysts, a map was quickly displayed, showing the Blackjacks and cruise missiles' combined range. The entire eastern half of the country was colored red.

Maurice inhaled slowly. "Good speech. Well delivered and reassuring. Americans believe this president. It'll buy us some time."

The telephone rang. Maurice lifted the receiver from the end table and said hello. He said "yes" and "I understand" several times, then returned the phone to the table.

He sat glumly until Rosa asked, "What's the matter, honey?"

"That was Jack Cantrell. Our satellites have just detected a course change in a Russian naval fleet that had been on maneuvers in the South Atlantic. The fleet is now headed to Cuba."

Victor Fedorin did not like personally overseeing the transfers, but if trouble occurred, bluster from a Russian always smoothed things out. More than once, when the Havana police pulled one of his trucks over or walked into a warehouse to ask questions about the late-night operation, a bit of bombast and rank pulling settled matters quickly. Faced with an angry Soviet official, Havana police patrolmen withered quickly. There was risk, Fedorin knew, in being anywhere near his operation, but his tactic of hovering near the transfer had paid off several times.

Fedorin stood in a doorway across from the old United Fruit Company wharf. In the dark night, his post was even darker. There were no streetlights and the few neon signs on Desamparados Avenue had broken years ago. He wore his front uniform, a Soviet army major's. From somewhere up the street came recorded *guajiro* music, folk songs young Cubans scorn. There were a few dilapidated apartment buildings here, but this was an industrial neighborhood, with docks and warehouses and an electric plant, and cement and coal silos. Fedorin could also hear the distant ringing of a train's bell. Havana's central terminal was three blocks west. The street was shiny with that evening's rain. There were no ships moored at the dock, but a Soviet freighter was due tomorrow. Fedorin's goods would be in Leningrad within two weeks.

He held up his watch. Eleven-fifteen, and right on time the truck turned from Habana Boulevard onto Desamparados. Cubans called such a vehicle a *rastra,* one of thousands of Russian trucks in Havana. *Rastra* graveyards, each filled with dozens of worn-out trucks, were located on many city lots. This truck looked as if it were just one broken axle or a thrown rod away from the *rastra* cemetery.

The truck was olive green, with a square cab and soaring fenders. It was a flatbed, but canvas sides had been rigged on a frame above the bed. The brakes squealed, the pads almost gone, as it slowed in front of the wharf's warehouse door.

The driver's side door opened. A man in a black rain slicker jumped to the street. He brushed back the slicker to dig in his pants pocket for a key. He opened the warehouse's customer door, located below a chipped and faded painting of a bunch of bananas. A moment later the loading door began rolling upward as the man pulled hand over hand on the circular control chain. The interior of the warehouse was dark. The driver climbed back into the cab. He must have been nervous, as he missed the gear, and the gearbox ground loudly before the *rastra* began backing toward the door.

Fedorin did not see the second man, who had hidden somewhere in the street's murky shadows, until the man was rounding the *rastra*'s cab to jump onto the running board. The man yanked open the truck's door and appeared to dive inside. The truck veered and bounced off the warehouse's door frame, wrenching it out of line with a rattling creak. Under the canvas, bottles crashed to the bed.

The driver was hauled from the cab, his arms lashing out at the intruder. They hit nothing, and the driver was thrown onto the street, his slicker fluttering after him like a tail. The attacker's hand rose into the air. It held a sap, and it was aimed carefully. He struck the driver's head once, and the driver lay still.

Only after a moment did the event register on Fedorin. His truck, with its fortune in rum, was being hijacked. Such things didn't happen in Cuba. Hadn't Fidel eliminated street crime? Not, apparently, in the wharf district. Fedorin pulled his Tokarev pistol from his pocket and sprinted across the street. His boots slapped at puddles of water.

The hijacker was behind the wheel before Fedorin reached the *rastra*. He jammed the pistol through the open window into the driver's neck and ordered, "Get out of the truck."

Instead, the hijacker tried to yank the gearshift into first. The Russian cracked the pistol's barrel across the driver's nose. "Next time I'll use this gun like it was intended. Get out."

His hands at his broken nose, and tears of pain flowing down his cheeks, the driver swayed in the seat. Fedorin threw open the *rastra*'s door and dragged the hijacker off the seat. The man bounced off the running board to the street.

Fedorin swore under his breath. He returned the Tokarev to his pocket and pulled the hijacker away from the flatbed, skidding him through water on the street. The Russian was breathing hard, less from exertion than from impending panic. Two people lying in the street, a truckload of black market liquor, and himself—a Soviet officer with no good reason to be here—in the middle of it all. He breathed deeply, trying to maintain his control.

If he couldn't get his driver to come to, he would have to drive the truck into the warehouse and, worse, would have to unload the rum cases. The driver was rolling to his knees, his head in his hands. He groaned lowly. He wouldn't be worth much. Fedorin cursed again and lifted a foot to the running board.

Metal bit into his neck, roughly prodding his head forward. His cap fell to the cab floor. From behind him came a voice in Spanish, "Put your hands over your head."

Fedorin froze with fright. The pistol barrel dug painfully into his ear. "I said put your hands over your head, and back away from the truck."

The Russian did as told. He raised his hands, dropped his foot from the running board, and turned slowly. First the driver, then the hijacker, now him. Slapstick. A grisly rhyme from his childhood: Three fat babushkas all in a row/Scarfs, shawls, and coffins in tow. Fedorin had an insane urge to laugh. He turned to see two Havana policemen.

They wore green uniforms, rock-crushers, and pistol belts. The policeman holding the weapon was at least six-two, with a mean thinness to his frame. His angular face lost some of its resolve as he recognized the Russian uniform. The pistol lowered fractionally. The second policeman stood over the hijacker, who was sitting in a puddle, his fingers covering his nose and blood splashing onto his shirt.

Havana police. There was hope. Fedorin drew himself up and jutted out his jaw. "You have no idea the trouble you are in." Fedorin let his Russian accent carve his words, lest the Cubans have any doubt.

He started to lower his hands, but, incredibly, the pistol came up again and pressed against his nose. This was already longer than any other Havana *policía* had lasted. He barked, "Lower your weapon."

Still nothing. A moment passed, then the big policeman's mouth turned up. He said politely, "May I see your papers, please?"

Fedorin was conditioned to Cuban deference and fear, and he was outraged. He sputtered, "I am an officer in the Soviet army, and I'm on duty. Give me your name."

The policeman's voice would not quaver. "I must insist on seeing your identification."

Fedorin trembled, some anger, some a building fright. "Further, I am assigned to the Soviet embassy, and have diplomatic immunity."

"This looks like an *elefante* to me," the policeman said, wagging his pistol at the truck. "Elephant" is Cuban slang for a large swindle. "I'm not going to ask again. Your papers."

"I will not—"

The cop tapped Fedorin on the temple with the butt of the pistol, staggering him, then spun him around and threw him against the *rastra*'s fender. The Cuban roughly spread Fedorin's hands and legs and placed his foot alongside Fedorin's right instep, ready to kick the leg away and topple him should he move. The frisk was rapid and professional. Out came the Tokarev and a wallet and a vinyl documents packet, which the policeman quickly leafed through. He held the papers at an angle to catch the dim night light. The hijacker had climbed unsteadily to his feet and was being placed in handcuffs by the second policeman. Fedorin's driver was still down.

"You match your picture in your army ID," the policeman conceded, allowing Fedorin to lower his hand to reclaim his wallet. "What are you doing on the streets beyond the curfew?"

Another flare of hope. Again trying to frighten the Cuban, Fedorin said in a coarse voice, "The curfew doesn't apply to citizens of the Soviet Union."

The policeman backed away from the Russian, and Fedorin straightened himself. He tried to return dignity to his features, but he was still afraid. Most Cubans loathe Russians and view their presence in Cuba as an occupation. They were willing to make trouble at any opportunity. Danger was still present.

"You've heard that Cuba is the largest country in the world, Major?" the policeman asked.

Fedorin spread wrinkles out of his uniform coat and shook his head. He resisted the need to touch his pulsing temple.

The policeman gave the punch line: "Our capital is in Moscow and all our people are in Miami." He laughed and handed the pistol back to Fedorin.

213

And just when the Russian thought he was out of it, the Cuban lifted a notebook from his breast pocket and began jotting down information from Fedorin's document pack.

"What are you doing?" Fedorin asked cautiously.

"I'm arresting that man"—the policeman nodded at the hijacker—"and I'm filling in a report on the crime."

Fedorin said unconvincingly, "There has hardly been a crime here."

"Robbery with violence. A felony, Major. With your testimony at this man's trial, we'll rid the revolution of a leech."

"I'm in a hurry to return to my quarters. There's no need for an arrest or a report." The Russian spread his hands appeasingly. "A slight incident. I don't even intend to report being beaten by a Havana policeman."

"There will occasionally be misunderstandings between socialist partners," the policeman answered dryly.

After he examined the cargo—giving a whistle of surprise—the policeman completed his report and returned the notepad to his pocket with a flourish. He offered Fedorin an insultingly casual salute. The hijacker was then led away by the two policemen.

Fedorin's driver staggered drunkenly to the truck, where he sank onto the running board. His slicker glittered with water. He explored a bruise on his chin.

Fedorin's stomach cramped with fear. The Cuban police would forward the report, including his name and a description of the cargo, to the embassy. The ambassador and the internal security officer could hardly miss the implications.

He pushed his driver off the running board and climbed into the cab. His hands trembled around the steering wheel. He negotiated the *rastra* into the warehouse. He had a long night of work ahead, and he needed a convincing lie for the ambassador by morning. The KGB was unkind when its own were caught trading in the black market.

* * *

Midnight, and the warehouse office was crowded with people and thick with anticipation. They had all been called back after the president's speech. Jack Cantrell stood between the director of the Central Intelligence Agency and the secretary of defense, briefing them on progress at the warehouse.

They had listened to the speech on the jet but had already known its contents. They were now in a hurry. The director and secretary had each brought along several assistants, and they waited on both sides of the door to the loading lot.

Maurice sat inconspicuously on a folding chair against the far wall. Gerard Jones was next to him, the first time Maurice had ever seen him away from the Apollo. Constantly shifting his feet and wetting his lips, Jones looked uncomfortable without a keyboard in front of him. He was working on a roll of Necco Wafers.

"Look at the director," Jones said in a confidential voice. "Crummy sports coat, bucket of mud face, wet eyes. He looks like a wadded-up paper towel."

Jones might also have been describing himself, Maurice thought.

"If you cross him, you find out he's no paper towel, and fast," Jones went on. "And the secretary of defense. I think he uses hairspray on his hair, then on the rest of himself—suit, shoes, face, the works—so he won't wrinkle."

He pushed a Necco into his mouth. "The lady looks pretty nervous, Bill. This's going to be tough on her. Coronary arrest time, if we've done our job."

Standing near the water cooler was Mirta Merrero, one of Fidel Castro's cousins. She and her husband had come to the United States in 1986, given the choice between emigration or prison. Castro suspected her husband, a vice minister in the Ministry of Light Industry, of making inquiries in the United States about building a computer-chip factory in Cuba. United States profit, exploited Cuban workers. That's what his revolution had been all about, Castro had lectured the weeping Mirta the day he'd banished them to Florida.

215

Jones said, "Mirta's husband found a good job at Federal Express, but she still feels like a foreigner here. Misses Cuba terribly. She adored Fidel, now she rages against him. Still loves him, but feels betrayed."

With her wild brunette hair and wide eyes, Mirta Merrero appeared baffled and frightened. She had not been informed why she was required at the warehouse, nor who all the people were, nor anything about the room's equipment. Something to do with Cuba, she had been told.

Mirta wore no makeup, and her damp eyes looked as if she had cried it off. She was a light-skinned *criollo,* of direct Spanish descent. Her features were exaggerated, with a prominent nose and a broad mouth. Her raven hair was a mass that flared uncontrollably behind her. She wore a yellow print dress that was inexpensive but well cared for. A leather bag hung from her shoulder. Her eyes flickered nervously around the room.

One of the agents, a Cuban American, tried to make Mirta comfortable, but she refused the chair and the offer of a cup of coffee. She did not know that after this evening, the agency would watch her closely. Any attempts to contact Cuba would be intercepted.

Cantrell joined Maurice and Jones. "We ready?"

Maurice replied, "I've given the okay. Any moment now."

"The director just told me the latest. This morning's issue of *Pravda* had a vicious attack on the president. Warmonger and traitor to peace."

"That's not too unusual," Jones commented.

"But this was pure vitriol," Cantrell said. "And, ominously, the Soviets have flatly denied that Blackjacks are in Cuba."

Maurice looked up sharply. "No equivocation? No barrage about the inviolability of state secrets?"

The DDO shook his head.

"Nothing about Cuba being an independent country capable of determining its own defense needs? That's what they usually do when caught with their pants down."

"It's a flat denial."

Maurice paused to digest the news. Finally, "Didn't Adlai Stevenson's performance at the UN, photos of missile sites in hand, teach the Soviets anything?"

Another shake of his head. "The director views this as the worst news possible. The refusal to admit the bombers' presence doesn't allow room for dialogue. Nobody is talking."

"Except Senator White, screaming for their removal," Jones said. "He's got some of the powers on Capitol Hill behind him now, calling for a Kennedy-style ultimatum. Either the bombers are removed or the United States will take appropriate action."

"Where's Castro, Gerard?" Maurice asked.

"Right now he's playing dominoes with some of his cronies in his suite at the Habana Libre Hotel."

"Have you detected any unusual changes in his schedule because of all this?"

"Castro won't change his schedule. It's a matter of machismo and honor with him."

Maurice pursed his lips. "Well, I think we'd—"

The door to the factory swung open, bouncing loudly against the doorstop. With a rush, Fidel Castro swept into the room, beaming, nodding his head, grinning, stretching out his hand to the nearest CIA operative, giving him a pat on the shoulder, shining good cheer.

And it was Fidel Castro. He was in his brown-green dress uniform, with the red-bordered epaulets on the shoulders and gold branches on the lapels. Castro had never been one for tailors, and the jacket fit loosely over the white shirt and black tie. His pants were stovepipes, breaking sharply above the boots.

Castro moved around the room, playing to the crowd, shaking hands, offering encouragement. To those whose most vivid memories of Castro were of photographs from the 1960s and 1970s, his beard and hair were shockingly gray. He had outlawed Christmas, and it was his curse that he was beginning to resemble Santa Claus. Castro's nose was bent but strong, his lips pendulous and moist, his teeth crooked and stained, his eyes riveting, teasing, cajoling.

The secretary of defense was heard to gasp, and the CIA director involuntarily took a step back as Castro approached.

Castro pumped the secretary's arm, then chucked his chin and said in Spanish, "Keep up the good work, Mr. Secretary. I'm keeping my eye on you."

Next he vigorously shook the director's limp hand. "Finally we meet," he said, glowing. Always physical, Castro put his arm around the director's shoulder and brought him to his chest. Castro leaned down, forehead to forehead. "You've caused me a lot of trouble over the years, you devil." He laughed loudly.

The director did not speak Spanish, but he was dumbfounded, his mouth open, spit collecting on his lower lip. Years of intrigue disappeared from his features. He was transfixed.

Even the agents sitting around the warehouse office who had worked on the transformation were stunned. They had seen bits and pieces of the metamorphosis, not the entire package. And Eduardo Mederos had saved himself for this performance. A moment before, he had been nervous, pacing, unsure of himself, an actor before the curtain rises. But when he walked through the door, Mederos had disappeared inside Fidel Castro.

Mirta Merrero fell apart. She burst into tears and buried her face in her hands. Sobbing, she looked away from Castro as he walked to her.

He gently put his hands on her shoulders and said, "Now, now, Mirta. You understand I had no choice. You'll do well here."

She gazed up at him. "Please, Fidel. . . . We should have—"

He put his finger to his lips. "No more, Mirta. You'll be all right."

Castro patted her shoulder and walked away. Maurice said, "He fooled her completely. He passed the acid test."

Castro shook more hands, grinning, sharing a joke here and there, saying he would take care of things, saying he would not forget the people here today.

The CIA director's eyes followed him. He had still not collected himself and would undoubtedly be embarrassed by it later. He had spent much of his adult life conspiring against this man. And here Castro was, in the same room, spreading good cheer, everything forgiven. When he walked by Maurice, Cantrell, and Jones, Castro winked.

At the end of the circuit, Castro stopped at the door to the factory and turned to raise his right hand in the classic Castro gesture. Then he disappeared through the door.

The room burst into applause. Cantrell patted Maurice's shoulder, then quickly left his chair when the director crooked a finger at him.

Gerard Jones said, "Honest to God, that was sensational." He dug in his pants pocket for a Tootsie Roll. "And it was great partly because Eduardo didn't give anybody too long to examine him or listen to him."

Maurice was giddy with Eduardo's success. He controlled it by measuring his words. "Sure, but that's exactly how we'll work it in Havana. Nobody is going to have the time to fix on him long."

Maurice could see the secretary and director nodding at Cantrell, and the director squeezed the DDO's elbow. An agent opened the door to the loading lot for the director and the secretary. They and their assistants began filing out.

Cantrell hurried back to Maurice and Jones. His face was alight. "It's a go."

"When?" Maurice asked, jumping out of his chair.

"Eduardo leaves tonight."

Chapter XV

Nico Galvez parked his Dodge pickup in a row of other trucks and four-by-fours. He was so immense that his adjustable steering wheel was always canted toward the dash. He pushed open the door and squeezed out. His door slammed into the next pickup, nicking it, but Galvez only grunted. He'd had a rough three days. He carried an athletic bag and a leash.

Ass End was in back of the pickup. The huge red dog was wearing a leather muzzle, and his slit eyes stabbed across the parking lot toward the pit barn. Over the past five days Galvez had dropped the dog from chain weight to pit weight by reducing its food and water. Dehydration lessened the flow of blood through wounds. And each morning Galvez had been "rolling" Ass End, keeping the dog on a short leash while it fought in three-second bursts with a friend's leashed dog. The animals were separated before any damage was done. Ass End was ready.

After the leash was secured to a chest harness, the dog leaped over the truck's gate and landed lightly on the ground. Galvez wrapped the leash several times around his wrist and walked toward the barn. He nodded at other pit men as they converged on the building. Security men wearing holsters were posted on each side of the door. No one was admitted unless recognized by the guards. One guard had a walkie-talkie and periodically checked in with the lookout stationed on the highway turnoff.

Ass End led Galvez into the barn. Acrid tobacco smoke was so thick it blurred the far walls. There were perhaps two hundred people attending the matches. Twenty or so had brought their dogs. The atmosphere was festive, with shouts of recognition and loud bunkum about fighting exploits or bloodlines. People made way for Nico Galvez, known to be as mean as his dog. Galvez paused several times to place wagers on Ass End.

The pit was in the center of the barn. It was a square, sixteen feet on each side, with thirty-inch wood sides. The floor was canvas, and white tape marked two scratch lines twelve and a half feet apart. Two dogs had just been taken from the pit, and the referee was writing in a pocket-sized spiral notebook, his foot near a puddle of blood. Around the pit, bettors were exchanging money.

Waiting his turn, Galvez held Ass End between his legs—the best way to control a pit dog when other animals were near —and ordered a Budweiser from a man with a vendor's cooler around his neck. He drained the bottle in three swallows and asked for another before the vendor had counted his change. This time he paused between gulps to survey the crowd.

Half Cubans and half Anglos, he guessed. In one corner of the barn was Hugh Jackson, an ex-con waving his fistful of money at a potential bettor, touting his peculiar sport. Jackson bought used-up racing greyhounds, four- and five-year-olds, for fifty dollars apiece. Two of the lanky dogs cowered on leashes near him, their eyes white and wide with fear. Jackson matched them against a pit bull and took wagers on how long the greyhounds would last. None had ever lived more than sixty seconds, and the heavy betting was around thirty to forty seconds. Jackson was the bank and handicapped the matches according to how the bets were falling. Galvez and many other pit men thought Jackson was running a freak show.

Across from Galvez, near a door to the latrine, was Will Phillips, a Miami dentist convinced that Akitas made good fighters. The dog on his leash was his fifth animal in eighteen months, a fortune in the rare Japanese dogs that looked like crosses between German shepherds and huskies. Everyone else in the room knew the Akita was lunch meat for the pit bull, but they were only too willing to take Phillips's money, happy he was a slow learner.

Under the elevated hayrack was Primitivo Lezcano with his dog, Buster, probably the largest, fiercest pit bull in the barn. Last time, when Lezcano couldn't get any bets, he volunteered to tie Buster's rear legs together for the match. Wagering was wild. Twenty minutes after the let-go, Buster made scratch, pushing his way across the tape with his bound legs, and his opponent failed to cross the line. Now Lezcano was walking around puffed up like a rooster, bragging about his dog, trying to tempt bets with even wilder handicaps. He wasn't having any success.

Next to a support post was Delio Yero, who was waving around a handful of fifty-dollar bills. Yero, an impoverished drunkard, was also wearing a new Hawaiian shirt rather than his usual layer of grime and stains. He was placing a bet with another bystander. A large bet, it looked like to Galvez. Something was going on if this *guajiro* had money. Galvez tugged Ass End toward Yero.

The Cuban had spent three days gleaning Little Havana for information. His brother, Carlos, had demanded it in a strident message the likes of which Nico hadn't seen since the missile crisis. Five thousand dollars had accompanied the message. Nico had pounded the pavement, made a hundred phone calls, beseeched his few friends and threatened others. He still had no hard information he could report.

But something was happening in Little Havana, no mistaking that. A crease on its surface. There was talk among the domino players at Maceo Park on Calle Ocho of the sudden vacations of two of the regulars. Gone to Darwin, Australia, for a tour, they laughed.

Another domino regular, a business liquidator who had once been a military policeman frequently assigned to the front door of the Habana Libre Hotel when Fidel was in residence, had told them he had just been interviewed by the Immigration and Naturalization Service. The INS still made the domino players nervous, even though most of them were naturalized American citizens. The liquidator had only shrugged when asked what the INS wanted.

Juan Ibbara, a waiter at El Pub restaurant who had floated to the United States in 1986 on a tractor inner tube, was asked to produce the Cuban work permit he had brought with him in a waterproof roll. The visitors had shown him identification, but he couldn't read English and didn't have the courage to ask. The permit was returned a day later.

A lecturer in Marxist-Leninist thought at the University of Miami was asked by the Library of Congress for the loan of her vast collection of recorded Castro speeches. Galvez had telephoned the library in Washington, D.C., but no one there had heard of the Castro tapes, much less of anyone from the library borrowing them.

Nieves Azua, once an official in Cuba's Ministry for Physical Education and Recreation who now owned a Miami sporting goods shop, had suddenly visited distant relatives in Buenos Aires. Just as well, some in Little Havana thought, because all Azua ever talked about was playing on Fidel's basketball team at the University of Havana in the 1950s and claimed to have once been Fidel's friend, the liar.

All in all, nothing Nico Galvez could assemble. But there was unexplained movement in Little Havana. Something was happening. And now the impoverished Delio Yero was flashing money around the dog pit. At this point, Galvez would grab at anything. He tugged Ass End over to Yero.

The little man sobered when Galvez arrived at his side. Nico Brava was *un abusador*, a bully. Yero had once owed him five dollars. The huge man with the singsong voice had slammed his fist through the wall of La Estrella restaurant, barely missing Yero's face. Right through all the plaster and wood, cracking the ceramic urinal in the men's room on the other side of the wall. Yero had quickly paid the money.

Just as quickly, Yero jammed his bills into his pants pockets. He nodded nervously to Brava. It was a contest as to who was uglier, Brava or his torn-up dog. Or who was more ornery.

"How about keeping Ass End on a short leash, Nico," Delio Yero said as the pit bull smelled up Yero's pants to his crotch.

"See you got some extra cash, Delio," Galvez said in his sweet voice. "You usually go through money like shit through a goose."

"Only when I bet on your dog." Yero was feeling braver. Not much the fat giant could do to him in a crowd.

"Where'd you get it?"

Yero hesitated, glancing left and right. He was cadaverously thin. His hands resembled claws, and his neck was no larger than Galvez's wrist. Yero's bulbous nose was covered with a fishnet of red veins. He had crimson, moist eyes. His shoulders were stooped protectively. He was wearing a silver ring that looked new.

Yero coughed to give himself time. He said tremulously, "Can't say, really. You know how things are."

Galvez was always drawn to weakness, and he sensed turmoil and irresolution in the smaller man. He inched closer. "Maybe you should rethink—"

"Ass End, owned by Nico Brava." The referee's call interrupted Galvez's threat. "Against Big Whitey, owned by John Gallivan."

"You stay right here, Delio," Nico Galvez ordered as he turned his dog to the pit. Ass End pulled at the leash. Around the pit, wagers were placed at a furious pace. Big Whitey had ten pounds on Nico Brava's dog, but Ass End was a trooper.

One of his fights had lasted two hours ten minutes before the opponent failed to meet scratch.

Ass End stared over the pit side, his muzzle pointed at Big Whitey like a compass at north, steady and calm. Only Ass End's hind legs, digging at the ground, gave him away. Held between John Gallivan's legs, Big Whitey was also braced on the pit side, looking for his opponent. Big Whitey was white all right, except for a black spot over his right eye that also covered much of his face. His owner was a Miami veterinarian who wore alligator-skin cowboy boots.

Galvez pulled towels and a blanket from his athletic bag, and after they had been exchanged for the vet's, Galvez said in English, "I want to taste water."

The referee scowled, but it was an owner's right to sample water from the opponent dog's dish, which was alongside the pit. The referee brought Big Whitey's dish over, and Galvez sipped from it. He spat onto the ground and nodded.

"I also want to see elbows," Galvez said. This caused a stir among the bettors. The rules provided that a handler may demand the opposing handler bare his arms, but it was considered bad form. And the veterinarian had never before been suspected of hiding a knife. The vet smiled and rolled his shirt up.

"Call it, Nico," the referee said as he tossed a coin into the air.

"Heads." A few muted laughs came from the audience at the giant's soprano cry.

The ref bent over the coin. "Heads it is. Choose your corner and your turn."

"This corner." Galvez pointed at his feet. "And Ass End will be washed first."

In some pits, a handler's corner man washed the opponent dog. Here the ref cleaned both animals. He began with Ass End, thoroughly running a soapy towel over the dog, then ordering it into a tub of warm water at the pit side. When Ass End was rinsed, the ref rubbed him with a towel. Without such precautions, pit men were known to lace their own dogs' hair with poisons, causing the adverse dog to go down quickly. Each dog was washed and dried with towels and blankets provided by the other handler, lest the towels be impregnated with toxins. The ref walked across the pit to do the same to Big Whitey.

After a moment the referee called, "Both corners ready? Face your dogs."

The rules were simple in a scratch-in-turn contest. The dogs fought until one turned to run. At that point, both handlers returned their dogs to the scratch lines. The dog that just turned would be let go first at the timekeeper's call. Again they would fight until one turned, and again they would be brought to the scratch line. The first dog that did not cross the scratch line in a charge at the opponent dog was the loser.

Ass End and Big Whitey were set in place, held tightly between their owners' legs at the scratch lines. To one side of the pit, the ref held a breaking stick. The timer yelled, "Let go."

A newcomer to the pit audience would be surprised at the lack of noise. Pit bulls do not bark at each other. They do not use threat displays, no baring of teeth or lowering the tails. Only the bristling hair on their backs and the lead-steady stares give them away.

And then the explosion. Ass End and Big Whitey shot at each other in a fury of muscle and fangs. They met and climbed each other, twisting heads to find the enemy's neck. Their combined force violently gyrated the dogs away from each other. They charged again. Hair flew into the air. A red dog and a white dog, spinning. A barber's pole.

Ass End found meat first. His fangs sank into Big Whitey's neck. Dobermans and German shepherds and most other breeds have had gameness bred out of them generations ago. They will bite, then, almost politely, withdraw to assess damage or flee. A pit bull bites, then releases only to bite higher at a more vulnerable spot, then again and again, crunching its way up through skin and sinew and bone. Ass End released and clamped his jaws shut again, then violently spasmed his body, jerking Big Whitey off his feet and throwing him against the pit side.

Big Whitey found his stance only to see Ass End charging. The dog looked at the vet and took half a step toward him.

"A turn," yelled the ref immediately, stepping in Ass End's path and poling him with the breaking stick. "Pick up free of hold."

Wearing a malevolent grin, Nico Galvez carried Ass End back to the scratch line. The vet was not as strong and had to goad his pit bull to the line.

"Face your dogs again."

The timekeeper allowed the required thirty seconds to elapse. Both dogs were positioned between the handlers' knees.

"Let go."

Again the lunge. This time Big Whitey raised a leg on his opponent, pushing Ass End's head aside, and sank his teeth into Ass End's shoulder. Galvez's dog leaped straight into the air and rolled back onto the vet's dog. Big Whitey's mouth opened as its body was pulled away from Ass End by the roll, but the tooth stuck under Ass End's collarbone.

"He's fanged," shouted Galvez.

The ref levered the dogs apart with the breaking stick while Galvez surrounded Ass End's muzzle in his huge hand and pried the tooth out from under the red dog's bone.

"No turn. Same scratch." He waited until Galvez and Gallivan nodded ready. "Let go."

The animals launched themselves again. A whir of motion, the clacking of canine teeth slapping into each other, saliva spinning thirty feet out of the pit and landing on spectators, the scrape of skin and pads on the canvas, and all the while the demonic eyes burning. Bettors cheered their respective dogs. Smoke in the room thickened, and at times the pit bulls appeared to be fighting in the clouds.

Most dogs fight for their masters, and the vet walked around the ring, positioning himself to always be in Big Whi-

227

tey's view, encouraging and cajoling. But Ass End fought not for his master, but because of a lifelong buildup of bile, Galvez knew. So he stayed in one corner, taking his eyes off the action only long enough to order a beer.

Twenty-five minutes into the bout, the sound of canvas tearing came from the pit. Not the canvas floor, but Big Whitey had peeled back the skin covering Ass End's rib cage, leaving a bloody flap trailing behind Galvez's dog, who, heedless, lashed out yet again at Big Whitey.

"Throw in the towel," the vet shouted over the spinning dogs. "Yours is going to bleed to death."

Galvez sneered, and his voice sounded much like the skin tearing. "I'm going to shoot him if he loses, so he'd better keep going." A bullet was the fate of many pit bulls who lost. Once broken, they were no longer as game, and with more than several losses, they weren't in demand for stud.

Big Whitey burst toward Ass End, but the red dog rolled away, leaving a smear of blood on the floor, and caught Big Whitey's left hind leg between his jaws. Ass End clamped down and spun, crushing Big Whitey's leg. Ass End bit higher, and a shank of broken leg bone burst through Big Whitey's muscle and skin, sticking through Ass End's lips like a toothpick. Blood foamed in Ass End's mouth. The white dog clawed toward the pit side.

"It's a turn," the referee yelled. He pushed Ass End away with the stick. "Face your dogs."

The outcome was now obvious to the ringsiders. Cash began changing hands amid the winners' whoops and the losers' groans. Nico Galvez laughed, a high-pitched sound like wind chimes. He bent over Ass End, trying to keep his pants away from the raw and bleeding side. The flap of skin hung almost to the ground. At the scratch line, the vet nodded glumly.

"Let go."

The audience nodded its approval when Big Whitey tried to charge, but his leg crumpled under him, and he could not push himself across the line.

The ref sang out, "He can't make scratch. Ass End is the winner."

The vet carried Big Whitey from the pit. The Cuban returned Ass End to its harness and attached the leash. Panting hard, the dog tried to lick its ragged flank, but Galvez pulled him over the pit side. The Cuban paused to collect bets, pushing the bills into his shirt pocket without counting them. No one dared cheat him.

Any hope Delio Yero had that the man he knew as Nico Brava might have forgotten him in the flush of victory was forgotten when Galvez pulled his pit bull toward him.

"I asked you a question, Delio. Where'd you get the money you've been waving around?"

Ass End dropped to his haunches to tend to himself. Each lick brought away blood.

"I can't really—"

Galvez lowered himself to his dog. "This dog just won me a bunch of money, Delio. I should take real good care of him. But you know what happens when I get sore? Well, I'm sore at Ass End because it took him near a half hour to bring down Big Whitey."

Galvez took the flap of Ass End's skin in one hand and yanked it back, tearing away another three inches of skin. This time the ripping sounded like a zipper. Not a whimper came from the dog. Bred for stoicism, Ass End only looked balefully at his owner. Most pit men believe their dogs don't feel pain. They do.

Galvez squeezed the flap of skin, which still hung from his dog. Blood drained to the barn's dirt floor. "Now, if I'd do that to a valuable property like this dog, you can only imagine what I'd do to you if you got me sore."

Delio's face turned the color of an old newspaper. He backstepped into a post. "Jesus, Nico . . ."

"Where'd you get the money?"

"I was talked to by a couple fellows five, six days ago. Lots of questions about Havana and Fidel and a lot of other things in the old days."

"Who were they?"

Delio was trembling. "They didn't say."

"Did they show you any identification?"

A nervous shake of his head. "They wore suits and ties, and that was good enough for me."

When Galvez rose to his feet, the spavined little man hurried on, "But my kid was waiting for me out on the sidewalk. He recognized one of them. Went to his house a couple times before we moved north."

"The name."

"William Maurice."

Galvez blinked. "Maurice?" He breathed heavily, his enormous chest halving the distance to Yero, then falling back. "You come with me, Delio. We need to talk out in my truck."

They had been sitting on the bottom of the sea for three days. Cramped and smelly days full of frozen food, fitful sleep, tired jokes, and barked shins and bruises. NR-3 rested a few yards from the reef at Bahía la Mulata, its tiny wheels sunk into the sand and its manipulator arm folded away. The coral reef was visible on the monitor in the control station, looming above the submarine. If the camera were turned, the gap in the reef thirty yards east could also be seen.

Wearing a gray Naval Academy T-shirt, running shorts, and New Balance shoes, Commander Edward Waite jogged in place in a puddle of sweat behind the helmsman's seat. He wore headphones and carried a Sony Walkman in his right hand. On each exhale he breathlessly sang along with Lionel Richie.

Behind the commander, Charles Brickell endlessly adjusted the station's controls. Once, on a lark stemming from boredom, Brickell had lowered the oxygen content of the air circulating in the sub while Waite jogged. He'd laughed hard when the commander started to stagger. Now Waite glanced frequently at the atmosphere dials as he exercised.

Eduardo Mederos sat in the minuscule galley next to Mouse Bretcher, the SEAL. Mederos was also wearing a Walkman. The other SEAL, Miguel Sosa, kneeled on the deck op-

230

posite the galley bench. He had taped a rubber-and-leather pad to a bulkhead support and was repeatedly striking it with his right hand, each time exhaling fiercely. The first hour out the commander had ordered Sosa to eliminate his striking scream, which had unnerved the crew, sounding too much like a metal hull collapsing under the sea's pressure. Sosa was absorbed in the exercise. The calluses on his knuckles were half an inch thick, making him look arthritic. Sweat ran down his arms and dropped to the deck from his elbows.

NR-3's ten-man crew had been reduced to seven. But Eduardo and the SEALs had been added, and a cardiovascular surgeon, and a radio operator. The operator was trained in the TACAMA (take charge and move out) communications system that connected NR-3 to the navy's newest and largest plane, the E-6, a modified Boeing 707 that normally was a platform for communicating with the Trident submarine fleet. The TACAMA and an air lock had been installed on NR-3 just before departure. The E-6 was lazily circling the Caribbean.

Extra bunks had been jury-rigged high in the main passageway, forcing the reactor engineers to crawl to their work. The marine biologist had been left in Miami, to the applause of all. The surgeon was asleep on a narrow step between the jogging commander and the pilot's seat. He wore a black mask over his eyes and earplugs. A six-foot-long plastic tarpon, eerily real with its skillfully painted gills and eyes, was suspended from the main cabin's overhead plumbing.

"What are you listening to, Eduardo?" Mouse Bretcher asked.

"Cubans talking. I'm learning."

"I thought you were Cuban."

"Spanish in Cuba has changed since the revolution. It's now part Spanish, part Marxist buzz words. But Miami Cubans speak Spanish as it was spoken in Havana thirty years ago. New emigrés think it's quaint. Plus Miami Cubans have added Yankee words. The mix is called Spanglish. So I'm relearning my own language."

Miguel Sosa paused in his ritual. The back side of his hand

231

was red. His first language had been Mexican Spanish. He said, "You Cubans talk too fast. That's part of your problem. You have never understood that to be Latino is to take things a little easier than everybody else." Sosa struck the pad lightly. "What's for dinner? The same frozen crap?"

Bretcher nodded.

"Why didn't they stock some Mexican food? Some enchiladas and refried beans."

Mederos said, "Beans on a submarine, Miguel? Think about it."

Sosa resumed striking, this time with his other hand. "When I get back, I'm quitting this chicken outfit and going pro."

"What's that you're looking at?" Bretcher asked, nodding at the photograph Mederos had pulled from a pocket.

"Questions and more questions. Are you still trying to find out if I'm Fidel Castro?" Mederos asked accusingly. "Didn't the admiral tell you my name, and something of our mission?"

Sosa said, "You look too much like Castro not to be Castro."

"Fine, so I'm Castro. Believe what you want."

"If you're Castro," Bretcher said, "I'd be tempted to stick my thumb in your eye right now. I hate that bastard."

"I'm Eduardo Mederos," Mederos exclaimed quickly. "Ask the commander."

"The commander is a submariner, and they don't know shit. If they did, they wouldn't be submariners." Bretcher flexed his biceps. Both Sosa and Bretcher wore nothing but swimming trunks. They looked like sculpture, with veins close to the surface and muscles clearly defined. "So what's that photo?"

"A girl I once knew," Mederos replied. His voice lowered. "A long time ago."

Bretcher reached for his cup of coffee. "Yeah? Looks like an old photo. Know her back when you were still in Havana?"

"She was a student with me at the university there."

"You must miss her, to carry that photo. You going to visit her in Cuba?"

Mederos didn't say anything.

"You know," Bretcher went on pensively, "I should've gone to a university. Imagine all the poontang walking around the campus. I read in a *Playboy* interview that Joe Namath screwed three hundred different girls when he was at Alabama. Can you imagine?"

"Three hundred?" Sosa asked. "How many is that a week?"

Mederos held up a hand like a traffic policeman, trying to end the conversation.

Commander Waite wiped a towel along his arms. The headset dangled around his neck. He laughed. "How's it feel to be trapped in a metal cocoon with two adrenal glands, Eduardo? SEALs are all the same."

Mederos smiled. "I have a hunch they'll do their job."

"You count on that." Bretcher returned the grin. "You're all right, even if you are Fidel Castro."

Mederos slid out from the bench, passed Sosa, who was still pounding the pad. The Cuban approached Waite, who was now toweling his legs. "I've got to ask a favor, Edward."

The commander was still breathing hard. He stripped off his white socks. "Sure, Eduardo. What's up?"

Charles Brickell said over his shoulder, "Something's coming in from the A-6, Commander. I'll run it through the decoder."

Mederos was wearing olive fatigues. He was heavier than he had been three weeks before, with a slight paunch. His feeding program had continued on NR-3. "I want to take this photograph with me."

Waite lowered his towel and studied Mederos. "That's against all our training, Eduardo. It could really foul things up."

"Maybe in a plastic pouch, a Baggy. I could pin it inside the swimming trunks."

"Jesus, Eduardo. What if someone on the boat sees it? You could blow the whole plan."

Mederos scratched his beard, attached with pinpoints of glue, a miracle of cosmetics. Waterproof and somewhat pull proof. It itched all the time. "I never thought I'd do this, but here." Mederos folded the precious photo in half, then in half again. Carmen Santana's face was creased. His hands shook as if he were chilled. "There, now it's a lot smaller. Can we hide it?"

"I don't know, Eduardo. I think—"

"If I'm the *jefe supremo* of Cuba, I can do any goddamn thing I want, it seems to me."

Waite pursed his mouth. "I'll find a plastic bag. You're going to have to be fast with your hands to make the switch."

"I'll be quick," Mederos promised.

Brickell handed a message to Waite and said, "Better read this, Commander."

Sweat from his hands soaked through the thin paper before Waite finished reading it. His mouth pulled back in a grimace.

"What's going on?" Mederos asked. The men aboard NR-3 had not been informed of world events while they were submerged.

"There are suddenly three Soviet ALFA-class attack submarines patrolling the area. We've been ordered to use evasive maneuvers on our return. And the *Sunbird* won't be towing us part way home, as it did when we came south. We'll be underwater all the way."

Waite read further, then said gravely, "And listen to this, the president has just announced that the Soviets have forty-eight hours—until Tuesday at four P.M.—to remove the Blackjacks, or the United States will remove them."

"I wonder what's happening up there," Brickell said from the helmsman's seat.

"Not our concern," the commander replied without conviction.

Mederos said darkly, "But it'll soon be mine."

* * *

Gerard Jones leaned closer to his Apollo monitor. He had been tracking world newspapers as they came in. He could call up the front page of any major paper in its original format, the stylized logo included. He flipped through them. "These headlines are getting larger."

Maurice nodded wearily. Eduardo Mederos was aboard the submarine. Behind the office, the warehouse factory was being rapidly dismantled. The booths and the electronics and the tank were gone. The wiring was being torn up, the lights removed.

The frantic activity in the office had subsided. Agents were posted at their terminals, waiting and listening, but the rushed meetings and the running about had ended. Boredom and tension mingled in the room. Jack Cantrell was still on the secured phone most of the time, talking with the White House or the Pentagon or CIA headquarters. Gerard Jones endlessly played with his computer, chattering like a baseball catcher. Maurice leaned back in his chair against the wall near the Apollo, rubbing his chin, crossing his legs, pinching the bridge of his nose, cracking his knuckles, waiting.

"Get this, Bill," Jones said, turning his monitor so Maurice could see it. "Reuters reports that the Doomsday clock just clicked to two minutes to midnight."

"What's the Doomsday clock?"

"An outfit in Paris called the Committee for Peace, made up of three Nobel winners and some journalists, keeps an imaginary clock, and sets it according to the level of world tension, midnight being the end of the world. It's usually at ten or twelve minutes to midnight. It's been creeping up this past week."

"Sounds accurate," Maurice said gloomily. It was Monday morning, thirty-one hours until the president's deadline.

In the three days since Mederos had left Florida in NR-3, the world had begun to tremble. When the Soviets continued to deny that the Blackjacks were in Cuba, the Defense Department released photographs of the plane. The Soviets

235

countered that the CIA had obtained the photographs inside the Soviet Union. So the Defense Department displayed satellite photographs of the work being done on the Blackjack hangar in Cuba and compared features in the satellite photo with those in the 35-mm camera shots. Same scene, different angles. No question remained.

The Soviets had been stung. The Soviet premier was quoted as saying an American attack on Cuba would be the end of imperialism.

When news of the Soviet fleet turning toward the Caribbean had made the newspapers two days ago, the president in an electrifying announcement called up two hundred thousand reserves. He adroitly avoided questions as to precisely what the United States would do were the Soviets not to remove the Blackjacks and the cruise missiles, but reiterated that they were unacceptable in Cuba. In what some journalists were saying was a deliberate slap at Castro, the president had also said that Blackbird flights over Cuba were being resumed. Exile Cuban groups in Miami were forming combat units and calling for an invasion. Amid all this was the constant screech of hawkish politicians, led by Senator White, calling for an immediate sea and air blockade of Cuba.

And there was the ominous announcement from the Kremlin that the Soviets would ignore the deadline.

There was also much the public did not yet know. Soviet attack submarines were now routinely following Soviet freighters, anticipating running a blockade. A second Soviet navy carrier group, this one in the eastern Atlantic, had just changed course, steaming toward the Caribbean. The president had secretly ordered the transfer of more air force combat, intelligence, and electronic warfare units to south Florida. Navy vessels were leaving Norfolk and Charleston and forming offshore. And the State Department was quietly seeking approval of the Organization of American States for unspecified activity against Cuba. None of this could remain secret long. Those in the warehouse could only watch the international situation with growing dread. There was no way to help or hinder it.

The Apollo signaled an incoming message. Jones swiveled on his chair toward the screen. He said urgently, loudly, "It's a translation from Castro's helicopter pilot, a radio signal to the tower at Martí Airport."

The room electrified. Newspapers and snacks were thrown down. The agents scrambled back to their desks. Maurice and Cantrell leaned over Jones's shoulder.

His voice rising with excitement, Jones announced, "The Hormone pilot is clearing his flight to Las Paz. 'The Stallion will be aboard,' he says."

Jones grinned widely. "I was right when I said Castro wouldn't do anything differently just because of a Caribbean crisis. To do so would be to admit weakness."

Maurice said jubilantly, "And he's finally decided he needs a little exercise."

Chapter XVI

Eladio Arrinda stood well away from the window so the sun would not reflect off his binoculars. Even these tiny villages had the meddlesome CDRs. He was careful, as rumors were sweeping Cuba of arrests by the hundreds. G2 breaking down doors in the dead of night. Someone had talked. Probably an American agent. To his shame and regret, Arrinda knew all about the damage a talker could cause.

His view of the fishing village was limited to the market with its cobblestone square, the wharf, and the school and its baseball field. There was not much more to Las Paz. Several dozen workers' *bohíos* and a small fish-processing plant for the bonefish, marlin, and rock lobsters. The cigar-rolling factory burned down six years ago, and its blackened foundation still stood next to the school.

Arrinda's cousin, who was doing service in the territorial militia, had gladly loaned him the two-room house for the week. The cousin didn't ask questions, not for the hundred pesos Arrinda paid him.

It had been a dull week for Arrinda. He was not sure why he was posted at the window dawn to dusk, binoculars in one hand and the curious radio in the other. Not a radio, really, but a button with telescoping antenna on it. And not a hand, but a rounded, shiny stump that ended an inch below his left elbow. He kept the radio squeezed between the stump and his rib cage, always ready to flee.

Day after day Arrinda had watched the town. The task was a *jamón,* a ham, slang for an easy job. He stood near the window or sat on the rocking chair. The chair always creaked under his weight, as did the floor. Arrinda had almost starved to death during those years when he had no job. He was making up for those hungry times now. His heavy paunch had rubbed the shine off his belt buckle. His face was puffy, and his mustache was pinched between full lips and his nose. He put down the binoculars to rub his eyes. Too much staring into the sunlit square. He lifted the glasses again.

The town's day always unfolded in the same centuries-old way, from the fishermen and the baker gathering at the cafe for coffee at five in the morning to the last light out at night, always in the priest's window. He seemed to need little sleep. In between, the market filled and ebbed with Las Paz's citizens. The poultry vendor arrived early on his bicycle, chickens hanging by their claws on a wire rigging above the wheels. The banana salesman came, clumps of the fruit attached to a pole he carried over his shoulder. And the waterman, pulling his cart with its water drums, stopping at the huts. Usually the only motor vehicle seen during the day was the cooperative's truck, arriving midafternoon to haul away that day's catch. And there were always the strolling couples and idlers of every Cuban village. Arrinda was born and raised in this town, precise down to its last detail, except that it was ninety miles away, east of Havana.

Arrinda lowered the binoculars to his lap to rub his stump.

239

His phantom hand often hurt, right where the axe had hit first. The doctor had said it was common for a limb to ache, even if it wasn't there. The pain was in his head, Arrinda knew. But the agony in his missing hand was real enough, by Christ, sometimes making his eyes tear over. The ghost of his hand. His reward for being an *alzado,* a rebel, those years in the Escambray mountains.

It is little known now in Cuba that Fidel Castro, just victorious from his guerrilla war in 1960, had to fight one himself. Over three thousand soldiers hid in the Escambray mountains, fighting Fidel just as Fidel had fought Batista, struggling to dislodge Cuba's newest dictator. Without support of the peasants—they were still charmed by Castro—the war was hopeless from the outset, and within two years the guerrillas were crushed.

Arrinda had been the Central Intelligence Agency's contact in the Escambrays, bringing in American arms for the guerrillas. When he was captured he was brought to Carlos Galvez in the Morro Castle prison. Twenty minutes and one arm later, Arrinda was babbling like a child. He told of every CIA meeting, every name he knew. He kept the stenographer busy for an hour.

After eight years in prison Arrinda was released in one of Castro's propaganda amnesties. Arrinda tried to contact the CIA again. He either failed to find them or they would have nothing to do with him, Arrinda had never determined which. Couldn't blame them. By talking to Galvez, he had undoubtedly destroyed much of the Americans' Cuban network. For several years he could not find a job, not a one-armed traitor to the revolution. Until William Maurice contacted him.

He hadn't met Maurice when he was in the Escambrays. And he didn't know how the American found him once he was out of prison. Yet through an exchange of letters—always to a Santiago de Cuba address—Maurice had hired him and told him he would find him a cover job. Arrinda was soon accepted as a dispatcher at the 26 July Trucking Department, in the

240

Havana harbor office. He had been working for the department, and for Maurice, since.

Arrinda arranged the shipment of some of Maurice's Cuban exports. It was easy, safe, and well paid. But now this alarming business, stationed in a Las Paz window with a button he was to press only if Castro's snorkeling visit was not routine. Maurice had sent a long description of what would happen when Fidel visited Las Paz. Press the button if things are peculiar. All right, he would. He'd probably never know anything more about it.

As Arrinda shifted on the rocking chair, a distant hammering came from the hill to the east of Las Paz. It was a throaty fluttering that gained volume. A helicopter. A moment later it soared over the huts, its nose pulling up as it neared the baseball field. Its blades pounded the air, sounding like cannons. Dust blew off the dirt field, briefly obscuring Arrinda's view of the helicopter.

No markings, double props, and no tail rotor. It matched the description in Maurice's letter. This was the Hormone. Four men emerged from the cafe and hurried to station themselves around the ballpark. Two carried submachine guns. So that's who those men were who had arrived earlier by automobile.

The helicopter landed gently between the pitcher's mound and second base. The door slid aft, and a ladder was thrown out the hatch. A bodyguard was first out, looking left and right, running across the field to home plate. Another guard emerged to stand near the hatch. Prop wash whipped his jacket.

Fidel Castro stepped into the sunlight, ignoring the guard's offer of his arm. Carrying a duffel bag, he jumped to the field and walked quickly toward Las Paz's market. Arrinda noticed that he stood rigidly erect even while under the Hormone's blades.

The familiar surge of hatred washed over Arrinda. He had lost more than an arm to Castro. His hand began to shake with

241

the emotion, and he had to lower the binoculars for a moment. He found new calm by crossing himself, then raised the glasses again.

Maurice had written that a limousine never met Castro, that he would walk from the helicopter to the wharf, and that he carried his own equipment. All routine so far.

Arrinda focused the binoculars. Despite the fatigues, this wasn't the firebrand revolutionary whom Arrinda had seen harangue a crowd at the Plaza de la Revolución twelve years ago. Here was a heavy, sagging man, walking stiffly as he unwound his legs from the flight. Wrinkles cut deeply into his face and silver beard. There was some justice in the world. Castro wasn't going to live forever after all.

His elemental power had not diminished. Arrinda could feel it even at this distance. As he nodded to a handful of villagers who rushed to home plate to greet him, Castro moved as he always had, with utter confidence, cloaked in his authority, a man sure of his destiny. He was a medieval world unto himself, around which all the universe revolved. Arrinda cursed him for it.

Castro waved away other villagers who tried to approach. He was known to occasionally grant a request on the spot. A job, an apartment authorization, a pardon. Bodyguards moved warily between the president and his people. Castro walked across the cobblestones, passing a gear shed and two mules tethered to a lamp. Chickens scattered out of his way. He threw his pack over his shoulder as he stepped onto Las Paz's wharf. Guards moved with him, their eyes restless.

Maurice had written that there would be no special preparation of the dock. Castro dodged poles over which were draped drying fishing nets and hundreds of sponges placed in rows to dry. Fishermen repairing nets stood as he quickly passed them.

Arrinda guessed the boat moored at the end of the pier was about forty feet long. With its size and gleaming paint and cabin-top antennas, it had little in common with other Las Paz fishing boats. It was a sportfisher, with two stacked, glassed-in decks and equipped with two mounted Gin poles, a fighting chair, and a tuna door. An inflatable raft covered much of the foredeck. The pilot and a guard carrying a Kalishnikov automatic rifle were posted on the flying bridge. This boat was the fastest in Cuba.

Arrinda heard the diesels turn over. Black smoke spewed from the stack and dispersed slowly to leeward. Castro stepped over a gunwale onto the boat's aft deck. He lowered the bag and entered the cabin. Three bodyguards followed. Others remained on the wharf.

A crewman dressed in a striped T-shirt slipped the lines from the cleats. The engines roared, and the boat pulled away from the dock. With the aid of the binoculars, Arrinda read the legend on the stern: *Ernest Hemingway*. The boat headed for the reef.

Arrinda stood to stretch. He was to wait until the boat returned and Castro flew out of Las Paz. He would gladly wait. He was curious. And Maurice always paid.

"Nothing from Eladio Arrinda?" Maurice asked urgently. He didn't trust his voice above a whisper.

"If he activates the radio, it'll be on this screen instantly, and we'll abort," Jones said testily, staring at the Apollo monitor. "Two keystrokes on the machine, and everything's off. But we're all right so far."

Jones was so nervous he had forgotten to open a box of Goobers he had pulled from the workstation drawer. It was the first time in their days together Maurice had seen Jones with his mouth empty. It increased Maurice's anxiety.

Jack Cantrell drank from a bottle of mineral water. He had switched from Pepsi to Perrier, but nothing would keep his mouth from getting dry. The Apollo beeped, and he lurched forward so quickly in his seat that it almost rolled out from under him. "The navy has the sonobuoy signal. Loud and strong."

243

Two days before, a submarine tracking buoy had been dropped from a Phantom near the Bahía de Mulata reef.

A new message arrived on the screen. Jones smiled. "It's Castro's sportfisher."

A computer at Fort George Meade had just matched the sonobuoy's signal with a confirmed recording of the *Ernest Hemingway*'s engine noise.

Cantrell and Jones turned to Maurice. It was his decision now.

Maurice said, "Tell them it's time."

Eduardo Mederos had heard nightmarish things about Caribbean coral. If it cuts a person's skin, it will grow beneath the surface forever, a granular, scratchy parasite. No way to remove it, and after death it lives on in the corpse for years, happy in the dank darkness of a coffin. He wasn't sure he believed it, but he shivered anyway.

He was in a coral canyon at the reef front, thirty feet below the surface. The coral grew in pods that resembled bloody brains. Behind him was the open sea, dark and filled with vague, slow movements just beyond the range of clear sight. NR-3 was out there, also waiting.

Mederos stood on unstable coral debris, which felt like a pile of kindling. Miguel Sosa floated easily next to him, grinning around his mouthpiece and occasionally giving Mederos a hearty thumbs-up signal. Higher on the reef, Mouse Bretcher peered around a coral outcropping into the landward lagoon. Immediately after leaving the sub, Bretcher had disappeared around the reef with the plastic fish and had returned without it.

The SEALs were as calm as the water's surface, but Mederos was nauseated with fear and afraid he would vomit into his face mask. With acid clarity, Mederos could remember every moment of his wait to disembark at the Bay of Pigs. This was worse.

Bretcher and Sosa were wearing wetsuits, but Mederos had

244

on swimming trunks, cut like a loincloth so he could kick out of them quickly. His photograph of Carmen Santana was pinned against the front. All were using Daxon rebreathers, each with two square tanks. Spent air was circulated back into a tank, so there were no bubbles. They all wore weight belts and boots and gloves to protect their hands from the coral. Mederos's ears hurt from the water pressure.

Next to Sosa on the coral debris was an underwater propulsion unit, manufactured by Water Trek and modified by the navy with blue-gray camouflage paint and a stronger electric power plant. It was now capable of eight knots when submerged and pulling five hundred pounds. The UPU was the size and shape of a dolphin. The navy had also attached longer handles and grips, which protruded from the unit just behind its nose. The operator rode it like a horse, and the passengers lay along the UPU's body as it carried them through the water. The UPU's controls were much like a motorcycle's, with handlebars and a twisting accelerator. The propeller was in a cage at the stern, below which was a small rudder, but most of the steering was done by the riders' fins.

Mederos felt they were underequipped. There was no spare rebreather. Neither of the SEALs carried a weapon except for the Tekna knives strapped to their calves, and Sosa's fists, of course, which resembled bludgeons. Mederos thought he heard him say "chicken outfit" around his mouthpiece.

From above them, Bretcher gave the alert signal. Their target was in sight. Tension clamped around the Cuban's throat, and he concentrated on long inhales and exhales as he had been taught, the sound of his breathing amplified by the equipment.

He flicked away a blue-and-yellow trigger fish that was attracted to his mask. Mederos chided himself for his fear. In his training with Bretcher and Sosa, he had learned they could simply do anything, endure anything, laugh off anything. They weren't normal human beings, not anybody he would want a daughter to go out with or even be in the same state with. But their competence was evident in every move in the warehouse tank and off the Florida coast where they had trained. Even their infantile acts of bravado impressed Mederos, from Bretcher's holding his breath for two and a half minutes on a dare to Sosa's bending a quarter in half with his teeth. These guys were a half step away from a padded ward, but until then Mederos was content to be in their hands.

Bretcher signaled again, his eyes alight through the mask. Sosa quickly lifted the UPU from the coral. He mounted it and twisted the accelerator. As he had practiced dozens of times, Mederos gripped the left handle and brought his body against the machine. It lifted them from the seabed, stirring fragments of coral. The UPU rose quickly, and Bretcher grasped the side opposite Mederos as it passed.

The tide was high, allowing them to crest the reef near the gap. A few seconds later they descended to the sandy bottom. A large stingray, as flat as a plate and its pectoral fins rippling, flew along the ocean bed away from the UPU's shadow. A school of silver fish flickered away from the divers, sunlight sparkling off their skins. The water was warmer here. It leaked into Mederos's mask, and he blew it out. His hands and arms ached as the UPU swiftly pulled him through the sea.

The UPU slowed abruptly, and Sosa and Bretcher used their fins to turn it. Suddenly Mederos saw Fidel Castro, floating lazily on the surface in the tidal current. He was forty yards above and ahead of them. The UPU was in his blind spot. Castro moved his fins slowly, swimming near the reef, watching for fish that fed there. A catch net was attached to his wrist and trailed alongside him. A knife was strapped to his leg. He held his speargun with both hands. He was skin-diving with a mask and snorkel, not using tanks. He jackknifed and dove to a depth of six feet, but the fish, a three-foot grouper, darted away along the edge of the reef. Castro returned to the surface and blew the snorkel. He continued his easy patrol.

The UPU slowly closed the distance, remaining behind and slightly below the target. Mederos looked at Sosa, then at

Bretcher on the other side of the UPU. They were riveted on Castro. Mederos felt as if he were just along for the ride.

Another moment passed. The decoy was ahead. Castro was getting closer. Mederos glanced over his shoulder. The hull of the sportfisher was out of sight behind them. The reef was alive with fish of every color and shape, reminding Mederos of jewels. They seemed unconcerned with the parade of humans. Above him, the surface was a swirl of silver and blue. Mederos thought it odd that in this world of water his throat was painfully dry.

Sosa patted him twice on the arm. The final signal. They were nearing the decoy. Castro abruptly changed course, and his fins began slapping vigorously at the water. Mederos renewed his grip as the UPU gained speed.

Thirty seconds passed, and Castro again increased his pace. He left a trail of churning white water behind him. Mederos could not make out his features against the backlight, but he did see him reach back on the shaft to throw off the gun's safety. They knew that Castro used an American-made Shaftmaster speargun. Gas-propelled, it could launch the spear forty yards underwater.

Castro dove, now also using an arm for propulsion, keeping the speargun on point. Sosa twisted back the UPU's accelerator and swept after Castro in a descending arc. Mederos saw the decoy, the silver plastic tarpon that looked as if it should weigh two hundred pounds, a spearhunter's lifetime trophy. It was motionless, except for its tail, which drifted with the reef current. Castro approached it from the rear, and he slowed himself, perhaps knowing the tarpon could feel a nearby commotion through its scales. A few bubbles escaped Castro's mouth to drift to the surface.

As Castro closed in on the tarpon, readying his speargun, the UPU rushed in on him. The current coursed over Mederos, fighting to tear him off the machine. Thirty yards, then twenty.

The tarpon was still. Castro slowly righted himself in the water, maintaining his depth ten feet above the sandy bottom.

He sighted down the gun. An acre of gray fingerlings drifted overhead, partly blocking the sun. The UPU raced toward the diver. They were going too fast. Mederos braced for a collision.

Sosa spun the accelerator off, then violently twisted the UPU away in a rehearsed maneuver that left him and Bretcher floating free and facing Castro. Their fins dug into the water. Seven feet, then four.

No one at the Central Intelligence Agency denied Fidel Castro was a courageous man, at times recklessly so. He never shrank from a physical challenge. They did not foresee that he must have had tarpon in his blood. He sensed the kidnappers, spun toward them, and instantly fired the speargun.

Bubbles blasted from the weapon. The spear spat across three feet of water, shooting through Mouse Bretcher's thigh, then trailing a thin stream of blood behind it as it drifted limply to the sand below.

Bretcher did not even wince. As Castro pulled the knife from his calf sheath, the SEALs swarmed over their target. Castro lashed out, and the blade found Bretcher's forearm, splitting it open.

Despite Castro's size and strength and daring, he did not have a chance, not against two men who had done nothing for four years but harden themselves. As he propelled himself at Castro, Miguel Sosa used a side block with his right arm, deflecting Castro's second knife lunge, and roughly turned him. Sosa clamped his arm around Castro's throat, applying a sleeper hold, and with his other hand flattened Castro's mask against his face.

Oblivious to his wounds, which were turning the nearby water pink, Bretcher caught Castro's knife hand and twisted it sharply, forcing the hand to open. The knife slipped toward the sea floor. Castro struggled futilely against the arm across his neck, but it only gripped tighter. Sosa was an expert at how much pressure could be applied to make one light-headed.

Castro tried to kick Bretcher, but his fin slowed his leg. He scraped it off against his other foot and tried again. His foot

248

bounced against the SEAL's thigh. Bretcher caught Castro's other hand and turned to nod at Mederos.

Mederos acted from training. He pulled off his boots and gloves, then inhaled hugely and opened his jaws to release the mouthpiece. He slipped the rebreather's straps from his shoulders and passed it to Bretcher, who roughly grasped Castro's nose and yanked it back, at the same time inserting the mouthpiece between Castro's lips.

His lungs full, Mederos unhooked his weight belt, then swam toward the three men. His hands shaking, he gripped Castro's trunks. The SEALs had endlessly joked about Castro's reaction to this part of their plan. Castro, the embodiment of Hispanic machismo, stripped of his swimsuit.

Bretcher had told him over and over not to be polite. Yank the damn things hard. Mederos followed instructions. Castro flailed out with his feet, but Sosa increased the pressure, and the effort was short-lived. With typical Cuban modesty, Mederos looked only at Castro's trunks as he pulled them from Castro's feet. Bretcher removed Castro's knife sheath.

Mederos slipped out of his own shorts, careful to avoid further wrinkling the precious photograph in the plastic bag. His lungs began to ache as he fumbled with the safety pin. His shaking fingers kept slipping off the pin. He yanked the pin. Not knowing about the photo, Bretcher frantically waved at him.

Finally it came free. He pushed his ankles into Castro's trunks, then spent another ten seconds—Bretcher angrily gesturing at him all the while—securing the plastic bag to the inside of the trunks. He tightened the waist cord.

Mederos kicked to the surface. He casually floated above them for a moment, a picture of calm, before diving again. He swam to the bottom to pick up Castro's speargun. He could not find the knife until Bretcher pointed. Only the handle knob protruded above the sand and coral debris near the UPU. On his return, Bretcher handed him the catch net and helped him with the sheath.

Mederos began again toward the surface but was startled by a tug on the speargun. They had not noticed that a fine length of wire connected the spear to the gun. It ran through Bretcher's thigh and trailed away to the lost spear below.

Bretcher peered down at the glistening wire. He shrugged, lifted his knife from his leg, and cut the gun free. Bretcher might have been cutting bread. Sosa would spread the word among their compatriots. This topped the mouse.

Mederos glanced at Castro. He was breathing raggedly, but every time he raised an arm or leg, Sosa pressured his neck. Bretcher gave the final thumbs-up. Mederos swam toward the surface.

Gerard Jones had chewed much of the skin off his lower lip. As always, he was studying the Apollo screen. "We should've heard by now."

"Not yet," Maurice replied. "We don't know—"

Jones stood suddenly. "There's the message from NR-3." He inhaled sharply. "They've got him."

Cantrell whistled and picked up the secured phone. Maurice let his chair drop to all fours. His face was pinched with worry, his empty gaze on the far wall.

The office was silent, all the agents staring at Maurice.

He said lowly, "I thought I'd applaud when the switch was made. Suddenly I don't feel like it."

The sound of the returning sportfisher woke Eladio Arrinda from his nap. He was still in the chair at the window overlooking the square and the wharf. The room was warmer and smelled of burning wood from an open-air brazier below. He ran his tongue around his mouth, then reached for a cigar in his pocket. He lit the match—a feat, with only one hand— and rolled the slender panatela in his mouth to evenly burn the tip. He inhaled gratefully and raised the binoculars.

Before the crew had fully secured the boat, Castro jumped onto the wharf and strode by the fishing gear, then into the market. His guards formed loosely around him. The fishing or diving or whatever Castro had been doing must have done him good, because he appeared refreshed, moving quickly. Still carrying his duffel bag. Didn't look like he had caught anything. Or maybe he had given his catch to the crew, which La Prensa said he often did. Castro strode through the town square, passing a number of villagers once again hoping to gain his ear.

The Hormone's engine whined to life before Castro got to the ball field. Arrinda moved the binoculars in a wide sweep, knowing he was missing something, wanting some reason to press the button. But all was routine. He hoped he hadn't failed.

Castro disappeared into the helicopter, followed by several guards. Its engines immediately roared, and the ship lifted off the field. A moment later it disappeared behind the eastern hills.

Arrinda crushed the tiny radio under his shoe and pushed the pieces into his pants pocket. He wrapped the antenna into a knot and also hid it in his pocket. He would scatter them on the side of the road back to Havana.

He quickly left his cousin's room and started down the stairs to the street. Arrinda fervently wished he knew what role he had just played, what plan he had just been a part of. But, whatever, it was the least he could do for William Maurice.

Chapter XVII

Three black Mercedes-Benz limousines swept into the Plaza de la Revolución and sped along the wide central boulevard, where during interminable state ceremonies the troops marching on review outnumber the spectators. The automobiles sped by a five-story-high portrait of Marx, Engels, and Lenin against a field of red and another, even larger, of Che Guevara, which, with the distant gaze, beard, and peaceful countenance, resembled a parish portrait of Christ, save of course for the beret.

Castro had once used Oldsmobiles, but he quickly became accustomed to the perquisites of his office, despite constant La Prensa articles otherwise. He switched to Mercedes-Benzes as quickly as he seemingly could after the revolution. The first and third limousines contained *barbudo* guards. Eduardo Mederos was in the backseat of the center Mercedes.

Maurice had told Mederos that Castro's staff would carry

him. They knew Castro was moody and could lapse into week-long brooding silences. During these times, the Cuban government and Castro's day-to-day life ran on momentum, as his aides made the decisions just as Castro would, were he not in ill humor. You can coast, Maurice had assured him.

True so far. Mederos had snorkeled for a while, then had swum to the sportfisher. Nobody had told him that one of the guards would rush up to him and insert drops in his eyes and nose. Without a word, Mederos then went below to don Castro's uniform. Mederos knew Castro always wore an undershirt, and—in a release of tension—he laughed aloud when he found it to be silk.

The boat returned to Las Paz. He did not have to give the Hormone pilot instructions. He laughed again when he saw that the helicopter had an oak panel interior. He did not need to give orders to the limousine driver at José Martí Airport. Mederos was being swept along by Castro's routine. He had been president of Cuba for two hours and had yet to say a word.

His Mercedes drew up to the Palace of the Revolution. A guard on the curb hurried to open the rear door. Mederos stepped into the tropical heat and walked swiftly toward the massive doors of the palace. The guards sprinted to form a protective gauntlet. Mederos was tall enough to glance over their heads to the plaza, a vast staging area surrounded by Warsaw Pact–style cement buildings and grudgingly few palm trees. The square was dominated by the monument to José Martí, which was mounted on a star-shaped foundation and rose over four hundred feet, sculpted by Sicre. Mederos thought it resembled a power pole from an electrical substation. The National Library and Theater and other government buildings were also in the plaza. The offices of the Central Committee of the Communist party adjoined the palace. The area was too large and hot for strolling during midday, and it was almost empty of pedestrians. The cars and trucks had been rerouted for a few moments while the president was in transit.

A guard held open the door, and Castro walked into the palace. He was braced by chilled air. Castro usually wore a green campaign uniform made of heavy cloth. He insisted on the low temperature, and his staff often complained—but never, never to Castro—that they had to wear jackets against the air conditioning.

Just inside the door, Mederos was met, as he had been told he would be, by Dr. Vicente Legro, his secretary. The doctor, known throughout Cuba by the toddler's nickname Chico, had replaced Celia Sánchez when she died in 1980. Legro was an implementer, jotting on his notepad every command Castro gave, from ordering a bowl of ice cream to sending another brigade to Angola. Legro was with Castro or outside his door every one of Castro's waking moments while he was in Havana. The secretary's office was on the second floor, and Castro's instructions kept Legro's staff of six working long hours.

Legro limped along next to Mederos as they crossed the grand hallway, their shoes echoing. The doctor had joined Castro's forces in the second year of the war and, in the days of critical medical shortages, operated without anesthesia on his own leg, removing a .38-caliber bullet, which was now in a glass case in the Museum of the Revolution. The doctor was a small man, little higher than Mederos's breastbone. Legro was bald, with a horseshoe of gray hair and a bulbous nose resembling a gourd. He perpetually wore a harried expression, with good reason, because he received the brunt of Castro's frenetic energy.

Legro was not one for making small talk. "*Comandante-en-Jefe,* the Soviet ambassador is waiting for his meeting, as are Comrades Galvez and Rabassa."

Mederos nodded. For the first fifteen years of his rule, Castro had refused to use the building's elevator because it was built by the American company Westinghouse. Then the Westinghouse equipment was replaced by an East German elevator, and now he enjoyed taking the elevator to his third-floor office, the one week in any given month it was working. Legro started toward the stairs.

Mederos tried his voice. "How long has Sokolov been waiting?" Too much quaver. His deadening fear had returned, and Mederos knew it was pinching his voice and constricting his hard-learned Castro strut. He breathed deeply several times, trying to shake the tentacles of his fright. Mederos had been told Chico Legro was so intent on capturing all of his boss's pronouncements that Legro could appear rude, even to Castro. Perhaps so intense he missed any trouble with Mederos's voice.

Legro did not look up from his pad as they climbed the marble stairs. "About forty-five minutes."

Mederos tried again. "Give me a moment, then show him in." Better. Brusque and forceful. As he had been taught, Mederos had roughened his voice on NR-3 by harshly clearing his throat again and again, making him hoarse. He would do the same every morning of his stay in Cuba. The voice was the weakest part of his act. His language and mannerisms would have to carry him.

"You wanted me to remind you first thing of Cipriano Mesa's request."

They gained the third floor. Mederos knew the layout, walked along the hall, and passed half a dozen uniformed guards toward the reception room, behind which was his office. He had no idea who Cipriano Mesa was, but Maurice's people had trained him to cold-read a question. "Grant it, but tell him I want a report in a month."

Legro jotted in his notebook. "Ambassador Sokolov has been pacing at an unusual rate today."

"Good. He can use the exercise." Talk, Maurice had said. Of all Castro's complex traits, his talking and talking and talking was the most notable. He talked to anyone about anything at great length and with much vigor. Words escaped him in an unending spill, a rush of enthusiasm and, occasionally, knowledge. He listened far less well.

Mederos said, "There is a frigate lieutenant, one Enrique Pascual, stationed at the Havana Naval Base, attached to the torpedo boat flotilla. I want him brought to me immediately."

"Yes, *Comandante-en-Jefe*." Legro made a note.

Mederos asked, "What's scheduled for the rest of the day?" He grimaced at his own words. A mistake. He had known it before the sentence was fully out.

Legro looked up from his pad. "Why, anything you'd like, *Comandante-en-Jefe.*"

"Of course." A feeble rebound. "I'll see what Sokolov has to say now."

They walked quickly through the reception room, empty but for a burgundy cherry table to one side, a dozen uncomfortable pressed-back chairs against a wall, and a rust-colored Oriental carpet on the floor, a room used for nothing but walking through. Not allowed to miss an utterance, Legro left Mederos only at the door to Castro's office.

Mederos would have to congratulate Maurice. The CIA replica of Castro's office was precise. The desk was massive and made of oak stained almost to black, with an inlaid leather top. Three leather chairs were near the desk and a swivel rolled and pleated chair behind it. Two brass lamps, one with a circular shade, the other rectangular, were at the desk's ends. A modern Seth Thomas clock was near one of the lamps, as was a brass nautical barometer-hygrometer set and a frequency-preset radio tuned to the United States Spanish-language national weather service station in Miami. Ever since Hurricane Inez had devastated Cuba in 1967, Castro had closely followed the weather. A cigar lighter set in a bull carved of wood and an in-and-out basket were also on the desk. Mederos moved to the seat and rested his palms on the desk. They left damp prints on the leather.

Behind the desk was a sideboard on which were three telephones, an Aiwa tape player, and a dozen photographs of Castro with Soviet-bloc and third world leaders. On the wall were photographs of Castro as a university student playing basketball and another from the Sierra Maestra mountains, showing him with his famous scoped rifle slung over his shoulder. Raul, Juan Almeida, Ramiro Valdes, and Ciro Redondo stood beside him. On the floor near the sideboard was a stack of *New York*

Times. Castro understood written and spoken English well but hesitated to speak it. A Replogle globe stood at the end of the desk.

Mederos walked to the bookshelf built into a side wall near the windows. Castro was a voracious reader. Works of Shakespeare, André Maurois, Lenin, Victor Hugo, Charles Dickens. Mederos lifted a copy of García Llorente's *First Lessons in Philosophy.* It was well worn. Near Karl Marx's *A History of Economic Theories* was a selection of Gary Larson's *The Far Side* paperbacks and a copy of *Cecelia Valdes* by Cirilio Villaverde. A collection of antique wood humidors lined the top of the bookshelf. Between two humidors was a cup, the bowl made of silver and the stem of boar tusks, presented to Castro by Bulgaria's Todor Zhivkov.

Mederos replaced the volume and turned away from the books. On the opposite wall was a floor-to-ceiling map of the world, framed by maroon curtains. An old map, as someone had erased the dividing line between North and South Vietnam. Angola, called Portuguese West Africa, was full of red pins.

Mounted on the door wall opposite the desk were gifts given Castro. A Mosin-Nagent rifle from Khrushchev, an ornate, knobbed war club from Ghana's President Kwame Nkrumah, a framed gold friendship medal from Egypt's Gamal Abdel Nasser, and another from Prime Minister Nehru of India. Also framed and hanging on the wall was a letter to Castro from Franklin Delano Roosevelt. Copies of these trophies had decorated the Miami training office.

Mederos lowered the Venetian blinds covering the three bulletproof windows overlooking the plaza, then pulled the cords to close them. He flicked off the overhead light. Only one lamp on the desk remained on. He tilted the shade slightly so the bulb would be visible to those in the chair. They would not be able to closely examine his face.

He sank into the swivel chair. This room was Castro's office and his den and his retreat. It was full of his intimate and quirky mementos. It even smelled as he would, of tobacco, sweat, and scented soap. More so than during the underwater switch, Mederos felt as if he were violating the man. He said aloud, as he had hundreds of times during his training, "The bastard deserves it."

Vicente Legro escorted Ambassador Sokolov through the door and quickly turned to go. With Sokolov was the translator Victor Fedorin. Without standing, Mederos waved them into the chairs. Castro could be just as rude as he was charming.

"Thank you for seeing me, comrade," Sokolov said with biting sweetness. The Russian would have known that he was kept waiting for a snorkeling excursion. Sokolov's hair was shockingly white, with dog-tooth yellow at the roots. He might have been handsome once, but age had given his skin a sallow tinge. His eyes were sunk deeply and bagged, and they gave away nothing. His square jaw was softened by wattles. His smile was oblique and cynical. He was wearing a gray suit, and he carefully tugged the pants at the knees as he lowered himself onto the chair. He put his briefcase on his lap.

Sokolov said quietly, "I said I would report back to you as quickly as I learned anything new. I have just received a message from Moscow, and I want to pass it along."

The ambassador's mannerisms reflected his vanity. He straightened his tie and pulled his cuffs. "To put it shortly, the situation in the Caribbean is deteriorating quickly."

Victor Fedorin translated at the appropriate pauses. The major was wearing his army cover uniform. Fedorin looked more peaked than in the photographs of him Mederos had seen at the Miami warehouse. Strain seemed to be pulling at his features. Perhaps he was just exhausted. The Soviet embassy in Havana must have been frantic the past two weeks. Mederos had thought that Fedorin's flat face was due to the photographs. But the major indeed had features on a single plane, as if he slept on them.

Mederos was silent, so Sokolov hurried on, "We believe the United States is moving at least ten thousand marines into Florida."

258

"How certain are you?"

Sokolov waited for the translation, then replied, "We have had it confirmed that most of a marine amphibious brigade is moving south from Camp Lejeune. At least three infantry regiments so far. The rest is educated supposition. We think another division may be preparing to move south from Virginia."

"What would three U.S. Marine regiments be prepared to do?"

Sokolov pointed limply at Fedorin, who replied, "They would have fifty light and medium mortars, over ninety machine guns, grenade launchers, TOW weaponry, and their new MK19 grenade machine guns."

"In other words," Mederos said, "they are outfitted to do what U.S. Marines always do, hit the beaches."

Sokolov nodded.

"Are the *norteamericanos* planning an invasion?"

The ambassador replied, "Against your FAR, proven in Africa and armed with our matériel, it is not conceivable. They would never even establish a beachhead."

"What else?" Mederos knew the Soviets would be forthcoming with virtually everything they knew. During the missile crisis, which Cubans call the October crisis, Castro was made a bystander by the superpowers. Khrushchev deliberately kept Castro in the dark, acting without consulting him, bargaining away the fate of Cuba. Castro admired Kennedy's bluff during those weeks, but he had never forgiven Khrushchev for the humiliation of dismantling the missile installations. At a rally at the University of Havana, Castro had charged that Khrushchev lacked *cojónes* and had led students in singing a new tune, "Nikita, Nikita! *Lo que se da, no se quita.*" What you give away, you shouldn't take back. A decade passed before Cuban-Soviet relations returned to their pre-1961 level. But Castro would never again fully trust the Kremlin. The Soviets had learned the lesson—as well as history ever teaches them anything—and although they might not follow Castro's wishes, they would keep him informed.

Sokolov said, "Our intelligence is that the U.S. Atlantic

Fleet is shifting west at the rate of eight hundred kilometers a day. Fifteen warships of Cruiser-Destroyer Group Two are now within twelve hundred kilometers of Cuba, as are major components of their Service Group Two. Their Carrier Group Four, with the *Nimitz*, is off the coast of Georgia, and is under full steam south. Not far behind it is an amphibious group. Carrier Group Five of their Pacific Fleet will be at the Panama Canal in two days. A portion of their Middle East fleet, including their battleship, the *New Jersey*, has just left the Persian Gulf, presumably also heading this way."

Mederos rubbed the bridge of his nose, a well-known Castro mannerism. It was still tender. And his beard itched.

"As you know, we currently have a task force off your coast, with the aviation cruiser *Leningrad*, three new UDALOY-class destroyers, and fourteen other ships. Our Pacific Fleet North is also en route."

Mederos dipped his chin noncommittally.

"You asked for a listing of troops that we could supply Cuba." Sokolov opened his briefcase to pull out a manila folder. He slipped out the contents of the envelope and said, "As you know, there are two fleets steaming toward Cuba. Each has a naval infantry brigade." He paused to let Fedorin speak and went on, "Each brigade has a tank battalion consisting of over thirty Pt-76 amphibious light tanks, and ten medium tanks, three amphibious APCs, and about one hundred sixty riflemen. There is also a reconnaissance company, with nine BRDM reconnaissance vehicles . . . "

Sokolov droned on, telling Mederos of the antitank and rocket launcher batteries, and the naval infantry battalion with each fleet, of the transportation, supply, maintenance, and medical companies, and of the naval infantry's weapons, the SAM launchers, SAGGER manpack sets, the 120-mm mortars. Castro had a lifelong fascination with armament, and the ambassador obliged. Mederos caught Fedorin glancing at his wristwatch and was tempted to do so himself. The major appeared distracted, glancing at the ceiling between translations. Mederos wondered why.

The ambassador wound down, "And the chemical defense company has three CBR decontamination vehicles and two recon trucks." He gestured with his palms up. "Of course, comrade, we cannot be specific as to what circumstances these troops would be released to your command."

"Tell me more about the North Americans." Mederos knew Castro repeated this phrase often. His repertoire of invective for the United States was vast, but all his life he had been intrigued by Americans, and he could not take his eyes off the country. "What is their president doing?"

"The president is in continual meetings with his cabinet and his National Security Council and the Foreign Intelligence Advisory Board, and of course with the heads of the CIA and NSA. But we don't believe the president is going to push us on this thing."

"That's what Khrushchev said in 1961, but you were pushed around plenty. Made to look like fools."

"Out of the October crisis, we received a guarantee from the Americans they would never invade Cuba." Sokolov's voice was tight. "You have never given us credit for that, comrade."

Mederos ignored the barb. "Tell me what you think he'll do."

"We don't believe he is preparing to use force, not over a few Blackjack bombers."

"The president is bluffing?" Mederos asked.

"That's our best estimate."

"Half the goddamn U.S. fleet heading toward Cuba doesn't sound like bluster to me." Mederos had learned to be profane. Castro cursed frequently, even in friendly conversation, and insisted his profanities be accurately translated. He had enjoyed seeing U Thant and Nehru avert their eyes. Nixon had given it right back to him, to Castro's delight. Nixon was the only American president to figure Castro out, and Castro knew it. He respected him for it, despite Nixon's snub of Castro during a New York visit.

"They are trying to frighten you, comrade."

"So tell me the Kremlin's estimate of how I'll react." A

vintage Castro challenge. "Do your masters think those bastard Americans will scare me?"

"Absolutely not," the ambassador answered with fervor. Castro permitted no other response. Sokolov waited for Fedorin to translate, then continued smoothly, "The president has scheduled another speech to his countrymen for six o'clock Havana time tonight. He is being pressured by the press and public and the Congress into making the United States's position more definite. We believe he will do so in tonight's address."

Mederos drummed his fingers on the desk top, which Castro's aides knew meant the meeting was about over. "What is your government's position?"

"The same as when we spoke yesterday. We will stand behind your decision to allow the Blackjacks on Cuban soil."

Mederos smiled thinly. "How long will you stand by me?"

"Our countries have been friends since the revolution. The premier has assured me that nothing will change that relationship in the next few days."

A diplomatic nonanswer. Castro would know, as did Mederos, that this was all he was going to get from the Russians.

Mederos stood, the signal for Sokolov and Fedorin to do the same. "I want another report tomorrow."

"Of course." Sokolov straightened himself and brushed unseen lint off a cuff. "I realize that an air of normalcy is important, comrade, but the situation in your Caribbean, and indeed the world, is as tense as it has been in thirty years, and you might want to stay near Havana in the next few days, rather than snorkeling. Perhaps you could get your exercise closer to the city."

After the translation, Mederos stared coldly at the Soviets. It was enough. They quickly turned and left the office. Chico Legro instantly appeared in the doorway to announce Aristides Diaz Rabassa.

Rabassa fairly pushed Legro out of his way. Mederos knew that Rabassa, head of DGI, thought Legro was too influential, that he restricted access to Castro.

Rabassa settled himself into the chair with the ease only *Granma* veterans were permitted. He was in plainclothes, a white shirt open at the neck and gray slacks. He carried a briefcase.

"I heard all Sokolov said," Rabassa began, opening his case. "It's fairly accurate, as far as I can tell."

So the office was wired. Maurice hadn't been sure on that one. There would undoubtedly be a switch somewhere on the desk so Castro could cut off the listeners.

"What the Russian didn't tell you was the state of the American public, and their politicians." Rabassa swept his eyes over a report he had pulled from the briefcase. He held it farther away from him, then finally had to pull eyeglasses from his shirt pocket. He looked somewhat like Castro, a tall man with an athlete's build. His beard was red, and he was sometimes known as Barba Roja. Unlike Castro's, the beard was cropped close. His nose was broad, and Mederos knew Castro teased him about the red welts on both sides of it, indicating he was wearing his glasses more and more. In his youth his hair had also been red, but now it had grayed and was receding, making his forehead high. Over the years he had settled into being a bureaucrat, and now he carried too much weight. But Rabassa still projected a vigor, and after three decades he continued to run the DGI with energy.

The DGI, the Dirección General de Inteligencia, began in the early 1960s as a training school for Latin Americans in guerrilla warfare and subversion and had expanded to become Cuba's Central Intelligence Agency. Its headquarters in Havana was called Centro Principal. Like many nations' intelligence agencies, the DGI was divided into sections, which were in turn composed of desks. For example, Section II-2 was the European operation, with seven country desks, each with ten to twelve officials, all stationed at Principal Central. This section oversaw centers located in Cuban diplomatic posts in Geneva, Lisbon, London, Madrid, Vienna, Paris, and Rome. Section III handled the United States. It operated through the enormous Cuban Mission to the United Nations, which was Castro's

263

espionage center for North America. From the United Nations building in New York, Cuban DGI maintained contacts with subversive elements in the United States, tracked activities of Cuban exile groups, funneled propaganda into the country, and collected intelligence on American politics and the military. They did not, however, kill people. That was left to G2.

"We just received copies of eight U.S. newspapers, and we continue to monitor a number of radio stations. This business —it has been dubbed by the American press the Cuban bomber crisis—has become a singular preoccupation of the American public. Although there is some dissent, the vast majority of Americans appear to be behind their president."

"The Soviets believe he is bluffing, that he will not resort to military action to remove the Blackjacks. What is your estimation?"

Rabassa replied, "Under no circumstances will he allow himself to suffer by comparison to the president his countrymen are comparing him to now, Kennedy. So he will, if it comes to this, erect an air and sea blockade of Cuba, meaning he will not allow further Blackjacks to arrive here. As you know, we are expecting another two of them shortly."

"And what will he do if the Soviets use military force to run the air blockade with an escorted bomber?"

"I do not know if this president has a backbone, *Comandante-en-Jefe*. Nor do I know what he will do if he demands the Soviets withdraw the Blackjacks from Cuba and they refuse."

"What else do you have?"

"We are moving quickly for a General Assembly vote against the United States. At this point, I don't know what form it will take, but we have a good chance of success." He read down his report. "In tomorrow's edition, *Pravda* will have a full-blown attack on the president, calling him a harbinger of doomsday. This week's *Time* magazine cover will be of President Monroe."

Mederos grimaced, as he knew Castro would at the mention of Monroe, a president hated more than malaria in the Caribbean and Central America.

"And, finally, our people have found out that the last two Blackjacks have arrived in Mozambique, and are awaiting Soviet instructions to make the ocean crossing."

So that was the bombers' route, a southerly one, avoiding the North Atlantic and the high level of American detection ability there. The CIA and the Defense Intelligence Agency had suspected as much. And Rabassa, rather than the Soviet ambassador, informing Castro of the Blackjacks' route also meant the Soviets did not inform Castro how the planes were shuttled into his country or the precise timetable for their arrival. Castro would have been outraged.

"Russian bastards," Mederos said vehemently. "I want to hear from you again in six hours."

The DGI chief gathered his report and quickly left the office. Again the omnipresent Chico Legro stepped into the room. He said, "The lieutenant is here, and Carlos Galvez is still waiting."

"The lieutenant."

Legro stood aside and motioned with his hand. The lieutenant moved smartly into the office, stood squarely in front of the desk, and snapped to rigid attention. He was dressed in the navy's white working uniform and carried a briefcase. He was a black Cuban in his early twenties, with prominent cheekbones and a flared nose.

"*Primer Teniente* Enrique Pascual reporting as ordered, *Comandante-en-Jefe*." His dark eyes shone with knowledge and amusement. Pascual's father, a political science instructor at the University of Havana, had been a CIA *agente informativo*, captured in the G2 sweep following the Bay of Pigs. William Maurice contacted Enrique eight years later, after he was drafted into the Cuban navy. Counting on the son's continued bitterness from his father's execution, Maurice suggested Enrique reenlist and work for him on the side. Over the years Enrique supplied Maurice with information on

265

Cuban MGR shore patrols and impending crackdowns on black-marketing coasters.

"You have something for me."

"Yes, sir." Pascual handed the briefcase over the desk to Mederos.

"Dismissed."

Pascual turned smartly on his heels and marched out. Mederos flipped the briefcase locks, pulled it open, and removed a Sony multiband radio, available in the United States for $120. But Sony had only made the shell of this radio. Ninety thousand dollars' worth of CIA refinements were inside. Mederos opened the top left drawer. He raised his eyebrows at the blue Colt government-model pistol lying there, its hammer back and safety off. Perhaps on occasion Castro had to rely on more than his argumentative skills to persuade his subordinates. Or maybe he was afraid. Mederos laid the Sony next to the Colt.

Chico Legro appeared again in the doorway. Mederos said, "The lieutenant is to be added to my office staff as an adjutant, effective immediately. Now bring me Galvez."

The G2 chief immediately walked into the office and stood at casual attention, awaiting the signal to sit. Galvez was a stocky man, the power in his arms and thighs visible under his khaki clothes. His black walrus mustache and heavy eyebrows helped the ferocious appearance he cultivated. His dark eyes were lost under his low brows and seemed to emit red sparks as the room's low light caught them. His was a bully's face, square and full, with pug ears and hair combed back with oil.

Mederos stared at him until Galvez looked away, and Mederos felt an unthrottled surge of power. He had expected his first meeting with the G2 chief to be frightening. For three decades this man had been Castro's brutal right arm, a man beyond any law and any compassion. But Mederos was dead calm.

When Galvez took a half step toward the chair, Mederos commanded, "Remain where you are."

He let Galvez stand for a moment, then on impulse said, "I want the Malecon between Belascoain Avenue and the Hotel Deauville closed to all traffic for the next three hours. And the light posts there are to be painted white during that time."

Galvez nervously chewed his lip. "It will be done right away."

His face was carefully composed, but Mederos exulted. Maurice had been right here, too. A nonsensical order would be hastily followed. Anything, to anyone. Mederos's leeway in the next two days would be remarkably wide. Castro was known to act on the slightest whim, to be impulsive, sometimes irrational. Over the years his quicksilver moods and absolute authority had taught Cubans to defer to him instantly and totally. Castro brooked no interference or criticism. He had taught his subordinates to expect and accept utterly anything, any quirk, any odd pronouncement or unusual behavior, any mood. Castro was a chameleon, with constant, unpredictable changes. It made being Castro easier.

"Begin your report," Mederos ordered abruptly.

Galvez exhaled with relief. "We are still working on two fronts. The CIA arrests are continuing, but at a slower pace. Only three more suspects were gathered up today, all in Havana. This is the fifth cell we've found. We are learning all they know, but things are winding down. You will of course continue to receive full reports on the interrogations."

Mederos asked, "You are aware of the crumbling world situation today. Can you guarantee I am safe from the North Americans?"

Galvez paused, perhaps sensing a trap. Finally he hedged, "As safe as you've ever been, *Comandante-en-Jefe.*"

"Precious little assurance, Galvez." Mederos knew that Castro never called the G2 chief by his first name.

"But if I may be so bold, *Comandante-en-Jefe,* I am confident we have broken the CIA's back in Cuba. My arrests have left them nothing here. I have cleaned them out as thoroughly as we did back after the Bay of Pigs."

"And the other front?"

"Here I am less certain," Galvez admitted.

Mederos had no idea what Galvez was talking about.

The G2 chief held his hands in front of him, as one might a basketball, encompassing the situation with his blunt fingers. "As you know, my brother, Nico, reported a few odd occurrences in the exile population in Miami. I pressed him, and he's stirring the pot in Little Havana. And I've put other people on Calle Ocho on it. We've found a few more things, and they're beginning to add up."

"To what?" Mederos asked, too weakly. His chair suddenly seemed to be embracing him from behind, squeezing the air out of him, as Mederos's fear returned in strength. Miami was shot through with Galvez's people. Had G2 tripped over the operation?

Galvez pursed his mouth, seeming to weigh his words as he spoke them. "William Maurice is rooting around on the Calle Ocho."

That name would mean something to Castro, who never forgot and never forgave. Mederos played safe and said only, "Maurice."

"As you know, we now think he was the mastermind behind the Bay of Pigs, not Kennedy or Dulles. He thought it up and sold it to the American administration. His wife died in one of our actions after the invasion, the one where the traitor Jorge Gonzalez was liquidated."

Castro would know this. Mederos nodded and waved away the explanation. "What is he doing?"

"As far as we can tell, he's talking to a lot of exiles about you. How you live, your daily activities. We don't know why."

Mederos flinched. Maurice's goddamn plan was too ornate and fragile. A house of cards, and Mederos was sitting in the middle of it.

He asked with what he hoped was an incredulous tone, "Is Maurice working for the CIA again?"

"I don't think that's probable, not with the way he blundered three decades ago. But then, with their agents here in prison, the Americans are undoubtedly desperate."

"That desperate? Maurice is a bungler." Mederos said it with some conviction.

"I do not pretend to understand the Yankees, *Comandante-en-Jefe*. I have told my brother and others in Miami to dig further, and I am sure they'll have something shortly."

"You don't have much to go on, an ex-CIA operative asking questions about me."

"Of the smallest parts large puzzles are solved," Galvez said with satisfaction.

The assurance worried Mederos, and it would haunt Maurice. Carlos Galvez was very good at his job.

Mederos pulled the photograph from his shirt pocket and handed it to Galvez. "I want you to find this woman."

The G2 chief bent the old photo to the meager light from the desk lamp. His brows furled, and he was about to ask a question.

Mederos said, "Her name is Carmen Santana. She was a student at the University of Havana in the late 1950s, and she went to the United States after the victory of the revolution. She returned as a medic at the Bay of Pigs, and was captured by the FAR. She was imprisoned a number of years at La Ruda before she escaped. I believe she is still in Cuba, a fugitive now."

"May I ask—"

"I have told you all I know about her. Find her."

"Well, I'll put some of my men on it and—"

Mederos slammed the desk with his fist and growled, "You will personally search for her. You will use all the manpower you need, and you will have her in this office within two days. Do you understand?"

Galvez might have been slapped. He jerked suddenly erect, his eyes straight forward. "Of course, *Comandante-en-Jefe*."

"Two days, Galvez, or I'll find someone else to do it. Dismissed."

Chapter XVIII

Maurice stood on the bridge deck of Mario Plata's *práctico* as the boat entered the headwater of the Havana channel. The rollers ended here, and Maurice could take his hands from the portal frame. Behind the wheel, Mario Plata talked effusively, telling Maurice of his life and how it had improved since they began doing business together years ago. Maurice knew Plata's friendly chatter was hiding trepidation. No question, though, that Plata's bear hug when Maurice was lowered from the navy helicopter onto his boat was genuine. It might have been tempered had Plata known then that Maurice wanted a ride right into the city.

Plata's *práctico* had modern instruments and ornate trim that few other Cuban pilot boats enjoyed. Brass dials, a gyro-compass, and a digital wind-speed indicator were near the wheel. The deckhouse was trimmed in Thai teak, and the elevated helmsman's chair was covered with Argentine leather.

Plata had been careful not to overdo the boat's exterior, as it would have aroused jealousy and suspicion. Most of his pay for working for Maurice was in a Miami bank, but he hadn't been able to help himself dressing up his boat a little.

Plata chuckled at a joke Maurice missed. The pilot rested his thin frame against the wheel's spokes. Every time he adjusted the *práctico*'s course, he had to push himself away from the wheel. Plata had a narrow face, devoid of interest, giving him the appearance of one incapable of guile. He had used it to his advantage over the years.

To their right as they plowed into the channel was the Castillo de la Punta and to their left the Castillo del Morro. Morro Castle was as plain as the rocks on which it stood. Waves crashed over the stones, sending spray against the walls.

Maurice asked, "Ever been inside Morro Castle?"

Plata shook his head. "I've heard the dungeons are so dark and dank that a week in one will drive you mad. I've also heard that many of those arrested over the past several weeks by the G2 are being kept there. And in the Príncipe."

The boat passed a Soviet bulk transport ship, probably carrying sugar, headed to sea. A moment later the *práctico* rolled in its wake. Now on the city side was Avenida de Céspedes, with few cars but trucks of all descriptions: flatbeds, two-tonners, some with no doors, some in green-and-tan camouflage. And across the channel from the avenue, on the east bank, was La Cabaña, another fortress, this one built in the mid-1700s, after the Spanish regained control of Cuba from the British. It, too, had served as a prison and execution ground. Since the revolution it had been a military academy. Every evening at nine o'clock a cannon was fired from La Cabaña, a tradition dating from times when the shot signaled the city gates were closing.

The *práctico* veered toward the west bank as it approached yet another fortress, the Castillo de la Fuerza, Havana's oldest. The structure resembled a blockhouse, with thirty-foot-high walls twenty feet thick. It was now a weapons museum. Just

271

beyond the castle, at the foot of O'Reilly Street, was the old ferry landing, where launches departed for La Cabaña and Casablanca. Plata's boat drew near the landing.

As he had when he studied photos and computer displays of Havana with Mederos in the warehouse, Maurice sensed that Havana was stuck in time. He had visited the city half a dozen times before and during the revolution. That was over thirty years ago, and nothing looked different. The skyline behind the shoreline drives remained the same, with the newest buildings—the hotels and tall offices—being from an unsightly time in architecture, the late fifties. The wharves in the Havana harbor—the Santa Clara, the Machina, and the San Francisco docks—were the same, with no new ones. The few automobiles Maurice could see along the avenue were also from that time, now with everything but the glass painted garishly. American cars from the 1950s were still the unofficial symbol of Havana. And the strollers. With few other recreations available, Cubans in Havana walked along the waterways, with their cooling breezes. And the haze. A brown smudge obscured the city, softening its edges and making it seem smaller than it was.

The *práctico* rubbed against the dock's bumpers. Maurice jumped from the gunwale to the cement landing. He held his hand out to the police lieutenant and the one-armed man there to greet him. Neither had met Maurice before, and their faces fell.

"Something wrong?" Maurice asked in Spanish.

Eladio Arrinda said, "I . . . I was expecting an American."

"How should I have looked?"

"You know, with a nice wristwatch and a gold chain, and pants with creases. A necktie and a shiny belt buckle." He added with a quick grin, "Maybe a stereo box on your shoulder and some nice Florsheim shoes."

"You've been watching too much Miami television." Maurice was wearing a coarse cotton shirt, blue serge pants, black brogans, and a cracked leather belt. His haircut looked cheap, spiky, not short or long enough to be fashionable, even in Cuba. He looked Eastern European.

Maurice glanced along the shore. There were four militiamen near the Castillo de la Fuerza, but they were unarmed and appeared interested only in the two young ladies who were asking for directions. Two Havana policemen were walking idly in his direction along de Céspedes, but they were eating sacks of fritters, called *croquetas,* and watching a coaster steam out to sea. Other than Arrinda and the policeman, no one seemed interested in his arrival.

The lieutenant said with distaste, "You look like one of the Russians who crowd our streets."

"My nationality depends on who asks me," Maurice explained as they crossed de Céspedes toward the Plaza de Armas. "You're going to accompany me, Eudy, to reduce any chance I'll be stopped by the police or militia or G2."

"We don't stop Russians," the lieutenant said. "There's hell to pay if we do."

"I'm counting on that. I have both Soviet and East German papers in my pocket. I don't speak either of those languages. If a Russian asks me something, I'm a German. *Spreche nicht Russki.* If a German asks, I'm a Russian."

"That doesn't sound too convincing," the policeman said.

"It's the best we could come up with on short notice. And it's up to you to be believable if I'm stopped, Eudy."

Lieutenant Eudy Puentes nodded doubtfully. He wore a pistol on his Sam Browne, and his khaki blouse was crossed with a diagonal strap. He was as tall as Maurice, but much thinner, with a sharp cast to his face. With the prominent Adam's apple and sunken cheeks, Puentes would always look hungry. His shaded eyes suggested distant Asian ancestry. Chinese were brought to Cuba to work on the sugar plantations after slavery was abolished in 1865.

"Who's 'we'?" Arrinda asked as they approached the plaza. "I thought you worked alone, for your own company."

"I've been asked by my government to help them out."

Puentes stopped abruptly. "Your government? The only part of your government that ever has anything to do with Cuba is the CIA. You mean the CIA?"

Maurice nodded reluctantly.

"Goddamn it, Bill," Puentes said sourly. He took his cap off to run his hands across his brow, as if he could wipe away the new knowledge. "I hate those bastards."

Arrinda was so startled with the revelation that he staggered over a curb. "What?" He blinked rapidly several times. "I've been working for the CIA all these years?" He was almost shouting, and he waved his stump apoplectically.

"Calm down, you two," Maurice said stiffly. "You've been working only for me all along, for my shipping company. You know what you've done, arrange transshipments of cigars and rum and fruit and textiles. Does that sound like the CIA to you? And you've prospered doing it."

"Holy Christ, but they've got their claws around you now," Puentes said, his voice mournful. "What are they making you do? It's got something to do with all this craziness in the Caribbean, doesn't it? And the G2 arrests?"

Maurice's answer was cut off by a siren. A police motorcycle turned off Obispo and passed them, headed toward de Céspedes. Three flatbed trucks bearing bulging gunny sacks followed the motorcycle.

"Fidel is sandbagging government buildings," Puentes said. "Just like during the October crisis. And yesterday he ordered a partial mobilization. My son, Marcelo, had to report to his reserve headquarters this morning. I'm worried sick. So are most Cubans."

Arrinda said to himself, "The CIA. I don't know who I hate worse, them or Fidel."

"We won't be working for them long."

"The CIA," Arrinda repeated miserably. "Jesus."

"I have a taxi waiting for us," Puentes said, pointing at a dilapidated checkered yellow sedan near the corner.

"I want to walk a little," Maurice replied.

Puentes and Arrinda glanced nervously at each other, then hurried after Maurice toward the plaza.

Maurice slowed under the shade of a royal palm. Plaza de

Armas dated from the early 1500s and looked European with its marble benches and wrought-iron railings and its statue of Carlos Manuel de Céspedes. On the Fuerza side of the plaza was the Palacio del Segundo Cabo, with its strong colonnades, formerly the headquarters of the Spanish governor of Cuba. Maurice and his escorts continued west toward the city center, passing the block-long museum and a restored pastel-blue house that had plants hanging from its balcony.

They turned south along Mercaderes, which had once been a raucous shopping street and now looked like a browsing street. There was not much buying in Cuba these days, Maurice knew. Heading west again, on Obispo Street, they soon passed the Johnson Drugstore. Through the window Maurice could see the mahogany shelves dating from the Spanish occupation, just as he remembered, except for the poster on a wall reading "Nobody Surrenders Here." A Fiat bus, manufactured under license in Russia, roared past them. It was missing its muffler and was so crowded that two passengers were squeezed precariously in the open door each with a leg hanging out over the passing pavement. The Fiat spewed so much black exhaust that Maurice had to turn his head away.

At first Maurice had felt the confidence of familiarity walking along old Havana, with its carriage-width streets and buildings with their alcoves, columns, and iron lattices. The great wash of the revolution had left this corner of Havana unchanged. There was an abidingness, a constancy, to a great city. Unlike a lost friend, met again after several decades, who returns with deep wrinkles, a fallen stomach, a world-weary cynicism, Havana had remained the same. Cheerful, bright, home of the endless carnival. It met his memory, and Maurice was grateful to the city.

Only after several blocks did he begin to notice the changes. Earlier in the century, old Havana was where rum and women were found. Pimps and lottery vendors and pornography sellers. There was no evidence of these now. Nothing lost there, Maurice supposed. But other changes were more

275

telling. It wasn't cheerfulness Maurice noted, only movement. He had confused Havana's former gaiety with its current urgency. Pedestrians were in a hurry, something Maurice thought alien to Havana. The gaudy awnings and rainbow-hued cafe umbrellas had been replaced with red-and-blue Communist party posters pasted on the sides of buildings. There was once a fluttering quality to the city; pennants swirling from flagpoles, women's showy skirts waving in the wind, advertising signs swinging above shop doors. The signs and pennants were gone, and the women were all wearing pants. And where were the legendary Havana smiles? Those Cubans passing Maurice seemed muted, staring at the sidewalk.

Maurice said, "I've never seen so many grim faces in my life."

"They think you are a Russian," Puentes answered. "No one smiles when our friendly occupiers can see them."

They came to the Floridita restaurant. Maurice remembered the lobster *mariposa* he had eaten here long ago. *Esquire* magazine had once called the Floridita one of the world's best bars. He left Arrinda and Puentes on the sidewalk and pushed his way through the door. It was too dark inside to see much at first, but Maurice recognized the tawdry French decor, the red velvet and intricate candle holders. He thought he could smell the almonds, pineapple, and butter that flavored the lobster. In a drawer at home, Maurice still had several Floridita swizzle sticks with "Cradle of the Daiquiri" stamped on them. Hemingway drank here. Of course, most Havana bars made that claim. Truthfully.

He walked to the bar. There were no customers. Maurice smiled at the bartender, who was standing next to a bust of Hemingway. The bartender was wearing a tattered white apron and was polishing a glass.

Maurice asked, "Still make the best daiquiris in town?"

"The ice machine is broken, comrade. We hope to get new parts for it next month, maybe."

This couldn't be the Floridita, not without the daiquiris.

He walked through the restaurant. The enormous gold-framed mirrors were gone, replaced with revolutionary art. Slogans on lips, rifles carried on high. The room was empty. From a weak speaker came Carlos Puebla, billed as "the singer of the revolution," crooning "Hasta Siempre," his fawning tribute to Che Guevara. There were no lovers bent low over the tables and no schemers penciling plans on tablecloths, fixing deals with handshakes, as Maurice remembered. He almost tripped on an edge of torn carpet on his way out.

They passed the Lorca Theater, with its four towers and baroque facade with the outstretched angel on top. One of the few photographs Rosa had from her childhood showed her on the steps of the Lorca Theater wearing her parochial school uniform and an enormous grin. Whenever Maurice thought of his wife as a girl, the Lorca was in the background.

Maurice and his escorts moved along the Prado to the Capitolio, a precise replica of the Congress building in Washington, D.C., except that it was purposely six inches taller. Cubans regarded it as the most flagrant example of *americanizado* in their country. The Capitolio is the home of the Natural Science Museum. Maurice knew that on school days, long lines of children would be waiting to enter the museum. But because of the emergency, schools in Cuba had been closed, as most of the teachers had to report to their reserve units.

"I've seen enough for today," Maurice said. They gathered under the shade of a laurel tree. "Our meeting is in Vedado."

A moment passed before a cab came down the Prado. Arrinda waved, but the cab did not slow, as they often did not in Havana. Only when Puentes, in his uniform, stepped onto the street to signal sternly did the cab begin to slow.

"Can you tell us why we're heading to Vedado?" Puentes asked as the taxi stopped.

"We're going to visit Fidel."

Arrinda laughed.

Puentes smiled and said, "You have what every Cuban needs these days, a sense of humor."

Maurice grinned back. "No, I don't."

The cab, a 1958 Plymouth, smelled of old cigarette smoke and motor oil. The rear seat's padding had been worn away, and a sheet of plywood covered the springs. The three men bunched themselves along it, and Maurice gave an address in Vedado a few blocks away from their destination. G2 routinely examined taxis' trip logs.

The cab's transmission sounded as if it had gravel in it, and judging from the fumes, the exhaust pipe emptied directly into the cab. Maurice rolled down a window, but it stuck at halfway. The cab drove along the west side of the Capitolio toward the sea. Moments later they were on Malecon, the bayside avenue that rings Havana. The cabdriver whistled to himself, tapping a rhythm on his steering wheel. Maurice squinted against the radiant blue of the Gulf of Mexico on the other side of the seawall. To their left were old buildings painted random colors. There were few cars on the road.

Maurice spoke normally, confident the cabby could not hear him over the grind and rumble of the car. "Things have changed, haven't they?"

Arrinda gingerly rubbed his stump before answering, "I hardly remember Havana *antes*." Cubans called Batista's era *antes*, before the revolution.

"Tragedy does that," Puentes said. "Eladio here lost more than his hand. Two of his brothers were taken away by G2 after the October crisis. Disappeared into one of their prisons. He never saw them again."

Arrinda shrugged. "Cubans push those things away. It has always been that way for us."

The lieutenant lit a *suave*. "When I was in the FAR in the early days, I visited East Berlin and Leipzig and Moscow for political training. Those cities are like Havana. Clean streets, painted opera houses, museums of industry. During those visits I learned what the revolution did to Havana. The city is without a soul." He exhaled loudly and tapped the ash onto the floor. "It breaks my heart."

When the cab passed the bronze-and-marble statue of Antonio Maceo, Arrinda said, "You can tell there's a crisis in Havana when there aren't any kids playing baseball here." The park around the statue was empty.

They drove by the Hotel Nacional, where the casino was once famous. The hotel was an imposing ten-story white structure with two bell towers atop its roof. The grass boulevard approaching the hotel was lined with tall palms.

Maurice said, "Well, at least Fidel got rid of the American gangsters who wintered at the Nacional."

Arrinda shook his head with anger. "The Mafia, yes. But gangsters still dominate Havana. The G2. Same mentality, same brutality, but now they are Cuban and have Fidel's sanction."

The taxi left the shoreline, turning onto Linea, a wide, tree-lined avenue bordered by apartment buildings from the 1950s, now with their colors faded and marred by rust streaks under broken air conditioners. Castro nationalized the entire retail sector in 1968, and many of the shops along Linea were still boarded. After a few moments they turned onto a side street, passing a group of *becados,* children brought into the city for their education. They all wore orange armbands.

Vedado was once Havana's wealthiest neighborhood. Most of the larger homes, which had names like Villa Rosa and Villa Santa Maria, have been appropriated by the government. When the owners fled to Miami, they unwillingly left their houses to ICAP (the Institute for Friendship among Peoples), UNEAC (the Writers and Artists Union), and other abbreviations. Many of the other homes had been divided into apartments. Some were dormitories for the *becados.* But a few were still owned by Havana's affluent. Despite thirty years of revolution, a few wealthy citizens remained in Havana. Eudy Puentes was one of them.

A Cuban police lieutenant made 270 pesos a month, 20 more than a schoolteacher, 30 more than a tobacco roller, by no means enough to own a home in Vedado. Puentes had earned his money working for Maurice, and unlike the cautious Eladio Arrinda, the lieutenant saw little reason to make money if he could not spend it. For many years Puentes had walked a careful line. Because of the plausible story concocted by Maurice and documented by Dallas Lyle, some extravagance was allowed by the Cuban government. Puentes had proof that his maternal grandmother, a Spaniard, had bequeathed him a sizable sum held in trust in a Madrid bank, which forwarded money to him in quarterly installments. The Cuban government could not confiscate the money in Spain, and as it had not resulted from the exploitation of Cuban workers, they left Puentes alone.

In truth, Puentes's father had been a member of Batista's infamous Rural Guard and had been executed shortly after Castro came to power. Puentes was ten years old at the time and knew nothing about what role his father may have had in the guard. His mother died shortly after of a wasting disease, loneliness, Puentes had suspected all his life. He had never forgiven Fidel Castro. He met Eladio Arrinda in the FAR, and Arrinda introduced him to Maurice by letter in 1968. Maurice needed someone in the Havana police force. Puentes quickly joined and rose to a lieutenant's rank.

Even with the forged documentation, Puentes could not risk living the life of a sybarite, or even a North American. He did not own a car. He did not leave Cuba on vacations to the Black Sea or Leningrad like a few prosperous Cubans. His off-duty clothes were subdued. He worked for a living. His home and its contents—mostly Cuban art—were his extravagances.

When Maurice had sent a message requesting Puentes to allow his people to make a few interior alterations in the house, the lieutenant had not hesitated to hand it over. He had been living with Arrinda for the past week and doing a few errands for Maurice.

They approached Puentes's residence from the north. It was enclosed by a wall covered with crimson bougainvillea that heavily scented the air. Puentes pushed open the iron gate. The neighbors' views of the patio were blocked by a masonry wall and a glade of tall bamboo growing in front of the walls. The exterior of the house was white stucco. Movable panels made of wood slats, called *persianas,* hid the windows and allowed ventilation.

They crossed the brick patio to the massive wood door. A stained-glass *mediopuntos* was above the door, a full 180-degree arch, the glass fanning out like a peacock's tail. In the middle of the door was a *postigo,* a small window, also of stained glass, which could be opened from the inside. Below that was a brass knocker resembling a lion's head.

Puentes said, "I don't know if I should knock on my own door."

"They know we're here," Maurice said.

The *postigo* opened. Roberto Ramos peered out, then tilted his head back so Maurice could see his smile through the *postigo.* "Welcome," Ramos said as he pulled open the door.

Ramos politely held his blued Beretta behind his buttocks as he waved them in. They entered a courtyard, open to the sun, around which rooms were arranged. A gallery lined the second floor, and baskets of Indian goldenrain hung from the railing. Around the pillars supporting the gallery were climbing green congea. Near a table in the center of the court were four pots of buddleia, called the butterfly bush, Cuba's national flower, each purple bloom with three spikes like a trident. The hum of insects filled the courtyard. Shielded by a pillar, another agent whose face Maurice could not make out lowered his Heckler and Koch assault rifle.

Ramos's features were too large for his face, with a nose thick through the bridge, ears that stuck out from his head at a sharp angle, and an ear-to-ear grin. Maurice had noted in training that Ramos's quick smile always carried a physical challenge. Ramos was born in Miami, served in the navy, and had since worked at the CIA, with only four months' leave in 1980 to train for the Olympics, where he placed fourth in the judo half-heavyweight class. He led them through the door into the sitting room.

The room was decorated with Puentes's collection of paintings: a cityscape by cubist Marcel Pogolottis, a river scene by Esteban Chartrand, a new art painting by Portocarrero, a painting of Afro-Cuban symbols by Wifredo Lam, and others. Vibrancy seemed to be the only theme to the collection. The room shimmered with their presence. It was more than a gallery, as the chairs were worn and a pile of newspapers covered an end table.

They walked through an archway into an expansive dining room, then down a flight of stairs into the basement. It once had been lit by a single bulb on the ceiling, but auxiliary lighting had been installed, and the basement was as bright as the courtyard. To one side was a work bench, on which were a laptop computer and a bank of coding and communications equipment in backpacks. Hung above the bench were a pair of pruning shears, a crosscut saw, and two Uzi submachine guns. A pile of discarded wallboard, two-by-fours, and acoustical insulation lay in a corner. An agent wearing a *guayabera* sat near the bench, earplugs in place, playing with the radio dials.

A vault had been added to the basement, looking at first glance like a large wine cellar. The door to the chamber was of iron, and it had a portal on it the size of a plate. An air conditioner had been installed in a wall to the chamber, with iron bars encasing it so it could not be pushed out. The air conditioner controls were on the inside of the vault. A one-way mirror, two inches thick and bulletproof, was in one wall, and Ernesto Pazos was sitting on a folded chair looking into the vault. He rose as with a relieved grin when Maurice and the others reached the basement.

Pazos wore a black trimmed mustache above narrow lips. His eyes were pale brown, and one eyebrow ended in a purple scar, resembling a length of red ribbon, going halfway to his ear, which Maurice knew was the result of an experiment with a pipe bomb when Pazos was ten. Pazos had on tan pants and a T-shirt with "Che" printed on it. In hot and humid Havana, there were few places to hide a weapon on one's clothes, and Maurice knew that Pazos wore his pistol in an ankle holster.

When Maurice raised his eyebrows, Pazos said, "No problems. He's reading. Asked who we were, but otherwise hasn't said a word. And we haven't told him anything."

Maurice stepped to the one-way mirror and peered inside. The vault contained a bookshelf with several dozen volumes. Carefully folded blankets were on a cot against the end wall. On a table near the bed were a lamp, a radio, a small television set, a computer chess game, and a box of typing paper. On a small serving table near the door was a plate containing the remnants of a meal and a spoon and fork. A straw mat covered most of the floor. A toilet and sink were in a corner.

In the center of the room was an occupied rocking chair. Maurice could see only the back of the prisoner's head. He was wearing a U.S. Navy work uniform. As Puentes and Arrinda joined Maurice at the mirror, the prisoner stood to walk to the bookshelf. Undoubtedly knowing he was watched, he glanced at the mirror.

Puentes and Arrinda gasped as one. Puentes put his hand against the vault wall to steady himself and exclaimed, "Mother of Jesus, what have you done?"

Arrinda crossed himself, and his face began to mottle, like a fruit left too long in the sun. He wavered and had to step to one side to catch himself. No one in the room noticed his immediate trembling, and he clasped his hand around his stump to hide it.

"I've been meaning to tell you about this," Maurice said, leaving them to their astonishment and turning to the agents.

Pazos indicated the radio. "We've installed the dish on the roof walkway, hidden by pots of plants. It's only two feet across anyway, and it can't be seen by neighbors or low-flying aircraft. We're about to test the connection, and we—"

The sound of a blow and a grunt of pain cut off Pazos. Maurice turned to see Eudy Puentes fall against the cell wall, then slide to the floor. The flap on Puentes's holster was open. Maurice turned farther, toward the cell's door.

The pistol was pinned against Eladio Arrinda's rib cage by

283

the stump, and with his hand he was desperately yanking at the cell door's portal cover. His face wore a madman's rage, and bits of spittle flew from between his exposed teeth. A searing hiss escaped him, as if he were fighting pain. He screamed with exertion, and the portal sprang open on its hinges.

Maurice lunged at him, but before he could cross the four feet of floor, Arrinda jabbed the pistol barrel into the opening and yanked the trigger three times. The concussion filled the basement. The ejected casings clattered onto the cement floor.

Maurice's head rammed Arrinda, bowling him off his feet. The pistol, caught for an instant in the port, fell back onto the floor. Maurice landed on top of Arrinda, who screamed a curse. He kicked wildly, trying to free himself, and his hand swept the floor, searching for the weapon.

Pazos quickly stepped over both of them and jerked Arrinda's arm into a painful wrist lock. Maurice rolled off Arrinda to sit on the floor. His breath was knocked out of him, and he swallowed and gasped and pressed his sternum and coughed.

By exerting pressure on the wrist, Pazos forced Arrinda to his feet, and Arrinda brayed with the pain. Pazos pushed Arrinda against a wall. The other agent in the room covered Arrinda with a pistol he had pulled from somewhere. Puentes had been more startled than hurt by the cuff to his head. He walked over to his handgun, picked it up, and replaced it in the holster.

Pazos ran to the mirror and took a deep breath of relief. After a moment Maurice could draw a breath. He pushed himself to his feet. "Did he get hit?"

"Amazingly, no," Pazos said. "There're some holes in the back wall, and he's standing with his hands on his hips, grinning."

"No one said he wasn't brave," Maurice said, dusting off the knees of his pants. He looked at Arrinda. "What the hell, Eladio? Goddamn it, you just about—"

"I swore . . ." Arrinda was gulping air, and his entire body shook with emotion. "I swore if I ever had the chance, I'd kill that bastard. . . ."

"Jesus, Eladio . . ."

"I'd get even for all the pain and misery he's caused me and my family and Cuba. I never thought I'd get close enough, and suddenly I'm two feet away from the monster." His words rattled to an end, and he turned away, quietly sobbing.

Maurice went over to him. "Eladio, listen to me." He turned him so they faced each other and put both hands on his shoulders as if he were a child. "We've got to have your help over the next couple of days."

"I owe you so much, Bill, but I can't. . . . He had my brothers murdered."

"What we'll do to him will be worse than shooting him."

Embarrassed, Eladio ran a sleeve across his cheeks. He tried to turn away, but Maurice held him.

"Are we going to have to watch you, Eladio?"

He shook his head. "I'm sorry, Bill. I don't—"

Maurice held up his hand. "We'll forget it." Rubbing his chest, he walked to the port and bent slightly to look inside the cell.

He was startled to see the prisoner, similarly stooped, staring right into his eyes. The prisoner said something in a low voice, something about the CIA.

"Pardon me," Maurice said, feeling the weight of history. He leaned closer to the viewing port, an act of intimacy. He was oddly flattered the prisoner would speak to him. "I didn't hear you."

With ferocious energy, the prisoner stabbed the fork through the portal. The tines shot into Maurice's cheek with such force they broke off a molar. Pain flooded Maurice's head. He staggered back, then fell to the floor, his legs splayed out awkwardly.

Puentes rushed to him, rolling him onto his back. "Jesus, Bill, you all right?"

On the bench, a radio beeped twice. The agent grabbed for his headset.

Blood spurted from the hole in Maurice's cheek. His eyes were watering so much they blurred his vision. He was in such

285

agony, he could not recall what had just happened. He gritted his teeth. Arrinda steadied him. He exhaled, and the incident came back to him, with increasing waves of pain that seemed like electrical currents swirling between his ear and neck.

The agent on the radio called, "It's the Miami warehouse. They want a report."

Maurice felt for his cheek. The fork was still embedded in his gums. He gripped it firmly and yanked it out.

"Tell them things are going smoothly," he said. He spit out the tooth, blood with it. "Very smoothly."

PART THREE

Al loco y toro dale corro.

(Always make way for bulls and fools.)
CUBAN PROVERB

Chapter XIX

With the exception of three rooms used for diplomatic purposes, the Soviet Union's embassy in Havana was entirely a KGB residency. Soviet residencies the world over follow a strict, uniform floor plan, and when Victor Fedorin was transferred to Havana, he could have found his way around his new station with the lights out.

Behind the reception area, a hallway divided the building on the first floor. To the left were rooms for computer and communications equipment. In a cramped room on the right were twenty desks for case officers who oversaw operations. Farther along the hall on the right were two offices, the first shared by the head of Line X and the illegals support officer. The second was occupied by the Line KR chief, the security officer, and Fedorin.

In these rear offices of any Soviet residency, three to a

room meant one of the occupants was on his way out. The head of Line KR, an ambitious Georgian whose uncle was a Politburo alternate, and the security officer, a major who had served with distinction in Afghanistan, were still rising and would probably soon receive assignments at the Center in Moscow.

Fedorin knew he was the odd man out. His desk was against the inside wall under the clock, clearly the inferior position in the room. With the Caribbean about ready to detonate, the others in the office were working twenty hours a day, and the operations room was in constant uproar. Only Fedorin had time on his hands.

Time to study his wife's telexed letter. The telex was a perquisite of KGB foreign service, and it made all messages from home look official. He read it again and ran a nervous hand across his mouth. Alexandra reported that two investigators of Napravleniye (Direction), a division of the KGB's Second Chief Directorate charged with investigating corruption, had visited their apartment unannounced. They interrogated her for three hours, asking about the family's income and expenses. Hundreds of questions, but they all reduced to one: How does a KGB major afford a two-bedroom apartment on Prospekt, an automobile, the piano, the carpeting, and a Sony stereo system? The investigators had made an inventory of their personal possessions, opening drawers, fingering through her wardrobe, counting the pieces of sterling silver, and demanding she turn over her ruby ring for appraisal. She had no choice but to give them the family ledger.

Alexandra decried the impertinence of the Direction, asking such things of a KGB major's wife, and in the next sentence asked what would become of them. She was overcome with worry. Could he take care of things, like he always did?

Fedorin scowled. His wife thought he ran Moscow Center. At least she did if she believed all his tales.

And, good God, the Napravleniye. Those bastards were thorough. Corruption was a crime for which Soviet citizens were often shot, and their widows would read about it in

Pravda the following day. The punishment awaiting a KGB officer caught using his position to pilfer from the state would be certain.

Fedorin's back was damp and his stomach leaden. A persuasive but unspoken attraction of KGB service was that it was one of the few enclaves in Soviet society where fear of the secret police was not endemic, as the KGB *was* the secret police. Fedorin had not been truly afraid for years, until he had a fresh taste of it when the Havana policeman tripped onto his trucking operation. And now, after reading Alexandra's letter, fear returned in a rush of ugly memory.

His telephone rang. He lifted it and listened for a moment. He clenched his jaws so tightly crescents formed at the corners of his mouth. He glanced over his shoulder and whispered, "I'll be right there."

The major weakly pushed himself away from his desk. He was deathly tired—a reaction to fear he had forgotten—and his knees wobbled as he walked to the office door. The chief of Line KR, a colonel in charge of penetrating foreign intelligence, was yelling into a secured telephone. On the wall behind him was a chart outlining the CIA's Havana organization as revealed by the recent G2 arrests.

Fedorin left the office and pushed his way through the embassy's fortified front door. He tried to walk briskly, but his fear and bewilderment slowed him like a headwind. Sultry tropical air wrapped around him, suffocating him, giving his panic a physical presence. By the time he reached the Club Sharad he was frequently glancing over his shoulder, expecting to see Direction officers following him. He forced a grin. It hadn't come to that yet. He had scrambled before. He could do so again. Fedorin stepped into the Club Sharad with renewed confidence.

It vanished the instant he saw Justo Cantillo's battered face. The club owner's eyes were purpled, and droplets of blood from his nose were splattered along the top of the bar from one end to the other. His lower lip was split and exposed, and blood was leaking down his chin. A rag on the bar he had used to dam his nose was soaked through with blood. Near the rag were his shattered spectacles. Cantillo was gripping one hand in the other and grimacing, in so much pain he did not hear the Russian enter the bar. The room was empty.

Fedorin recognized the work of the KGB as readily as if Cantillo wore a sign. Loose teeth, broken fingers, a dozen bone-deep bruises and cuts, but still awake. Knowing the precise edge of consciousness was a KGB art.

He skipped the preliminaries. "What'd you tell them?"

Lost in his pain, Cantillo was so startled he almost slipped off his bar stool. He recovered only by catching his elbows on the bar, unable to use his wrenched hands. The Russian pushed him upright.

Cantillo sputtered with pain and indignation and tried to wave the Russian away. He winced with the effort.

Fedorin resorted to compassion. He lifted the bar rag and tried to dab at Cantillo's chafed face. Cantillo ducked him and slurred his words. "I told them as little as I could."

"How little?" Fedorin asked in a small voice.

"Just about every goddamn thing they wanted to know. And you go ahead and tell me you'd have been braver." Cantillo challenged him with a bloodshot glare. "Go ahead."

Now Fedorin needed the support. He slid onto the stool next to the Cuban. He kneaded his forehead with a fist. "Justo, what did they ask? I mean, were their questions aimed—"

"They didn't waste any time. Showed me a photo of you dressed in your nice army uniform, cap and all. I said you might've been a customer here once or twice, but couldn't be sure. That's when they started bouncing their fists off me and walking on my fingers. And that's when I started remembering."

"The rum sales?"

"That's right," he said defiantly.

"I mean, they know I often buy for the embassy here to get a good price. Did you tell them more than that? About the extra crates?"

"They started grinding my face into the bar, so I kept talking."

Fedorin flushed with fear. "What about the truck I send around to take delivery?"

"That, too."

Fedorin inhaled slowly, trying to calm himself. It didn't work. He stood slowly and saw Carla enter from the back room. She was wearing a sheer dress that clung to her like cupped hands. She smiled invitingly, but he rushed out of the Club Sharad into the Havana heat.

Mederos had been president of Cuba for six hours and had not left the third-floor office of the Palace of the Revolution. Only after he had met with the Soviet ambassador and Rabassa and Galvez did he realize how foolish he had been.

Maurice had instructed him to immediately isolate himself, to separate himself from those who might notice the small things, might cast a questioning glance at a mannerism gone wrong. Yet on entering the palace, Maurice had found them waiting for him and in an impulsive act of showmanship had met with the Russian ambassador and Castro's key advisers. A masterful performance, he congratulated himself at first. Now he was not so sure. The G2 and DGI chiefs had known Castro since his exile days in Mexico. The ultimate test of Mederos's act should not have been the first test. After Galvez's departure, Mederos had told Chico Legro he wasn't to be bothered. He hadn't been, not for six hours.

During that time, he had expected Galvez and his agents to crash through the office door at any moment, pistols in hand, to arrest the impostor. Hopelessness had saddled him during the afternoon, compounded by a renewed sense of absurdity. Maurice had fooled him into thinking his preposterous scheme would work, and now he was embroiled in it with no way out.

But the afternoon had worn on, with Mederos doing little but casually reading reports from Castro's in-basket and staring at the office door, and nothing had happened. The dread had dissipated. Maybe Maurice was right, as hard as that was to believe.

Mederos lifted one of the telephones. "Come in, will you, Chico."

The secretary was standing in front of Castro's desk fifteen seconds later, his pad and pen ready.

Mederos leaned back in Castro's chair. His confidence returned in a giddy rush. He could pull this off *a seco*. Castro was known to disappear for ten days or two weeks. Rumors would sweep Havana, and he would just as suddenly reappear, all smiles, no explanations. Usually hunting or fishing trips, the CIA knew. But occasionally he would visit his villa on the Isle of Pines or his sanctuary on Cayo Piedro and apparently do nothing but brood. No one in Cuba could call for an explanation. An enigmatic, powerful man received vast leeway.

Mederos said roughly, "Tell Raul I'm sending him to Moscow for a clarification of our comrade-in-arms's positions on the new Caribbean crisis. He is to leave immediately."

Chico Legro's face twitched, as much of a reaction as he was allowed. He said hesitantly, "Excuse me for suggesting, *Comandante-en-Jefe,* but shouldn't we make a request for such a trip through the normal channels? I mean—"

Mederos's thin smile was sufficient to interrupt. "Send Raul, and have the Ministry of Foreign Affairs do the niceties while he is en route. He is to leave immediately."

"He will want instructions," Legro said meekly.

"I just gave them to you. He is to determine the Soviet position." Mederos pulled at his beard, as Castro would. "I want Aristides Rabassa to send reports to me every four hours. I won't need to meet with him personally."

Legro made notes and did not so much as raise an eyebrow. Castro had walked unusual paths many times before. Legro would not ask why.

Mederos asked, "When am I meeting with General Labrada?" Arnaldo Labrada was chief of the armed forces general staff.

Legro said, "Whenever you—"

"Of course, Chico," Mederos said harshly. "Whenever I want. I'm asking you when he thinks I'm meeting with him."

"In thirty minutes, *Comandante-en-Jefe*."

"Cancel that. He is to submit a written report on preparations every four hours. The same with Negrin, Betencourt, Fonseca, and Acosta." The commanders of the Territorial Militia Troops (MTT) and Cuba's three standing armies. Mederos had read their reports, written in response to Castro's order the day before to fortify a number of Cuban beaches, including Matanzas, Mariel, and the Bay of Pigs. The beaches and harbors were being mined. Barbed wire was being unrolled. Mortar entrenchments and machine-gun nests were being set up to sweep the beaches. Castro had always feared the U.S. Marines.

"I want my bodyguards rotated out," Mederos went on. "Bring in new people who haven't been nodding off because of the palace's routine, who'll be sharper."

"I'll tell G2 immediately." Legro wrote furiously.

"And when did you last have any time off, Chico?"

The question brought the pen to a sudden stop. "Pardon me, *Comandante-en-Jefe*? Time off?" Several seconds passed. "I don't recall."

"I want you to get away from Havana for a week. You've got a little place near Tarara you almost never see. Go and relax."

Legro was aghast. "But now of all times? Shouldn't I be at your disposal to—"

"Install Frigate Lieutenant Enrique Pascual in your office, and go."

"Have I done anything to displease—"

"Not in the slightest," Mederos said with equanimity. "You are loyal and trusted. But the very fact you question my order tells me you need rest. So go, and be prepared to work even harder on your return."

"Yes, sir," Legro said doubtfully. He limped toward the door.

"One last thing, Chico. I want to talk with Galvez."

The secretary disappeared through the door. After several moments, one of the telephones chirruped. Mederos lifted it and said only, "Yes."

Telephone conversations, where he was without his reinforcing appearance and gestures, were Mederos's most vulnerable activities. He had been told to keep them short.

"This is Galvez, *Comandante-en-Jefe*." He must have been in one of the distant provinces, as his voice cracked and faded over the line. And he must have jumped at Mederos's call, as he had not taken time to find a linkup with his helicopter radio.

Mederos waited, and Galvez hurried ahead, "The woman you are looking for, Carmen Santana, was sentenced to an indefinite term for her part in the imperialist aggression at the Bay of Pigs. She served six years of the sentence at La Ruda. She appeared to be no trouble for the camp administrators and worked in the infirmary there. She was then assigned to a UMAP, where she was a field nurse, tending cane cutters. After attending an injured prisoner during the *zafra*, she escaped. The camp *jefe* thinks there was no subterfuge, she just walked down a cane row into the hills. She was a fugitive for several weeks, and was recaptured by G2. She was then interned at El Príncipe."

Mederos's heart pounded, making his entire frame shudder. Many did not survive El Príncipe. Was she still alive?

"She appears to have been adept at escape. Three years later, while again on a UMAP harvest detail, she walked away. I have spoken personally with the warden there, Daniel Lafour, who was then assistant warden. He has no recollection of Carmen Santana, but he remembers supervising the investigation of her escape. He concluded only that should she be found, she should not be allowed back on work patrols. She has been out of the penal system since."

Mederos melted into his chair with relief. El Príncipe, the last cruel stop for generations of Cubans, had not been the end of her.

Galvez waited for a comment, received only silence, and went on, a nervous splinter in his voice. "Since then she has roamed eastern Cuba, mostly in Oriente and the Sierra Maestras. We have found that she lived in Buey Arribe, Las Mercades, Ocujal, and a number of other villages. People were at first reluctant to talk about her, out of a misguided sense of loyalty. It seems the few friends she made as a fugitive were unaware of her treasonous past, and knew her only as a midwife and nurse. We asked if it did not appear odd that she was itinerant, did not speak of her past, and did not have work papers. We had to reprimand one of our countrymen who replied that there were enough G2 interrogators in the country without his villagers acting like them."

Galvez may have been searching for a laugh from his superior. Again, he heard nothing. He finally continued, "She was easily accepted into the *batays,* and she was eagerly sought out for health care. She is quite skilled, as she almost had her medical degree before she abandoned the revolution by going to the United States."

"So she has been an escapee all these years?"

Galvez hesitated, perhaps sensing a rebuke. "This woman appears to have a trait shared by a few political fugitives, the ability to generate a quick loyalty among the uninformed masses. They trust her and are willing to overlook her lack of a history. But she also has repeatedly crossed the tracks of loyal Cubans, who have reported their suspicions to the CDR or the militia. She has had to flee again and again. This woman has not had an easy time of it."

Mederos sensed the danger of his next question. In Miami, he had listened with Maurice to a CIA tape of a conversation between Castro and Galvez playing dominoes on the Isle of Youth six years before. As always, Castro was holding forth, expostulating with a dilettante's enthusiasm and lack of study on a range of subjects. Punctuated by the sharp slap of dominoes, the one-sided conversation turned to the nature of humanness. Castro said he was intrigued by the problem of other minds, wondering increasingly as he became older if there was a consciousness behind others' body envelopes, behind the facial expressions and mannerisms, for he could find no empirical evidence of it. Castro said that Marxist-Leninism would benefit from proceeding as if this consciousness did not exist. The tape had a few seconds of silence, during which Maurice said, "University of Havana, Philosophy 101. Castro got a B in it."

Mederos had replied, "Sounds like it should have been a D."

Galvez had next spoken on the tape. "I view as proof of the other mind that I can read others' thoughts before they have formed. It has been a singular key to my modest successes in ridding Cuba of counterrevolutionaries. If there were nothing behind the faces, there would be nothing for me to know in advance, before the others' thoughts were fully formed."

The argument had droned on, but Maurice and Mederos had believed Galvez. In charge of G2 since 1959, he had lasted longer than any other secret police chief in modern history. Most were quickly swallowed by their own revolutions. But intuition, combined with his chronic suspicion and his dark ability to exploit weakness, had made him indispensable to Castro. Mederos had taken Maurice's warnings about Galvez to heart. He was not to be toyed with.

But Mederos had to know. He asked in a roughened voice, "Is she married?"

Another pause on the line, then Galvez answered, "No, not that we know. But she had a son, who is twelve now. We don't know anything about the father. She has never traveled with a man, as far as we know."

"What's the boy's name?" Try as he might, Mederos could not keep the wistful note out of his voice.

"Segundo."

"Have you found them?"

Galvez let the question hang a moment, capitalizing on the power his knowledge gave him. Then he said triumphantly,

298

"We have just discovered they are in Montellano, where she has been for only a few days."

Mederos tried to control his breathing, but he sounded like a blowing quarterhorse. "Do you have her in custody?"

"Montellano is a village of only three hundred people. G2 does not have an office there, but fifteen minutes ago I ordered the Montellano militiaman to arrest her. He assured me he would do so immediately." Galvez paused, then said, "One moment, *Comandante-en-Jefe*."

Mederos heard a background voice over the telephone. He could not make out what was being said.

Galvez returned to the phone. He said with professional calm, "The Montellano militiaman has just reported back. He has Carmen Santana under arrest."

Galvez paused again and may have been disappointed when no praise came over the line. He added quickly, "My helicopter is already warmed up. I will be in Montellano within twenty minutes."

"Bring her to me," Mederos ordered, then gently placed the telephone on its receiver.

His thoughts racing, Mederos was only marginally aware of the muted sound from the radio in the desk, which had suddenly switched itself on. It was tuned to a Havana station playing a postrevolution song, a *nueva trova*, by Silvio Rodriguez. Mederos had been instructed to keep the radio at his side. Maurice wanted something.

The ringer ignored it. Maurice could wait. Mederos wondered how Carmen had changed after all these years. Could they bridge those lost years? Would she want to? He had once thought of his love for her as thirst but now knew it to be a wound. By going along with crazy Maurice, he had done all he could to heal it. He was bringing them together again. Now it would be up to her.

The radio had been programmed to subtly increase its volume twice. The Rodriguez song became louder. Planning his future with her, Mederos heard nothing.

Carmen Santana was slumped against the coarse concrete wall of the jail cell. Her head was lowered, and she stared at her hands clasped across her lap. The cell was so humid that droplets formed on the concrete and ran to the floor. But she was chilled, and goose bumps on her arms resembled the texture of the walls.

She was weeping quietly, her shoulders quivering, not for herself, but for her son. The last she had seen him, he was lying facedown in the road, blood from his mouth and nose puddling next to him, his legs jackknifed under him. He looked as broken as anything she had ever seen. Segundo was all that remained of her life, her reason for running. To see him injured, sprawled in the mud, motionless, had eviscerated her.

Her pants were muddy to the knees. Segundo had tried to free her. The boy had run at the militiaman from behind and hooked his hands around the man's neck. The militiaman had trampled her to the dirt road, grabbed Segundo's hands, and twisted him off his back. He'd held the boy in the air by his scalp and smashed his fist into her son's face again and again. He'd tossed him aside, picked her up, and continued his journey to the jail.

She had thought they were in a safe place, at least for a few weeks. She had heard Montellano was a town where the revolution had been unwelcome and still had little influence. She and Segundo had found sanctuary with a *santero*, the leader of an Afro-Cuban cult, who had spent five years in a camp after Castro came to power. His name was Virgilio Acosta, and his kindness had been a balm for Carmen and Segundo. His granddaughter lived with him, a nine-year-old named Teresa, who quickly established Carmen as her best friend, and who looked away in confusion whenever Segundo caught her staring at him.

Acosta's crime, as he had explained to Carmen, was that he believed in something other than the revolution. He was an elderly black man, one of the many descendants of the Nigerian Yoruba in Oriente. When asked, he claimed to be a Roman Catholic, and the ceremony she and Segundo had witnessed in his small home contained the Lord's Prayer, the Hail Mary, lighted candles, and a wood statue of his favorite saint, Peter, whom he viewed as his ancestor and guardian. He presided over divinations, during which members of his congregation were loudly and hysterically possessed by *orishas*, spirits who took over the parishioners' bodies with distorted facial expressions and gestures instantly recognized by others at the service. The *santero* dispensed advice and magic charms and received small donations.

For those few days after she fled San Roque, the old man's home, with its darkness and scents and mystery, was peculiarly comforting. With its piles of sacred stones, enormous earthen jars of herbs, primitive paintings of saints on the walls, the carpet of dry cane leaves called a *paja*, and the quiet murmurs of comfort Acosta offered to the stream of faithful behind a bead curtain that acted as a confessional partition, the house made her feel as if it could be nestled in, that it would hold her and Segundo and would shut out the world.

Using a word he had picked up from American radio, Segundo said the place was creepy. All his life, Segundo had wanted to go to the United States, and his vocabulary was peppered with as much Yankee slang as he could put in it. But his mother loved the permanence of the *santero*'s home, something she had not felt for years.

Then the militiaman had stepped through the beads. He'd pushed aside the protesting old man and roughly grabbed her by the arms. The stench of his breath—tobacco, beans, and blackened teeth—was disorienting, and she'd next found herself on the road to the jail. The militiaman had offered no explanation, just chortled at his own good fortune. A block from the jail he'd said jubilantly, "The Green House will be grateful. Who knows what they will offer."

The Green House was slang for the secret police, after its old headquarters. Only then did Carmen know this was not a

301

country policeman's attempt to extort sex or money from a transient, a common hangover from Batista days. G2 had caught her again. Her meager hopes for herself and her son, rekindled for a few days in the warmth of the old *santero*'s home, had been struck down. And a moment later, when Segundo had wildly attacked the policeman and was badly beaten, she'd withered.

Over the years she had begun to think of Segundo as invulnerable. He seemed charmed, with his quick wit, extraordinary courage, and easy manner. Despite their life on the run and the hurdles thrown their way, he had survived, grown, even prospered in the little ways allowed them. That her son would fall was a preposterous, foreign notion. Yet he had, and he was still lying there for all she knew, in the filth of a Montellano road. She gasped as she again pictured him there. She felt as if she were a husk, the outside of her brittle, ready to crack, with nothing inside. Her reserves were exhausted.

The militiaman rose from his ancient swivel chair that shrieked like a cicada. He was a ponderous man, his belt hidden by the folds of his stomach and his thighs pushing against each other as he trundled toward her cell. It was a short walk, as the building was only twenty feet long, the last third of it her cell. Set close and corrugated by rust from a century of service, bars divided the room. Her *calabozo* contained only the cot, a bucket of water, and a reeking hole in the floor under the barred back window. His side of the room had a desk made of banana crates, the chair, a wood file cabinet, and a shotgun in the corner near the door. Bolted to the wall and connected with a padlock, two lengths of chain secured the shotgun through its trigger guard. The militiaman was wearing a revolver on his hip. Cuba has never been short of guns.

"I am Aldo Torras," he said with a rumbling voice, as if it came from his ample stomach. His uniform had once been olive but was stained brown and black by years of abuse. The few hairs of his mustache hung damply over his upper lip into his mouth. His ears stuck out at right angles from his head. His

302

tiny eyes, lost above his bulging cheeks, sparkled with avarice. "Maybe you were wondering how I found you."

She was silent, still looking sightlessly at her hands.

"There's only one CDR member in Montellano, and he reported you to me this morning. Said he saw a stranger helping that *santero* with some washing. I always hear about new people in town. Tell me what you've done. Maybe I can help."

She looked away, through the bars at the back of her cell. She could see only the sky, where the day's light was quickly failing. She heard the cough of a nearby automobile. She was surprised the town had anything but donkey carts.

"Must be something big, as I spoke on the town's telephone with a G2 major, and I heard him address General Carlos Galvez in person. He doesn't often toy with us simple *campesinos* all the way out here in Montellano. You must be a real prize."

She wrinkled her nose. His odor overpowered the jail's privy. He put a toothpick between his meaty lips and twisted it thoughtfully. "Must have been your boy who climbed all over me out there. I had my hands full with you, or I would have really taken care of him."

A new idea was as unusual for Aldo Torras as a clean shirt. His face twisted with the puzzle as he stared through the bars at the cell's ceiling. His head jerked left and right, as if the errant thought were nudging it. After a moment he said slowly, letting the idea form, "If G2 wants you, they probably would also like to talk to your boy."

Another moment passed, as the thought settled on him. He grinned evilly. "Don't go away. I'm going to get that little bastard."

Carmen stood shakily, joyous that she would soon see her injured son, fearful that he would soon be in the cell. Just as Torras stepped through the door to the road, she heard a scrape against the iron bars behind her. A length of a chain dropped into the cell. A thin arm reached after the stout links, pulling them around two of the bars. The links rattled as they were dragged over the iron.

She rushed to the window. In the weak light, she made out a blood- and mud-caked face. Segundo whispered, "Stand away from the window, Mama."

He was bent over the chain, attaching two end links together with barbed wire. He wrapped the wire quickly, oblivious to the stabs made at his hands by the barbs. The chain disappeared under the fender of an old black Ford sedan, the car she had heard. Its engine was idling roughly.

"Segundo," she cried, "are you hurt badly?"

He glanced at her. His nose was too flat and pointed at his right cheek. One eye was visible through a slit of puffed skin. "I'm sure I look worse than I feel, Mama." His words were terse and slurred, as if his jaw muscles hurt too much to move. He tested the chain by yanking on it. "I saw this in an American movie. I'm going to jerk the bars right out of the wall."

"The militiaman is after you, Segundo."

"Get away from the bars, Mama."

They had never owned an automobile, but Segundo had learned to drive when he was ten. Many of the old cars in Cuba had had their failed ignitions wired around, as new parts were impossible to find. The boy had searched Montellano until he had found a car with a makeshift switch hanging below the steering wheel.

"Segundo, run. . . ."

As the boy opened the Ford's door, Aldo Torras entered the jail again. He growled, "Your son isn't where I left him."

Startled, she took a jerking step away from the cell window. She turned to the militiaman.

"Where's he gone?" he demanded.

She looked at him directly for the first time, trying to hold his attention. "Maybe he's—"

The Ford's engine howled. Torras cocked his ear at the sound, then brought his eyes to the cell's window. Even in the low light, he could not miss the chain wrapped around the bars.

"What in hell?" He rushed out the door.

Cuba's succession of dictators had apparently wanted its

prisoners to remain in their cells more than the Ford Company had wanted its axles to remain on its cars. When the Ford shot forward and the chain sprang off the ground, the grinding screech of torn metal filled the cell. Segundo was thrown against the steering wheel. Its rear end dragging, the Ford bounced to a stop. The axle and wheels had been stripped off the car and now lay on the ground four feet behind the rear bumper. The chain still connected the axle with the intact cell bars.

"Uh-oh," came from the car.

Carmen ran to the bars and cried, "Run, Segundo! Get away from here."

The boy had never abandoned his mother, and he would not begin now. His nose bleeding again, he launched himself from the car and sprinted along the side of the jail toward the street.

Aldo Torras also ran, in the opposite direction, toward the prisoner's son. He pulled the revolver from his holster as he neared the rear of the building.

Segundo had seen the move in another American movie, one about a Notre Dame football coach. A lineman's block. The militiaman was bringing up his pistol and trying to come to a halt in front of the blurred, onrushing boy, when Segundo charged toward Torras's lower legs. Segundo's shoulders plowed into the man's shins. The militiaman toppled heavily as Segundo rolled under him. The boy was on his feet and sprinting again almost before Torras hit the ground.

He churned around the corner of the building and sped through the door. He leaped to the cell door. Of course it was locked. It was an antiquated latch that, judging by the keyhole, required a huge key, the kind worn on a metal loop hanging from the jailer's belt. Panicked for the first time that night, Segundo raced to the desk to pull open drawers. There was no band of keys.

"Mother, it's not—" His words stopped abruptly when his frantic gaze found the shotgun standing on its stock in the corner. He ran to it and lifted it off the floor, stretching the chain. He pulled desperately on the double barrel, but the chain would not give.

"Mama, I can't get the gun." His voice carried fear and resignation.

Carmen tried to find the words that would make him run. She knew he would not.

In a mounting rage, he held the weapon as far away from the wall as it would go, about a foot, and kicked savagely at the chain. The links were solid. He brought his foot down again, then again, lifting himself from the ground with the effort. And he cried out victoriously when a bolt popped from the aged wall. As he bent to bring the chain through the trigger guard, Aldo Torras limped into the room.

The business end of the shotgun barrel and Torras's mean gaze locked together. He blanched and backpedaled, bringing up his hands as if to plea. He was holding his revolver. Then he saw who was behind the gun. The boy, the prisoner's son, the one he had dropped into the mud. No taller than his shoulders and sickly thin. And frightened. The barrel was swaying.

The militiaman steadied himself. "I thought I left you out in the road." He smiled thinly. "You must be tougher than you look."

Segundo said nothing. The sound of his mother's harsh breathing filled the building.

"You probably never shot a gun in your life." Torras held out his hand. "And you aren't likely to begin now. Hand it over."

"I want the keys to the cell." Segundo's words waved like the shotgun's barrel.

Torras chuckled. "Looks like I'm going to have to teach you another lesson."

He stepped toward Segundo. The barrel lowered several inches. Torras renewed his grin, perhaps thinking it was a motion of surrender. He was wrong.

Fire spewed across the space between them, and thunder

chased itself around the building. Torras's right knee vanished. A window opened between his thigh and his calf. The militiaman screamed and fell backward, flailing his arms uselessly. His severed foot and ankle remained upright, a gory post. An unrecognizable portion of his leg had skidded to a rest against the side wall, below a small circle of buckshot.

Segundo let the weapon clatter onto the concrete floor and ran to the writhing militiaman. Avoiding the flailing arms, the boy searched Torras's pants. There was only one key, no ring. There weren't many locks in Montellano. He lifted it out of the pocket and hurried to the cell. A few seconds later, his mother was free. He took her hand and led her running from the building.

Carlos Galvez landed in Montellano five minutes later. He raged at the injured militiaman as he was loaded onto a stretcher, and he yelled at his men as they began a house-to-house search of the town.

Few of the villagers remembered seeing the woman, didn't recognize the photograph. The old *santero* said he had offered her a place to sleep, and she did a few chores for him. He didn't remember anything about her, what with his failing memory. And none of the townsfolk knew where she and her son might have gone.

Chapter XX

All his life, Maurice had come instantly awake as his eyes opened. He put his feet on the floor and dragged his hand across his chin, then gently touched the bandage patched to his cheek. His broken tooth made the entire side of his face hurt, and he tasted stale. His wristwatch read seven o'clock. Tuesday morning. They had let him sleep. He was wearing the same clothes as the day before, and they stuck to his skin as he rose from the cot. Even his shoes were still on. His knee sounded like a rusty gate. He crossed the basement to the bank of communications equipment, now arrayed with purpose along the bench.

"Anything?" he asked.

Ernesto Pazos was wearing earphones. He didn't look up. "Not a word from Mederos."

Maurice absorbed the news. It made him ache with impatience and frustration. "Can it be your equipment, Ernesto? I mean, can you tell if it's working?"

Pazos looked balefully with his dull brown eyes at Maurice. "It's self-diagnosing, Bill. I'd know if it were on the fritz. Same with Eduardo's radio. It'd tell me if it weren't working. It'd even tell me if it'd been blown apart." Pazos looked back to his equipment and asked in the tone of an afterthought, "You don't suppose Eduardo's been discovered, do you?"

"We would have heard from Pascual." He scratched his chin, absurdly wondering how he would shave around the bandage. "Eduardo is still in there, in charge."

Maurice turned to the basement's vault. Roberto Ramos sat on the chair in front of the one-way window. He was balanced on the back two legs of the chair, perhaps to keep himself awake. He looked over his shoulder at Maurice and smiled. The window was bright, but Maurice could see only the back wall of the cell.

"What do the newspapers say this morning, and Televisora Nacional?"

"Not a thing along the lines we had planned."

Maurice felt like grinding his teeth. "Damn it, Eduardo was supposed to release a Castro statement to his press last night."

"He hasn't, and that's all I can tell you."

"Is his Sony on right now?"

"He turned off the music alarm last night about midnight," Pazos answered. "I've tried to raise him since then, but he has the override switch on."

"I want him to hear my voice," Maurice said. "Right now."

"Override the override?"

"Whatever you call it, Ernesto." A fierce anxiety tugged at Maurice. This was the simplest part of their plan, one dependent on reliable CIA technology, something controllable. Yet even it was going awry.

"That's dangerous, Bill. What if he's in a meeting?"

"This early in the morning? Besides, we've told him to cancel Castro's meetings. Mederos should have isolated himself."

Pazos lifted headgear from the counter and passed it to

Maurice. Mounted on one earphone was a thin microphone that hung to the corner of the mouth. Maurice adjusted the gear on his head.

Pazos pressed a button on the console in front of him. "You're on."

"Mr. President, may I speak with you?" Maurice waited. His sentence was digitalized, mixed, transmitted in a split-second burst, bounced off a satellite to Mederos's Sony, which unscrambled and returned the message to its voice form, all in an instant. Maurice closed his eyes. He was in the grip of tension as tight as that quivering moment between when a son or daughter is born and when the baby cries. He said, again in Spanish, "Mr. President, can you hear me?"

"My confirm line says Mederos's Sony is broadcasting your words," Pazos said.

Maurice jumped when he heard "I hear you, Bill" from the earphones. Coming from both earphones, Mederos's voice seemed generated inside Maurice's head.

Maurice's dread abruptly turned to anger. "What in hell is going on, Mr. President?" When Pazos vigorously shook his head, Maurice added quickly, "I presume you can talk."

"I can talk," Mederos said. He sounded weary.

"Then will you tell me why you haven't acted as planned."

"I've put back your agenda a bit, that's all," Mederos said.

Maurice wanted to tap his headphones. He couldn't have heard that right. But Pazos's scarred eyebrow rose, verifying Mederos's words.

Struggling to sound calm, Maurice asked, "Putting back the agenda? What are you talking about, Mr. President?"

"I've got something I've got to do before we can proceed."

A hundred of Mederos's little quirks suddenly fell into place for Maurice, magnified by Maurice's fear. Each odd word Mederos had said since that day in the swamp, every unusual item of his history, every peculiar, human thing he had done in training, seemed to point to his fickleness, perhaps his craziness. Maurice should have seen it. He tried to rein in his veering thoughts. "Tell me what it is, this thing you have to do."

310

"It'll be resolved shortly," came over the radio. "Then we can get back to your schedule."

"Goddamn it, do you realize what you're saying? Do you understand what hangs in the balance?"

"Fully."

Maurice ran a hand through his sparse hair and over the headset brace. He exhaled loudly, puffing out his cheeks. He had no other choice. "Mr. President, I'm leaving now for the Palace of the Revolution. You and I need to talk."

"You'll have a hard time getting in, what with all my guards. G2, Havana police, the militia. I've got the works here."

"I'm going to arrive with a Lieutenant Eudy Puentes of the Havana police force. If you haven't cleared the way, and if we're not immediately escorted to your office, I'm going to tell the first guard who tries to stop me everything I know about you."

"He'll laugh in your face," Mederos said, doubt clipping his words.

"Not when he knows who I work for." Maurice ripped the earphones from his head, unwilling to listen further to Mederos.

Maurice raced by the cell without looking in and charged up the stairs. Puentes was in his dining room, with a cup of coffee and a roll in front of him. He was in uniform and rose from the table when Maurice walked quickly by and pointed at the door. The policeman caught up with him as Maurice passed through the gate to the street. They walked several blocks as Maurice explained, then the lieutenant commandeered a cab as he had done the day before.

The driver balked at the destination, the Palace of the Revolution, saying they wouldn't even get close. But Puentes assured him otherwise. Maurice wondered. Mederos had the power to throw them into prison. They would just disappear. Ten minutes later they entered the plaza.

The lieutenant whistled at the military activity. "This place isn't this busy except on January Second's Day of Victory celebration."

The older weapons were the farthest from the palace. They passed several Soviet-made Model 1931 antiaircraft guns.

Puentes commented, "Those guns fire fourteen-pound shells to thirty thousand feet. They're antique, of little use other than to let the citizenry gaze upon."

More serious protection was closer to the palace. They passed four camouflaged trucks, each with twin 57-mm dual-purpose guns mounted on the flatbeds. Closest to the government building were Soviet GECKO surface-to-air missiles, with ranges of about six nautical miles. The Russians did not trust the Cubans with the missiles, as Soviet troops—the elite Soviet naval infantry, with their berets and new AK-74s—surrounded each emplacement. FAR soldiers manned half a dozen spotlights, each as large as an automobile and, in the age of electronic air warfare, utterly worthless.

The cabdriver said to his passengers, "Damned Russians and Americans are dragging us into it again. Look at all this. You'd think the next war was going to happen right here."

The cabbie cursed when he was signaled by a militiaman standing near a portable blockade. The soldier shaded his eyes against the eastern sun to peer into the cab.

The lieutenant said, "I am Lieutenant Puentes," and passed him his police identification.

The militiaman immediately gave it back and waved them through.

Maurice breathed with relief. Mederos had cleared them. Twice more they were stopped, then waved on. At the entrance to the palace they were met by Frigate Lieutenant Enrique Pascual, whose apprehension had frozen his features into a solemn mask. Pascual led them into the cool interior. He had been installed the day before as Castro's secretary, and the palace guards let him pass with his guests. They climbed the stairs, their footfalls echoing. Pascual and Puentes waited in the reception room.

Maurice entered Fidel Castro's office to find Mederos sitting behind the large desk, wearing a slight smile. Two slim, yellowed folders were in front of him. Maurice's anger and anxiety were abruptly pushed aside by a surge of pride. Here sat Fidel Castro, surely. The slightly crooked teeth, the thin beard, the damp lower lip, the bulk and the aura, the confident Spanish hidalgo carriage as he stood to usher Maurice in. Here was the precise replica of Castro, their film footage come to life. He and his team hadn't missed a thing.

"Let me get you a chair." Mederos moved a guest's chair to the side of the desk, near the globe.

The voice wasn't quite right, of course. Nothing they could have done about that. A bit too polite, too sweet. It brought Maurice back to his purpose.

He said, "I want to know—"

Mederos cut him off with a short wave. He pulled the Sony from the desk drawer and turned it on loudly. He pointed at the walls, gestured Maurice closer, and said, "Quietly. Who knows what electronics the *jefe supremo* has had installed here. I turned off the mike I found, but there might be others."

Maurice leaned close and whispered fiercely, "I want to know what you think you're doing. Son of a bitch, the world has a short fuse, and you're sitting in this fancy office day-dreaming or solving crosswords or playing with your pud or something. What in hell is going on?"

"I'm looking for someone, Bill."

"What?" No other response came.

"Her name is Carmen Santana. I knew her when I was a student at the university here. She and I were at the Bay of Pigs together."

"Am I hearing you right? You've delayed our plan to search for someone? Listen to me closely, Eduardo. In eight hours American planes are going to try to destroy the Black-jacks, and the Soviets are going to put up a fight, and God only knows what happens then."

Mederos moved even closer. "She's the only reason I came to Cuba. I'd better tell you about her."

He did, about their time together in Havana, their love for

313

each other, which was carried to Miami after Castro entered Havana, about the disastrous invasion and her mysteriously endless internment. He told Maurice that she had now been a fugitive for fourteen years, and that he had ordered Carlos Galvez to find her.

Maurice felt himself coloring during the narration. He wanted to grab Mederos by his uniform's lapels and shake sense into him. Instead, he remained rooted to his chair, staring hard at the Cuban, trying to see behind the carefully reconstructed face. Maurice was fascinated. His impostor was speaking longingly of a lost love, of a woman he had seen only once in thirty years, and then through a pair of binoculars, as if this love somehow weighed against the Soviet fleets steaming to Cuba and the U.S. Navy and Marines moving into Florida with their landing crafts. Each hour, the world's safety increasingly depended on Mederos, and he was sitting there sadly recalling a woman he probably wouldn't recognize if she walked into the room. Mederos didn't seem to see the grotesqueness of it.

"I've got most of G2 looking for Carmen. Galvez thinks if he doesn't find her, he'll end up at El Príncipe." Mederos ended his story with his arms wide, like the pope, spreading understanding and forgiveness, seemingly sure Maurice could abide by his actions, as if his candor had placated Maurice.

Maurice was dumbfounded. "You're not normal, Eduardo. Christ, no one lets an obsession hound him for three decades. You've got to pull yourself together."

Mederos smiled indulgently and whispered, "An accurate diagnosis. An obsession. I suffer from it willingly. But unlike others, I've managed to do something about it. I have no doubt Carmen is going to enter this room."

"You fooled me, Eduardo. You hid your craziness well. You took us all in."

"You never quite managed to resolve your obsession, Bill. Or to do anything about it, like I'm doing."

Maurice was lost in his desperate thoughts. They had planned for endless contingencies. Alternative plans could be instituted immediately. Gerard Jones had even written a project management program designed to accommodate mischances. But they had not factored in the ringer falling off his rocker.

Mederos's words finally registered over music from the Sony. Maurice asked, "My obsession?"

"How long did you look for the killer of your first wife? A year, I heard. Did nothing but prowl Miami streets, trying to pry loose information."

"What're you talking about?" Maurice inched closer, as if trying to read Mederos's thoughts. Their foreheads almost touched.

"But you were a pariah on Calle Ocho. Miami Cubans weren't about to talk to you, not after your role in the Bay of Pigs, not when their relatives were languishing in Cuban prisons while Fidel crowed over them. You flapped your gums and wore your shoes out and twisted a few arms, and you didn't learn a thing."

Resenting that he had to follow Mederos, whose sanity he now suspected, Maurice said, "The bomb was ordered by Castro, and undoubtedly planned by Carlos Galvez. Retaliation for Jorge Gonzalez's role in planning the invasion."

"Of course," Mederos said. "Everybody has always assumed that. But who actually planted it? And how? These questions obsessed you for years."

Maurice tried to wave away this talk, but the Cuban grabbed his hand and held it like a child's. "You couldn't find the answers, but you were able to crawl away from your obsession. You've lived a life since then. I couldn't find the answers about Carmen Santana, and, unlike you, I wasn't strong enough to get away from it. I've lived with it like an addiction all these years."

"Jesus, Eduardo . . . " Maurice said below the music.

"You've just forgotten what it was like to be swallowed up. That's why you don't understand what I'm going through, why I came to Havana."

Mederos released Maurice's hand to lift the folder from the desk. His voice turned cruel. "I let you come to the palace today so you could be reminded." He passed one folder to Maurice. "That's G2's file on the assassination of Jorge Gonzalez and the incidental killing of Anne Maurice. It tells who and where and why, questions you've pushed aside for a long time. You'll note that one Nico Galvez planted the explosives."

He gave Maurice the second folder. "And this is G2's file on one of their Miami operatives, Nico Galvez, brother of Carlos. You'll find it interesting reading."

Maurice held the files as one might fragile glass. Mederos rose magisterially, as Castro would, indicating the meeting was over. Maurice stood, opening the first file, touching the onionskin paper. His pulse roared in his ears, and he could not resist Mederos as he led him to the door. Maurice was afraid of these files.

The Cuban said, "And when you've read those, try to tell me you don't understand an obsession, or remember yours."

Mederos gently pushed Maurice into the reception room. He said, "And the minute I learn of Carmen Santana, I'll return to your plan."

He closed the office door behind Maurice. The file was still open, and Maurice's head bowed as he read. He followed Puentes and Pascual from the reception room toward the palace's stairs.

Jack Cantrell struggled with the safety seal on a bottle of Maalox. "At my girl's junior high school, they had a nuclear war evacuation drill yesterday. Scared the bejeebers out of her."

The Miami warehouse was fully staffed, with an agent at each desk. But the room was almost silent. Most eyes were on Cantrell and Jones and Rosa Maurice. Throats cleared nervously and fingers drummed. Everyone was awaiting word.

Jones didn't look away from his Apollo monitor. "I remember doing that in 1961 during the missile crisis. During homeroom announcements at Sacajawea Junior High School. Right after an item about refraining from popping our milk bottle tops in the lunchroom came the announcement about possibly boarding buses that day to be driven to Rosalia, south of Spokane, but only if there was a nuclear war. Single file, don't bother taking your books. Our parents would meet us there when they could. Then the teacher went on about boys' choir after school. She didn't miss a beat. It's still the most disturbing moment in my life, sitting in homeroom wondering where Rosalia was."

"How're you doing now?"

Jones glanced at his boss, unaccustomed to the kindness in his voice. "I'm frightened, like everyone else. But I can push that to one side while I'm working, so I'm grateful for the long days, I suppose. You?"

Cantrell swallowed the antacid, then removed his glasses to wipe them with his tie. He said finally, "I don't know how I'm doing. The president's quarantine announcement last night sent a chill up my back. He has ordered the navy to turn back Soviet or other Warsaw Pact ships or planes suspected of carrying Blackjack parts or supplies or fuel. Christ, Gerard, I don't know what to be more worried about, the impending collision between our country and the Soviets, or that you and I and everyone else involved in this brainless plan will go down as some of history's greatest villains."

. "My husband has already had that distinction once, after the Bay of Pigs," Rosa said. She was wearing a black skirt and jacket with a red bow at her neck, work clothes. Her hair was tied behind her head, accenting her burgundy mouth and dark eyes. "That affair has eaten at him since. Not a day goes by . . ."

"You can be comforting, Rosa," Cantrell said dryly.

"Is he supposed to have contacted you?" she asked.

"Well, we're in constant contact with his team. It's just that certain things aren't happening."

The sound from the Apollo alerted them to an incoming message. Jones read aloud, "The U.S. Navy reports that a So-

317

viet heavy-lift load carrier, the *Stakhanovets Yermolenko*, thirty miles northeast of Cuba, refused a command from a navy cruiser to halt and allow an inspection. The cruiser fired a Standard antiship missile across its bow, and the freighter hove to. The cruiser's marine company has boarded the Soviet freighter and are conducting a search." Jones paused while the screen redisplayed. "The Defense Department will announce shortly whether the ship must turn around."

"The heat just went up a notch," Cantrell said, lowering himself onto the swivel chair next to Jones.

Another sound came from the Apollo. Jones read for a moment, then said, "And now the Kremlin has protested the interference in its maritime activities on the high seas, and said the boarding of the *Stakhanovets Yermolenko* is an act of belligerency."

Jones rolled his chair away from the computer, as if to distance himself from its stream of bad news. As if in sympathy, the monitor sounded again and produced a heartening message.

Jones scooted back to the screen and said, "Here's something. Raul Castro was seen an hour ago in Conakry, Guinea, presumably on his way to Moscow. Our reporter there says the visit is unexpected, and that Raul's plane was on the ground only for refueling. And here's something else. Carlos Galvez has been seen a number of times in the Oriente, a long way from Havana."

"He usually doesn't get much beyond Castro's elbow. So Mederos is closing the doors around himself according to plan. Then why didn't he make the announcement this morning?"

"Don't know, boss." Jones found some Rolos in his desk. He opened it, made sure no foil stuck to the chocolate, and put one in his mouth. He offered the roll to Rosa, but she declined. He said, "Our reports from your husband aren't as encouraging as we'd hoped."

"An understatement." Cantrell stared at the clock a moment, then added glumly, "But Bill might not know what's going on at the Palace of the Revolution. Maybe Mederos has been discovered or is somehow out of control."

Rosa blinked several times, her eyes shining. She said nothing.

Cantrell put his hand on her shoulder. "Things haven't fallen apart yet. And Bill is resourceful."

Again the Apollo sounded. Jones read, "The general secretary has announced that the Soviet Union will do everything in its power to avoid a conflict, but that an attack on Cuba will be regarded as an attack on the Soviet Union."

Cantrell rubbed his temples. "Jesus, what next?"

A surface-to-air missile launched from a Soviet KASHIN destroyer was next.

Navy Lieutenant Commander Robert May patrolled at twenty-five thousand feet ten miles southwest of his carrier, the *Nimitz*. He was loaded. His F/A-18 Hornet carried seventeen thousand pounds of armament, including Sparrow III and Harm missiles on nine stations. The Hornet's GE low-bypass turbofan engines could generate sixteen thousand pounds of static thrust, but he was throttled back, cruising at only six hundred miles an hour.

May had begun his service life as a Sea Cobra helicopter pilot. He was reformed now, his fighter pilot friends on the *Nimitz* liked to say. He had never told them that the Hornet was easier to fly than the Cobra. They wouldn't have wanted to hear it. But the plane was a breeze. Much of the conventional instrumentation was missing from the plane, replaced by eye-level readouts that allowed him to take the measure of his plane without taking his eyes off the target. And the on-board computers could damn near fly the Hornet on their own.

May was almost six-four, and his shoulders rubbed uncomfortably against the sides of his cockpit and his legs cramped quickly soon after the start of any mission. Once, because of the sharp angle of his long legs, the surgical tubing running between his condom and the bag strapped to his leg had been pinched off. The rubber burst, and he'd had to fly with a damp crotch for the last hour of the flight. All because he was tall for a fighter pilot. Fine with him. He'd sacrifice for the job.

The Hornet's radar was displaying eight other planes. His sidekick, Jeff Lorber, was out the starboard window in his Hornet. An EA-6B Prowler was flying below them and off three miles. Cruising the same perimeter, two navy Tomcats were six miles ahead. And fourteen miles ahead two Soviet fighters, probably Forgers, were hovering over a portion of the Soviet fleet. May knew a full Soviet fleet was fifteen miles southwest of him, but he couldn't see any of the ships in the low haze.

May heard over his phones, "Eagle-Red-One, edge a little closer to the main body. Bossman wants a test."

"Roger, Alphabase."

Eagle-Red-One and -Two were the Tomcats. May saw them begin a slow close on his plotter.

After a moment May heard, "This is Eagle-Red-One. I've got a visual here. Closing at an angle. Twelve, thirteen ships, heading east by southeast. May be more in the haze."

"Roger, Eagle-Red-One."

"I also read the two old bogeys at seven thousand distance, and a new reading just off a carrier."

"Got them, Eagle-Red-One."

There was a long pause. May had nothing to do with this chatter. He glanced over his right shoulder. He could see a blaze of sun reflected off Jeff's face mask. Jeff cheerfully wagged two fingers at him as he always did.

Eagle-Red-One's tone brought May's head around. "This is Eagle. I've got some jamming coming at me, Alphabase. Bearing two-seven-oh."

"This is Eagle-Red-Two. Same here. Looks like it's coming from the new bogey."

May glanced at his screen. The Soviet jamming appeared as a conical yellow strobe coming from the southwest.

The Tomcat leader said, "Alphabase, I'm pulling in jamming now from the water also. One of the ships. Take a guess what's going on. I've got no idea."

"We're looking at it, Eagle-Red-One. Pull away from there, both of you."

"Glad to, Alphabase."

May saw the Tomcats veer slightly north on his screen. He tried to see the planes through the windshield, but the brilliant sky and reflecting sea merged seamlessly together in the distance without a visible speck anywhere.

"Alphabase, Eagle-Red-One, I'm getting a faint blip from the south, dead center in the jamming. It looks like it's closing." The voice was steady. "Are we being shot at?"

"Can't confirm, Eagle-Red-One. Ditch the mission. Get out of there."

"Aye-aye, Alphabase."

"Eagle-Red-Two here. That blip just had a baby. We've got two incoming, probably launched from the jamming ship."

May's screen still only showed one blip. As soon as his computer recognized it, it would take a form, a stylized plane or missile or helicopter. The jamming was confusing his reader.

"Eagle-Reds, our assessment is that you've got two SA-N-1s coming at you. Flood the area and execute Plan Basic."

That meant turn on all your fuzz and get the hell away from there. May's screen suddenly carried cones of snow as the ship and fighters jammed and counterjammed.

"This is Eagle-Red-One. I'm pulling out in burn, but I show an incoming following my exhaust."

"Ditch him, for Christ's sake, Danny." That was One's mate. "Flare it, and roll down and away."

"A done job. But he's closing."

"It didn't take the flare, Danny. Drop now."

"Alphabase, this is Eagle-Red-One. Intruder is closing." A long second passed. "Right on my tailpipe. That's—"

The earphones broadcast a brief burp. May's eyes swept the horizon. He saw it, a blast of orange and black, a fireball almost instantly extinguished by its own speed. He looked again at his radar. Eagle-Red-One had disappeared.

Over the phones came a fogged voice: "Danny's gone. No chute."

"Eagle-Red-Two, this is Alphabase. Continue Plan Basic. All other craft remain on station."

May breathed for the first time in a minute. His flight suit was soaked. He looked again at his wingman. Lorber's fist was balled. Me too, May thought. Bastards. A moment passed. May studied his windshield projections and concentrated on even breathing.

"Dog-Red-One, you read me?"

"Yes, Alphabase," May said into his mask.

"You and Dog-Red-Two are to take that ship out. Do you copy?"

May suddenly felt as if he'd pounced on the afterburner. The order pushed against his chest. "Repeat, Alphabase."

"The bossman has ordered us to rid the lake of that ship. Do you read me?"

"Aye-aye, sir."

"Our best info is that it's a KASHIN-class guided missile destroyer, carrying two twin SA-N-1 SAM launchers and four SS-N-2s. And the Gatlings fore and aft. Thirty-five knots. Take your wingman in with you. Mirror Five will provide the fuzz."

Mirror Five was the Prowler. May asked, "You got that, Mirror Five?"

The Prowler pilot instantly said, "I'll soak them."

The Prowler was a Grumman EA-6 electronic warfare plane, a four-seater carrying the AN/ALQ-99 Tactical Jamming System (TJS), which housed five integrally powered pods, two under each wing and one under the fuselage. Surveillance receivers were in the fin-tip bulge. The plane was capable of spot, dual-spot, swept-spot, and noise jamming. The TJS had three modes. On automatic the computer selected the threat and took the necessary action. On semiautomatic, the computer ranked the threat in order of danger either to the Prowler or to any other planes or ships in its range. On manual, the back-seaters carried out the search and jamming. The Prowler was the best in its business, that of throwing a blanket over the enemy's eyes.

"Let's go, Jeff," May said.

May powered his Hornet from the sky, banking south toward the fleet. His ground radar now showed fifteen Soviet ships. He said, "Alphabase, light my target."

One of the ship symbols, the KASHIN-class destroyer's, glowed red. "That's it," said Alphabase One. "They'll throw flack, Dog-Reds."

"Thank you," May said with difficulty. He was dry. He tried to swallow, but his tongue caught. "You okay, Jeff?"

"Breathing fast, but I'm here."

May pushed the stick, and the digits climbed quickly past a thousand miles an hour. Lorber kept with him, right on his wing. If the Soviets could see anything, it'd be one blip.

"You on, Mirror Five?" May asked.

"You're bathing in it," returned the Prowler pilot. "That destroyer captain down there can't see his hand in front of his face."

The haze lessened, and May could see four ships in the distance. He refocused his eyes to a closer point so he could see the radar readout. The second from the left was their target. "Arming." May flicked a Harm missile switch.

"Ditto," his wingman said.

"You're close enough for visuals now," the Prowler pilot said over the phone. "They may be on to you."

"Roger," May replied. To confuse the target as to their intentions, the Hornets were streaking for an imaginary point east of the Soviet ships. The Soviet captain, unsure whether this was harassment or a strike, might hesitate the needed ten seconds. The risk was that it opened their profiles, giving more reflection for the KASHIN's radar.

"Bogeys closing at oh-nine-five, seven thousand feet," Lorber said. They were the enemy Forgers, V/STOL (Vertical/ Short Take-Off and Landing), probably from the *Kiev*. They were slow, but they carried a department store of armament. "Orders, Bob?"

"Take after them. I'll keep going in."

"Roger."

Red-Dog-Two instantly peeled off May's wing and soared due west, quickly gaining altitude. In only a few seconds its wings and fin were no longer visible, just the red ball of its exhaust. May turned back to target.

His gaze found two sparks of fire. He said into the radio, "They've launched two SAMs. Coming in." May was amazed at the calmness of his voice. This was his first combat mission, and he knew all the pilots and ships in the area were listening more to his tone than to what he said.

"Give them a couple seconds," the Prowler TJS tech said over the radio. "Hah. They're lost. They don't have you. Ignore them."

May's Hornet streaked to the reengage point. "Turning now," he said.

He knelt against the control. The fighter raised a wing. May accelerated and felt the gravitational pull push him back into his seat. At the end of the turn, the KASHIN was off his bow ten miles in front of him.

He said, "Do their Gatlings have me?"

The TJS tech said, "No. We're swamping their aiming radar. They'll have to go manual. And you're still out of their range."

The Gatling was an ADMG-630 six-barrel 30-mm AA gun designed to throw a wall of depleted uranium projectiles between its ship and anything incoming. It was the destroyer's last defense. When he tasted blood in his mouth, May released his cut tongue from between his teeth.

"Launching." He pulled the Harm's trigger. His right wing bounced slightly as the weight left it. He caught only a brief glance of the missile before it stole away. May banked sharply east and threw in his afterburners. Then he pulled his nose up, climbing away into the sun, away from the guided missile cruiser and the other Soviet ships.

The Harm, an antiradiation, defense-suppression missile, streaked in at the Soviet ship. It carried a laser terminal, and at this range the destroyer was an easy mark. The destroyer's Gatlings searched for it, black smoke pouring from their snouts, but with their aiming radar blurred, they threw long arcs of rounds that found nothing but water.

The Harm shot into the destroyer, detonating the missile's 146-pound warhead. The ship shuddered, and its middeck ruptured skyward.

"It's a hit," the Prowler pilot said. "A Technicolor beauty. George Lucas couldn't have done better."

"Red-Dog-One, this is Alphabase. Plan Basic."

May looked behind him. A spume of fire climbed from the Soviet ship. It billowed and rolled, and only the fore- and aft decks were visible under the flame.

"Can I get a report on Dog-Red-Two, Alphabase?" May asked, wanting to savor his victory, but unable to, with his wingman out of sight.

"Reporting in the flesh," Lorber cried over the radio. "Two Sparrows launched. One bogey killed, and the other ran away." Lorber's radio didn't hide the primal joy in his voice.

"Plan Basic for you also, Dog-Red-Two," Alphabase said.

"Thanks for the umbrella, Mirror Five," May said, pulling through fifteen thousand feet.

"Our pleasure," the Prowler pilot replied. "Let's go steady someday."

Let's not, May thought. A peaceful man by nature, he fervently hoped this was the last action the navy would see in the Caribbean that day. But then, that depended on the politicians, and he didn't trust them a bit.

Chapter XXI

Carlos Galvez bent over the desk, using a blunt finger to trace across a map of the Santiago de Cuba region, a province of Oriente. The map's flat relief did not show the broken mountains and dense valleys of the area. Cubans said Oriente was thinly populated because there weren't that many places to gain a foothold. Galvez asked, "This road to La Prueba?"

"Blockaded, General," a G2 major replied. He was wearing a green-and-khaki-camouflaged field uniform, as were five other G2 officers and Galvez, who crowded the militiaman's office in Montellano. They formed a circle around Aldo Torras's unstable desk.

"And this to Mayari Arriba?"

"Also closed off, general," another officer responded. "No one can get by there."

"And you have assured me that these barricades were up within an hour of her escape?"

"Yes, general," several answered.

"What about horse trails in these hills here?"

"We know where they are," the first officer said. He drew them with his finger. "They too have our people on them."

"Could she and her boy have taken off across country? I remember this area from our days during the revolution, and it doesn't seem likely, does it? At least, not far and not fast."

"Most of the flat land in the area is planted with coffee," the first officer said. "Unless they cross those fields, they won't make five miles a day. And we're patrolling the fields with DAAFAR helicopters."

Galvez looked squarely at his officer. "What you are saying is that she must still be within five miles of Montellano."

"Yes, general."

"How quickly is that circle closing?"

"We have over seven thousand men in the field. Our people, FAR, and militiamen. They are searching house to house, bush to bush, so their progress is slower than we would like."

Galvez stroked his mustache. "Too slow. But there are other ways. Where's that *santero* with the convenient memory?"

"We have him under house arrest, general. We can—"

The officer cut off his words as Vicente Legro walked with his uneven gait into the jail. Galvez and the others instantly straightened themselves and slammed their feet together, preparing to salute. When no one followed Legro into the building, Galvez peered over Legro's shoulder. Except for Galvez's bodyguards, the dirt road outside was empty.

"May I have a word with you, General Galvez?"

Galvez dismissed his officers with a curt nod. They hurried out, but not without backward glances. They had never before thought of Chico Legro as having an existence apart from Fidel Castro. He was Fidel's shadow, not there unless attached to the *comandante-en-jefe*.

The G2 director said, "You are a long way from your office, doctor. What brings you into the field?"

"My failing vision, general. At least, I presume it's failing." Legro carefully sat on a rickety wood chair, extending his game

327

leg out full. The two men eyed each other, neither willing to look away first. Both had undoubtedly wondered which of the two was more powerful in Cuba, Galvez with his innumerable undercover agents or Legro with his constant access to Fidel. For years they had known that neither would ever rise higher, and neither could do the other's job, so they had entered into an unspoken truce. Neither sought to undermine Castro's confidence in the other. Still, they were wary of each other, and always alert.

"You have me at a loss, talking of your vision, Vicente." Galvez pulled at his mustache.

"Yesterday I was relieved of my position at the Palace of the Revolution."

"Relieved?" Galvez said with genuine surprise. "Impossible. Fidel has utmost trust in you."

"Well, he terms it a holiday. One week of seaside air. Same thing as being relieved. And I must need it, because I'm having visions." Legro was a short man, rather withered, and he suffered by comparison when in the same room with the burly G2 chief.

"Why don't you come right out with it, Vicente?" Galvez asked, his mustache partly hiding his smile, like a half-concealed knife. "What have you seen that you're blaming your old eyes on?"

"Have you cooked up some scheme for Fidel, that you and he are pursuing in the revolution's interest, that I know nothing about? Or has the *jefe supremo* undertaken his own mysterious plan?"

Galvez glanced impatiently at the map. "You know everything that goes on in Havana, Vicente. Why don't you stop speaking in riddles and come out with it?"

Legro rubbed his bum leg. "I could not leave my office for this holiday without taking care of a few things this morning. And I think I saw William Maurice enter Fidel's office."

Galvez's head came up. His eyes glittered like a cat's, as if lit from within. "Maurice? Enter Fidel's office? That simply cannot be."

328

"Precisely. But I think I recognized him."

"We have all studied the photographs of the enemies of Cuba's revolution," Galvez said, turning to stare at the bars. "Our photos of Maurice are decades old. I'm not sure I'd recognize him either, or why I'd have occasion to."

Legro ran a hand across his bald head. "I might be wrong about seeing him. But are you aware of any reason for him to be in Havana?"

"You give me too much credit, or none at all, Vicente. That William Maurice would be meeting with Fidel could not be my idea, as such an event is an historic impossibility. There would not be a reason on this earth for it to happen. And Fidel would strangle him outright. Maurice tried to topple Fidel, and the *comandante-en-jefe* never forgives, as we both know."

With a deliberate motion, Galvez slowly drew his hand over the map, as if trying to rid it of creases. His words were just as deliberate. "Why come to me, Vicente? Why not mention your concern to Fidel?"

"Would you, general? I can say without criticizing our supreme commander that he brooks absolutely no second-guessing. I am not in a position to inquire of him why he is meeting with a particular person."

Galvez pensively chewed his lower lip. "Nor am I, nor is anyone else in Cuba." To do so was to invite a tirade and perhaps dismissal, as both men knew.

"Yet this was not an apparition I saw. I thought Maurice's meeting with Fidel might be your business, and I was going to warn you of the dangers of dealing with the American, and suggest we approach Fidel about those dangers." Legro removed a tape cassette from his breast pocket. "A year ago, at your behest, I impressed on Castro the necessity of obtaining a voiceprint machine. I know you have one. Tell me how it works."

"I am not a professional," Galvez said. Technicians are termed professionals in Cuba. "Our voiceprinter is a frequency-spectrum analyzer built by AT&T Technologies, a company in the United States. We procured it through a

329

French firm. It breaks the spoken voice into a frequency window, and prints out a graph showing the intensities of sound in given ranges. The way a particular sound is pronounced is called a phoneme, which shows up as a characteristic pattern which can be compared to a known recording of the speaker."

"I find it hard to believe that voices are as singular as are fingerprints," Legro said. He was sweating, as the morning sun had begun to cook the building. His head glistened, and a damp spot appeared along the button line of his shirt.

"My people assure me they are. The configuration of an individual's vocal cords inside his larynx, his throat, mouth, and sinus cavity produce a unique phonation. It cannot be disguised."

"You know of one taping system in Fidel's office. He often shows a visitor the switch, and with a grand gesture turns it off, assuring confidentiality. But there is another sound system, voice-activated."

Galvez shifted on his feet. "I was unaware of the second system."

"Our president is conscious of his place in history. He wants his every word saved." A lame explanation, but Legro continued, "The system is always on. Fidel and this man who resembles William Maurice turned up a radio a few seconds after the visitor entered the office, so most of what you'll hear on this cassette is music."

"Turned on music?"

"Fidel does that frequently, when he doesn't want his recorders catching what he says, despite the demands of history," Legro said without sarcasm. "Yet there are a few words recognizable on this tape. Perhaps you could use the voiceprinter and determine if it was Maurice I saw."

"As I said, we would need a control tape, a known recording of Maurice, for comparison. We don't have one."

"Ask the Russians," Legro suggested. "I would imagine they have an extensive inventory of that sort of thing."

Galvez nodded. "If they have it, they can send it via satellite. We will have it quickly."

Legro stood, requiring concentration. He made his way to the door. "You think Maurice is back at work? For the Americans?"

"Doesn't sound probable. But I've studied his methods. His planning of the invasion at Bahía de Cochinos and the attendant uprising in Havana was better than most know, probably including him. I won't take him lightly."

Galvez followed Legro from the jail. He squinted against the white tropical light and said, "I'll speak with my headquarters and arrange an immediate request to Moscow. We'll know shortly if we can run a test on your tape."

Legro said, "My suspicion that Maurice entered the presidential office is laughable, you must admit."

"William Maurice has come to my attention once already in the past several days. I have some people in Miami looking into things. Perhaps, just perhaps, it is less humorous than you think."

Maurice read one torturous line at a time, page after page of the file on the G2 operation that killed Anne and Jorge Gonzalez. He was sitting at Ernesto Pazos's bench in the basement of Eudy Puentes's home, and he was in turmoil.

Pazos manned the communications and coding equipment to Maurice's right. Roberto Ramos was at his post, watching the prisoner shadowbox. With nothing else to do, Puentes sat on a stool near Ramos, cleaning his handgun. They were all waiting. Brought on by Mederos's sudden delay of their plan and the report over Pazos's radio moments before of the deadly skirmish between the Soviet and United States navies in the Caribbean, the tension in the basement was palpable.

Except for Maurice. He had forgotten the Blackjacks and Fidel Castro. He was so intent on the file's pages that he was unaware he had scratched a long gouge into the wood of the bench with his thumbnail.

So new was the revolutionary government then that many of the documents were on typing paper without logos and on paper where the printed office had been torn off the top, little more than scraps. Some of the documents were handwritten by Carlos Galvez. Maurice gingerly lifted the typed order, apparently dictated by Galvez to a secretary for coding, ordering the killing of Jorge Gonzalez. It used the euphemism "take care of." He read it several times, slowly, like a child memorizing a lesson. Shaking, he returned it to the folder. He had to roll his head left and right, unwinding his muscles, before he could continue. He studied a yellowed page from the *Miami Herald* reporting the bombing, an order transferring money to a Miami address, and other papers.

Maurice picked up the last document, several pages stapled together, typed with what appeared to be an old machine. Maurice was instantly gripped by the pages, a detailed postmission report from Nico Galvez to his brother. It was written in a curiously whining, bragging, pleading, technical tone that spoke of a complicated relationship between the brothers.

The report contained an enraging surprise for Maurice. The FBI speculated the bomb was detonated by a switch attached to the car, but the car's engine compartment had been too mangled to tell with certainty. But according to Nico Galvez's report, he had used a radio detonator, which meant he had seen his target Jorge Gonzalez enter the car before pressing the switch. Which also meant he had seen Anne Maurice and Jorge's wife also get into the car. Nico Galvez had set off the bomb anyway.

"You doing okay?" Pazos asked, pulling an earphone away from his head. "You look bothered."

"I'm all right," Maurice said tremulously. He nodded in what he hoped was a reassuring way.

In recent years his anger and frustration over the murder of his first wife had receded, replaced somewhat by a feeling of guilt, because he could now recall his anguish and rage better than he remembered Anne. His day-to-day life with his first wife was remembered only vaguely. He found it difficult to recapture her in his mind. Forgetting her was an insult to her memory, to their time together. She was fading, but he could bring back in vivid detail those days he patrolled Miami's streets looking for clues to the bomber, recalling clearly his reckless, frantic attempt to get even. She wasn't his most vivid memory of her. His rage was. He didn't want to know that about himself.

He turned to the file on Nico Galvez. It was much thicker, as it had been updated as late as the previous month. The Cuban still lived in Little Havana, at an address not far from Calle Ocho, and he still did odd jobs for G2. Maurice read of Galvez's capture by Batista's troops, of his mutilation, his return to Fidel's rebels, and his assignment to the United States. There was a sheaf of messages from Nico Galvez to his brother, asking when he could return to his homeland. Some of the letters approached begging. There were also copies of Carlos's vague responses and his congratulations on missions well done. Maurice also saw that Jorge Gonzalez's car wasn't Nico Galvez's only successful bombing in Miami.

An old photo of Nico Galvez was attached to a page. The Cuban's face was devoid of angles, an empty face. His skin was doughy, as if a finger could be poked deeply into it and it wouldn't rebound. There was a hint of femininity to his spare eyebrows and of cruelty in his louche lips. It was a face Maurice would remember.

"We've got something coming in," Ernesto Pazos said.

Maurice dragged himself away from the file. "From Mederos or Washington?"

Pazos held up a hand for silence while he listened. A moment passed, and Pazos's lips pressed together and changed color. He removed the headset.

He said, "A message from Cantrell. Questioned by reporters, the president has just confirmed that there will be no changes in his zero hour. If the Blackjacks are not removed from Cuba in four hours, they will be destroyed."

Maurice returned to the file.

Pazos went on, "He'll use air strikes against the Blackjack hangars, which are guarded by Soviet soldiers. God only knows what the Soviet response will be. That doesn't give us much time."

Maurice finally turned to his radioman. "I'll try to talk to Eduardo again this morning, and hope it turns him around." His voice had an uncertain, distracted quality.

He left the stool, headed upstairs to confer with Eudy Puentes, but his thoughts were still on the Galvez brothers.

They had spent the night in a plantation shack, a dilapidated *bohío*, abandoned since the revolution, used since by *guajiros* only as a shelter from the rain. The *bohío* was one in a row of shacks, wedged between the field and the ring of tall cedars planted to protect the coffee trees from the sun. Sensing she and her son were fugitives, the old priest had told her their first day in his home of the *bohíos*, a dry place, good in an emergency.

Through gaps in the roof's thatch, Carmen Santana had watched the sky much of the night. She did not know how long she had slept, as she drifted in and out. They had found a bail of thatch outside the hut, probably blown from the roof, and had spread it across some of the hut's dirt floor. Segundo slept next to her on the thatch. They had no blankets, nor food. Last night, knowing better, they had broken off stalks of sugar cane to suck the juices. Now she was more thirsty than ever and had blisters on her tongue and lips from the rough stalks. Segundo had carefully buried their cane stalks, knowing that Fidel and his army were almost captured when Batista's soldiers followed the trail of the parched rebels' discarded cane.

The sky shifted to indigo with the first light of false dawn. The stars dimmed. Segundo said something in his sleep, sounding like a lost child, making her inexpressibly sad. She put her arm around him, feeling him tremble with the early-morning chill. Her thoughts again turned to their escape from the Montellano jail. The militiaman had bragged that G2 had ordered her picked up, said she was a prize. How was that possible after all these years? She had begun to hope the vast organization was capable of forgetting, that they would have more important people to chase. Wasn't Castro always railing against the American CIA? Why didn't G2 run them down? Instead, the militiaman indicated Carlos Galvez himself was organizing the search for her. It seemed inexplicable, all that effort for her, when she had been on the run for fourteen years, and when she should have been sent back to the United States with the other Brigade 2506 members. The chase just didn't seem to fit the crime.

There were moments when Carmen could look back to the days before her flight to Florida, before the Bay of Pigs and her internment. Sometimes her years in prison, with their droning, oppressive sameness, and the years of numbing hiding could be condensed, almost squeezed from her mind, making those years at the university seem close and vivid. She once thought of them as the good times and would be filled with melancholy and happiness. But with her parents dead and her one-time fiancé Eduardo Mederos in the United States for so long, she had no reminders of those sweet days. They were so long ago, and she had forgotten what it was like to be secure, so those memories had become foreign to her.

During long evenings Carmen would often build her life again, from the day she and Eduardo left Cuba. An ordinary life, constructed one fervent wish at a time, of a home, of Segundo and other children. Days of work at a hospital as a physician, evenings of quiet, of errands and cooking, and affection. So fervent were these daydreams that often when she woke, a brief, blissful time would pass when the echo of her wistfulness the night before would linger with her. Those moments were her only truly happy ones. Then, always with a heartrending jolt, her life would swarm back.

Her part of the sky through the thatch was turning blue. Still sleeping, Segundo bumped against her, his legs almost up to his chest for warmth. She gently pushed back a lock of his hair, and her fingers jabbed him as she flinched at her name sounding in the distance.

She bolted upright, staring through the open door into the dense forest at the edge of the field. Segundo rolled to his feet and crossed to the door.

"I heard someone call me," Carmen said, following him.

Segundo peered around the door, cut in the palm fronds that made up the side of the *bohío*. He squinted into the morning mist that clung to the hill bordering the dirt road.

"It's Virgilio Acosta," he said, his voice bright with relief.

The boy waited a moment to make sure no one was following the *santero*. Little of the winding, tree-lined road could be seen behind the old man. Segundo stepped from the hut. Belying his age, Acosta approached quickly over the rough rocks in the road, which Cubans called dog fangs. He was wearing a *guayabera* and black cotton pants with a rope for a belt, with the ends swaying in front of him. Acosta's dark hair was peppered with white, as was his full beard. He had no upper front teeth, and his lip blew in and out as he breathed. "Carmen. Segundo," he called.

The boy stepped from the hut. "Hello, Virgilio. We're here." He went to his tiptoes to flag the old man with his arm. Carmen brought up a smile for him.

The *santero* would not meet their gazes, staring instead at the road. Segundo called again. Acosta kept coming, but when he wouldn't look up, they knew they had been found.

From the trees behind the priest came uniformed G2 troops, AK-47s across their chests, two with German shepherds on leashes. They ran along the road, swept past the old man, and closed in on Carmen and her son. Segundo grabbed his mother's hand and yelled, "Come on. Up the road."

A helicopter suddenly swept in from behind the hill and hovered over them like a low cloud, blowing leaves and dirt into the air and cutting off the boy's escape route. It flew a dozen yards up the road, then descended. Soldiers dropped from the bay doors.

She clutched her son and said, "Not this time, Segundo."

He tried to pull away, but she held him tightly. The soldiers spread out around them, keeping away from Segundo and covering him with their automatic rifles. They had heard what he did to the Montellano militiaman.

With a black, veined hand, Virgilio Acosta wiped tears from his cheeks. "Please forgive me, Carmen. I couldn't watch them do it anymore."

Carmen could only make out a few of his words as they were washed away by the helicopter's bellow. Then one of the G2 men pushed Teresa Acosta toward the *santero*. He gathered her in, lightly stroking her broken face. Both the girl's eyes were swollen shut, and her right jawbone was crooked where a white glimpse of bone showed through her skin. Her entire face was blue black and lumpy, resembling a bunch of grapes.

Carmen tried to tell the old man she understood, but it was too much effort. She felt utterly nothing as the soldiers led her and Segundo to the helicopter, and still nothing when she saw the man wearing four gold stars of a G2 general on his shoulders. He was waiting for them in the belly of the helicopter.

Chapter XXII

Victor Fedorin's career and perhaps his life were slipping away, and it seemed he could do nothing about it. His wife's letter of the day before had been followed that morning by a cable from Moscow Center that a KGB Direction unit had arrested her for corruption. The message came from the head of the Second Chief Directorate, with an eyes-only code on it. They were keeping Fedorin's disgrace and imminent arrest quiet. But the coding clerk knew, and he wouldn't look at Fedorin as he handed him the message.

Surely he would be arrested. God only knew what Alexandra was telling her interrogator at the Lefortovo prison, if that was where they had taken her. She didn't know much about his business, but what she knew was enough to end him. That his first concern was himself, not his wife, didn't cross Fedorin's mind.

He was nearing panic. He glanced over his shoulder every few seconds, spasmodic movements that threw sweat away from his face. He was fairly running along Linea Avenue, ignoring hostile glances from Cubans, who instantly knew him as a Russian. Even the embroidered insignia on a building in almost every street indicating the local Committees for the Defense of the Revolution made him nervous. They must be watching him. He turned into the cool marble entrance of the Golfo de Mexico Bank, built in 1928, which, with the exception of the obligatory party posters in the lobby, still resembled an old-money New York bank. A moment later he was allowed into the safe deposit vault.

Perspiration chilled him as his shirt stuck against his back. He turned his key at the same time the clerk twisted his, and the Russian swung open the box. The clerk retreated. Fedorin slid out the inner box and rested it on the counter while he removed five bundles of United States currency. They were wrapped in brown paper. He pushed them inside his shirt, shoved the box back into its slot, and closed the steel door.

He emerged from the bank onto Linea and twenty minutes later entered the Club Sharad, panting with fright. Were he to believe his eyes, he saw forty or fifty Direction agents following him. He slipped onto a stool and tried to calm himself. There weren't nearly that many Direction people in Cuba, and he'd probably recognize them. Officers of the Second Chief Directorate didn't frequent the embassy, but like Fedorin they roomed at the dingy Hotel Deauville on Galiano Avenue, where most KGB personnel in Havana lived. And Fedorin had taken instruction at the Surveillance College in Leningrad. He'd know if he were being followed. No one was after him yet. He might ride this through. At least he tried to let that thought soothe him, because try as he might he could think of no way out if his business enterprise was discovered. There was no escape from Cuba for a KGB operative. Nowhere to flee.

When the barman approached, Fedorin ordered a rum.

"You want cola with that?" A Cuba libre.

339

"Just a shot."

The barman poured Aquardiente Carta de Cano into a glass and pushed it over to the Russian. Fedorin threw it back gratefully. He lowered the glass and inhaled sharply, the burn in his throat making him feel better. "Get me Justo, will you?"

The barman stepped into the storage room. After a moment Justo Cantillo walked down the bar toward Fedorin. The club owner's face was patched with bandages, but Fedorin could see through gaps in the tape black and purple skin around the Cuban's eyes. His spectacles were taped together.

Cantillo's hands were wrapped in white tape, the fingers rigidly jutting out. "If you ask me how I wipe my ass, you'll only be the tenth person to do so today."

"I don't have time for jokes, Justo." Fedorin signaled the barman for another shot. "We've done business a long time, haven't we?"

Cantillo nodded his head doubtfully. "A while."

"We've learned to trust each other over that time, wouldn't you say?"

"As much as I'll ever trust a Russian, yes."

Fedorin waited until the bartender had refilled his glass, then once again drank it in one swallow. "I need you to hold some money for me." He dug into his shirt to pull out the bundles. "I don't know when I'll be back for it."

Cantillo fretfully glanced around his club, but it was empty, the girls and patrons having left to listen to their radios. Cubans throughout the island were posted at their radios, waiting for the Americans and Soviets to make the next move. There had been much grumbling in the bar the previous days about Cubans again having to watch while others decided the fate of their island. Bystanding was Cuba's fate, they complained.

Cantillo wouldn't touch the money. "Why don't you get a safe deposit box?"

"I know for a fact that G2 has duplicate keys to every box in Cuba. I'm in . . . I may be in a little trouble, and the embassy may ask G2 to discover if I have a box, and they'll be into it shortly. I can't risk that, not after all the work I did for this money."

Cantillo fingered a bundle, flipping through the currency as if he were rifling cards. "There'll be a twenty percent bailment charge."

"Ten percent, you robber."

"Done." Cantillo scooped the bundles off the counter and put them on a shelf below the bar. "I've got just the place for the money. I'll move it tonight."

"And if I don't return . . ." Fedorin paused. His face bunched as fear gripped him again. With visible effort, he peeled away the fright, breathed evenly, unclamped his hands from the bar edge, and pulled his mouth into a smile. He stood to walk to the Club Sharad's door. He said as casually as he could, "I'll be back."

But when he saw the car parked at the curb outside the club, he knew he would not. It was a late-model white Volvo. With their muscular Chaika engines, these cars were the fastest in Cuba. They were only driven by KGB Direction officers.

The Volvo was empty, but that offered no hope to Fedorin, as a deep voice behind him said, "You're under arrest, in the name of the state and by authority of the Second Chief Directorate."

Fedorin tried to turn to talk reasonably with the KGB policeman, a laughable idea, he knew. Rough hands grabbed his arms, pinning them behind his back. He felt the chilled metal of handcuffs. He saw only a blur from the corner of an eye as another officer stepped around him to open the Volvo's back door. His head was pushed down, and he was thrown into the car's backseat. The door slammed.

He pushed himself upright. There were no interior door or window handles. A thick plate of glass was between him and the front seat. The two officers climbed into the car. They didn't speak another word or even glance at him.

Utter resignation calmed Fedorin. Whether it ended with

a bullet or a prison cell, he was finished. The jaw-grinding tension of the past few days was over. His fate was out of his hands, and he was relieved. The engine turned smoothly over, and the car drove away from the club.

Carmen Santana had heard only rumors of G2 procedures, most of them brutal. She did not suspect she and Segundo were being handled differently from other G2 victims when the general himself escorted her to Havana in his helicopter, nor when she was whisked through the town in a black Zil with the general in the front seat. He did not offer explanations. Trying to reassure her, Segundo gripped her hand so tightly it was aching.

Like joy or hope, fear also fades. She had been afraid so long it had worn away. Fear required effort, and she had nothing to give. Instead, she was jolted by memories as she passed through an unchanged Havana. The ubiquitous red-and-blue party posters were new, but the rest—the Spanish buildings, the narrow streets, the tropical tenements called *solares*—were unchanged from her childhood. And they passed the ancient, monumental steps at the University of Havana, where she had stood with Eduardo and Fidel Castro and hundreds of other students, demonstrating against Batista, struggling for Cuban freedom, not knowing what Castro would become.

The G2 general had been silent the entire journey. Now his first words startled her. "I do not have authority to question you, but I am curious. Would you tell me your connection to our president?"

"Our president?"

He stared angrily at her. "President Castro. Why does he want you?"

She sighed. "He has hunted me for thirty years. It seems that an escape from one of Fidel's prisons is such an affront to him that he will track a fugitive endlessly. No matter how much time passes, he will be after the runaway. The *plantados* must be taught their lesson. Revolutionary justice will pre-vail."

Segundo grinned fiercely. His mother was brave.

The G2 general bit his mustache with his lower lip. He said finally, "I'm not talking about the continuing search for all escaped prisoners. I want to know why the *comandante-en-jefe* wishes to speak to you personally. Tell me why he would order me at all costs to find you and bring you in."

Carmen laughed hollowly. "Perhaps one of his women is having a baby. I'm good at that, coaxing the little ones into the world."

One of Galvez's brows rose. "What I'm saying isn't even registering, is it? You have no idea why you're here."

Carmen shrugged. Curiosity had also been deadened. For now, Segundo was with her, and she was so grateful for these last moments with him that she thought no further.

The Zil rushed into the Plaza of the Revolution, new since her last time in Havana. She was startled by its vastness. The automobile passed several new military installations, antiair-craft batteries and spotlights, frantic with activity. Carmen did not know that the building they stopped in front of was the Palace of the Revolution. She had never seen a photograph of the building, as they were never published in Cuban news-papers.

A G2 guard opened the Zil's doors, and Galvez stepped into the sun. Carmen and Segundo followed Galvez, with guards behind them.

A navy lieutenant met them at the palace's front door. He said, "I'll take them in from here, General Galvez."

"Who are you?" Galvez demanded.

"MGR Frigate Lieutenant Enrique Pascual, sir."

"You're Chico Legro's replacement?"

"That's right, general."

"I should present the prisoners to the president, Lieuten-ant."

"I have been instructed to escort them to his office without other assistance."

"President Castro will see me," Galvez said in a stainless-steel voice.

"No, he won't. Now, if you'll turn over the prisoners."

Galvez's eyes bored into the MGR officer. "I'm going to remember you, Lieutenant."

"I have no doubt, General." He held his arm out, across Galvez's chest, showing the way to Carmen and her son. They passed the G2 chief into the building toward the stairs.

Moments later they crossed the carpeted third-floor reception room. The lieutenant knocked on a door at the back of the reception area, stepped inside another room, said a few words Carmen could not hear, and returned.

"Please go in."

This room was smaller, an office. Comfortable, with wood furniture and leather books and an old globe. A radio played Cuban folk songs. And across the desk from them was Fidel Castro.

He was standing, but stooped, his palms on the top of the desk, as if steadying himself. Carmen blinked, but the vision would not dissipate. Fidel Castro stood in front of her. The giant. The first Cuban statesman to be known beyond Cuba. The world-renowned revolutionary. Murderer of countless Cubans who would not bend to his will. Her great tormentor. It simply could not be.

"I'm not who I look like, Carmen." His voice fluttered, sounding little like Fidel's, heard over the radio during his inexhaustible speeches.

She stared, not knowing what was expected of her and Segundo, not having the remotest idea why they were brought to the president's office. Her confusion was so intense it dizzied her. Segundo leaned into her, supporting her.

"I am Eduardo Mederos."

So implausible were Castro's words that they did not touch her.

344

"Your fiancé, Carmen. I've come to take you away from Cuba."

She still could not make sense of his words.

"That isn't Fidel," Segundo said, pointing to Mederos's glistening face. "Fidel would never weep, Mama."

Then she knew.

Vicente Legro had never been in the basement of the G2 building, where Technical Section was located. The halls were institutional green with a brown carpet worn to the pad. The doors along the hall had no name or number. The glass in most of them was opaque. Armed sentries were posted at both ends of the hall. Legro was escorted by a G2 guard.

The guard, in plainclothes, knocked lightly on one of the doors. At a sound from within he opened it and nodded Legro into the room. Carlos Galvez stood near a stack of cassette machines, which were piled next to a bank of reel-to-reel recorders. Other electronic components Legro did not recognize filled the room, taking every table and bench. Several technicians in white coats worked at a video monitor at the far end of the room. Another entered information into a computer at a desk. They all glanced repeatedly at Carlos Galvez.

"Moscow Center was forthcoming with several samples of William Maurice's voice," Galvez said without preliminaries. The G2 chief was studying two sets of graphs on the table that separated him and Legro.

A moment passed, and he said nothing further. Legro had never seen Galvez's face without its usual confident set. The G2 chief imposed his will on others, a luxury that allowed him to be perpetually composed. He was always acutely conscious of himself, always on the stage. But now Galvez was lost in thought. His face was blank with the puzzle.

"Well?" Legro asked.

Galvez did not look up. "You were right, Vicente. That was William Maurice you saw enter Fidel's office. The voiceprints match."

"What should we do? Ask for an appointment with Fidel? Try to find out what he's doing? Lay out the dangers?"

Galvez finally looked up. "Both voices on your cassette were tested."

Legro waited, wondering at Galvez's hesitation. If Legro didn't know better, he would have sworn the G2 chief was squirming.

Galvez said tensely, "The second voice on your tape was not recognized by the professionals here. It didn't match any of their graphs."

"There were only two voices on the tape. Fidel's and William Maurice's. What other voice are you talking about, general?"

"Listen to me, Vicente," Galvez said slowly, as he might to a child. "The second voice, Fidel's, didn't match Fidel's."

Legro smiled. "You are making it difficult for me to follow you."

"The Technical Services staff has walked me through the voiceprint method. I have threatened them with Angola if I discover they made a mistake. They adamantly stick by their conclusion, and they've convinced me. That isn't Fidel Castro in the Palace of the Revolution."

Legro stared hard at the G2 general, looking for some hint of a grand joke. "Then who is it, up there with the face and body of Fidel?"

"Christ on the cross, Vicente," Galvez bellowed, "does it matter a whit who it is? All I know is that William Maurice has planted a fake as president of Cuba. A ringer."

"Take this with due respect, General Galvez," Legro said equably, "but you are talking nonsense."

The G2 chief slapped his fist on the graphs. "This is the work of those bastards in the CIA. I'm going to arrest both Fidel and Maurice."

Legro's eyes widened. "Are you listening to yourself? Do you know what you're proposing? Nothing less than a palace

346

coup. Of all the people in Cuba, you know best what happens to those who try to topple Fidel's government."

Galvez gestured angrily. "I'm telling you, that isn't Fidel up there."

"You've got a bug in your voiceprinter. It's broken. And if you run off to do crazy things, you won't live through the day."

"That impostor must be dealt with."

"You're going to rush into Fidel Castro's office and point a gun at him? Try to put him in handcuffs? Take him to one of your G2 dungeons?" Legro chuckled derisively. "Fidel was wrong in sending me to the beach. It is you who needs the vacation."

"That is why I'm a general and you are a secretary," Galvez said heartlessly. "You want to stall for more information and more analysis. Stall and wait and study. And you'd watch while the revolution was stolen from us. Not me. I'm going to fix William Maurice."

"How will you find him?"

"I don't need to. He left his weakness in Miami, and I know how to get to him." Galvez's voice was so hard Vicente Legro stepped back a pace. "And then I'm going to tear the mask off the impostor."

Two hours later Nico Galvez sat in the cab of a garbage truck near a parking lot a block from the Miami Herald Building. The order from his brother had said to do it immediately. Easy enough, he figured. He had been studying her for days.

The truck was a rear loader with a hydraulic compactor, capable of carrying five tons of garbage. The truck was sea blue and clean. He hadn't wanted a filthy rig, smelling like the gut wagons of his childhood. Those two Miami Disposal employees at the cafe on Calle Ocho wouldn't miss their rear loader for another half hour. He'd be done by then, Nico Galvez figured. The woman was ruled by habit. Her home, the Herald Building, the warehouse. She hadn't been anywhere else for days. Galvez had hoped to find her husband by tracking her. No luck on the husband. But his work had paid off. His brother now wanted her.

She arrived right on time, pulling into the lot in her silver Honda. She had a reserved spot at the west end of the lot. When a Ford followed her into the lot, Nico Galvez grinned narrowly. He reached over and chucked the pit bull's muzzle. "Doing pretty well today, aren't we, Ass End?" The dog was wearing his red collar with the brass studs. The skin of his rib cage had been crudely stitched together.

Galvez's caution had also paid off. He hadn't seen her guard at first, two days ago, when he'd decided to follow her. She was always guarded, he had quickly learned. He had driven around her neighborhood in Coral Gables for hours, but never passing the home on Granada. He approached from side streets, parking a good distance away, using his binoculars. Then dressed as a gardener he had walked along the golf course in back of her home.

Her protectors were doing a credible job. At least four men were posted at her house. He assumed as many watched her at work. The warehouse area was crawling with the same types. He had determined that she could only be reached while she was in transit, when there was only one bodyguard following her.

He started the engine. The truck had no air conditioning, and his damp hands slipped on the steering wheel. He wiped them on his dog, then pulled the shift into first. The Honda aimed for its spot, a Ford thirty feet behind it.

Galvez turned the truck into the lot and cut over to the center aisle between rows of cars. The truck was moving no more than five miles an hour. He turned again at the back of the lot, and the Honda, coming toward it, had to veer out of the truck's way. Only when the Honda was passing him did Galvez stomp on the accelerator. The garbage truck roared ahead, plowing into the Ford. Momentum carried Ass End into the dashboard, where he bounced hard, then fell to the cab's floor. Galvez laughed.

It could hardly be called a collision, as that implied some equality in the projectiles. The truck simply sank into the front end of the Ford with the loud sound of tearing metal. The truck suffered only a scratched bumper and a broken headlight, but the Ford's grill was smashed back almost to the wheels. The front end resembled an accordion.

Nico Galvez threw open the cab door and jumped to the pavement. He rushed to the Ford. The bodyguard was only now responding, wiping blood running into his eyes from a gash on his forehead and drawing his pistol from his coat.

Galvez wadded his fist and shot it through the glass of the driver's window. The window fragmented and blew inward, raining on the dazed agent. Galvez grabbed the man by his hair and with vicious force yanked his head out the window. He rammed the head downward so the glass fragments still in the window frame slashed into the agent's neck. Blood cascaded down the door. The man died soundlessly.

Galvez had known what the good samaritan's reaction to the collision would be. Rosa Maurice ran back to the scene of the accident.

"Are you all right?" she cried as she rounded the front of the garbage truck. She saw the blood, but it was too late.

His brother had said to seize her. He didn't specify her condition. He grabbed her by the throat, almost lifting her off the asphalt. Her scream was choked off as he dragged her to the rear of the truck. He swung her off the ground like a sack of grain and tossed her into the rear loader. Rosa yelled with outrage.

Nico Galvez flipped down the hydraulic operation lever on the side of the truck. The massive packing blade dropped from the roof of the bin and swept in at her, whirring, then grinding the tin cans and milk cartons as it began to compact the load in the bin.

Galvez waited until the blade hid her, then flipped back the lever. Only one of her hands showed under the blade, almost hidden by soda cans, paper, and brown fruit peels.

"Looks like that'll keep you," he said cheerfully as he returned to the garbage truck's cab.

Chapter XXIII

Maurice was taking his turn at the vault window, watching the prisoner and waiting. He knew that Mederos's delay was easier on him than the others in Eudy Puentes's home and the people back in Miami, because he had something new and bitter and distracting to chew on. Nico Galvez. Reading the G2 file on the assassination in 1962 had made the memories swarm back, bits and pieces of that terrible time that he had so carefully tucked away in their uncomfortable corners over the years. Now, with the fresh evidence of cruelty, they were all back. Anger and sadness and remorse had flooded Maurice, making Mederos's intransigence and the crumbling Caribbean situation almost an aside. Try as he might, he was having trouble focusing on his reason for being in Havana.

For hours the prisoner had done nothing but attack sheets of paper with a ballpoint pen, using immense handwriting, and casting one full page after another onto his cot. He worked with ferocious intensity, never crossing out lines, sure of his words. Castro wrote *History Will Absolve Me* while he was in prison after his failed attack on the Moncado barracks in 1953. The volume was based on his courtroom defense of his bungled attempt to overthrow the Cuban government. Full of references to Montesquieu, Rousseau, Milton, Locke, Paine, even St. Thomas Aquinas, it became a legendary document of the Cuban revolution. Maurice supposed he was writing a second volume, dredging up similar references from his prodigious memory.

Maurice closed his eyes and squeezed the bridge of his nose. The Galvez brothers. He was fighting it, trying to close them out. They were of no relevance to his reason for being in Havana. He could not imitate Eduardo Mederos's erratic performance in the thirty hours since the switch. Cantrell and the others in Miami now suspected Mederos was mad, diverted from his momentous mission by the memory of a woman he hadn't seen in thirty years. Maurice had to keep to his purpose. The stakes were too high for him to be derailed. He had to tear himself away from ugly thoughts of Carlos and Nico Galvez.

"Boss, it's for you," Roberto Ramos said from the bench. "Miami."

Maurice changed places with Ramos and picked up the headset. "Yes?"

"We've got a lot of bad news here," Jack Cantrell said over the headset. The DDO's voice was reedy, the consonants cut short, processed through code and burst equipment.

"With our operation stuck on hold here, I can well imagine."

"No, you can't. It's worse. There's a war impetus in Congress here, a stumbling momentum. And with Eduardo not cooperating, we in Miami are spending more time fearing unfolding events in the Caribbean than doing anything productive. What's the latest from him?"

"Nothing since the last time we spoke." It had been only

an hour. "G2 found this Carmen Santana, and Eduardo is meeting with her."

The equipment did not disguise the exasperation in Cantrell's voice. "And that's what everyone from the White House to the Pentagon to the agency are all waiting for?"

Maurice cleared his throat. "That's it. I think he'll come around, though."

"Jesus, Bill . . . " Cantrell paused so long Maurice tapped the headset. "Well, you'd better know the latest. We've got the air force and the navy fighting in the Pentagon over who's going to test those defenses and knock out the Blackjacks. Whichever service it is, they're taking off from carriers or bases in Florida in two hours. The Blackjacks will be knocked out."

"What will be the Soviet response?" Maurice asked. He touched the stump of his broken tooth with his tongue.

"That's the subject of endless meetings at the White House. The Pentagon figures the Soviets know they cannot win a naval or aerial battle in the Caribbean, but from all their equipment there now, it looks like they're going to put up a good fight. And they've already pulled all the diplomatic stunts. Calling their ambassador home, joining Cuba in a push for censure in the General Assembly, instigating an emergency meeting of the Warsaw Pact command."

"What's left to them?"

"You know what's left. The president believes there is no way the Soviets would risk a nuclear confrontation over Cuba. They proved that in 1963. But, Bill, NSA satellites have shown us that twenty minutes ago they began pulling back many of their missile silo covers."

"Any compromise on the horizon?"

"Not from the U.S. end. The president won't go down in history as unable to do what John Kennedy did. One way or the other, the Blackjacks have to go, and that's not negotiable."

The radio was silent a moment. Probably Cantrell taking a long breath. He said finally, "Christ, Bill, this country is holding its collective breath, expecting things to happen, not knowing there's a way out, our plan. And it all depends on Eduardo. You've got to get him off his ass."

"I'm working on it," Maurice said unconvincingly.

"You don't have long to work," Cantrell said. "Here's more bad news. We picked up a Soviet transmission of your voice, aimed at Havana, we think."

"My voice? How do they have my voice?"

"Don't know. It's a conversation taken at some point during the missile crisis."

"G2 has a tape of me taken in the past day or two in Havana, and they asked the Soviets to send a voiceprint control."

"That's what we figure," Cantrell replied over the radio. "G2 knows you're in Havana."

"Is Eduardo blown? Voiceprint on him?"

"That's the big question. We don't know. But you can assume G2 is looking for you. And with their CDRs, those watchdog block committees, they can distribute a photo or a drawing, and every block will have eyes, so you'll need to be even more careful."

"Is that all?"

Another long pause. "Bill, we debated whether to let you know this. The director said the information would distract you. But I can't keep this from you."

Maurice wondered what could be worse than what he'd just heard.

Cantrell said, "Rosa has been taken."

An iron hand seemed to lock itself around Maurice's neck and begin to clench. He could hardly get out, "What?"

"A messy but very convincing job, Bill. Her tail, Rolando Cubalo, was killed, and they picked up Rosa. Kidnapped her. We don't know who took her or where she is."

"Jack, you told me she'd be protected." And Maurice had convinced her.

"Goddamn it, we had eight people assigned to her. Whoever took her figured it out, found us where we were weakest."

Maurice's head was light, and he had to plant both elbows

on the bench. "It's G2. They know I'm here and up to something, so they took her for leverage. You must have figured that out."

"That's Jones's theory, and I've come around to it, too," Cantrell admitted.

"The Galvez brothers," Maurice said stiffly.

"It fits Carlos Galvez's style. Brothers?"

"He's got a brother in Miami." Maurice's mouth was sawdust dry, and his chest wouldn't draw air. Fear for his wife was strangling him. "I've got to meet Carlos Galvez. He can free Rosa. Nico takes orders from his brother." His voice sounded almost dreamy.

It must have alarmed Cantrell. "Bill, get Eduardo off the mark. You can't go off doing other things now. As important as Rosa is—"

Maurice removed the headset, cutting Cantrell off. He turned to Ramos. "Roberto, get Eudy Puentes. We're going back to the palace."

Mederos had talked for an hour, telling her of his life in Miami, of his endless search for her, of smuggling himself into Cuba and gazing at her through the binoculars while she was a prisoner. He did not temper his obsession but played it out for her, baring himself. All the while he kept his voice below the level of the radio.

Then she started, taking another hour, telling of her time in the camps and prison, and of her fugitive life. Mederos stared at her throughout, not even looking up when Lieutenant Enrique Pascual offered to show the bored Segundo the palace and the Plaza de la Revolución. Segundo was happy to leave.

Mederos studied her face throughout her narration, finding little changed in thirty years. A few lines around her eyes, some silver in her hair, but her beauty matched his memory of her. He had last seen her as a girl. She was now a mature woman. He had missed all the years in between. Yet little in her face had changed.

Only when she spoke did Mederos understand Carmen

was not the woman he had left in Cuba. His most vivid memory of her was of her animation. There was none now. She talked in a monotone, using no gestures, keeping her eyes on the office's wall. Much of what she said sounded rote, as if she had prepared it for an interrogation. Mederos sensed she was leaving out much of her thirty years, as a crime suspect might skip the incriminating. He prompted her several times, but her tale was unleavened, village after village, year after year. He had to coax her to talk of her escapes. He also asked of Segundo's father. She said she had forgotten him, couldn't even remember what he looked like. Mederos believed her.

"So that's my thirty years, Eduardo." She was sitting on a chair next to his, both behind Castro's desk. "Not much to it, really. Except for Segundo, very little has happened to me in all the years since my last escape."

"But you've changed." Mederos ignored the Sony, which was suddenly louder in the drawer. "Your story is of torment and heartache, and you should shed tears. Yet there are none. When I knew you before, a limping dog would make you cry."

Mederos felt a surge of relief when her upper lip curled, the slight, sardonic smile he remembered so well. He proclaimed, "See, you aren't dead."

"No, not yet, I suppose."

He reached for her hand, the first time he had touched her since that day on the beach. She did not respond. "I never stopped loving you, Carmen."

He waited, but she said nothing. She didn't nod or purse her lips or blink with misty eyes. She studied the wall just above his head.

He said, "I've waited so long that—"

"I gave up long ago, Eduardo. I never thought I'd see you again. And I'm still not seeing you. All I see is Fidel sitting across from me. A huge irony, don't you think? The man who imprisoned me and made me run for thirty years now tells me he loves me." She laughed mirthlessly.

"So you stopped loving me?"

"I loved a memory, and it kept me going for many years. I could not sustain it."

"I did."

"It's unfair of you to think I could. Look at your life, Eduardo. You say you own auto parts stores, quite a few of them. You said you live in a house in Miami. You probably even own a car. I've heard how successful Cubans in Florida live. You've had the luxury and time to look back and fan old flames."

"You never daydreamed of how our life together could have been?" he asked.

"Yes, I did, but during many nights I used those dreams instead of food and a roof over my head. And I imagined us together as a substitute for a future." Her voice rose. "But do I still love you? Eduardo, I just—"

"You deserve to be angry. I left you on the beach."

She slowly moved her head left and right. "I've never thought you deserted me, Eduardo."

"Leaving you was the worst decision of my life," Mederos said.

"I have no idea what happened, how we became separated."

Mederos told her of the mortar blast, of trying to help her, and of the corporal ordering him up the beach.

She said, "I always believed that's how it happened. You wouldn't have left, but you were a soldier, and you did what you were told."

Mederos was insistent. "You haven't said you don't love me. Not exactly. And you haven't said you won't leave Cuba with me, go to Miami."

A spark of life entered her as she smiled. "That last is easy. Of course I'll go to the United States. I've been trying to get there for thirty years. And Segundo would give his right arm to go."

"And me? Us?"

She shrugged, and the corners of her mouth turned down.

"Will you try, at least?" he asked ardently.

"Try to love you? How do I go about doing that?"

With exasperation he waved his hand. "I don't know. You let me be with you. We spend time together. We didn't intend to fall in love at the university. But we did, because we were together in class and in the political groups. Just be with me."

She pressed his hand and leaned toward him. She hesitated, then bent even closer until only a few inches separated them. It was an awkward movement of one not used to confiding in another. "Yes, I'll be with you. And I'll try."

His grin was huge. "Then I've won you. I'm still as lovable as you used to say I was. You won't be able to help yourself."

She dropped her eyes to his gray beard, then back to his widened nose. "You don't look like this normally, do you?"

"This is thousands of dollars of plastic surgery, and the beard is fine synthetic. I've always been better-looking than Fidel. Nothing has changed that way."

"Well, your ego certainly hasn't."

Mederos couldn't restrain himself. "I've won. You don't realize it yet, but I have."

He stood, and she followed him up. He was about to put his arms around her when Carlos Galvez pushed open the door and walked into the office. He carried a Mosin-Nagent pistol, and it was pointed at Mederos's left eye.

Mederos straightened, jabbed a finger toward Galvez as if it were a knife, and bellowed, "You dare enter my office with a weapon in your hand? You've made a mistake, Galvez."

So convincing was Mederos's instant switch to Fidel Castro that Carmen cowered away from him, heedless of the G2 general who had brought her to Havana.

"You and William Maurice almost did it," Galvez said, his voice silky and gun hand steady. He moved toward the desk. "Almost got away with it. Tell me, is President Castro dead?"

Mederos glared at Galvez imperiously, but he could feel Castro's will and courage seeping from him.

Galvez stepped around the desk. He stared at Mederos with cold surmise, then said, "You're a miracle. I've seen the *comandante-en-jefe* almost every day since his exile in Mexico, yet you fooled me. I must hand it to, whom, the CIA? Maurice is back with them, isn't he? He's your control, am I right?"

Carmen Santana drew against Mederos, but he pushed her away, wanting only himself as Galvez's target.

The G2 chief pulled his mouth into a vulpine grin, made more ominous by the mustache. "You will talk to me, believe me." He glanced fractionally over his shoulder. "Arteago, bring in the equipment."

Romarico Arteago was a young G2 recruit, as they never lasted long at this job. He was a muscular man, a requirement, as the *verdugo*'s garrote was heavy. Arteago turned sideways in the door to have enough room to lift the garrote into the office. The equipment was packed in its traveling case. Arteago lowered it to the floor. Beads of sweat covered his forehead. He had a dull, round face, without expression. The pink, hairless skin of his cheeks looked like a baby's. Galvez had carefully prepared Arteago for this assignment, lecturing him on his proof that this man was a ringer. Still, Arteago's eyes grew wide at his first sight of Mederos. He opened his mouth to say something, when a quick, deadly look from Galvez brought him back to his task.

Arteago flipped the clasps and opened the cabinet, then righted the wooden center block. The short steel bar with its two prongs held the neckrest. The iron collar, the garrote, swung loosely. He positioned the condemned's stool in front of the post. Arteago absently clucked his tongue as he worked. He might have been patching an inner tube.

"What are you going to do?" Carmen Santana stepped forward to intercede.

Galvez lashed out, clubbing her temple with the butt of his pistol. She collapsed to the floor before Mederos could catch her. Blood pooled beneath her head. When Mederos knelt to help, Galvez whipped the barrel across the back of his head. Mederos staggered to his hands.

The general ordered, "You, whoever you are, get onto the stool."

Mederos opened his mouth for one final bluff.

Galvez pushed the Mosin-Nagent's barrel into the impostor's lip. He snarled, "If you say one more word as Fidel, I'll kill you outright. Get into the chair."

Mederos struggled to his feet. He rounded the desk. When he stopped, Galvez jabbed the pistol into his neck. Arteago reached over the post to guide Mederos into the seat, then quickly placed the straps over his arms. Galvez grabbed a fistful of Mederos's hair, holding the head up so Arteago could bring the choke bar around Mederos's neck. The *verdugo* spun the bolts, then stood behind the machine. He twisted the lever so the screw pulled the bar into Mederos's neck. When Galvez signaled with a finger, the bar stalled.

Galvez put the pistol into the holster on his belt. "Tell me where William Maurice is."

Mederos stared glassily at him and said nothing.

Galvez nodded, and Arteago turned the lever ten degrees. The choke bar was pulled into Mederos's neck below his Adam's apple. Mederos's head was pinned against the metal neckrest.

Another short chop of Galvez's chin. Arteago again turned the lever. Mederos's eyes bulged and his tongue squeezed out between his teeth. His eyes rolled back and his jaw slipped open. A half moment passed before Galvez signaled. The bar was released slightly.

"I'm going to black you out and bring you around. Again and again. You'll never know which is your last time. But one silence too many, and you'll never wake up."

Mederos tried to spit at Galvez but couldn't generate saliva. Then he tried to curse, but his larynx was crushed under the bar.

The general said lowly, "Let's try it again."

The *verdugo* turned the handle. Mederos's eyes fluttered close and his lips colored blue.

Galvez said to the unconscious man, "You'll talk to me. Have no doubt. Release him, Arteago."

The room shuddered from two sharp percussions, so loud

that three of Castro's framed photographs fell from their nails to the floor, the glass breaking, sounding like a girlish giggle after the roar.

Two bullets passed entirely through Romarico Arteago. Spots on the front of his shirt bloomed red like opening flowers. Galvez grimaced with surprise and pain as one of the bullets, not quite spent, shattered a knuckle on his right thumb. Arteago sank to the carpet, vainly scratching at the garrote's post for support, but dead before his head reached the floor.

His Smith and Wesson at eye level, William Maurice said, "You talk too much, general."

He fired again, the bullet smashing Galvez's right elbow and spinning him around. Galvez grunted and caught himself from falling. When he tried to pull his weapon from the holster, Maurice pulled the trigger again. This time Galvez's thigh was punctured through, throwing blood against the front of the desk. The general fell heavily.

Maurice tested the garrote handle, then spun it counterclockwise. The choke bar opened.

Galvez pushed himself to a sitting position. Blood poured from the thigh wound. He coughed wetly. "We have your wife. Kill me and you'll kill her."

Rage renewed itself, and Maurice's gun hand trembled. "Nico has her?"

Galvez must have found courage in the question. "Yes." He inhaled sharply from the pain. "And he does what I tell him."

Maurice glared at Galvez. Then he smiled. He fired twice more, once into the general's chest, once into his stomach. Galvez did not change expression as he died.

Mederos gulped air and licked his lips repeatedly. Maurice unhooked the bands across his arms. The Cuban tried to rush to Carmen Santana, moaning behind the desk, but he couldn't find his legs. Maurice helped him off the stool. Mederos rubbed his neck as he hobbled to the woman. He helped her sit against the wall and dabbed at the cut on her temple. A trickle of blood ran down her neck.

Mederos put his arm around Carmen's shoulders, steadying her. He asked Maurice, "You knew Galvez was coming here?"

"Miami told me they were on to me and maybe you. I set a record crossing town. Enrique Pascual carries a pocket linkup, and he was told over it to meet me at the plaza's outer barricade to escort me past the guards in the plaza and the building. He's out in the hall with Segundo."

Carmen's eyes fluttered open. She put her hand on Mederos's arm. Her eyelids lowered again.

"I feel sorry for you, Bill," the ringer said, rocking Carmen slightly. "You wanted Galvez dead more than you wanted to find your wife. You must hate in a way even I can't understand. I thought I was the crazy one."

"I'll find her," Maurice said. "But you're right. I wanted him dead pretty bad." He bent to examine Carmen's wound. "Leave her to me. You've got work to do." He looked at his wristwatch. "American planes take off for La Panchita in eight minutes."

Maurice was greeted by turgid martial music when he descended to Eudy Puentes's cellar. "Workers Marching for the Revolution" played on Radio Havana. The first Cubans learned of most important world events was the music heard on the radio. By the time a series of funereal or military tunes had been broadcast, the entire country was listening, anxiously guessing who had died or what disaster had occurred. Martial music had been on the air continuously for the past four days, punctuated by shrill announcements from the broadcasters.

Maurice glanced into the cell as he passed. The prisoner was still writing his new treatise. The sparse beard rested on his chest, and he mouthed a few words as he wrote. He glanced up at the wall clock to gather his thoughts, then began a new sentence. His pile of finished pages was half an inch thick. Ramos had said that every hour or so he would put his pen down to square the pages, then would begin again. The prisoner was listening to Radio Havana.

Roberto Ramos was still at his row of communications equipment. A portable television set was to one side of the bench. It showed only a tape of a Cuban flag waving in the wind. The audio was also of military music. Ramos asked what had happened at the palace.

"I think we're squared away with Eduardo. We'll see soon. Anything new?"

"He knocked on the cell door to ask for a copy of José Martí's *Nuestra América*. Eudy went to his bookshelf upstairs to find one and passed it through the door to him. And when I asked what he wanted to eat, he replied spaghetti. Does that sound normal?"

"It's one of his favorite foods. He'll eat about three pounds of it in tomato sauce."

An urgent voice came over the television set. "Please stand by for an announcement from President Fidel Castro Ruz."

Ramos turned up the set. "Is this it?"

Maurice nodded. "Turn on the set in the cell."

Ramos pressed a button on a console to his right, then turned to the cell. Ernesto Pazos was on the chair in front of the one-way mirror. He nodded that the screen of the set inside had brightened with the same footage of the Cuban flag. Maurice crossed the basement to the window.

A puzzled expression crossed the prisoner's face as he looked at the television that had apparently come on of its own volition. When the unseen announcer said, "Comrades, speaking from the Palace of the Revolution, President Fidel Castro Ruz," the prisoner stood to face the screen. Forgotten, his writing slid from his lap to the floor.

The screen filled with Fidel Castro sitting at his desk at the palace. "Fellow countrymen and workers of the Cuban socialist revolution. It is with a heavy heart that I come to you tonight. Yet it is also with renewed hope, as the process of the revolution has become even clearer to me in these past few days of crisis in the Caribbean."

The prisoner pointed at the screen, his face turning white, then pink, then a splotched purple.

"Goddamn, Eduardo's good," Pazos said, watching the set in the cell through the one-way mirror.

"We aren't broadcasting simultaneously on radio, as is Castro's usual procedure, because the voice alone might not carry him." Maurice paused, staring at the screen in the cell but listening to the speech from the bench television, as the cell was soundproof. He said as calmly as he could, "The voice still needs work."

But he was jubilant. The impostor's voice was rough like Castro's, and the syllables were overpronounced, just as Castro carefully molded his words. The articulation might not have fooled anyone long had not Mederos been a precise stamp of Castro. The man in the cell might have been looking at a mirror rather than a television screen.

The prisoner yelled at the television. Maurice could not hear it, but the pulsing vein on the prisoner's neck and his balled fists left little doubt of the context.

Mederos said into the camera, "The events of this week have taught all Cubans that we did not fully learn the lessons of the October crisis of almost thirty years ago. That lesson was that our friend, the Soviet Union, often acts without consultation and without regard to the wishes of its loyal allies."

Eudy Puentes descended the cellar stairs. There was a crowd at the cell window, so he watched the set on the bench. He said, "Ambassador Sokolov is watching, you can bet. I'd give anything to see his face in the next few minutes." He turned up the volume.

Mederos said, "History has repeated itself. Our comrades in the Soviet Union have once again unilaterally acted in a manner that directly affects Cuba and our revolution. We were not consulted before the recent fleet maneuvers. We were only informed afterward."

The impostor spoke for a few more minutes, outlining the diplomatic chess game in the Caribbean and the military bluff and the counterbluff. Then he said, "I have concluded that it is unwise to rely totally on our Soviet friends. They must act in their interest, which, as we have seen, does not always coincide with Cuban interest. The seemingly inevitable war we have seen brewing these past few days between the North Americans and the Soviets will be fought in our sea, and perhaps on our land. Just like during the October crisis, Cuba will be forced to stand by, watching its fate decided by those who do not have Cuba's best interest at heart."

The prisoner's jaw was open and his face was flaccid and inanimate. He was dumbfounded.

The speech continued, "As a result, I have ordered the Ministry of Foreign Affairs to review our treaties of friendship with the Soviet Union, with a reduction of its influence in Cuba as the goal of such a review."

Mederos paused dramatically, then said in a lower voice, inviting the viewer to lean closer to the television. The prisoner did just that. "Comrades, I am going to reclaim Cuba for the revolution, for Cubans. I am going to bring Cuba back from this brink." He laid aside another page of his speech and glanced at the next page. "As your *comandante-en-jefe*, I have been forced to make decisions today to defuse the crisis in the Caribbean. For a number of months the Soviet Union has used an airfield near La Panchita for its new weapon, the Blackjack bomber. This plane has had a destabilizing effect in the area that I confess to you I did not anticipate."

Maurice whispered as if he were in Castro's office with Mederos, "We wrote that in because Castro occasionally admits a mistake. It only endears him further to his followers."

"As a result, I am ordering the Soviet Union to remove the bombers within twenty-four hours."

The prisoner's chest heaved in rage. He lifted the Martí volume from his cot and flung it against a wall.

"I understand," Mederos said with a carefully rehearsed

hint of whine in his voice, "that four minutes ago fighters and bombers departed the United States and are approaching the Cuban coast. I ask the president of the United States to call these planes back in light of my own directive removing the Blackjacks."

The prisoner screamed at the television set.

"Further, I am ordering that the number of Soviet military and technical advisers in Cuba be reduced by three-quarters."

His muscles taut with rage, the prisoner staggered to the television set. He lifted it in both hands, bringing the impostor's face up to his.

"To further our goal of establishing a careful balance in the Caribbean, I am today instructing Foreign Minister Berreda to explore the possibility of renewing diplomatic relations with the United States. This, I believe, will fully restore a balance in the area that will best protect our people."

The prisoner swayed with rage, the set still held in front of him. His chest was rising and falling like a bellows.

"Finally, comrades, let me make a solemn pledge to you. I am rededicating the revolution to peace in our area. All nations in the Caribbean owe it to peace to act as responsible world citizens. As a token of my efforts for peace, I will destroy a symbol of war."

"Here comes the kicker," Maurice said.

The impostor pulled a rifle from the side of the desk into view. "You all know this is the weapon I carried during the years of the revolution." It was a .30-06 with a telescopic site. Castro was deeply attached to it.

Mederos pulled the bolt from the rifle and dropped it dramatically to the desk top. "As a symbol of my renewed efforts to strike a peaceful balance in the Caribbean, I will destroy this weapon of war." He twisted two nuts and the telescope fell to the desk.

The prisoner's mouth pulled back into a gargoyle's grimace.

"I pledge that I will—" Mederos's voice cracked. "That

I will burn this rifle." He quickly wiped a tear from his cheek.

Fidel Castro weeping in front of all Cubans. The man all Cubans, friends and enemies alike, called the Stallion. A man's man in the Latin tradition. Crying before his public.

The prisoner snapped. He flung the television set to the floor and smashed his shoe through the screen. He tried to tear the manuscript in half, but it was too thick, so he flung it against the wall, where it flew apart, pages filling the cell in a blizzard. Next he ripped the mattress from the cot and spun it into a wall. He worked with furious energy.

Five minutes later there was nothing unbent or unbroken in the cell. The prisoner collapsed on the floor, blowing air like a runner, his face still contorted with seething anger.

Ramos asked, "Is he pissed or what?"

Maurice had watched the frenzy dispassionately. He said finally, "We're not done with him yet."

Chapter XXIV

Wreckage covered the cell floor. The television set was in a hundred fragments. Slats from the back of the chair and its legs were scattered about. The computer chess game had been smashed underfoot, and its electronics were in a scrambled pile. Book bindings had been torn from the pages and flung about. The metal cot frame had been twisted into a knot. The toilet bowl was in two pieces, one still attached to the plumbing, the other resting near a wadded blanket. Ceramic chips, chess pieces, and eating utensils littered the floor. Spaghetti sauce was splattered against the door.

The prisoner was slumped on the floor, leaning against the back wall of the cell. His face was shiny, and beads of sweat dotted his beard like rain on a bush. His tantrum had ended fifteen minutes before, but his chest was still heaving. The prisoner's eyes were glazed with exertion. He had a madman's stare, unfocused yet riveted.

The muffled sound of a shot, then a series of them, did not bring him around. Only when automatic fire erupted, heard clearly in the cell despite the acoustical insulation, did the prisoner turn his head toward the door. It was answered by another light-caliber automatic weapon, a tinnier, more persistent sound.

There was a slight pause in the shooting, then the crackle of a firefight came again, seemingly from the floor above. The closer sound of a sharp explosion, perhaps a grenade, brought the prisoner to his feet, moving like an athlete despite his age. The roar of an entire clip came from just outside the door. In the cell the sound of the scream was muted. Several more shots, and it was over.

The prisoner bent to look through the grate just as the door was pulled open. A man in a white *guayabera* held a Kalishnikov assault rifle on the prisoner for two seconds, then raised the barrel to the ceiling.

The man said with professional calm, "Lieutenant Amel Frias, Seguridad del Estado, sir."

The prisoner rushed passed Frias into the workroom. His trunk covered with blood, a jailer lay against the wall under the bench of radio equipment. A submachine gun lay next to him. Another had fallen at the base of the stairs. His arm ended bloodily at the elbow, and the remnants of his forearm and hand rested on a step. The radios and coding machines had been destroyed by bullets. Bullet pockmarks stitched the wall above the bench. The room smelled of powder and new blood.

Another G2 agent descended the stairs and smartly saluted the prisoner. He said, "The third floor is secured. There is a lot of radio broadcasting and receiving equipment on the roof."

The prisoner demanded, "Where's the bastard Anglo who was running this operation?"

Frias replied, "There's two more bodies upstairs, Comrade President, but I don't think they were *norteamericanos*. Looked Cuban to me."

"How did you find me?"

"General Galvez gave us the location. He said he had caught one of the CIA messengers, who told him where you were being held. We expected him to arrive here to plan the assault on the house, but he didn't show, so we took the initiative. I don't know where General Galvez is."

The prisoner swayed left and right, as if the floor were cresting under him. He squeezed his eyes shut, and his entire frame trembled.

The G2 lieutenant asked, "You all right, sir?"

"When I get my hands on that whore's son . . ." The prisoner abruptly rushed up the stairs.

The gunmen stared after him, then looked at each other. The lieutenant shrugged and slung his automatic rifle over his shoulder. He stepped carefully over a puddle of blood to the body under the bench.

The black Zil swept into the Plaza of the Revolution. The antiaircraft battery crews were less hectic than an hour before. Soldiers stood idly near their posts, smoking and chatting. The *estado* mayor general had removed the alert. Seeing the car approach at high speed, the sentries at the outer barricade lifted themselves from their haunches and straightened their belts and caps. They expected G2 officers or ministers, who drove the Mercedes and Fiats and Zils in Havana. When they saw the *comandante-en-jefe* through the windshield, they went to a rigid salute. Once through the barricades, the car sped toward the Palace of the Revolution.

Chico Legro was running out of the palace when Fidel Castro jumped from the limousine. Legro hesitated twenty yards from Castro, then retreated a step.

"Where's the impostor?" Castro yelled.

Legro cocked an ear at the voice.

"Mother of Mary, Legro, get over here."

Reassured, he rushed to Castro and blurted, "Carlos Galvez is dead."

Castro grabbed his secretary by the shirt collar. "Tell me where the impostor is."

"He ordered a car and driver ten minutes ago. I don't know where they went."

Castro released his secretary and twitched with impatience. "Is his CIA controller with him?"

Legro nodded. "His name is William Maurice. The impostor also has a woman with him."

Castro's face contorted into a mask of chagrined rage. "Legro, I want the armed forces, every CDR, every militiaman, the Youth Labor Army, every policeman and Young Pioneer and postman to be looking for my Mercedes. Bulletins are to be immediately released by Televisora Nacional and the radio stations. Cuba is to come to a standstill until they are found. Do you understand?"

"Of course, *Comandante-en-Jefe*," Legro gushed with relief. This was indeed Fidel. Issuing orders as fast as his lips could move. And no doubt about the gravelly, impassioned voice.

Castro turned on his heels and sprinted forty yards to a FAR jeep that was guarding an antiaircraft missile installation. It was a GAZ field car with a .30-caliber machine gun mounted behind the driver and a fifteen-foot radio antenna attached to the back gate. The driver, a twenty-year-old FAR private, jumped from his seat to give a smart salute. A corporal posted at the machine gun imitated him.

"Corporal, patch me through to Arnaldo Labrada."

"Sir?"

"Chief of the General Staff."

"I know who he is, *Comandante-en-Jefe*. I don't know how to patch anyone through to anyone else."

Castro reached over the side of the GAZ to lift the handset. He barked, "This is President Castro. Put me through to General Labrada immediately." He turned to the corporal. "That's how you do it."

A moment passed. Castro did not return the salute, so the soldiers remained as if they were starched. Finally Castro

371

shouted into the set, "Arnaldo, I will be sending you coordinates shortly. I want you prepared to dump soldiers and weaponry into that area. Three people are trying to escape Cuba by air or sea, and I want them stopped at all costs. I suspect it'll be in the Central Army District, perhaps even Havana. I want you at Code Alpha until I give the stand down."

Castro paused, then he bared his teeth and said, "What do you mean I ordered you and your soldiers away from the docks?" His head jerked back with anger. "Mother in hell, that wasn't me. I rescind that order. Get your men out there."

Castro listened for a few seconds, then inhaled a huge gulp of air. "Arnaldo, don't you know a nonsensical order when you hear it? Why would I have directed two hours ago all MGR patrol boats away from the Havana harbor? . . . Christ, no, I'm not telling you to disregard my orders when you think they are crazy." Castro closed his eyes with frustration. "Listen, Arnaldo, your job is not to ask questions. Deploy your people immediately. Am I understood?"

He tossed the headset to the corporal, who lowered his salute to catch it. Castro started back to Legro, then spun again to the GAZ. The impostor's Havana destination must have revealed itself because he climbed in, fairly pulling Chico Legro after him. He pushed Legro into the backseat next to the machine gun. He was known to take the secretary when momentous events were to occur, the better to record his stewardship of the revolution.

He ordered, "Get us to the harbor, private." Then he yelled over his shoulder, "Use your radio and have an escort move in front of us, something with a siren. Looks like the plaza is full of them. Get on the goddamn two-way radio, Corporal."

The corporal, who at twenty years old already had the calluses and sun-baked skin of centuries of Cuban peasants, nervously twisted the radio dials. He had been drafted off the commune, had never been to a Castro speech in this plaza, much less shared the same jeep. But he was a quick study. He said, "This is an assistant to President Castro. Immediately assign a vehicle with a siren to the south entrance to the plaza. It will be escorting the president."

Chico Legro was almost thrown from the jeep as the FAR private accelerated through the gears. The secretary had to grasp the machine gun's mount for support.

"Your pardon, Mr. President?" the corporal shouted over the engine noise and rush of wind. "You said something?"

Castro ended his muttered string of curses to say, "Just get me to the docks, soldier."

As the GAZ reached the Havana City Hall at the southern corner of the plaza, a Zil pulled in front of it and turned on its siren. They might have recognized Castro from the beard flowing in the wind over his shoulder. The GAZ and its escort roared down Avenue Salvador Allende toward Plaza de la Fraternidad. Havana streets were deserted, as Cubans were still in front of their radios and televisions.

As the jeep rolled by block after block of central Havana, Castro bellowed orders into the handset. The police and military were to converge on the shores of the Bay of Havana, certainly their escape route.

Moments later the GAZ rushed from Muralla Avenue to Desamparados, the dockside road. The vehicle slowed, and Castro gripped the windshield for support as he stood to survey the bay. The three largest docks in Havana jutted a hundred yards into the water. They dated from the days of United Fruit Company's dominance of the waterfront. Two-story warehouses covered the docks. Loading roadways ran the docks' perimeters. The revolutionary government had resisted changing the docks' names. They were, from south to north, the Santa Clara, the Machina, and the San Francisco. Just north of the San Francisco dock was the mile-long canal to the open ocean, the entrance guarded by Morro Castle.

Visible to Castro through the Santa Clara and Machina docks was a United States Navy gunboat accelerating quickly toward the canal and the sea. Castro's face was a knot of rage.

He batted the driver's head as if he were a tank commander alerting the driver. "Into the gates. Hurry." He pointed to the Machina dock.

The GAZ lurched forward, through the ornate gates into the dark warehouse. The temperature dropped, and the air inside the building was dank. The warehouse had been neglected since the revolution, and patches of water could be seen through cracks in the floorboards. The GAZ veered left toward the light. It sped through a side door to the mooring slip, then raced along the dock's perimeter drive, past pallets and mooring bits. There were only two ships in Cuba's merchant fleet, and neither was moored at the dock.

The FAR private knew his vehicle. He pushed its engine. Chico Legro opened his mouth to shout a warning and gathered his legs under him to jump. But the GAZ's brakes shrieked, and it came to rest a foot from the end of the pier.

The gunboat was abreast of the Machina pier. Its wake, trailing behind the boat in a half circle, indicated it had picked up its passengers at the Santa Clara dock and that it had stopped dockside, if at all, for only a few seconds.

Its new passengers were scrambling aft along the port walkway, heading for a hatch midships. A sailor wearing a blue windbreaker and carrying an M-16 followed them. Castro recognized himself. The size, the walk, beard, the olive field uniform.

He roared, "Fire at them!"

The corporal had already pulled the breech. Chico Legro knelt at the side of the jeep. The gunner brought the weapon's heavy barrel down and stared over the crude Partridge sight at his target.

He hesitated. "Sir, that's you, isn't it?"

"Goddamn it, fire your weapon or I'm dropping you off at the Príncipe."

The corporal resighted. It was an old gun, a Goryunov 43, with a sideways-tilting locking action and, as a result, a complicated metal link-belt feed system. But it worked well enough.

The gun spewed bullets. A stream of ejected shells splattered against Legro.

Because of chronic ammunition shortages, the gunner had fired his Goryunov only once before, on a firing range. The bullets threw up geysers of water thirty yards short of the gunboat.

The order was Castro's mistake. The boat was a Pegasus-class hydrofoil missile ship, 133 feet long, bristling with weapons, capable of forty-eight knots foilborne, with a crew of twenty-five, most of whom had fingers on assorted triggers and were bored with intercepting drug runners. As the gunboat gained foilspeed and rose eerily from the water to its wings, it flashed smoke and fire. Harpoon missiles almost instantly crossed the short stretch of water between the gunboat and the docks, streaking into the Santa Clara and San Francisco docks, to Castro's right and left, leaving trails of rocket exhaust as straight as beams of light.

The missiles each carried five hundred pounds of high explosive in a blast penetrator warhead. The seaside fifty yards of each building blew apart in balls of fire and debris. The fire clouds roiled outward, seemingly reaching for the GAZ. Lengths of wood and steel shot into the air.

At this close distance, the GAZ's passengers felt rather than heard the concussion. Their clothes fluttered with the blasts. Small pieces of the warehouses rained on them. At the same moment, the hydrofoil's 76-mm gun opened up, loosing one shell after another into the water a few yards short of the Machina dock, soaking Castro and his men.

The FAR corporal and private leaped from the GAZ to the deck, covering their heads, bracing for the next missile, surely aimed at their dock. Chico Legro fell over the jeep's side and cowered behind a rear tire. But there were no other missiles.

When the smoke had drifted away and the wall of water from the cannon had settled, the gunboat was already well into the canal. It seemed to be flying, throwing a tail of water behind it.

Castro had never ducked in his life. He was still standing next to the driver's seat, gripping the window frame. He said in a low voice, bitter with sarcasm, "Cease firing, corporal."

Thirty minutes later Castro was pacing his office, issuing a torrent of instructions to Chico Legro. His hands were bunched behind his back, as if he did not trust himself not to ram a fist into his desk or wall or secretary.

"And Raul is in Moscow?"

"You sent him there. Or at least we thought it was you when he left."

"Get him back." Castro turned again on the carpet, pulling up in front of Legro. "For God's sake, Chico, the impostor was running Cuba for less than a day and a half. The damage he has done is . . . is incalculable."

"Yes, sir."

"And humiliating. Do you realize he made me look like a weak-willed, bumbling fool during that broadcast?"

"I realize that."

"How many years have I cultivated a strong image, one necessary to lead my people away from the foreign domination that has been Cuba's only history until me?" Castro's voice rose. "To have it ruined . . ." He trailed off.

Always helpful, Legro suggested, "Your reputation is too secure for that, *Comandante-en-Jefe*. Tarnished, perhaps, but not ruined."

"And how many of my enemies had a good belly laugh, watching me buckle under pressure from the United States?" Castro put both hands to his head, pressing it, an uncharacteristic gesture. "And to have them watch me wipe away tears. I can just . . ."

He lowered his hands with what seemed like a draining effort. He squared his shoulders and resumed his pacing, back and forth in front of his secretary, oblivious to the dampness of the rug where Carlos Galvez had died.

Castro said, "I've got to handle those bastard Russians first.

I'll meet—" He interrupted himself and again turned to Legro. "You know, Chico, I have never trusted the Soviets, not since they left Cuba adrift during the October crisis. And the goddamn apologizing I had to do for them after Czechoslovakia and Afghanistan. If they didn't have Cuba by its throat with their money and equipment, I'd deal with them far differently, believe me."

"Are you going to tell them about the underwater switch, the impostor, all of it?"

"Christ, no. I only tell them what I have to. I'm going to assure them that the deadline to remove the Blackjacks from Cuba has been eliminated."

"The ambassador has been trying to see you for a full day. He is here again. Shall I show him in?"

Castro nodded. "First make sure the recording system is working."

Legro closed his notebook and left the office. Castro brushed his tunic. Dust from the explosion blew away with each stroke of his hand. He walked around the globe to his chair. He asked no one, "How in a virgin's nightmare did the *norteamericanos* think they could get away with this? Goddamn them."

The door opened and the secretary ushered Ambassador Sokolov and his translator Victor Fedorin into the office. Castro stood quickly to extend a hand, an unusual offering to the Russian. Sokolov's face was pale and his mouth compressed. He looked ready to deliver a long lecture on the nature of Soviet-Cuban friendship and Cuban obligations thereunder. Fedorin stood to one side as always, his stricken face perhaps a comment on Castro's unilateral announcement.

The ambassador began without waiting to be offered a seat. "Comrade Castro, the general secretary has been urgently attempting to contact you for most of the day. It has been difficult for us to react in an informed way to your announcement today when—"

Castro backstepped so suddenly he bounced against the

377

sideboard. He held one hand up. Sokolov may have thought it was to interrupt. But the ambassador's gaze followed Castro's to the interpreter, who had drawn a pistol from his uniform.

Victor Fedorin fired quickly. He squinted, turning his head partly away from his target. His hand shook. The roar of gunfire filled the office, one peal rolling over another.

A bullet tore into the desk, raising a line of wood chips. Another spun the globe. Castro dropped to the floor behind the desk. Bullets opened holes in the wood. Fedorin squeezed the trigger until the hammer fell on an empty chamber.

Sokolov had not moved. His face registered shock and horror. He turned his head slowly to his interpreter but was mute.

Fedorin dropped the weapon and bolted through the office door.

Fidel Castro had always recognized that extraordinary luck had played a pivotal role in his ascendancy and rule. During a life filled with revolutionary struggle and the evasion of assassins, the only injury he'd ever received was a hairline fracture of his skull from a policeman's club while he was leading a demonstration at the University of Havana.

So he was perhaps not astonished when he found he could crawl up from behind the desk. Several seconds passed as he waited for some part of him to bleed. But he was unhurt. Completely unscathed. Not one bullet had found its mark, thanks to the rugged desk.

"My God, Mr. President, my God," the ambassador sputtered. He held his hands out, beseeching Castro and trying to calm both of them.

But Fidel Castro was not to be calmed. The past few seconds were entirely clear to him. And the force of the betrayal rendered him incapable of movement. He clung to the edge of his desk, staring malevolently at the ambassador.

Loyalty was the value Castro admired above all others. He possessed a dogged and endearing faith in his friends and allies, and he expected, indeed extracted, no less from them. Those who breached that trust paid dearly.

Castro's voice had the tone of a hammer ringing upon an anvil. "The Blackjacks meant that much to you? You thought I had ordered them out of Cuba, and this is how you resolve it?"

Sokolov moved his mouth but could not speak.

Castro leapt to his feet. He brushed by the ambassador and disappeared into the reception room.

Sokolov turned to follow him, bawling out, "Mr. President, don't jump to conclusions. . . ."

Chapter XXV

Ponce had quickly become accustomed to the extra minutes Esteban Martinez paused over the bluff each day. The donkey was quiet in his traces as Martinez stepped to the cliff overlooking the sea to cross himself and say a short prayer for the family he had seen die on their raft. The sea glittered with late-afternoon light. One body had washed to shore, to be whisked away by the militia. The others had never been found. Nor had anyone on the dairy commune learned who the hapless family had been. A tragedy, so casually dispensed by the FAR soldiers. Martinez shuddered.

He stepped away from the bluff over clumps of salt grass to the road. Ponce snorted and began again toward the commune and his shed. Martinez scratched the animal behind an ear, which was the price Ponce exacted for the delay at this turn in the road. If Martinez forgot, the donkey would abruptly halt and not take another step until his ear was tended to.

Martinez clucked at Ponce as they walked alongside the airfield. Milk cans clattered together on the cart. He had never again glimpsed the black airplanes inside the hangar. He may have heard them, as occasionally a big plane with a deeper roar than a MIG could be heard above the commune. Always at night, only when it was cloudy.

Could his photographs have started this crisis? Radio Marti had named the airfield at La Panchita and had called the big planes Blackjacks. Had the Americans discovered them because of his photographs? He thought so. Had the photos led to the confrontation, to Fidel weeping on television? He thought so, too. Martinez chuckled. The things a lowly dairy farmer could do. Fidel crying in front of his countrymen.

"Well, he has made a lot of us cry," Martinez said into the donkey's ear. "What goes around, comes around, eh, Ponce?"

Martinez turned to the sound of a klaxon. It seemed to be coming from the control tower, and it wavered with the ocean wind. Men ran from the barracks on the rise across the runway. They tried at the same time to don jackets and helmets. One was yanking at his zipper. They wore darker uniforms than Cuban DAAFAR pilots.

"Russians," Martinez explained to Ponce. "They're running like their pants are on fire."

Hangar doors slid open, revealing four Blackjacks. They reminded Martinez of sewing needles, long and sharp. Tugs were attached to lead wheels, and the first bomber was pulled from the hangar. The tugs had begun their work before the pilots had climbed into the craft, and the Russians ran alongside, trying to find handholds to pull themselves aboard. The pilot of the first Blackjack yelled at the tug driver, and the procession stopped. Ladders were rolled to the planes so the pilots could board.

381

"Looks like they're in a big hurry," Martinez said, patting the donkey's rump as he lifted aside a milk can and removed his camera. He stood behind the animal's flank to focus the lens on the hangar. He snapped the shutter, and the film advanced. "You know, Ponce, I was listening to Fidel on the commune's television today when he ordered those planes back to the Soviet Union. I thought he gave the Russians more time. You'd think that—"

The wail of jet aircraft suddenly came from behind Martinez, closing quickly from the west. And for another terrible moment, he thought he had been caught. He lowered the camera and looked over his shoulder. A wing of MIG-25 fighters swept along the coastline, only a few seconds behind the sound of their engines. Aimed at Martinez, they seemed suspended above the water, growing larger rather than moving.

He laughed with relief. "It doesn't take a bunch of fighter planes to capture a dairy farmer, Ponce."

When the first fighter veered sharply from the formation, Martinez saw Cuban markings on its fuselage. It climbed and banked above the seaside end of the airfield, then dove from the sky toward the runway. For a few seconds, Martinez thought the plane might be landing. But it seemed to be accelerating as it fell from the sky. Above the sound of its screaming engine came a sharp hiss as a missile shot from under its wings. The Soviets had outfitted these Cuban MIGs with AS-7 missiles, which had the NATO code name KERRY. The missile sped away from the MIG, leaving a thin trail of white exhaust behind it.

The KERRY rushed the length of the cement. It slid into the runway with a ferocious explosion fifty yards short of the Blackjack. Fire and smoke from the blast blew quickly to leeward, against the hangar. A three-foot-wide crater had opened at the edge of the runway.

"Cubans shooting at Russians?" Martinez whispered, daring to raise his camera again. "Things have changed, Ponce."

The first Blackjack's engines roared, and the tug had to hurry out of its way. The bomber rolled to the south side of the runway and was moving so quickly when it turned for its takeoff run that its left wing almost dipped to the cement. Its twin engines flared, and it began its run, ponderously at first, then quickly gaining speed.

Not quickly enough. The second MIG plunged and loosed a missile. The KERRY slanted toward the runway and found the base of the Blackjack's dorsal fin. The fin disappeared in a cloud of flame. The bomber skidded to the side, its left wheel mount buckling and the wing dropping to the runway. Sparks flew as metal ground against cement. The fuselage trailed boiling black smoke.

The Blackjack shuddered to a stop midway down the runway. Four crewmen dropped from the fuselage and sprinted toward the hangar. As they reached the edge of the runway, the Blackjack's fuel compartments detonated, obliterating the bomber in fire and blowing the slowest crewman to his knees. He scrambled to his feet and chased after the others toward the tower.

"Why would Soviet-made fighters be destroying Soviet-made bombers, Ponce?"

If the donkey knew, he was saying nothing. He rattled his bit and stamped the ground. His oats were more important than this.

The second Blackjack had just cleared the hangar when a missile ripped into its right wing. The plane toppled to its side. The tug continued its work for a few seconds, dragging the crippled plane away from the hangar until the tug operator leaped from his rig and ran from the flames.

A new sound was added to the mix. Martinez looked landward to see a helicopter hovering above the bluff. He had never seen such a craft, with two main props, one on top of the other, but without a tail rotor. He didn't know that it was a Soviet-made Hormone.

The remaining two Blackjacks did not make it out of the

hangar. Three MIGs soared east, banked over the coast, and swept in perpendicular to the runway, one after another. Their missiles raced ahead of them, crossing the runway over the burning Blackjack and into the hangar. The blasts filled the hangar, then blew off its roof.

"Hell on earth," Martinez said, snapping one photo after another.

The hangar's eruption had finally caught the donkey's attention, and it gazed at the explosions. If it didn't promise food, Ponce was not interested. It brayed and started toward the commune. Martinez slapped its rump and said, "Hold on, Ponce. We've still got film in the camera."

The donkey unhappily settled again in its traces. Flame billowed from the hangar, consuming everything between its north and south walls. Remnants of the roof collapsed into the fire. The bombers inside were hidden by the orange-and-yellow blaze. A fire truck tried to get close to the conflagration but had to back away.

As the MIGs circled the airfield, the helicopter lowered gently to the runway opposite the hangar. Martinez swung his camera to the copter as its passenger emerged from the waist hatch.

"I'll be damned," Martinez said. "That looks like Fidel himself." He took another photograph. "Looks like he was sitting up there in the air directing the attack."

Six GAZ patrol cars rolled onto the runway from the south, swerving around the first Blackjack's burning husk. Fidel ran to the lead vehicle and gestured wildly. Martinez guessed Fidel was yelling, but he could not hear the *jefe supremo*'s words because of the crackling of the fires and the distance. The jeeps rushed toward the Soviet pilots' barracks, rounding up Soviet crewmen and maintenance workers who were watching the fires. The GAZs surrounded the barracks, forcing the Soviets inside.

Another fire truck approached the blazing remains of the

384

Blackjack near the hangar entrance. The firemen hurriedly rolled out the hose. Fidel Castro waved them away from the bomber. They quickly retreated.

"He wants them to burn, Ponce," Martinez said.

Burn they did. The two Blackjacks that had escaped the hangar seemed to sink into the cement as the fire reduced them. Tar-black smoke surged away from the wreckages. The hangar was consumed in fire, and the first fire truck used its hose to dampen the side of the nearby control tower.

Fidel Castro crossed his arms and nodded. He looked satisfied with himself.

Martinez said to his donkey, "Nobody's going to believe me, even if I send the film to prove it." He snapped the last shot on the roll. "Nobody."

In the darkness the small house near Calle Ocho appeared abandoned, with its overgrown lawn and peeling paint. Maurice had seen the G2 files and knew the house belonged to Nico Galvez. Maurice entered the yard from the rear alley, pushing open the gate in the hurricane fence, keeping his Smith and Wesson in front of him.

He swore under his breath when he saw the dog run. From the size of the doghouse on the gravel at one end, the dog was a big one. Maurice hoped it was an Irish setter or a bloodhound, something docile. He hesitated on the cement walkway, listening for the dog, but heard nothing. Maybe it was inside.

He stepped into the back porch and opened the screen door. He looked through the window into a tiny kitchen that resembled a recycling bin, with beer cans overflowing a waste basket near the sink and a three-foot pile of newspapers by the refrigerator. Six or seven dishes were stacked next to the sink, which was stained ocher. One of the sink's water handles was missing. The room was lit by a bare bulb overhead. Maurice carefully tried the door. It was locked with a frail handle lock, not a dead bolt.

Maurice and Mederos and Carmen Santana had reached Miami only thirty minutes before. The missile boat had docked at Key West, and a navy helicopter had picked them up. Carmen had helped Mederos remove the beard during the flight. Mederos had grinned the entire way. Jack Cantrell was waiting in the warehouse's parking lot when the helicopter touched down. He anxiously reported that his people had not found a trace of Rosa, but that they were still working on it. Maurice had not slowed his gait from the helicopter to his car as Cantrell talked. As Maurice started the engine, Cantrell asked where the hell he was going. Maurice's silence must have told him, because as the car pulled away Cantrell yelled, "Do you need help, some men?"

He didn't. He was going to pay a thirty-year-old debt on his own, and get his wife. Maurice pulled the hammer back on the revolver. He held open the screen door and slammed the bottom of his foot into the door under the handle. The door burst inward and bounced back against his shoulder as he swept into the kitchen. Three quick steps brought him to the main room.

Nico Galvez had been sitting on the couch, a can of beer in his hand and three takeout orders of nachos on his lap. He was almost to his feet when Maurice found him down the barrel of the Smith and Wesson. The nachos splattered Galvez's shoes.

Maurice was astonished at the size of the man. He blocked out most of the couch, all but the near armrest, on which was a pistol. Nico Galvez's face was that of a choirboy's, youthful and pleasant, with the skin of a peach. When Galvez glanced at the weapon, Maurice raised the Smith and Wesson slightly.

"Where's my wife?" he demanded in Spanish.

"In the next room, all bundled up. She's got a broken arm, so I didn't have to tie her hands too tight." Galvez had a startlingly sweet voice and a charming smile. "But you aren't going to get to her."

The Cuban slowly raised an arm to point at the bedroom. "You've got two problems. Me, with my gun two feet away. And that dog. You won't be able to get both of us before one of us gets you."

Maurice flicked his eyes left, and his gun hand wavered at the sight of the animal. A hundred-ten-pound knot of muscle, with scars, a missing ear, burning eyes in narrow slits. The dog's single ear was back on its head.

Nico Galvez's voice hardened. "Ass End, sic." It gained a note. "Sic him."

Maurice fired into Galvez's chest. The dog did not move.

A spot the size of a nickel opened on the Cuban's shirt. The big man did not even flinch. He charged and chopped at Maurice's jaw with his fist.

The blow almost lifted Maurice off his feet, launching him across the floor. He hit the side wall and slid to the floor, an arm flailing back against the rack of dog collars.

"You son of a bitch!" Galvez screamed at Ass End. His voice gurgled as his lung began filling with blood. A red bubble formed at the corner of his mouth. But the bullet didn't slow him. "When I tell you to do something, do it."

Galvez kicked Ass End in the rib cage as he crossed to Maurice, who was backstepping against the wall, trying to get his feet under him. The Smith and Wesson had skittered away and was in the middle of the room. Maurice fought darkness, which wanted to envelope him from all sides. His head seemed detached, floating in pain, useless to command his arms or legs.

He shook it off. He used the hat rack for leverage, frantically pulling himself up, but not before the Cuban's enormous hands found him. Galvez held Maurice's head like a basketball and began forcing his thumbs into his eye sockets.

Pain flattened Maurice's arms against the wall, and his right hand struck sharp metal. He instinctively grasped it. It was Ass End's spiked collar on its hook. He lashed out with it, and it whipped into the Cuban's face. Unable to see his weapon or Galvez and his eyes bombs of pain, Maurice ferociously brought his arm down again and again.

Pressure from the thumbs ebbed, and Maurice jammed a fist into Galvez's neck. It loosened the Cuban's grip. He coughed blood. The bullet was doing its work.

In a rage of pain and vengeance, Maurice slashed again with the collar. Then he grabbed the collar in both hands and inverted it. Galvez lunged for him, but Maurice knocked his arms away and sidestepped, bringing the collar around the Cuban's neck.

Two dozen studs, half-inch lances, bit into Galvez's neck. He grabbed at the collar, but it was too late. Maurice yanked it tight. The studs sank into the Cuban's fleshy neck, and blood oozed as if from a sieve, rolling down Galvez's shirt.

Galvez's neck was almost as thick as Ass End's. He could still draw half a breath. He screamed, "Ass End, sic him! Sic him!"

The pit bull sat on its rear legs and watched, its mouth open slightly.

Maurice kneed Galvez in the back to wrench on the collar. The Cuban sputtered, clawing at his neck. He began to sink, first to his knees, then to one side. Maurice followed him down. He kept the collar around him for another two minutes, warily looking at the dog. Ass End did nothing but pant in the evening heat.

Maurice released the garrote, stepped warily around the pit bull, and ran into the bedroom. Rosa lay on the bed, arms tied with clothesline to the bedposts. Her right arm was purple from the elbow to the fingers. Her eyes were wide, but they closed when she saw her husband. He removed the gag over her mouth.

"Did you kill him?" she asked tremulously.

Maurice nodded as he worked on the knot around her broken arm. The mattress was bare, and it stank from years of night sweats.

"I wish I could say I knew you'd come," she said as she sat up and held her colored arm with her good hand. She winced when she tried to make a fist. Her lips were cracked and her hair was matted. Her gray suit was rumpled.

He undid the last knot and helped her to her feet. They clung to each other.

She said softly, "I never once let him see me cry." And she sobbed quietly against his shoulder. He held her a long while, waiting for her trembling to subside, and his. Finally he walked her into the front room, past the Cuban's body and over the nachos. The pit bull was still sitting on its haunches.

They were to the front door when Maurice turned to the pit bull. "What about you? What happens to you?"

Ass End blinked and tilted his head.

Maurice opened the door. "Come on, then."

The dog immediately rose to his feet and trotted to them.

Rosa was weak but rallied to protest. "Bill, not that dog. It's the ugliest, meanest-looking thing I've ever seen."

Maurice gently helped her along the short walk to the street. The dog followed, the stub of its tail wagging. "Just for a while, until we find a home for him. Besides, you said you wanted a new dog."

"A cocker spaniel or a toy poodle."

They walked half a block to Maurice's Ford. She was dizzy and leaned into him.

He assisted her into the car, lifting her feet. When he opened the back door, Ass End jumped in.

Maurice climbed in behind the wheel. The dog sat on the backseat, inclined forward, its massive head between them. Spit dropped slowly from the corner of its mouth where the lip was missing.

"Besides," Maurice said, "as Edmund Burke said, 'Early fear and a dog are the mothers of safety.' "

He started the car and pulled away from the curb.

Her eyes were closed, and her head was against the rest. Her face was pale with pain from her arm. She waited until they reached a stop sign to say, "No, he didn't."

He lifted his wallet from his pants pocket and gave her five dollars, then turned toward Jackson Memorial Hospital.

Chapter XXVI

Mederos guided his jeep from MacArthur Causeway to Fifth Street in Miami Beach, then north along Collins Avenue. They passed the Raleigh Hotel, with its vertical panels of pink block, and the New Yorker Hotel, with its deco stepped parapet and fluted moldings.

Carmen Santana said, "Not much has changed since I was here as a girl."

"The art deco district is stuck in time. You won't recognize the rest of south Florida."

"Stop talking like Fidel," she said lightly. A small patch of gauze was taped to her temple where Galvez's pistol had hit her. It reminded Mederos of the gardenias she'd worn in her hair as a girl.

He smiled and shook his head. "It's hard to unlearn. I caught myself walking like him back at the warehouse a while ago. And I was still giving everybody commands. They wanted to begin the debriefing at the warehouse tonight, and I said it could wait until tomorrow, like I owned the place."

In the backseat, Segundo's head worked left and right, his eyes as wide as saucers. The lights on the marquees and storefronts played on his face. He alternatingly grinned and let his mouth fall with surprise. He repeatedly tapped his mother's shoulder to point out the new and exotic.

"You already look a lot less like Fidel, for which I'm thankful," Carmen said as they stopped at a light. "I'm glad the beard is gone, and you changed out of your military uniform at the warehouse, and left the glasses there. But what about the bump the plastic surgeons gave you?"

He touched the bridge of his nose. "I'm beginning to like it. And it'll keep my reading glasses from sliding down my face."

She laughed lightly. "Is your hair really gray?"

"Not a single strand of it. It's the same color you remember."

"Mr. Mederos, can we stop there?" Segundo's voice was urgent. He pointed to an arcade with a red neon sign that read "Rafael's Video Parlor." Inside, teenagers bent over video and pinball games.

"Maybe tomorrow, Segundo," Carmen said. "Eduardo must be deathly tired."

Mederos flipped on his blinker and checked the rearview mirror. The Cherokee crossed a lane toward the store. "If I'm going to be an overly indulgent friend to your son, which is precisely my plan, I'd better begin now."

He parked the car and bravely led them into the arcade. Mederos instantly knew he had made a mistake, at least for Carmen. She was dumbfounded, perhaps horrified, by the sights and sounds of the pinball machines and video games, the rock videos on large screens hanging from the ceiling and their pounding sound. She gripped his arm tightly. The games were filled with moving images of demons, commandos, motorcycles, and space ships.

Transfixed, Segundo stopped in front of a video game called Skateboarder. Sensing it was too late to turn back, Mederos gave the boy several quarters.

Segundo must have had a knack for the thing. Using the joystick, he steered the screen's animated figure on the skateboard around a series of obstacles. Segundo had never even seen a skateboard before. Occasionally a swarm of killer bees took after the skater, and a computer-generated voice boomed, "Skate or die." Segundo cheered or groaned according to the fate of his skateboarder.

Carmen said above the noise, "This place . . . Whenever I dreamed of hell, it looked and sounded like this. I've got to get out of here."

"Let's go, Segundo. You can come back tomorrow."

Segundo did not hear Mederos. He was completely absorbed in the game.

"Segundo," his mother called. "Come on."

Still no response.

"Your son has become an American rather quickly. Wait here, Carmen."

Mederos approached the man at the change booth. "You the owner?"

"That's right. You want change?"

"How much for the Skateboarder game?"

"A quarter, just like everything else," the man said. He was wearing a T-shirt and smoking a panatella with an inch of ash.

"How much did you pay for the game?"

"That's my business, don't you think, pal?"

As if he were still Castro, Mederos demanded, "How much?"

The owner said quickly, "Fourteen hundred dollars."

"I'll give you two thousand for it right now." Mederos pulled his checkbook from his pants pocket. "You can buy a new one tomorrow. Load it into my Cherokee out front."

The man blew a long trail of smoke. "Done." He signaled his employee at the soft-drink stand.

393

Carmen wore a dubious expression as they lowered the jeep's rear seat and lifted the video game into the rear compartment. Segundo was ecstatic.

When they continued their drive north on Collins, the boy sat in the front seat near the door, continuously glancing at the game, asking Mederos repeatedly if he was sure the skateboarder would return when the game was plugged in again. Mederos assured him he would.

Carmen was wedged between her son and Mederos. She said close to Mederos's ear, "This sets a very bad precedent."

Mederos smiled. "From what you tell me, he's never so much as had a baseball mitt in his life. Let me make up for it a little."

"Just this once." She watched the passing stores and apartments and hotels for a while. "Where are we going now?"

"I've made reservations for you at the Bal Harbor Sheraton," Mederos said, a bit formally. "You indicated you need to think things through, try to put things in perspective. Staying there will give you some time and a little distance from me."

She lightly ran a finger along the back of his ear. "Well, you certainly have changed, Eduardo."

"Other than the wrinkles and the extra weight?"

"When you were courting me, you pressed every advantage."

"Don't embarrass me in front of your son."

"I'm whispering and he can't hear me," she said, her lips almost touching his ear. "Remember? The moment my parents left us in the room alone, I was in trouble."

"I remember," he said, keeping his eyes on the road.

"Well, you aren't the same as in the old days. You aren't pressing your advantage."

It took him a moment. Then he said, "I lied. There are no reservations at the Sheraton, and they're always full. No sense even trying. You and Segundo are staying with me."

She smiled. "Now there's the Eduardo I remember."

* * *

The director and secretary were once again waiting in the hallway outside the Oval Office. These men, usually so disparate in appearance, had grown to resemble each other over the past several days. The prim secretary of defense, with his silk handkerchief and razor-sharp creases, was, for him, shockingly rumpled. His gray hair looked brushed against the grain. His suit was back on his shoulders, pushed out of trim by two straight days of wear. His jawline was sagging despite his plastic surgeon's guarantees. His eyes were a painful pink from wearing his contact lenses too long, and he was now wearing his glasses. And, surely unknown to the secretary, a spot of Dijon mustard was on his shirt.

In contrast, the CIA director appeared polished and ready for presentation. Good news did that to him. He was wearing a new blue blazer with brass buttons and cordovan shoes with tassles, a dapper yacht and golf combination. Years appeared to have been shaved off him, as his face was tight and animated. He smelled of Old Spice, which subordinates knew he remembered to apply only after a success. He rocked on his heels, anxious for their meeting with the president.

The DCI asked, "So the air and sea blockade has been lifted?"

The secretary nodded. "As of twenty minutes ago. No need for it now, as there're no Blackjacks left in Cuba for the Russians to send parts and fuel to."

"And we discovered that two more Cuban-bound Blackjacks made it as far as an airport in Mozambique before turning around, heading back to the Soviet Union," the DCI said.

When the president's voice sounded clearly in the hallway, the secretary of defense said, "I happen to know this door into the Oval Office is bulletproof and presumably soundproof. Yet we can still hear him. I doubt he has raised his voice this loud in all his years in the office. Who is he yelling at?"

"Don't know. He's a fearsome man when he's angry. The president is riled up when he should be basking in success."

"Your success," the defense secretary said graciously.

The DCI nodded, accepting the compliment as fact. "Where are you in the Caribbean?"

"A virtual instantaneous stand down. So anxious were both sides to avoid further escalation that once Castro announced the Blackjacks had to go, the U.S. and Soviet navies began steaming away from each other, and keeping their warplanes well in reserve. The aviation cruiser *Leningrad* and its three UDALOY destroyers are already eighty miles east of Cuba, distancing themselves from the Caribbean at full steam. Similarly, to indicate our peaceful intentions, we have ordered Carrier Group Four with the *Nimitz* to sail north. We'll keep Cruiser-Destroyer Group Two between Florida and Havana, but largely hugging our shore. Carrier Group Five is returning to Pacific duty. We've also canceled marine unit transfers, and the call-up of reserves has been canceled. We're through sending the Soviets signals for a while."

The DCI asked, "And the shooting down of the navy fighter and our reprisal sinking of the Soviet cruiser?"

"Moscow and Washington have exchanged protests, and it will end at that. Those navy pilots, Lieutenant Commander May and his wingman, will be up for Silver Stars. What are you about to tell the president?"

"The Politburo is meeting in several hours. The general secretary is scrambling, but he may be on soft sand. Cuba might have done to him what it did to Khrushchev. We won't know for a while yet."

"When is the president next addressing the nation?" the secretary asked.

"Tomorrow morning. As you know, his press secretary has already released that the navies are standing down, and that the Cubans have complied with his demand that the Blackjacks be removed from Cuba. The president's television speech is going to be a very confident talk, announcing that the Caribbean is calm and secure once again, due to the success of diplomatic endeavors."

The secretary of defense laughed. "Diplomatic endeavors? What this William Maurice did was no diplomatic endeavor. Have we heard personally from him yet?"

"Only one line, sent from the hydrofoil gunboat that picked him up. 'As George Custer said, "The defensive perimeter is a little understood art." ' "

The Oval Office door opened, and Senator Richard White scurried out. He looked dog-bitten, wounded, beaten. The president was known to lavishly reward his friends and severely punish his enemies. The catalog of things he could do to an errant politician of his own party was a long one, and White must have just heard the entire list. He glanced neither left nor right but fairly ran down the hallway away from the office.

Grinning with cold pleasure at the senator's retreat, the national security adviser waved them in.

The secretary of defense asked as they stepped into the Oval Office, "George Custer?"

The DCI replied, "We're not sure we decoded it correctly, so we're still working on it."

"So where's Fedorin now?" Maurice asked, sipping the light beer Rosa inflicted on him. It tasted like dishwater.

"At Langley," Jack Cantrell replied. "He'll be interrogated for quite some time. He's madder than hell about how we duped him, and he's sworn he won't tell us anything, but he'll only hold out a week or two."

"How do you know?" Rosa asked.

"We'll buy him. A car, a house somewhere, a job. That's what he was working for in Havana. We'll make it easier for him. All he has to do is tell us about the KGB."

Rosa held her broken arm across her lap. It was encased in a cast. A cracked radius. The orthopedic surgeon had wanted her to remain in the hospital at least overnight, but she had insisted on returning to Coral Gables with her husband. She had taken a Percodan and was feeling no pain. She asked, "How did you know to pick Fedorin?"

"We needed a Russian who saw Castro frequently, and someone who would be susceptible to our approach," Maurice said.

"To our blackmail," Gerard Jones corrected. He was alternating sips of beer with bites of a Snickers. Maurice had searched the refrigerator for something to serve. He had found black olives, banana peppers, cheese, and crackers. Jones had asked if he perhaps had something a little sweeter. Rosa asked Julie Porlocarrero, who dug the Snickers from under her schoolbooks in her backpack. A manila envelope was on Jones's lap.

"I asked a number of my contacts in Havana if they knew of any Soviet officers making money on the side," Maurice said. "Justo Cantillo owns a club there. I buy a lot of rum from him, and he told me he was also dealing with a Russian. Cantillo didn't know what Fedorin did at the Soviet embassy, but Gerard here knew. Fedorin was a procurements officer and, more importantly to us, a translator for the Soviet ambassador."

"We think Fedorin had his fingers in a lot of pies," Jones said. "He was shipping almost half a ton of goods back to Leningrad a month. Making quite a living."

"It didn't take much to convince Fedorin he was about to be arrested," Cantrell said. His tie was loose and his white shirt rumpled. The bags under his eyes made him look older than he was. "We started with the attempted hijacking of his truck and the arrival of the Havana police."

"We wanted him to think the policemen were going to inform the Soviet embassy," Jones said, taking another bite of the candy bar.

Maurice went on, "The hijacker was Roberto Ramos, and the policemen were Eudy Puentes and Ernesto Pazos. That started Fedorin's worries, and then we made it appear that the

KGB was closing in on him. They brutally interrogated the owner of the club where Fedorin did some of his buying. At least so it appeared. Actually, Ramos applied makeup to Justo Cantillo, to make him look like he'd been badly beaten. And he wrapped tape around Justo's hands. Ramos returned to the club later to lighten the makeup, giving Cantillo the appearance of someone on the painful road to recovery."

"Why did the club owner help you?"

"He and I have done business together a long time, and I've done him a few favors," Maurice answered. He was still wearing a small bandage on his cheek. "The message from Fedorin's wife further terrified the Russian."

Jones explained to Rosa, "Over a year ago the NSA learned to work its will on the Soviet's Molniya communications satellites. And occasionally they catch up to the Russians on one of their codes. At those times we can send messages from Moscow. At least a receiver thinks it's from Moscow. The NSA uses it very sparingly."

"So when Fedorin received the frantic news from his wife," Maurice said, "he ran to his bank, then to the club, where the KGB arrested him. The KGB agents were Puentes and Pazos, who don't speak a word of Russian other than what we had them memorize. They brought Fedorin to me for a talk. By that time he was frantic."

"I'll bet he was incensed when he discovered it was all a ruse." Jones chuckled and swallowed beer at the same time, producing a peculiar gurgle.

"What could he do? I proposed to bring him to the United States in exchange for a small favor. If he refused, we would give all our information about his black-market business to the Soviet embassy, and the awful events we had staged would actually begin. Fedorin would be arrested by the real KGB. He had no choice."

A burst of giggles erupted from the fireplace. Julie Porlocarrero and her two friends were again speculating on Aurelio

Moreno. Julie thought Aurelio had asked her for a date but wasn't sure. He had mentioned the word "movie" when he'd last spoken to her. She was repeating his sentence again and again, trying to find the invitation in it. The girls were going to vote. If it was voted an invitation, Julie would approach him in the basement and accept. The laughter was from their guesses as to what Aurelio would say. The girls kept their hands busy by braiding lengths of ribbon. Maurice had not asked what they were making.

Rosa asked, "And the escape from the basement cell?"

"Our people again," Cantrell said. "At that point, we had purposely made Castro so angry he wasn't thinking straight, not using critical judgment. We were counting on that."

"We made sure the rescue was realistic," Maurice explained. "I even had a fellow who works for me, Eladio Arrinda, who lost an arm years ago, do some of the acting. We made it look like his arm had just been blown off by G2 guns. Another body in the basement looked very dead, but that was Ernesto Pazos, holding his breath so his chest wouldn't rise and fall. And there was another of our agents on the first floor."

"Who were the G2 agents who rescued Castro?" she asked.

"Eudy Puentes, owner of the house, and Ramos." Maurice touched his tongue to his broken tooth. He had an appointment to visit his dentist in the morning. Ringing in the ears was a sign of too much aspirin. Maurice was hearing a constant A sharp.

Cantrell sipped his beer, then said, "You were more confident than I was that Fedorin's bullets would miss Castro. Christ, wouldn't that have been a disaster?"

"I told him that if Castro was harmed, he'd never hear from us again. He'd be left in Cuba, at the mercy of Castro and the KGB."

Rosa asked, "And how did Fedorin escape the palace?"

"Admittedly, that was a risk. Frigate Lieutenant Enrique Pascual had been Mederos's secretary. We thought that in Castro's anger and confusion, he wouldn't begin his purge of those he thought in on the CIA plan immediately, wouldn't have figured it out. And we were keeping him confused, making sure things happened to him, one right after another. So Pascual, supposedly Castro's new right-hand man, simply met the escaping Fedorin at the palace door, and escorted him to a waiting car. None of the palace guards thought anything was unusual. Fedorin and Pascual were gone before Castro could catch his breath. Mario Plata picked them up in his *práctico* at a dock near the Green House, and he was transferred to a navy ship a short while later."

"The purge has surely begun by now, though," Jones said as he tore back more of the wrapper around the Snickers.

"But who's left to purge?" Cantrell asked.

"Castro will find someone," Rosa said bitterly.

"But none of our operatives or contacts. Pascual and Justo Cantillo and Eladio Arrinda are on their way to Florida by now. Same with Eudy Puentes. And all the people we put into Cuba, Ramos and Pazos and the others, are out."

Jones crumpled the wrapper and opened the envelope. He pulled out several five-by-seven photographs. "A C-130 just snared these Big Bird photos an hour ago. We already had received photos transmitted by the satellite, but the dropped film produces better-quality shots. Take a look."

Rosa leaned toward Maurice to examine the glossy photographs. They were overhead photos of an airfield at several magnifications. They showed two raging fires on the runway and a building engulfed in flames. Smoke slightly blurred the images.

Jones pointed. "We think this person here, standing next to the helicopter, is Castro. We also just heard that we've got some ground-level photos coming in. They might show Castro's face. I wonder if he'll be smiling or grimacing."

Jack Cantrell said, "Destroying the Blackjacks wasn't quite enough to calm him. He has recalled his ambassador from Moscow, and has threatened to sever diplomatic relations with the Soviet Union."

"The messages between the Kremlin and their Havana embassy that we are intercepting are fun reading." Jones laughed. "The Soviets don't have the damnedest idea what went on."

"They'll figure it out," Maurice said.

"Eventually, sure," Cantrell said. "But no one is ever going to convince Castro that the Soviets didn't try to assassinate him. He saw it with his own eyes. And Castro loves a grudge like most men love a woman."

Cantrell and Jones rose. Maurice showed them to the door. He said he'd be in tomorrow to help wrap things up. They shook hands, as much congratulations as they would give each other. Maurice waited until they had driven out of the driveway before closing the door.

Maurice and Rosa returned to the couch in the den. They wanted each other's company. Ass End leisurely walked into the room. He had been in the basement, watching Aurelio shoot pool.

The pit bull looked left and right and was about to join Maurice when Julie called, "Come here, B.S."

The name was Julie's idea, short for big and sweet. Ass End had been the definition of docility, perhaps realizing his stay among these kind people depended on it. The ripped skin on his side was healing cleanly.

The dog stepped to the girls. They grabbed him and ushered him into their circle. He dropped to his stomach and tried to roll onto a side, but Julie held up his scarred head while Tessa Casuso wrapped the ribbon around his neck. They had braided a colorful collar. The girls returned to their talk of Aurelio. Julie rubbed behind Ass End's good ear, while Tessa scratched his rib cage and Maggie Suarez ran her hand up and down his nose. The dog closed his eyes.

"That animal has got to go," Rosa said, holding her husband's hand.

"I'll put a want ad in the *Herald* next week."

"You say that, but you won't. That dog knew a sucker when he found one. You've always been a fool for kids and dogs."

"And a certain Cuban woman," he added.

She leaned into him. "Well, you do have that saving grace."